Highest Praise for Gregg Olsen

The Girl in the Woods

"Frightening . . . A goose-bump read by a
very talented author. The characters are incredibly
real, causing each page to become a nail-biter, as
readers wonder who the killer could possibly be.
nd as the last pages come to pass, the final revelation
is truly unforgettable."
—*Suspense Magazine*

Olsen weaves an intricate thriller that begins with a
iissing girl and ends up in unexpected territory. The
characters of forensic pathologist Birdy Waterman
ind her colleague Detective Kendall Stark are both
ntriguing and compelling. The whodunit might be a
ig obvious, but the journey is still terrifying and the
riting is stellar. Readers will clamor for more stories
featuring Waterman and Stark."
—*RT Book Reviews,* 4 stars

Fear Collector

Thrills, chills, and absolute fear erupt in a story that
focuses on the evil Ted Bundy brought to society.
Readers will not see the twists and turns coming
ind, even better, they'll get the shock of a lifetime.
This author has gone out of his way to make sure
this is a novel of true and utter fear!"
—*Suspense Magazine*

"Excellent, well written, fascinating . . . an engaging story that will captivate from the very start. Olsen has combined the power of fiction with the stark reality of fact. It's a book you'll not easily forget."
—**Kevin M. Sullivan, author of**
The Bundy Murders: A Comprehensive History

Closer Than Blood

"Olsen, a skilled true-crime writer and novelist, brings back Kitsap County sheriff's detective Kendall Stark in his fleet-footed novel *Closer Than Blood*."
—*The Seattle Times*

"A cat-and-mouse hunt for an individual who is motivated in equal parts by bloodlust and greed. . . . Olsen keeps his readers Velcroed to the edge of their seats from first page to last. . . . By far Olsen's best work to date."
—*Bookreporter.com*

Victim Six

"A rapid-fire page-turner."
—*The Seattle Times*

"Olsen knows how to write a terrifying story."
—*The Daily Vanguard*

"*Victim Six* is a bloody thriller with a nonstop, page-turning pace."
—*The Oregonian*

"Fiercely entertaining, fascinating . . . Olsen offers a unique background view into the very real world of crime . . . and that makes his novels ring true and accurate."
—*Dark Scribe*

A Cold Dark Place

"A great thriller that grabs you by the throat and takes you into the dark, scary places of the heart and soul."
—**Kay Hooper**

"You'll sleep with the lights on after reading Gregg Olsen's dark, atmospheric, page-turning suspense . . . if you can sleep at all."
—**Allison Brennan**

"A stunning thriller—a brutally dark story with a compelling, intricate plot."
—**Alex Kava**

"This stunning thriller is the love child of Thomas Harris and Laura Lippman, with all the thrills and the sheer glued-to-the-page artistry of both."
—**Ken Bruen**

"Olsen keeps the tension taut and pages turning."
—*Publishers Weekly*

A Wicked Snow

"Real narrative drive, a great setup, a gruesome crime, fine characters."
—**Lee Child**

"A taut thriller."
—**Seattle Post-Intelligencer**

"Wickedly clever! A finely crafted, genuinely twisted tale of one mother's capacity for murder and one daughter's search for the truth."
—**Lisa Gardner**

"An irresistible page-turner."
—**Kevin O'Brien**

"Complex mystery, crackling authenticity . . . will keep fans of crime fiction hooked."
—**Publishers Weekly**

"Vivid, powerful, action-packed . . . a terrific, tense thriller that grips the reader."
—**Midwest Book Review**

"Tight plotting, nerve-wracking suspense, and a wonderful climax make this debut a winner."
—**Crimespree magazine**

"*A Wicked Snow*'s plot—about a CSI investigator who's repressed a horrific crime from her childhood until it comes back to haunt her—moves at a satisfyingly fast clip."
—**Seattle Times**

NOW THAT SHE'S GONE

A WATERMAN AND STARK THRILLER

GREGG OLSEN

PINNACLE BOOKS
Kensington Publishing Corp.
www.kensingtonbooks.com

PINNACLE BOOKS are published by

Kensington Publishing Corp.
119 West 40th Street
New York, NY 10018

All Kensington titles, imprints, and distributed lines are available at special quantity discounts for bulk purchases for sales promotions, premiums, fund-raising, educational, or institutional use. Special book excerpts or customized printings can also be created to fit specific needs. For details, write or phone the office of the Kensington sales manager: Kensington Publishing Corp., 119 West 40th Street, New York, NY 10018, attn: Sales Department; phone 1-800-221-2647.

ISBN-13: 978-0-7860-3866-4
ISBN-10: 0-7860-3866-7

First printing: December 2015

10 9 8 7 6 5 4 3 2 1

Printed in the United States of America

First electronic edition: December 2015

ISBN-13: 978-0-7860-2995-2
ISBN-10: 0-7860-2995-1

For Logan Jones

PROLOGUE

Janie Thomas studied the blue betta fish that her son had given her for Christmas the year before. In many ways she was surprised that the creature was still alive. She never changed the water, though it would have been so simple to do with the water dispenser ten feet outside her office. She'd forgotten to feed him for days at a time. Especially lately. Her mind was not on things like a pet. Her eyes darted to the scene outside her office doorway as workers collected their things for the night and departed one by one.

All were going home. All but her.

She observed the fish as it swam under the desk lamp next to her office computer. It had dark, iridescent fins and a penchant for hovering just below the surface.

Tears puddled in her eyes.

It struck her how that fish she unoriginally dubbed Sam was trapped in a tiny water prison. A small glass. It was no larger than the vessel that contained orange juice at the pricy Los Angeles Hilton where she and her husband had celebrated their wedding anniversary.

She wondered who would feed the fish when she was gone.

The irony of it all was that Janie was the superintendent of the only women's prison in Washington State. The boss. The warden. The keeper of the keys. She was all of those things, but like her neglected little fish, she was also trapped. There was nothing new about that. Not really. She had felt that way all her life. Every single second she'd lived had been a web of lies wrapped around her keeping her from really being able to breathe.

The fish puffed another bubble to the surface.

Janie refused to allow any tears to fall. She took a tissue from the box on her desk and dried her eyes. Her heart rate had quickened with the realization that she was about to change not only her own life, but her husband's, her son's. They might never fully understand why she was about to do what she had given herself over to. That would be a problem for them, a nasty gift that she was giving.

And yet, she felt she owed them something.

With no cell phones allowed inside the prison for security reasons, there was no way she could text a private message. She looked at her computer screen. Email was a possibility, but it would leave a trail on the institution's secure network.

Janie didn't want to leave any breadcrumbs. With all the uncertainty looming over her, she was at least steadfast in her conviction that she didn't want to be found. A fresh start would mean no loose ends. A fresh start would mean no more contact with her family.

To be truly free meant to accept that the beginning could start only with an ending.

She looked up from the fish, who was blowing bubbles to the surface of its prison.

"Good night, Karen," she called over to the last of the support staff as the woman who worked in the records department left for the night.

"Any big plans?" asked Karen, a tall woman with soft eyes and a smile that never knew when to quit. Even on the worst days ever.

"Same old, same old," Janie said, swallowing her lie in a big gulp.

Karen shrugged. "See you on Monday, Janie," she said.

"Right," Janie said, again another lie. "Monday."

Completely alone, Janie reached for a pen. Old school was the answer. She'd write a note and deal with the dilemma of having to deliver it later. Surely there would be time for that, right? The world would settle down and forget about her and what she was about to do.

She didn't use her husband's or son's name in her salutation. While the sentiment would be true, it just seemed too personal to lay those letters on the paper.

Just a teeny bit removed from things is how she used to live her life.

There is no way that you will really understand the reasons that I'm doing what I must do, but there are times in your life when you have a do-or-die moment.

She thought for a beat that those words might come off overly dramatic, but they were true. She was being dramatic because, well, what she was about to do was completely out of left field.

This is mine. I'm sorry that I'm leaving you with so many unanswered questions, but it is better that way. I'm sorry that the moment doesn't allow for time to pick up the phone and call you. To tell you that I love you. I do.

Just then another woman entered the office and Janie stopped what she was doing. The woman's long dark hair hung around her face like a curtain as she kept her head down. She spoke in a quiet, sweet tone. And yet, her words commanded genuine urgency.

"It's time now," she said.

"I'm ready," Janie said. "Just writing a note."

"A note?" the woman asked, her head still down.

Janie looked up. "To my family."

The woman let out a sigh. It was the sound of a tire slowly leaking air. It was the sound of a parent disappointed in the words of a child. It was the sound of judgment and disappointment all in one.

"Not a good idea, Janie."

Janie felt her heart rate pulse again. "I know," she said, trying to find the part of her that could stand up to anyone—the part of her that got her to the top of her criminal justice profession. It was gone. Long gone. "I just felt that I owed them an explanation."

"Let me see it," the other said.

Janie handed over the little slip of paper and the woman scanned the paper, then trained her gaze on Janie's now dry, but on-the-brink-of-tears again, eyes.

"Forget it. Forget everything." Her tone was icy and final. Her words were so brittle that if they shattered they'd be sharp splinters. Lethal.

Janie winced. "Don't be like that."

The woman dismissed her with a flick of an outstretched hand. "You don't get it at all. You'd make apologies to God for breathing. Such a pathetic thing. I don't know why I even bothered with you."

"Stop it, please. That's not fair. That's not who I am."

"Really, Janie? You're going to try that out on me? I know who you are to the last shred of tissue on your bones. You can never fool me. I see you for the weak creature you are."

Janie stood and reached out to the woman. "You can't mean that. You can't mean that at all. You and I. We've been through so much. Not together. Not at the same time. But we share a history." She stopped herself, thinking, before adding, "Not the same history, but elements of it all."

The woman rolled her shoulder and shook her head. Disgust turned her pretty mouth into an angry gash.

"There you go again," she said. "Trying to make yourself seem like you are better than me. Judging me for what I did. Hiding behind what was done to you. What made you the shell of a human being that you are."

The woman spun around to leave.

Janie stood. "Don't. Don't do this to me!"

The other kept going, letting Janie twist in the wind for just the right amount of time. Ten seconds that felt like ten minutes. Suddenly she stopped and turned around.

Janie went to her, dropping the note in the shredder. The blades whirled to turn her goodbye letter into confetti.

For the celebration that was about to begin. The new. The future. The chance to breathe it all in.

She put her arms around the woman and kissed her.

"I'm stronger now because of you," she said. "I'm not going to hide anymore. I'm not going to run from what I've been through. From what we've been through."

The woman embraced her and held Janie tight. She no longer kept the curtain of hair around her face. This was the moment she wanted to be seen. She looked up at the camera recording every second of the encounter.

Then she puckered her lips and sent a kiss in the direction of the lens.

BOOK ONE
TAMI

CHAPTER ONE

It had been eight days since his wife went missing. Erwin Thomas took down all of Janie's photos and loaded her things in large plastic totes that he'd purchased en masse from the Gig Harbor Target store three days after she vanished. The first day, he could barely breathe, and he certainly didn't believe anything that the authorities had told him. Janie would never, ever do *that*. Janie, he told himself over and over, loved him.

That same day, the news vans with their ten-foot-high satellite antennas planted themselves like a high-tech forest along the roadside in front of the Thomases' South Kitsap home. One reporter, a woman from CNN, complained that she had bladder issues and asked to use his bathroom. He let her do that only one time.

That evening he watched the news and the reporter showed video that she'd taken of the inside of his house— an "exclusive" that she'd bragged about.

The second day, Erwin, jittery from too much coffee and an overdose of worry, slumped on the gray leather sofa that had been clawed by their beloved cat, Luanne.

He could barely look Kitsap County sheriff's detective Kendall Stark in the eye as she offered proof that Janie had done what she did of her own volition.

"She couldn't, she wouldn't," he said, his tone just a little too insistent to be genuine. "She would never have fallen in love with that monster."

Kendall nodded. *Monster* was a good name for Brenda Nevins, a serial killer who cajoled, seduced, blackmailed, and left a trail of bodies all over Washington State.

Dealing with strangers in situations like the one occupying the detective and the shell-shocked husband was so much easier. Emotions were always part of the process, but with a stranger they simply didn't carry the same pain.

Kendall leaned forward. "We have proof, Mr. Thomas," she said.

Erwin blinked and slumped deeper into the sofa. "What kind of proof?" His dark eyes flashed a little anger, a little resentment. He turned away and watched Luanne as she rubbed tortoiseshell fur on the raw edges of a cat-scratching post. The distraction was like an extra breath of air. He needed it. Though he'd known Kendall since she was a student at South Kitsap High, he just couldn't believe her right then.

"A video," she answered.

Erwin looked right at Kendall, a kind of penetrating look that challenged her.

"What kind of video?" he asked.

Kendall thought about her words very carefully. The man across from her had the bottom fall out of his world and he didn't need to know specifically what was held in the less-than-hi-def images on the flash drive that had been recovered from his wife's bottom desk drawer at the prison where she'd served as superintendent. Someday, in a courtroom, she knew others would see the clip. Erwin, she had no doubt, would beg her to view it. He'd say it was his right to watch it . . . and ultimately that would be true.

But not right then.

"An intimate video," she said.

Janie Thomas's husband looked in the direction of the console behind the detective. A row of family photos played out like a tribute to their lives with their son, Joseph, a student at Boise State, who was now on his way home.

Erwin stayed mute for a very long time.

"Mr. Thomas," Kendall said. "I'm so sorry about all of this."

Erwin made a face, the kind that telegraphs one of those ambivalent emotions, but is really much more than that. Hurt pride? Embarrassment? Worry?

"I don't mean to be disrespectful, Detective," he said, "but sorry isn't going to help me much right now. So let's not be sorry. Let's find Janie."

Kendall stood to leave. "We're on it," she said. "I promise you, Mr. Thomas, we'll do everything to bring her home."

Erwin kept his eyes on Kendall. But he didn't get up. He stayed planted on the sofa.

"She's not coming back here, Detective," he said, his tone very firm. Very final. "I hope you find her and put her where she belongs, and that isn't here with me."

And that was it. Silence filled the room and Erwin Thomas indicated the way out with a quick nod. Kendall started for the door—with Janie's old laptop and iPad. She hoped that when and if they found Janie she'd plead guilty for what she'd done. She hoped that when Janie and Brenda were captured that justice would be swift.

That Brenda would go back to prison right away.

That Janie would join her.

Kendall Stark didn't want Erwin Thomas to ever see the contents of that video.

Indeed, she wished *she* hadn't seen it. It was one of those things that was unforgettable for all of the wrong reasons. It was like stumbling onto some site on the Internet and having it start playing vile images from which the click of a mouse cannot offer an escape.

When he first started the process of erasing Janie from his life after the detective left that afternoon, Erwin did so with a sad tenderness. He packed her clothes neatly. He carefully folded a lace top that she'd worn on their twenty-fifth wedding anniversary two months before. The high school guidance counselor who'd devoted his life to trying to help kids at South Kitsap had been utterly clueless that his wife had become involved with one of the inmates at the prison. He'd been trained to see when people were covering up, lying, trying to hide something. That she'd committed this terrible crime and facilitated a prison break for a serial killer was almost beside the point.

She'd made him into a fool. A laughingstock.

Over the next few hours, his tenderness turned to rage. Clothes, jewelry, papers—anything that belonged clearly to Janie—was dumped into those clear tubs. When he ran out of the containers, he started to pour

Janie's belongings into black garden-leaf bags. He was going to erase every trace of her from that house. She would never, ever worm her way back inside.

Just after nine p.m., Joe Thomas, twenty, pulled into the driveway in front of the family home on Long Lake and he hurried inside.

"Dad!" he called out, stepping past the tubs and bags of his mother's belongings. "What's going on here? What's happened to Mom?"

Erwin emerged from the bedroom and embraced his son. He did something that Joe had seen his father do only one other time—when his own father had died after lingering for days following a car accident on the interstate near Seattle.

Erwin started to cry.

CHAPTER TWO

Kendall Stark's world had unraveled and the last thing she needed was the constant calling, hassling, she was getting from a producer from *Spirit Hunters*, a television show that—according to the producer—"boldly searched for answers to unsolved crimes by going to the other side."

Or something along those lines.

The Kitsap County detective wanted only to focus on her problems, ones rooted in the very real world. Her husband, Steven, had taken a new job in the Bay Area developing an advertising program that was going to change the way the world shops.

Or something along those lines.

But there was more than a thousand miles of geographic distance between them. Something else, something more hurtful and deeper than what had undermined their now tenuous relationship. Kendall would call Steven and get his voice mail all too often. She dialed the direct line at the software company and an associate there said that Steven was gone and wouldn't be back for two days. He'd never told her he was going on a business trip. Cell phones are always with the person, not like the days when people had landlines, and if they answered the call one knew exactly where they were.

As Kendall sat at her desk in her small but neat office at the Kitsap County Sheriff's Department, she could not help but let her mind wander to the potential that this short-term estrangement—for all the right reasons—was more problematic than she'd allowed herself to believe.

She looked at a silver-framed photo on the wall behind her computer screen. Tears moistened her blue eyes, but she fought hard to contain the flood that would come later when she got home. The picture showed Steven and Cody, then five, as they sat on the edge of a dock at Kitsap Lake. The sun beamed through the little boy's hair, almost suggesting a halo. There was no such glow around the boy's father. Steven had his arm around his son's shoulder, pulling him in tight with the kind of protective sweetness that Kendall had never doubted would ebb. No matter whatever happened. They were solid, a family. A family that would be together forever.

What are we going to do? Kendall thought. *This can't be happening. Not to us. Not now.*

"Detective?"

She looked up. Brad James, the department's new public information officer, stood in the doorway. Brad was all of twenty-five. He had a kind of earnest face, one that conveyed sincerity when speaking with the media. Those in the office knew he was probably a better actor than a genuinely caring person. He pushed the edges of the department's dress and appearance code too. He had at least a three-day scruffy stubble and black hair that he sometimes gelled up so much that Kendall was convinced he'd leave a mark on a pillowcase.

"Hi, Brad," she said, knowing why he was there.

"Get my messages?" he asked.

"Yours and a dozen from Juliana Robbins."

"Did you call her back?"

"No," she said.

Brad slid into a chair and leaned forward. The light from her desk lamp played off his oversized and over-whitened teeth.

"Look, you have to do this show," he said.

"I don't want to, Brad."

"What's your objection?"

"Besides the fact that we have a major case to contend with, I think that shows like this prey on people's hopes in a demonstrable and cruel way."

He snapped his eyes shut, then opened them. "I don't get what you mean."

"The girl's been missing for four years and more than likely she's never coming back."

"How do you know that?" he asked, rubbing the scruffy edge of his chin.

Kendall knew what he was getting at. There really wasn't a lot to know for sure when it came to the case of Katy Frazier's disappearance. The South Kitsap High School student had simply vanished from her family's home. There was some evidence to suggest a potential abduction, but as far as Kendall knew there were other possibilities too. She hadn't actually worked the case. It was before her time as an investigator.

"I feel sorry for Mr. and Mrs. Frazier," she said. "Really, I do. But I don't think being part of some kind of psychic TV freak show is going to help anyone."

Brad leaned forward. "They've solved several cases, Detective. It's all on their website. Have you even been through the press kit I provided you?"

She glanced at the deep blue folder Brad had ceremoniously put on her desk three days after the producers started their relentless attack to get her on the show.

"I've been busy," she said.

"We're all busy, Detective," he said. "Sheriff wants the department to participate."

Brad was pushy and Kendall didn't like that. Not at all.

"Why don't you do it, Brad?" she asked. "You seem to be so eager to get someone on some cable show. Why not yourself?"

He made a face. "I'm not a detective," he said.

Kendall didn't balk. "I'm not a TV personality."

"Sheriff says you *have* to do it." A sly smile came with his second mention of the trump card that he wielded like it was some kind of checkmate move. Which, in a very real way, it was.

Kendall sighed. "What do the Fraziers say about the show featuring their daughter's case?"

"All for it," Brad said. "They want answers, Detective."

"I doubt they will get answers from *Spirit Hunters.*"

"Well, they never got any answers from us now, did they?"

Kendall never had liked Brad James. She *really* didn't like him now.

"Just so you know, Brad, while it was before my time, I can assure you this department did everything humanly possible to find out what happened to Katy Frazier."

Her face was a little hot, but she hadn't raised her voice. Maybe just a little. But not so much that Brad could trot off to the sheriff and say she'd been uncooperative and belligerent.

"Whatever," he said. "Ancient history. I'm all about helping this family and this is what Sheriff wants us to do. Read the kit. Check out the website. Dig through the old file. Bone up. Call Juliana Robbins and let her know you're going to be involved."

With that, he got up and left, leaving only a trace of the scent of his hair gel and an uneasy feeling in the pit of Kendall's stomach.

Kendall reached for the midnight blue folder. Stamped in the center was a gilt logo that indicated the production company and its flagship show.

PATHFINDERS PRODUCTIONS, INC.
Spirit Hunters
Starring PANDORA and WYATT OGILVIE

Kendall didn't know Pandora, the purported psychic, but the other half of the duo was well known by most in law enforcement. Wyatt was the retired—in disgrace—San Francisco homicide detective who'd had an affair with a juror during a major double-homicide case that had riveted the nation the decade before. Wyatt married the woman after sullying his career—and just about everyone else's involved in the case.

He gamely had tried to talk himself out of the mess, saying that he'd been a substance abuser and had fallen in love against his better judgment. In a way it worked. After the furor over what he'd done, he wrote a book, and started to make the rounds on TV shows—starting at the lowest rung, and with his undeniable charm, working his way up to the morning network shows. Finally, after writing a couple of flop novels, he ended up being paired with a psychic on an Investigation Discovery show called *Spirit Hunters*.

Kendall flipped through the press materials. A substantially Photoshopped image of Ogilvie faced her. He was in his fifties, but the electronic airbrushing of some photo geek at Pathfinders had turned him into a thirty-five-year-old. Gone were the red rims of his eyes, the bags underscoring them so majorly when Kendall had seen him on *Good Morning America*. Or maybe *The View*. In any case, for a purveyor of the unvarnished truth, he certainly had been varnished.

Pandora—no last name—was a strawberry blonde with green eyes and freckles over the bridge of her nose. Her hair was fashioned into a long braid that almost looked like a horsewhip. While Wyatt Ogilvie stood in the hero pose, arms folded over his barrel chest, his partner in psychic crime solving struck a more pensive, moody pose. She stood next to an angel statue in a cemetery, the wind tousling her braided mane, with a far-off look in her eyes.

Kendall skimmed through the rest of the pages, finding her eyes rolling enough to give her awareness that she was doing so. The format of the series was simple and, Kendall thought, utterly stupid. Wyatt would come to the location of the unsolved crime, camera crew in tow, to "seek the truth, to turn the stones that had been left unturned by those who should have done a better job."

Great, Kendall thought, *this show is all about making law enforcement look stupid and Wyatt Ogilvie is supposed to be the second coming of Sherlock Holmes.*

After the former cop now TV star turned said stones, Pandora would arrive on the scene and do what she did best.

"Seeing dead people is one thing, but talking to them is an entirely different matter. Pandora has the ability to enlist her guides in the quest for the truth. Viewers will have the opportunity to dial in to the other side as Pandora reaches over the spirit zone to unearth buried secrets and, more importantly, to provide closure to the loved ones of the dead and missing."

Kendall felt the urge to do one of two things—strangle that twit PR guy or throw up. *Spirit Hunters* was the very worst thing to do to a family, turning their tragedy into a spectacle.

Her phone flashed. It was Pathfinders.

"Detective Stark?"

"Yes," she said to the chirpy voice on the other end of the line.

"Hold for Juliana Robbins."

Before Kendall could say she didn't want to hold for anyone and should never have picked up the line, the call went to music. A few beats later, the producer spoke.

"Detective, this is Juliana. I thought I'd never have the chance to get ahold of you. You really had me worried."

The comment caught Kendall off guard.

"Worried?"

"Well, yes. I thought that you might miss the opportunity to do the show."

Kendall almost laughed. *Opportunity.* That was funny. More like nightmare.

"About the show," Kendall said, before being cut off again.

"Yes, I'm so excited that you'll be participating. I talked to both your PIO and the sheriff just now. Such nice men. And they both sound so handsome. Are they?"

"I don't—"

"Of course, you can't say. Wouldn't be professional."

There was nothing professional about any of this, least of all whether Brad James and the Kitsap County sheriff were good-looking or not.

"I don't know if I'll be able to do the show," Kendall said. "I'm in the middle of some major things right now."

"You mean the Brenda Nevins case?" Juliana let the words trail off a little, as though she was fishing for a little information. Maybe an upcoming episode in which Pandora could find the elusive serial killer by the use of her at-the-ready spirit guides.

While Brenda was certainly among the top items on Kendall's list, she wasn't higher up than what was going on with Steven.

"Among other things, yes," she said.

Juliana switched to a more understanding tone. It was swift and decisive. Like a light switch.

"No worries," she said. "I'll only need a little bit of your time. I told your boss that you'd only be on camera for a few minutes, but we need you there. Our show doesn't work if we don't have local law enforcement involved. Pandora and Wyatt insist."

We wouldn't want to disappoint them, Kendall thought—loud enough in her head that she was almost certain Juliana Robbins could hear it.

But she couldn't.

"What exactly do you need from me?" she asked. "And when?"

"I can tell you are less than enthusiastic," Juliana said.

Maybe you're the psychic, Kendall thought.

"We find resistance every now and then. I get it. Some cops act like if they can't find the answers, no one else can. But that's not true. And if you think about it, you'll have to agree with me on that."

"I've thought about it," Kendall said. "But I really don't see how a psychic and a former cop can swoop into Port Orchard and unlock a puzzle that hasn't been solved by top-notch investigators right here in this office. I'm not saying me. I haven't worked the case. But others here have."

"Have you looked at the press kit?" Juliana asked.

"Just doing that now. Before your call."

"That's awesome. I'm glad about that. Take a moment to review the section called 'Lost, Now Found.'"

Kendall fanned out the glossy pages.

"I see it," she said.

"Good. You don't have to read it now, but once you

start you won't be able to quit until you finish. There are three Pandora case studies there in which she solved the unsolvable. No offense, Detective, but don't slam something just because you're unfamiliar with it."

Kendall didn't like being lectured by anyone, but she let it pass as she skimmed the promo materials in front of her. There was no use in fighting it. There was no way she could wriggle out of taping *Spirit Hunters*.

"I'll read them later," she finally said. "When are we doing the interview?"

"Pre-interview tomorrow," the producer said. "That's with me. Then the real interview with Wyatt is the next day."

"Okay. Do you want me to call you?" Kendall asked, completely trapped.

"Nope. Let's just set a place and time."

"A place?"

"Yes, Detective. I'm in town. Staying at an adorable B and B in Southworth, Swallow Heaven. Couldn't find anything I liked in Port Orchard."

"The Comfort Inn is nice and convenient," Kendall said, finding herself in the role of Port Orchard booster. She hated when people made slights against the town that had always been home. It was not upscale, but decidedly working class. Its views were of the shipyard in Bremerton, not some huge snow cone view of Mount Rainier. Port Orchard was never going to be like nearby Gig Harbor with its quaint waterfront lined with boutiques and restaurants. It was, however, something that a lot of other communities weren't.

It was welcoming to new people.

"Oh, I didn't see that on TripAdvisor," Juliana said. "I only go four stars and above. Not that I can actually afford a five-star in a major city. The show doesn't have that kind of dough."

"I see," Kendall said. "In any case, I don't want to do it at my office. And like I said, I'm very, very busy."

"That's fine. How about a restaurant? You have to eat, don't you?"

Kendall did, of course, but she also had Cody to think about. She'd need to get him from school, get him settled in, and see if Marsha, his regular babysitter, could cover.

Plus there was another fact that this TripAdvisor snob might have a problem with. She didn't mention her son. That was none of Juliana's business.

"Not a ton of choices here," she said.

"Just looked online," said Juliana, clearly a multitasker. "How about Cosmo's off Sedgwick?"

Kendall knew the place well. Steven liked the restaurant's five-cheese ravioli. Cody liked buttered spaghetti noodles.

"Fine," she said.

"Tomorrow at six. The crew is coming to town as we speak and I'll have to babysit them to make sure they get done what they need to get done. We have a show to put on."

Kendall didn't like that last sentence at all. A show. It made what happened to the Frazier family so trivial. Their daughter had gone missing and while there was great mystery about it, it was hardly entertainment.

Nor should it be.

"I'll see you then," Kendall said.

"Bye, Detective. Oh, one more thing. If you want to bring your son, Cody, that's quite all right."

Cody's name being mentioned surprised her a little.

"How did you know I have a son?" she asked.

Juliana laughed. "It doesn't take a psychic to find out things like that anymore. I Googled you."

The line went dead.

Kendall sat there feeling sick to her stomach. She didn't want to do the show. She didn't want Roger and Brit Frazier, Katy's parents, to get their hopes up either. Pandora wasn't going to bring them closure.

At least she highly doubted that.

CHAPTER THREE

Kendall Stark and the county's forensic pathologist Birdy Waterman met in Kendall's office to cue up the videotape that the FBI had recovered from prison surveillance cameras. The pair were still in the midst of a cross-training program designed to improve the work and perception of the offices of the Kitsap County sheriff and the coroner—the result of a blunder that still had many embarrassed and angry.

"The FBI actually gave you something?" Birdy asked. "I think I'll faint."

"Don't faint, Birdy," Kendall said. "It's a total bone toss. But yes. They know that we don't have jurisdiction on the Nevins case and they want to play nice. You know, in case they want to blame us for something later."

"When was it recorded?"

"At seven p.m. the night before the guards and staff noticed that Janie was gone."

"And Brenda too."

"Right. Brenda too."

"Where did Erwin Thomas think his wife was, anyway?"

"That's a good one, Birdy. She told Erwin that she was attending a U.S. Council of Prisons conference in Philly. The subject was helping inmates achieve their full potential once they leave prison."

"That *is* good. Our government at work."

"This time the government gets a pass on stupidity. There was no conference. I checked. Not in Philly. Not anywhere."

Birdy's dark eyes flashed. "That means that Janie went willingly, didn't she?"

"More than willingly," Kendall said. "You'll see." She swiveled her computer screen, pressed PLAY, and joined Birdy on the other side of her desk where they could watch the video clip at the same time.

The images were black-and-white and slightly grainy, but certainly clear enough for any viewer familiar with the women to identify them. Brenda wore dark pants and a white top. Janie had on a skirt and patterned blouse. Glasses hung on a chain around her neck.

"It just occurred to me now, but what's Brenda doing in Janie's office, anyway?" Birdy asked.

Kendall looked at her drafted partner. "Special privileges, I'm told."

"Of all people in the prison," Birdy said. "Brenda Nevins? She should have a tattoo on her face that says 'Get the F Away from Me.'"

Kendall half smiled. "I know. It's utterly crazy that anyone would give her any special privileges whatsoever."

"But someone did. *Her*," Birdy said, tapping her fingertip on the screen.

"Yes," she said. "She was the only one who could."

"Do we need popcorn?" Birdy asked. "I'm hungry."

"You're always hungry. And no, we don't. Not unless you want to puke it up later. Just watch, okay?"

"Sufficiently intrigued, Kendall."

The images unspooled across the screen. At first it was as Kendall admitted when she called Birdy to join her for a screening—"A whole lot of nothing, but wait until the third act."

When the third act came it was everything that she'd promised.

"What's Janie doing?" Birdy asked.

Kendall looked at her friend. "She's taking off her clothes."

Birdy made a face. "I can see that. But . . . oh crap, she's not . . . Yeah, she is."

"Right," Kendall said. "She is."

"I can't get a man to do that to me," Birdy said.

Kendall glanced at her friend. "That's borderline TMI."

"I'm just saying," Birdy said, turning her head a little to improve her viewing angle. "Just saying."

"You sound like a teenager," Kendall said, still riveted to the video, even though it was her third viewing.

"Blame that on my nephew, Kendall. Elan's influencing me more than I'm influencing him."

The clip went on with Brenda doing what she was extremely proficient at—writhing in ecstasy. Tossing her head back. Running her fingers through her beautiful hair.

"How is it that I can barely get a date and Brenda can turn these women like it's nothing?" Birdy asked.

Kendall let out a short laugh. "I have no idea."

"At least you're married, Kendall."

Kendall almost said "for now" in response, but she held her tongue. She wasn't going to go there. Not until she heard something definitive from Steven. *Why doesn't he call? What is he up to?*

The video finished and Kendall looked at Birdy.

"Well?" she asked.

"I hope that Janie pulls herself together before Brenda decides that she's no longer worth the trouble," Birdy said.

"I figure Janie has the shelf life of an already ripe banana."

"I hope Janie's family doesn't have to see this."

"I'm almost glad that it's not our case just because of that," Kendall said. "I wouldn't want this played in a Kitsap County courtroom either."

Kendall's landline rang and she picked it up.

"Really?" she said, looking at Birdy with a strange expression on her face. The caller did most of the talking. "All right. I'll bring Birdy. She's with me now. I see. All right."

"What was that all about?" Birdy asked.

"Brad James says I have a visitor."

"He's getting on my nerves, Kendall. He asked me to speak to a kindergarten class at Mullinex Ridge about autopsies. As if I could or would do that. What's he making you do?"

"Beside that stupid TV show, *Spirit Hunters*?"

"Besides that."

"He says I have a visitor. Someone who I need to see

even though it's not really related to any case I'm doing."

"That's weird. Who is it?"

"Deirdre Holloway."

"Name doesn't ring a bell," Birdy said. "Who's that?"

Kendall stood. "Brenda Nevins's mother."

"I want to go too," Birdy said.

"I thought you would," Kendall said, heading out through the doorway. "She said no. Will only talk to me."

"I thought we were a team," Birdy teased as she departed for her office.

"We are," Kendall said. "For better or worse."

CHAPTER FOUR

The woman's eyes were familiar. They had the same coloring and shape as someone with whom Kendall had spent some time. They were older, wiser. And no doubt much, much kinder. Wearing a long, almost-black blue dress and a flowing, flowery pashmina over her left shoulder, held in place by a Tiger-eye clip, Brenda Nevins's mother would get looks no matter where she was. She was beautiful with high cheekbones accented by a nearly imperceptible touch of makeup. PR guy Brad James had made it very clear.

Brenda Nevins's mom is coming to talk to you. Says she has something important to tell you. You, and only you.

"I'm Deirdre Holloway," she said.

Kendall smiled at her. It was weak smile, meant to disarm and inspire interest in the woman.

"I'm glad you're here," she said as she met her by the reception desk of the Kitsap County sheriff.

"I can see that you are judging me," the older woman said.

Despite the fact that she'd arranged the meeting,

Deirdre Holloway was defensive. Kendall was all but certain that when it came to her daughter as a calling card, she'd had her share of rebukes and censures.

"I'm not," Kendall said.

Deirdre fussed with her pashmina. "I understand. Obviously I didn't do a very good job raising her, did I? If I had, we wouldn't be here." Her voice trailed off before she added a quick and sad postscript to the truth of her words. "And I would still have a grandchild."

Kendall led her to a conference room—a nicer one than the one she usually took suspects or witnesses to. It probably wasn't easy being the mother of a serial killer. In fact, she knew it *couldn't* be. Brenda Nevins had finally achieved what she'd long sought—notoriety on a grand scale. She's vowed she'd do so. Promised detractors. Cajoled the police and jailers over the course of her various stretches of incarceration. In running off with Janie Thomas, Brenda had unleashed a veritable media frenzy on the Kitsap Peninsula. There wasn't a parking lot that didn't have a satellite truck looming above the pickups and SUVs. She was out there. Somewhere.

"I'm sure you did the best you could, Ms. Holloway," Kendall said. "Some things are beyond anyone's control. I'm sure you know that by now. At least I hope you do."

Brenda's mother sat down and pulled out a crumpled tissue.

Kendall shot her a sympathetic glance.

"Allergies," Deirdre said. "Not going to cry, if that's what you were thinking. I'm all cried out. Have been for years."

Kendall had read the files about all that Brenda had

put her single mother through. The drugs. The running away. The men. And, of course, the murders. Kendall had seen so many mothers and fathers left to cope with the aftermath of destruction left by their progeny. None could hold a candle to Brenda's swath of destruction—which, of course, put Deirdre Holloway in a category of her own.

"You said you thought you could help," Kendall said.

Deirdre refreshed her lipstick. "Yes," she said, returning the black and gold tube to the open jaws of her purse.

"You've talked to the FBI, haven't you?" Kendall asked, already knowing the answer. They *all* had. Birdy had. The sheriff had. Kendall—as the last member of law enforcement to have a sit-down interview with the notorious killer—had a three-hour interview with two special agents and a stenographer. The FBI had pressed her hard as if she was supposed to know more about the plans that Brenda had been hatching with Janie Thomas. But she hadn't any information. Not really. The interview was a little on the awkward side, with Kendall pushing back as they fired their questions.

STATE'S ATTORNEY DAN WILSON: So you made a kind of connection with her, isn't that right?

KENDALL STARK: I don't know what you mean. I interviewed her.

SADW: It was more than an interview; you did some pretty deep soul-searching of the subject.

KS: Soul-searching? Not really.

SADW: I see. Well, she flirted with you.

KS: She flirts with anything with a pulse. Man.
    Woman. Dog, I suspect. Anyone she can use.
    That's what Brenda Nevins does. Don't you
    have Behavior Analysis guys in Quantico?
    Maybe you should talk to them.
SADW: You are being evasive and we want to
    know why.
KS: Evasive? I'm a local cop. I interviewed her
    about a case in which she was, as it turned
    out, tangentially involved.
SADA: She was very interested in your son.
KS: I didn't get that.
SADW: You didn't?
KS: No. But you've got my attention. What do
    you know?
SADW: I'm sorry. This is an active investigation.

Those familiar eyes staring at Kendall held steady
from across the conference table. Cool air pumped in
and the AC whirled. Behind Deirdre Holloway was a
large framed photo of a beloved deputy killed by a
meth head the year before.

"Yes," Brenda's mother said. "I've told them whatever they needed to know. I've talked to them before,
you know."

"Before what?" Kendall asked.

"Before Janie Thomas."

The detective was surprised, but she didn't allow any
emotion to register on her face. The feds never shared.
They only popped into backwaters like Port Orchard to
show the rest of the world they were on top of it and
that the local PD or sheriff didn't know how to investi-

gate a serious matter like they did. In part that was true. Outside of a few major American cities, none had the resources that the bureau lorded—sometimes irritatingly so—over them.

"What were they after?" Kendall asked.

Deirdre narrowed her gaze. "You don't know?"

Kendall shook her head. "No. I don't know."

Brenda's mother wiped her nose and wadded up her tissue.

"My daughter was corresponding with a couple of other serial killers incarcerated in Utah and right here in Washington."

"Corresponding?" Kendall asked. "That's not possible. Inmate-to-inmate mail is impossible."

Deirdre fiddled with the pashmina, smoothing out a wrinkle that had seemed to annoy her from the moment she arrived. "You obviously don't know Brenda as well as you think," she answered after a delay.

Kendall had read everything she could about Brenda Nevins. She'd followed her case during her murder and arson trial. Everyone did. But as a law enforcement officer, Kendall was supremely interested in the psychological makeup of the female killer. Outside of Aileen Wuornos, who murdered her customers in Florida, and a smattering of trailer park "black widow" killers over the years, there were few women who killed more than once. Brenda not only fit into that camp, she seemed to be the only one who reveled in the endeavor.

"How?" Kendall asked. "And really, why? That is, if you know."

As she spoke, something occurred to Kendall. Deirdre was a little like her daughter. She had a flair for the dramatic, and was all but certainly paying Kendall a visit to indulge in a little attention-seeking too.

"I don't know," she said, a little unconvincingly. "Not exactly. During a visit last year she told me about Connors and Reed. She said she'd managed to get correspondence out whenever someone was released."

Jerry Connors had murdered fourteen women—mostly street girls and weekend prostitutes—in the Seattle area in the early '90s. He wasn't a particularly brilliant serial killer, but one who managed to elude detection for a decade because his killings were so random. The ages and races of his women were across the board.

Cecil Reed was another matter altogether. He was devious, smart, good-looking. In another time and place he might have made the shortlist for TV's *The Bachelor*. While some serial killers, like Washington's Jerry Connors, were unintelligent and unattractive (the media called him a "dolt with a dark side"), Provo, Utah, ski lodge owner Cecil Reed was handsome and cunning. He also very specific. His targets were somewhat risky: lonely-hearted widows and divorcées who were looking for love on a ski weekend that his brochure promised "would be the trip of a lifetime where everything is taken care of . . . and romance is free of charge." Over the course of a five-year period, the handsome and evil man met six women looking for love and adventure with a penchant for torture. They were drugged, violated, and kept alive in a chamber he'd created underneath the Alpine Glow restaurant that he had managed before creating his own scheme for money and grisly satisfaction.

Sissy Crowley, a wealthy woman from Stonybrook,

Connecticut, would have been the seventh victim, but she managed to extricate herself from the dungeon by creating a small fire and sending smoke into the restaurant. Fire investigators found her, weak, nearly dead from smoke inhalation. After a lengthy trial, Sissy became a kind of spokesperson for victims. Cecil Reed emerged as one of the most evil killers of modern times. The lead investigator for the Provo police said they suspected he had killed more than the six who'd hit the slopes and landed in an underground dungeon.

"They were getting the messages out with the paroled inmates," Kendall said. "How?"

Deirdre offered a grim smile. "She called it 'where the sun don't shine' and I took that to mean a couple of places."

Kendall didn't need a picture sketched out, the sordid mental image came readily.

"I see," she said.

"Yeah, she said that no one ever does a cavity search when someone goes out of the institution. Why would they? My daughter was always smart. Smart and devious."

"What was she saying to Reed and Connors?"

"That I don't know. Not really. The FBI didn't tell me anything. I don't really care. That's not why I came here."

"Why did you come?" Kendall asked.

Those familiar eyes stared hard at the detective.

"Because of what she said about you," Deirdre said.

For the second time, Kendall kept her feelings in check. Inside, she felt a chill, but she didn't disclose it.

"And what was that? What did she say?" she asked.

"Words of anger," Deirdre said.

"What was she mad about? I barely spent any time with her."

"Like I said, you don't know my daughter. She was angry because your interview came at the worst possible time. She blamed you for killing her TV special."

The words gave Kendall another reason to hate TV even more.

"What TV special? I honestly don't know what you're talking about, Ms. Holloway."

"I don't know. All I know is that she blamed you and she blamed your partner, Dr. Waterman."

"What did Birdy Waterman have to do with anything?"

"You are expecting my daughter to make sense, Detective. I expect that you've researched the deviant mind before. In fact, I'm sure you have."

"Yes," Kendall said. "I've taken some training."

"Thought so. Then you should know there's no way to understand a girl like my daughter. You have to watch her, hopefully from a distance, like a wild animal, with the assumption that if given the chance, she'd chew your arm off. Maybe your face."

After Deirdre Holloway left, Kendall phoned Birdy, who immediately took charge of the conversation by telling Kendall the day was one of the worst ever.

"Husband and wife died in a wreck over by Sunnyslope," the forensic pathologist explained. "Baby in the other car hanging on by a thread at Harrison. Thank God the little one didn't take the brunt of the hit. I can't take another baby in the chiller."

"Alcohol?" Kendall asked.

"Oh yes," Birdy said, letting out a sharp and pronounced sigh. "Off the charts."

"I have something else for you that's a little off the charts," Kendall said, thinking that her segue was not as facile as she'd thought just before it came out of her mouth. Birdy had a way of taking over a conversation and Kendall needed to say what she needed to say.

"What's that?" Birdy asked. "Was it a bomb dropped by Brenda's mother?"

"Indeed. Seems that Brenda is mad at us," Kendall said. "Really mad at me, but your name came up too."

"Mad at us, Kendall?" Birdy asked. "What'd we do?"

Kendall looked down at some decidedly chicken-scratch notes she'd made while talking to Brenda's mother, Deirdre.

"Interviewing her about Missy Carlyle evidently cost her some privileges," she said. "That ultimately cost her some TV gig she was hoping for."

"That's not entirely a bad thing. I hate the fact that TV puts those people on for entertainment practically every night of the week. The worst. I hate TV."

"Me too," Kendall said. "Always have. Give me a book any day."

"A beer and a sunny day for me," Birdy said. "Maybe some jazz playing on my stereo."

"That sounds good too," Kendall said. "Anyway, I don't know that any of this truly matters. I do, however, find it interesting seeing how the special agents who interviewed me made no mention of it."

"Neither did my trio," Birdy said. "Guess they held that back for some reason."

"Guess so," Kendall said.

CHAPTER FIVE

Birdy Waterman looked up from her stack of paperwork. She smiled at Kendall. Birdy was a Makah Indian with dark hair and eyes—the opposite of Kendall's blond hair and blue eyes. And while they were nearly the same age, Birdy definitely had the edge when it came to hard-fought wisdom. She'd grown up very poor on the reservation at Neah Bay in the very western corner of Washington State's Olympic Peninsula.

Birdy's mother would be perfect fodder for any number of sleazy reality shows. She was cruel. She was jealous. She thought that there were limits on how much love to give and what should be given in return. She was everything that Birdy wasn't. Birdy was single. Since her nephew Elan had had shown up in Port Orchard to get away from his mom—Birdy's sister, Summer—she was doing her best to make a home for him.

Kendall's own parents were dead. Her sister lived in Portland. Her husband was presently in Sunnyvale, California, and she was raising an autistic son, Cody, temporarily on her own. So as different as they were, they found a connection that was deeper than finding out who'd killed whom.

"It's official. I'm stuck doing that *Spirit Hunters* show," Kendall said.

Birdy slid her reading glasses down the bridge of her nose. Her silver earrings dangled.

"I figured. I take it that you don't want to."

"No. I don't. There isn't time for it."

"Have you heard from Steven?" Birdy asked, taking the conversation where she thought Kendall needed it to go.

"Not since last night. It's not about that, Birdy. It's about taking advantage of people who don't know they are being taken advantage of."

"Katy's parents? Her sister?"

"Right. Them."

"I know the Fraziers, Kendall. They have been stuck in limbo for years. This might help them in some small way."

Kendall didn't know Birdy knew Roger and Brit, and she asked about it.

"They go to my church. I can't say that I'm close with them, but we've talked about Katy a few times. They aren't any different than other parents whose kids have gone missing. Sad. Heartbroken. Hopeful."

"No one knows what happened to Katy. I understand that. But, Birdy, Pandora and that cretin of a cop are never going to do anything more than exploit their grief for the cameras."

Birdy nodded. "Maybe," she said. "Maybe not."

"You don't believe in that crap."

Birdy didn't answer.

"Tell me you don't believe in that crap, Birdy."

Birdy paused, took off her glasses, and folded them into a black leather case. "I'm Native American, born on a reservation, and raised to believe that the spirit lives in all of us, in all things. Do I know for sure that Pandora can find out something the county missed? No. Is she probably a fake? Yes. But if there is a slightest shred of hope for a family who can barely hang on, I'm willing to take the chance."

"I can't believe you're saying this," Kendall said.

Birdy rolled her shoulder a little. She'd played tennis with Elan the week before and it was still bothering her. "Chalk it up to one of our cultural differences. It's part of who I am. It's the reason I sometimes sing quietly to the people who end up on my table downstairs. It's why I still pray for them. It's why I promise them that I'll do all I can to find out what happened."

Kendall knew Birdy did all of that. That didn't bother her at all. Birdy was sincere. It wasn't trumped up for the cameras.

"I know all of that," Kendall finally said. "I just don't believe Pandora is going to do anything good here, and I'm really mad at the sheriff for forcing me to be a part of it."

"He picked you for two reasons, Kendall."

"And what might those be?"

"You won't make the department look bad—and you weren't here when the girl went missing."

Birdy picked up a folder and handed it Kendall.

"This is all we have from the labs from the Katy Frazier case. Some blood work was done on samples from the scene. Some hair and fibers recovered. You need to do your homework."

Kendall made a face. She wasn't happy about that at all. She took Birdy's paperwork and folded it into the slender file she'd printed out from the department's computer system.

"Any Brenda sightings?" Birdy asked.

Kendall shook her head. "Nothing."

"Maybe Pandora will be able to find her too," Birdy said, offering a wry smile.

Kendall didn't return the smile. "Don't even say that, Birdy. That's the last thing we need right now."

"Talk to you tomorrow, Kendall."

Kendall started for the door.

"Wait," Birdy called out.

Kendall turned. "What is it?"

"Just wanted to tell you to break a leg. I've always wanted to say that to someone."

"I hope I do," Kendall said, this time smiling. "Then I won't have to do *Spirit Hunters*."

"I don't see that happening."

"So you're psychic now too."

"Everyone is."

Later that day, like a scratched CD that skipped without mercy, the interview with Brenda Nevins's mother came back to her. She wondered what it was that had piqued the FBI's interest in her single interview with the serial killer. What were they getting at when they kept trying to get information out of her?

There wasn't any.

CHAPTER SIX

The stark house in Harper, Washington, was as still as a slack tide. The old waterfront home was perched on a rolling hill overlooking the black waters of Puget Sound. It was after nine. Cody Stark was quiet as always when Kendall put him to bed that evening. The little boy was verbal, but often existed within his own world. He showed affection to his mother and father—there was none of the distance that other parents at the school complained about. Before Steven took the new job, Kendall thought that there was no one luckier than she. Certainly, her son had challenges that were beyond what some other parents could see themselves handling. But in reality, as far as the various shades of autism were concerned, Cody's problems were light. He didn't bang his head against the wall. He didn't let his frustration with the world manifest itself in destructive behavior. He was sweet and compliant. A pleaser.

Kendall poured herself a glass of sauvignon blanc, a wine that she had enjoyed immensely since Steven left. The only benefit of his departure. He'd always insisted that serious wine drinkers preferred only red. She didn't like that about him at all. It was like he was judging her for what she liked, as if her choices were not in line with what he wanted his wife to be.

There were other things on the list too.

She was too involved in her job.

Try telling a dead boy's mother that you don't have time to take her call.

She was too concerned with her appearance.

Only because he made such an issue of it.

She wasn't interested in his work.

What work? He was unemployed half the time. Selling ads for the magazine was a dead-end career and he should have seen it sooner.

She sipped the glass of wine and settled in at the kitchen table. A couple of raccoons scratched at the window.

And you should never have started to feed them.

Kendall hated what she was doing right then. She loved her husband. Steven Stark, she knew, was the love of her life. She didn't want to start to think of reasons why she shouldn't love him anymore. She didn't have the facts. She didn't know why he was dodging her. It might not have been a dodge after all. It might just be that he was busy in a new job trying to prove himself against some twenty-year-olds in a business that required around-the-clock devotion.

It was a new world, after all.

Kendall refused to get up to give the raccoons any marshmallows. Steven was definitely right about that. Wrong about the sauvignon blanc. She loved that wine and it didn't stain her teeth. Oh, wait a second, maybe he was right? Maybe she was too concerned about her appearance after all.

She shook her head, sending all those distractions to the far corners of the kitchen, and opened the file. Inside, she found interviews, one conducted by a detective long since gone to a new position in Idaho. She'd always considered Nick Mayberry a good deputy, and later a sergeant—one who peeled back every layer of a case. But this file was woefully thin in content. The interviews, Birdy's just-added forensic report, and some photographs taken at the scene. Kendall remembered the case. Everyone in Port Orchard did. A genuine mystery lingers forever.

Katy Frazier was co-captain of the South Kitsap tennis team—no small feat for a sixteen-year-old. She was a straight-A student. She was pretty with long dark hair and hazel eyes that looked almost too large for her heart-shaped face. Her parents were Roger, a former Navy commander who ran a small architectural firm in Port Orchard, and Brit, a school guidance counselor who at the time of her daughter's vanishing had just quit her job with the South Kitsap district to run a coffee shop that supported a clientele of homeless and at-risk teens. Second Cup, Second Chance was in a storefront in downtown Port Orchard. Katy had a sister, Naomi, four years younger, who started acting out and ended up in an alternative school—a blow to her mother, for sure.

The interviews with the parents indicated that both had been away on a trip to Portland, leaving Katy in charge. While Kendall knew others had chimed in about the inappropriateness of leaving a sixteen-year-old alone with her younger sister, Katy was hardly just any kid. She was mature, bright, and highly capable. When the couple arrived home late, Katy was nowhere to be found. Naomi was home, mad about her sister being gone, but seemingly unconcerned.

> Parents notified law enforcement when they
> arrived home. Ms. Frazier indicated that Katy
> had never disobeyed any family rules in "her
> entire life" and that "she would never leave
> Naomi alone, not even for an hour."

In Nick's report, there was a complete description of what he'd seen at the house, a glass cube that Roger had designed to take full advantage of the views of Seattle's skyline across Puget Sound.

> There is absolutely no evidence of a struggle,
> but two small drops of blood were photographed,
> collected, and sent to the lab for analysis. The
> drops were a quarter inch long, oblong disks.
> They were found on the bathroom floor. Also
> recovered from the scene were a hairbrush, a
> toothbrush, and some of the missing girls'
> clothing in case a canine unit will be deployed
> later and DNA analysis is needed.

Along with her sister, who really didn't know anything other than the fact that her sister wasn't home where she was supposed to be, Nick Mayberry also interviewed two of her closest girlfriends, Alyssa Woodley and Tami Overton, along with her on-again, off-again boyfriend, Scott Hilburn. There were transcripts for those interviews.

NICK MAYBERRY: When was the last time you saw Katy?

ALYSSA WOODLEY: At lunch. We were going to hang out after school, but she never called me. I'm still a little mad at her. I mean, now I'm sad. But at the time, I was mad.

NM: Was there anything going on in her life that would make you think she might be in danger?

AW: No. She has a perfect life. Everyone— including me—thinks so.

NM: If she had a perfect life, then why would she walk away from it? You mentioned before we started recording that you thought she just packed it in and left—your words.

AW: Being perfect isn't easy. I don't know how difficult, but I think it would be.

NM: Did Katy get along with her parents?

AW: I guess so. She and her mom went at it every now and then. Nothing outrageous. Her mom was always telling her, pushing her, trying to get her to be the best she could be. That kind of crap.

NM: You think that's crap?

AW: I don't know. It's always hard to live up to someone else's image of what you ought to be in life. I think that bugged Katy, but not so much she'd leave. At least I doubt it. She never said anything to me about it.

NM: All right. What about her relationship with Scott?

AW: Scott is hot and Katy and he made a cute

couple. Probably would be prom king and
queen if they weren't sophomores. They have
that kind of cred around here. Golden couple.
You know.

Kendall paused and let another sip of wine slide down
her throat. She had once been one half of that golden
couple. Everyone thinks that the so-called lucky ones—
those with good hair and teeth—have it made. That
everything will be easy for them and that their lives
will glitter to the end. Fast-forward a decade or more
and all of those things mean nothing. Gold tarnishes
just like tin.

She read on about the girls' friendship and how
they'd known each other since kindergarten at Manchester Elementary. They'd been inseparable until the
past year when Alyssa didn't make the cut for the tennis team.

AW: It bummed me out, but I didn't think it
    would make much difference to our
    friendship, if you were thinking I was jealous
    of her or something.
NM: Who said a word about jealousy?
AW: I don't know. I thought you did.
NM: No. I didn't.

Next, Kendall read the interview with the third prong
of the Katy trio, Tami Overton, also sixteen. It was
recorded two days after Alyssa's interview. Kendall
wondered why the delay in getting her to sit down.
That answer came a third of the way into the interview.

TAMI OVERTON: Sorry I couldn't come sooner. Been sick with the flu.

NM: I'm glad you're feeling better.

TO: Just a little. I still might throw up, but if I do I'll try not to make a spectacle of myself.

NM: Can I get you a 7UP?

TO: You have Sprite? I don't do Pepsi products. My uncle Hank works for Coke and it's been ingrained in us since childhood.

NM: No, sorry. Our vending machines don't feature Coke. Tell me about the last time you saw Katy. When was it? Where? What were you doing? What did you two talk about?

TO: It was at school. The day she went missing. We really didn't talk much. Like we were real close still, but not as close as we had been. I was sad about it, but she seemed to think everything was fine between us. Like she didn't judge me because I couldn't afford the best clothes like she and Alyssa. My parents just didn't have the means. My dad drives a bus for Kitsap Transit and my mom is an unpublished romance novelist. I mean, there was always hope that something big would break for her and we'd be able to move closer to the beach. Like, we never could have had a house like the Frazier place, but something nicer that the tract home we have on Long Lake Road.

NM: Did you think Katy would run away? Was there anything thing pointing to that kind of scenario?

TO: What's a scenario?

NM: Situation? A possibility?

TO: *(shakes head)*

NM: Can you answer directly into the mic?

TO: Ah yes. No, I never thought that. I mean there were times when she like acted all secretive, but, you know, I thought it was because she didn't want to hurt me. She didn't want to tell me something that would make me feel any worse than I already did.

NM: Why were you feeling so bad? Was it about Alyssa and Katy and Scott having a better life than you?

TO: How old are you, Mr. Detective?

NM: Forty-three.

TO: Wow, I thought you'd be older than that. You need Botox or something. My point—and I do have one—is that you can watch your life happen in front of your eyes and do absolutely nothing about it. You can see your own future and know that you're never going to get where some of the other people around you are going to go. Port Orchard is a town full of wannabes and people who have big dreams to make it to a job in Seattle. Maybe get in on the ground floor of a dot-com. Maybe even open a Big Lots store. But for most of us, that's never going to happen. Katy and Scott were different. Alyssa too. They were destined for something and I was going to be the girl they felt sorry for. The one who had a bald husband and a job at Walmart.

NM: That's a bleak picture you've painted.

TO: Well, I guess it's the truth, sir. *(Starts to cry.)* The thing is, I'm happy for her. I hope she escaped Port Orchard. I hope she got the F out of here and is living a better dream than the one her parents plotted for her. I loved her.

The passage was moving. Kendall couldn't help but think that the girl being tabbed had an undeniable sense of reality. Her assessment was simplistic and complex at the same time. Getting out of Port Orchard and doing something elsewhere was the best way back in. It was the only way to come back with an air of respect for the people and the place that depended on each other in the way that some isolated communities do.

Kendall was about to read Scott Hilburn's interview when she heard the familiar scuffling of Cody's footed pajamas over the hardwood floors. He was a few years older than most kids who wear that sleep attire, but it made him feel secure, and Kendall had found a shop online that specialized in footed sleepwear and that was a godsend. Anything that made her son feel comfortable in his own skin was something worth keeping.

"I want to talk to Dad now," he said.

She looked at the clock. It was after eleven.

"It's a little late, honey."

"I want to talk to Dad now," he repeated. His tone indicated there would be an endless rehash of the same statement unless she made an attempt to reach Steven. She swallowed the bottom inch of wine in her glass with a big gulp and punched the button for his number.

This time was met with a bit of a surprise. Steven Stark answered.

"Hey, babe," he said. "What's up? Kind of late to call."

"I've tried three times today," she said, immediately hating her tone. "Anyway, Cody got up missing his father."

"I miss him too. And you. Put him on."

"Daddy."

"That's me, son. How are you doing? How is school?"

"Legos day. Fine. I made about sixty-seven little cars."

"I'd like to see them when I come home. Don't you be taking them apart until I do."

"Okay."

"What else is going on?"

"Mommy's sad."

"She is? Well, I miss Mommy too. Just so busy here, buddy, I'm trying to stay in the game here and it isn't easy, I'll tell you that much."

"Okay. Did you know there are two hundred and two tissues in a Kleenex box?"

"No, I didn't. But I'm glad that I know now. Thanks for sharing. Put Mom back on, will you?"

Kendall reached for the phone and motioned for Cody to get back to bed.

"Our son seems to be doing pretty darn good," Steven said.

"He'd do better if you were here."

"You know I can't be in two places at once, Kendall. I have to do this. This is my shot. You don't understand because you're doing what you've always wanted to do. Fight monsters. I just want to make money. Is that so wrong?"

"When you put it that way, it seems a little shallow, to be honest."

Steven took a moment to reflect. "It is. But I don't mind. I want to take care of you and Cody."

Kendall looked at the wine. Another glass beckoned. "You're never around, Steven."

"I'm busy." This time his tone shifted. She couldn't tell if he was angry, annoyed, or maybe a little resentful. All were good bets. It was, after all, a conversation they'd had before.

Kendall didn't want to be the suspicious wife. She didn't want to be any of those things she despised about the ladies at the gym who found nothing but horrendous things to say about their spouses—everything from the size of his manhood to the condition of his underwear. Yet, she found herself crossing over into that territory.

"I called earlier in the week and you were at a trade show. You never mentioned you were going to go out of town."

"Last minute. I tried to call but there was no cell service. You know how bad our carrier is—works in Port Orchard but nowhere else."

That was true. The cell towers in Port Orchard seem to have an aversion to T-Mobile.

"Maybe we should go back to Verizon. Maybe a landline," he said.

"Maybe tin cans and a string," she said.

Steven laughed and that was good to hear. She missed him so much. She hated that she was being so selfish when he was doing exactly what she would have done—gone for the big prize. Never settle.

Stay golden.

"I love you, Steven," she said.

"I miss you and Cody," he said before hanging up.

Kendall wondered for a split second if missing was the same as loving. She was losing it and she knew it. She was being one of those women who dissected every word in search of a hidden meaning. Never a good one. Just the kind of meaning that was meant to stab and hurt.

Cody was fast asleep, and she turned off his tugboat lamp. The room was still bright from the six nightlights Steven had installed when their son first said he was scared of the dark. His room smelled of rotten bananas and she retrieved the peel of one from under his pillow. There were a million things about her son's world that she'd never understand, how at age six he knew there were 4,021 tiles in the bathroom floor. How he'd fashioned snowmen out of lint from the lint trapper of the dryer and made faces on each one that made the trio resemble his family—perfectly. The hair on his mother's snowman was the yellow lint from a set of yellow flannel sheets. His dad's dark hair was from a sweatshirt that he'd had since high school. Cody's own curly blond hair was fashioned from his own hair. Not hair that he'd plucked from his head, but strands that he'd collected from his pillowcase every day for six months.

She would never, however, even try to understand how it was that her son found it necessary or even appropriate to stick a nasty Chiquita peel under his pillow. That would never, ever happen.

She kissed his forehead and his eyelids popped open. He didn't say a word, but snapped them closed like the slow shutter on an old camera. A smile on his lips as he wriggled down under the covers.

*   *   *

When Kendall returned to the kitchen, the raccoons were back and she did what she knew she shouldn't do. She gave them a handful of mini-marshmallows. She justified it all by telling herself the animals were hungry and the marshmallows were stale.

The last couple of interviews were short—and there was no transcript to accompany them. Scott Hilburn said that he and Katy were "taking some time off" by mutual agreement and he had no idea where she'd gone. She didn't have any enemies "except those two bitches that call themselves her best friends" and "some weirdo, a security guard at the school who followed her around like a puppy dog." In Scott's estimation, his on-and-off-again girlfriend simply split Port Orchard because she had a "decent amount of cash" and a car of her own. Kendall wondered how much cash, where did she get it, and what kind of car, and what became of it. There was no further mention of either in the files.

Lastly she looked at the lab results of the hair sample and blood drops. The blood didn't belong to Katy, but the hair did. It also matched the DNA on her toothbrush, a first-generation Sonicare.

In the morning on her way in to work she thought she'd pay Ms. Frazier a visit at the coffee place. Later, she'd check in with Mr. Frazier. Then the girls, if need be. She probably had enough for *Spirit Hunters* to play her part of the representative from the sheriff's department.

Before she climbed into bed she loaded the DVR player with the DVD that the producers had included in the press kit. It was the story of a supposedly haunted house in Ocean Park, California. Wyatt Ogilvie was his blowhard self, so puffed up with his own importance that he didn't seem to even acknowledge that he was on the show to "uncover" the truth. The poor interview subjects had barely a moment to get a word in edgewise. He prattled on about how he'd solved this and that, how he'd bucked the system, how he was the original phoenix rising from the ashes of a life torched by haters and pointy-headed academics.

"I'm here for one damn reason only," he told a woman who thought that the hauntings were caused by her father's spirit, a man who'd died in a tragic train accident. "I'm here for the damn truth! I want to put a stop to your father's suffering and the pain that he feels every moment of eternity."

The woman started to cry.

"I don't know what Pandora is going to find here, but even I feel his presence," he said. "He's here roaming the halls, looking for justice."

"He can't roam," the woman said. "He has no legs. They were severed by the train."

"Pandora tells me that's a lot of bunk. In the spirit world everyone is young and whole, healthy and beautiful."

In the next scene Pandora, her mane flowing from what had to be an electric fan, came through the house. Her face contorted and she held her hands up high.

You're under arrest for bad acting, Kendall thought.

"Damn you!" she said. "I get it! You're pissed. You're angry! You need to leave here and go to the other side. Your legs are there. The rest of you is waiting. Go now!"

Pandora jerked and looked at the cameraman who

followed her from room to room. "Did you see that?" she asked, her eyes round and mouth painted in a red slash of lipstick, open to its widest.

The cameraman didn't speak. In the preamble to the show, the producers indicate that he cannot say or do anything that might affect the energy of what is occurring when Pandora is doing her job—reaching out to the other side.

It occurred to Kendall that if the cameraman was being shown in the clip, then there was another filming him. So much for the control measures promised by the producers.

"I want you to stop it now," Pandora said, appearing to speak to someone right in front of her. "I don't care what happened to you. You need to get a grip, damn it, and leave your daughter alone. She's in pain here. You are making me really, really mad, sir. I want you gone. I want you gone right now."

Then she let out a scream and fell to the floor. The camera went black. A beat later, one of the producers appeared outside the house.

"We don't know what just happened in there," said the young woman, who Kendall guessed was Juliana Robbins—the sound of her voice coupled with the slight impatience of a New York accent being her primary clues. "I want our viewers to know that Pandora is going to be all right. She's being checked out by our medical team right now. And from what I'm hearing, she's experienced only some minor scrapes and bumps. She insists that she needs to go on. She needs to fight the entity that she now feels is not the homeowner's father, but someone else. Someone who is consumed by rage and may in fact be holding several spirits prisoner—including some children."

Jeesh. Is this over the top. Way over, Kendall thought. *Who believes this crap anyway?*

Kendall fast-forwarded to the end.

The screen read: The Showdown.

Pandora stood at the top of the stairs holding a candle. The light from its flame flickered on her face as she contorted and spun around in a circle. Her breathing was either very loud, or the sound mixer had amped it up during post-production. It was all very, very dramatic.

"You can kill me, sir. I don't care because if you do, I will come after you with an army of spirits and you will go back into the hellhole from which you came. Take me on. I *bleep* dare you. I *bleep bleep* double dare you. You weren't a real man in the real world and you're a pussy in the afterlife. You don't want me to come after you. Trust me. No one wants that. But I'm *bleep* ready!"

With that the candle went out and there was a scream. A bloodcurdling scream. It was so authentic that it actually sent a chill down Kendall's spine. She hoped Cody didn't hear it.

In the next scene all the principals were seated around the family's kitchen table. Pandora looked like she'd been through hell. Her eyes were bloodshot and her hands shook as she sipped her coffee.

Wyatt Ogilvie spoke first.

"*Spirit Hunters* is about a lot of things, but not this. Not this kind of a war we had here last night. Pandy is lucky to be alive. We're all lucky to be alive."

Finally Pandora spoke. "Luck has nothing to do with it, Wyatt. We're alive because I was willing to fight to the death to get to the truth of what happened here. I'm convinced now that the evil entity in your house was your father."

She looked at the woman across the table. Her eyes were raining tears.

"The children were his victims. I'm sorry to say, but your father was a child molester. He raped and murdered those babies over most of his life."

"I . . . I . . ." The woman didn't know what to say. "I thought he died in a train accident and that he was here because he needed us."

"No," she said. "He was here because this is where he kept his victims, trapped for eternity. Trapped for all time. Trapped until someone—in this case me—came here to free them all and put him inside the gates of hell where he will rot and burn forever."

"My dad loved kids," the woman, now in full-on cry.

"Yes. Loved them for sex and torture," Pandora said. "Only when you wise up and come to grips with what happened here tonight—and only if you do—will you ever find peace for yourself and your family."

Pandora turned to her partner in crime. "Wyatt, let's go. This place sickens me."

"Me too. Nothing more to be done here."

Kendall was so appalled by what she saw that she got on her iPad and searched the Internet for the woman's name. There were a lot of hits. Many were from fan sites and, of course, YouTube clips featuring bits of the show. A couple—one from a newspaper and one from a mom blogger—caught Kendall's eye.

'SPIRIT HUNTERS' COURT CASE TOSSED OUT

An Ocean City woman who sued a reality show for portraying her father as a child molester has been left holding the bag. Her contract with the production company for the show "Spirit Hunters" doesn't allow any recourse for the productions they make.

"These people are good," Richard Button, the lawyer for the woman said. "They know how to write an ironclad contract. We didn't think we had a shot, but my client was so upset by the turn of events and the way the show twisted everything she'd said and done into something very ugly, she wanted to at least try to have her day in court."

There will be no appeal.

The next one was from a blog called Live & Learn. It was written by a consortium of mommy bloggers who took on the minutiae of life (how to make dryer sheets from scented paper towels, and a recipe for making fat-free tortilla chips with tortillas, cooking spray, and a microwave oven). Moms, Kendall knew, were always busy, and while she didn't need to know how to do either of those things, she didn't feel sorry for or superior to those who did.

The entry that led her there had nothing to do with any of those things at all. It was nothing about household tips, how to fix a daughter's broken heart, or how to ask for a raise from a skinflint boss.

Instead, the piece that provided the hit was written by a woman named Missy Moore Thanever from Nova Scotia, Canada:

I have no one to blame but myself for this debacle. I was stupid enough to believe the producers when they told me they were truth seekers and they believed that the washed-up cop and the psychic were really going to help. Stupid me. I dabbled with the tarot. I've had my palm read a time or two . . . and honestly, the things I learned were spot-on. That's my full disclosure.

Here's what happened. My little boy and his uncle went fishing two years ago. Charlie was six at the time. His uncle was a good guy and my husband and I trusted him—he's my brother so why wouldn't I trust Mickey? They went at first light to catch the tide out at the lighthouse not far from our house. I got up and gave them both a hug (and a kiss for Charlie), and off they went. Five hours later, my brother turned up on our doorstep. He was a complete wreck, shaking, crying, everything. I didn't have to ask. I knew something was wrong. I knew it. Sometimes I think I'm psychic because I had a little bad feeling that morning too. He told us what happened and, of course, our world was shattered. He said that Charlie was fishing from the bow when a rogue wave looped over the top of him and pulled him into the Atlantic. Mickey dove in and went after him, but he couldn't find him. No one ever did.

If you've lost a baby, then you know how I felt then and how I feel now. It just doesn't go away.

That was six years ago. After Charlie disappeared in the sea, people reported strange goings-on at the lighthouse. The lamp would go off and have to be started over and over. It got so bad that the lighthouse keeper who stayed there for sixteen years, because it was such an easy job with cool living spaces, up and quit. He told friends that he thought the place was haunted and he said all the trouble started a few weeks after Charlie's accident.

Enter *Spirit Hunters*. I wrote to them, so the fault for what followed, I guess, is mine. They make you feel that way, that's for sure. At first they act so nice and so sincere that you really do believe that they have your best interests at heart. I knew the cop on the show had some trouble in the past, but that made me like him even more. It was like he had something to prove and that was going to make him work harder. And about Pandora. What can I say that others who have written to me haven't? Besides, contractually, you can't say much of anything at all. You don't even get to meet her until after the sit-down at the end when they give you the big reveal—which incidentally was held in the cramped quarters of the lighthouse for what I presume was for maximum drama. Nothing better than a lighthouse in the middle of the night—or in this case early, early morning.

Okay, so it was me and my husband, my brother, and our eight-year-old daughter. Since I can't say much I hope you can read between the lines here. I'm considering this a warning to any of you. If you watch the clip, I can recap what aired. Basically Pandora told me that my daughter (leaving her name out here, for obvious reasons) was behind everything. She was only a two-year-old at the time, but according to Pandora, her jealousy of her brother getting to go fishing fueled a dark rage inside of her.

My daughter has no dark rage, though now she's in therapy for what happened and how some bloggers have called her the Bad Seed of Nova Scotia. I am crying now as I type this because I hurt so much for her. She didn't deserve any of this. I brought it on because I missed Charlie so much.

On the show, Pandora turned to my daughter and screamed at her that she "knew what evil lives inside" of her. In shock, my eight-year-old ran from the table crying to her bedroom.

Pandora smiled. My husband and I were stunned. But with the cameras rolling, there was some kind of weird control over us. It was like we didn't want to ruin their TV show because the producers had been so nice, the cop seemed to care, and the medium flat out said to me that her abilities at ferreting out the truth were the greatest the world had ever known.

"The girl needs therapy. She has to get help. Her envy manifested itself into that rogue wave."

We just sat there.

The producer, Juliana, pulled out a drawing that a forensic artist somewhere in town had completed under Pandora's direction. I wondered who that artist was. I didn't know we had any in NS. The drawing was a picture of my boy on the bow of that boat; the wave had morphed into a claw-like hand and was ready to grab him and pull him under.

We didn't say a word. At least my husband and I didn't. Mickey spoke up, saying this was the biggest piece of crap he'd ever been a part of, but they didn't air that bit. Instead they closed the show with Pandora's response.

"The truth is painful sometimes. Now you can go on with your lives. Get your daughter some help, or any one of you could be next."

I finally found my voice and yelled at them about taking advantage of people, putting something so nasty on the shoulders of a little girl who had done nothing to deserve it, but they cut that out too.

They'll probably look very closely at this site.
So I had my lawyer look at it. He says I'm good.
Here's the final tidbit and I'll not comment on it but
instead link to it. This is a video clip taken by the
lighthouse's security camera that night. It shows
Pandora, a producer, and the cop Wyatt Ogilvie
standing around smoking by the lighthouse door.

Kendall clicked on the link. A grainy black-and-
white video started to roll.

OGILVIE: Which way you gonna go here, Pandy?
PANDORA: *(laughing as she exhales on her cigarette)* I have two drawings. One with the uncle
molesting the boy, but legal says that's a tough
one. I really pushed for it. The other is the kid
being at fault.
OGILVIE: F me. Not the old Bad Seed deal. This
is season two and we're running out of ideas
already. You did that two episodes ago in New
Mexico. When we did the haunted
Farmington barn.

The producer, a middle-aged male, spoke next.

PRODUCER: We go with what works. And
honestly that Farmington show scored us our
best ratings this year. People love a bad seed.
We all want to make this show a success. I
mean, that's why we're doing this, right?
OGILVIE: You mean it isn't about helping people
get rid of their hauntings?

All three laughed.

Pandora crushed out her cigarette butt with the pointy end of one of her Manolos.

PANDORA: We're helping people, all right. I have no doubt that any direction I go is the right direction. You might laugh at my guides, but I can't help that I'm gifted. Tortured by them. Whatever you want to call it.

OGILVIE: How long will this be until we wrap? I need a drink.

PANDORA: We all do. Bad seeds can be so boring.

The tape ended and Kendall felt a wave of nausea roll to her stomach. How could anyone believe this crap? How could the Fraziers invite these people into their home to dissect their family tragedy? She scrolled though the hundreds of comments and there were only a very small handful of people who seemed to feel the same that she did. By far and away, the clip viewers were completely supportive of Pandora.

. . . this mom is a hater and I'm glad she got some tough love at the table from Pandora . . .

. . . people will say anything when they don't get their way . . .

. . . that kid had the eyes of a shark. Soulless. I think Pandora was spot-on as usual . . .

. . . did you notice how that dad and brother just sat there like they didn't even care about what happened to Charlie? If I were them, I'd watch out. I bet that daughter will drown one of them when she gets the chance . . .

*. . . it was so cruel of the mom to put up this
obviously edited video. It's no wonder that her
daughter is evil. The apple never falls very far from
the tree, you know . . .*

Kendall had read enough. She knew that her first stop
after taking Cody to the Cascade School the next morning would be Brit Frazier's coffee shop.

CHAPTER SEVEN

B renda Nevins hated the idea of cutting her hair. She loathed coloring, chopping, or changing her signature look more than anything she'd ever endured. More than being locked up in prison, which she considered to be the worst thing that had ever happened to her. She knew that she needed to alter her appearance, but at what cost? If she couldn't be the person the world expected her to be, what was the point of anything she was about to do?

She applied the black hair dye she'd found in the homeowner's medicine cabinet. She looked at the glint of the scissors and the knife and shook her head. There were a million uses for sharp objects, but cutting her hair was not one of them. She put her wet, black hair up in a clip, turned on the shower, and surveyed the scene.

It wasn't the Four Seasons, but she had stayed in far worse places than the one that was her refuge at that moment. She let the water from the shower pour over her, sending some inky blackness down the drain. She lifted her head back and let the spray of the showerhead run over her teeth. She missed her Waterpik. The prison rule-makers considered the device that sent a needle-sharp stream of water a potential weapon. Brenda had hated rules. Sonicare toothbrushes were allowed for "dental use only" but half the women in her unit at the prison used them as vibrators.

As the water caressed her body she ran her hands over her breasts and marveled that they felt so real, so unencumbered by scar tissue, as she'd read other women had supposedly endured. Her heart was beating slowly just then. She had that part of her personality that allowed her to compartmentalize her trauma and drama into separate spaces in which no part would touch the other. No overload. No crossed circuits. For how she lived her life, she needed more than anything to stay focused. Keep control. Aim high. Get what she wanted.

Brenda was free at the moment and she intended to stay that way.

She turned off the water, pulled back the shower curtain, which made a slightly melodic scraping noise, and stepped out. She reached for a towel and applied its softness to her face. So much better than those nearly crisp towels at the prison. Though it indeed wasn't the Four Seasons, she thought the towels smelled just like spring.

The mirror was fogged and she rubbed a washcloth over it.

She looked good with black hair. Her skin didn't fight with the change. It looked natural. She finger-combed it a little, considering one last time whether she should cut it or just leave it. Long hair was sexy. She was sexy right then.

She needed to stay that way too.

"I'll be out in a minute, babe," she called out.

Brenda didn't like to be rushed. Not when she was thinking about what to do next. She knew she had to think fast. Not move fast. Moving fast could get her caught. It was better to synthesize a plan that used her best attributes and left the excess baggage behind. Be nimble. Be ready.

Be cunning.

She tucked the towel around her body and wrapped another over her still damp hair. One last glance at herself in the mirror and she went toward the bed.

"You look scared," Brenda said.

No answer.

"Don't worry. It will all be over soon. I promise."

Janie Thomas didn't say a word. She looked at Brenda with the kind of haunted eyes of a fox caught in a leg trap. Tears oozed from her eyes.

Brenda produced a knife.

Janie turned away. Her heart was racing and she was all but certain that this was the way she was going to die.

"Don't worry, babe," she said. "I'm just going to cut a little hole in the tape so you can take a drink."

Brenda sat on the edge of the bed, admiring the sturdiness of the knots she'd made of the cut pillowcase—again the handiwork of the knife. She learned the skill of slicing and dicing with precision from Edna Hale, a woman imprisoned at the Washington Corrections Center for Women for attacking a boyfriend and making certain that he'd never cheat on her again. Lorena Bobbitt had become a quasi-celebrity when she'd sliced off her husband's penis for similar reasons, but not Edna. Slicing it off in a fit of rage, a bloody payback for betrayal was one thing.

Feeding it to the family's dog was something entirely too disgusting for mass appeal.

"Never hesitate," Edna had instructed Brenda when they were on kitchen duty one time, early in her incarceration. "That's the key. Go fast, go deep, and never look back."

"Good advice," Brenda said. "But you forgot one thing."

Edna wiped the sweat off her hairy upper lip.

"What's that?" she asked.

Brenda knew she'd made the same error. They were there together, pulling kitchen duty. Nevertheless Edna was too dumb to get it.

"Never get caught," Brenda said.

Janie Thomas started wriggling. It made Brenda think of one of those "Magic Fingers" beds she'd slept on when she was a child in a place two levels below the house that she and Janie were hiding out in.

Brenda let out a loud sigh.

"Look," she said, her tone suddenly sharp. "You want me to cut your lips? No one wants to kiss bloody lips. Hold still."

Janie shut her eyes.

Brenda repositioned herself over Janie to ensure that she didn't move so much and ran the blade down the center of the silvery duct tape and a sliver of red dripped down.

"Look what you made me do, you stupid bitch!"

Janie let out a muffled cry.

"I swear that you are almost more trouble than you're worth. If I didn't love you so much I'd cut your head off right now, babe," she said.

She knew she could do that. But not now. Not when she needed Janie. Useful Janie. Puppy dog Janie. The prison superintendent who had been her ticket out from the razor wire into the world of fresh air, quiet nights, men she could pick up, beguile, ride in the backseat of a car, and then . . . do what she did best.

Second best.

CHAPTER EIGHT

Second Cup, Second Chance was located on Bay Street in what had once been an antique shop and before that, a waterfront warehouse. Inside, it had been stripped of the doilies, old tables, and other questionable antiques and was outfitted with a distinctly modern vibe. It was as if Apple Computer had come in and taken over the space. The mix of the old wood with the brushed steel finishes of the tabletops and the Eames-style chairs (all white, with one turquoise one for a tasteful quirk) made it modern, fresh, and very teen friendly. In the back corner was the espresso bar. In the opposite corner, a gigantic flat screen showed teenagers' artwork on a rotating basis. Kendall Stark had never been inside before, and she was impressed.

Brit Frazier was talking to a teen.

"We have rules, Sammie, and they are simple. You can spend all day here if you like, but you cannot sleep here. The city won't allow that. You can take a shower. I do have meals at nine, eleven, and four. More than anything, I want you to work with a mentor to help you find your way out of your situation and on to your 'Second Chance.' That's what we're all about."

She looked up, caught Kendall's gaze, and nodded. She mouthed the words "just a minute" and motioned for Kendall to take a seat across the room.

A moment later, she came over with two cups of coffee.

"It's about the show, Detective Stark. Isn't it?" she said, sitting down.

Her directness surprised Kendall. She was probably adept at reading people; her history as a guidance counselor was a strong indicator of that. Also, in that moment with the girl Sammie, Kendall could tell that being direct, kind, and honest was probably the course Brit Frazier had always chosen.

"Yes. How did you know?" Kendall asked anyway.

Brit poured a packet of blue sweetener into her cup and swirled its contents with a spoon.

"Small town," she said, almost with a sigh. "Everyone's been talking about it. I know your sheriff had reservations about participating, but I convinced him. It isn't like we have anything to lose. It's been four years, you know."

Kendall sipped the coffee. It was a very dark roast, the kind she wanted and needed after a night of tossing and turning over what she'd read about *Spirit Hunters*.

"Mrs. Frazier, do you know anything about these producers, their tactics?"

Brit Frazier pulled a loose strand of her red hair and rested it on her shoulder. Her expression was hard to read and she didn't jump to answer right away.

"Do you?" Kendall asked.

"I heard you the first time, Detective. I have read the posts by those who are less than happy with the results of the show. There are an equal number if not more who feel that their circumstances shifted into something more bearable after *Spirit Hunters* came to town."

"More bearable? How do you mean?"

Brit drank more coffee. "You couldn't possibly understand and that's fine. I remember when I was counseling kids at South and telling them that I understood, I was lying. I wanted to understand. I said so. But you can't. You can't ever know how another person feels when the unthinkable occurs."

Kendall nodded. Brit didn't know all that much about her, but she was right about that. She'd interviewed countless people who'd undergone tragedy of immense magnitude and she held their hands, cried with them, told them that everything would be all right. That they'd survive.

"I'm not saying you don't empathize with me and my husband. I know you do, but let's face it. We're stuck in a limbo from which we cannot escape. If *Spirit Hunters* does anything with Pandora and Wyatt's help, then maybe we're a step closer to getting a little freedom from what's holding us down."

"You mean closure?" Kendall asked.

Brit shook her head. "No such thing. We both know that. But one thing I know and you don't is that every night I go to bed and wonder what's become of Katy. I wake up with the same thought. I'm stuck in a time warp. It's ruining my relationship with my husband and Katy's sister."

A teen with blue and orange hair came over to the table.

"Ms. Frazier, I finished cleaning the kitchen. Can I work in Katy's Place for a while?"

"Go ahead, Melissa. And thanks for asking," she said.

"Katy's Place?"

Brit indicated the corner with the big flat screen and the teen artwork.

"My daughter was good at just about everything. Classes. Tennis. She was also quite an artist. We put in the creative space for teens in her memory."

"That's lovely," Kendall said. "You said her memory. So you think—"

Kendall's words trailed off a little and Brit cut in.

"Yes, she's dead."

"But there isn't any evidence."

"My daughter would never have left us. She was happy. She was well-adjusted. An achiever."

"Maybe she felt pressure to be the best," Kendall said, echoing a note Nick Mayberry had made in the file.

"I've heard that theory before, Detective. And I don't buy it. That kind of theory comes from someone on the outside looking in. Katy was never pressured to be the best. She wanted to be the best because it made her happy. Not because Roger and I wanted it. We're not like that. In fact, I find beauty in all kinds of imperfection. Imperfection is not a weakness."

"But this show . . . you know it's fake, don't you?"

Brit shrugged. Her eyes lingered on Melissa before she looked back at Kendall.

"Maybe. Probably. I don't really know. I know only one thing that's good about it and that cannot be disputed by anyone."

"And what's that?"

Brit got up. "You're here, aren't you? You are work-ing this case now, aren't you? I begged the sheriff to put you on the show. No one else. I figured that just maybe a woman with a child of her own would dig in a little deeper to find out what happened to my daugh-ter."

"Nick Mayberry did a very thorough job," Kendall said. "I don't know that I could have done better. Not with what he had to work with at the time. There really wasn't much to go on."

"You can do better. I have faith in you, Detective. I have hope that you will find something that everyone else missed. Maybe with Pandora and Wyatt's help you'll do what should have been done four years ago."

Kendall didn't know what to say. It was a challenge and, in a weird way, a threat at the same time.

Brit made her way over to Katy's Place, turning to look in Kendall's direction one last time.

"Find out who killed my daughter. Find out. Let her rest. Let all of us rest."

Kendall gulped down the rest of her coffee, got be-hind the wheel of her SUV, and drove up the steep in-cline that was Division Street to the complex that housed most of the county's law enforcement agencies, including the sheriff's department, the jail, and the courthouse. She knew why she'd been tapped to do the show and no one else. Brit Frazier and the sheriff had a history. It was a long time ago, before either was mar-ried. When she called for help, he had only one choice and like it or not Kendall had been drafted. That pip-squeak PIO Brad James probably didn't even know about any of that.

Why would he? He was all about proving himself

on his own terms. He wanted to put Port Orchard and Kitsap County on the map. It was going to be a feather in his cap, the likes of which hadn't been seen since the remake of *Walking Tall* was filmed up north in the county.

Kendall dialed Birdy as she went inside the sheriff's office. "You want to do lunch today?" she asked.

"Sure," Birdy said. "You might be too big a star for that soon enough."

Kendall took a breath. How did everyone know what troubled her? "It's about that," she said, finally.

"I figured. Puerto Vallarta?"

"Sounds good. See you there at noon."

Puerto Vallarta has a great big red neon sign that proclaims IMMEDIATE SEATING and it was never—at least as far as anyone in Port Orchard knew—turned off. It wasn't because the place never filled up, because it was always busy. But it was large enough to get people to a table with scarcely a minute to wait. Birdy and Kendall were seated in the sunken fountain area, next to an automated tortilla maker. A pretty young woman named, quite appropriately, Bonita operated the machine, carefully stacking the corn and flour disks as they rolled off the heated conveyor belt into a wire basket.

"I cannot miss having one of those," Birdy said.

"Me too."

"Do you know what you want?"

"Yes, but I can't have a margarita."

"That kind of day already?" Birdy asked.

"Yeah. It's just a little of everything. All coming

at me at once. Steven. The show. Mrs. Frazier. Brenda Nevins. It's like a steady drip of disaster after disaster."

"More like a deluge," Birdy said.

"Right. More like that."

A waiter came and they ordered. Birdy got two soft chicken tacos and Kendall ordered the tortilla soup.

"And a basket of those," she said, indicating the mountain of corn tortillas that Bonita was putting into small flat containers.

After the waiter left, Birdy asked about Steven.

"That's got to be what's really putting you at odds with the world right now."

Kendall didn't want to cry, and she knew if she said too much about what she was feeling she'd dissolve into tears.

"I guess I can't talk about that, Birdy. I want to. I know that it would probably help, but I don't know much more than what I'm feeling and thinking and suspecting and I don't like living on assumptions."

"Of course. You want the facts."

Kendall looked down at the basket of chips and salsa.

"Yeah, I guess so."

"So let's talk about the *Spirit Hunters* show. What's the latest on that? Did you find anything of interest in the file I gave you, such that it was?"

Kendall shook her head. "Not really. I mean, who can be sure that the crime scene—if there was a crime—was actually at the Frazier residence? It could have been anywhere. Those blood drops don't tell us much—and we don't even know whose blood it was anyway."

"Right. It wasn't Katy's, that's for sure."

"Yeah, and according to the report they tested it against other members of the household and they indicated no match to the mom, father, or sister."

"Right. So I'd say that's a dead end. Unless we're going to test everyone in Port Orchard."

Their food came and they both picked at their plates. Neither felt particularly hungry. Lunch was seldom about eating anyway.

"What are you going to do?" Birdy asked.

"With the show?"

"Yes, the show, but also the case."

Kendall swallowed. "I'm meeting with the producer tonight. Dinner at Cosmo's."

"That should be interesting. When are you going to meet Pandora and Ogilvie?"

"I guess the show protocol is that no one meets Pandora until after their investigation. I'll go on camera with Ogilvie tomorrow."

"That should be fun," Birdy said with full-on sarcasm.

Kendall nodded. "Just what I've always wanted."

"And the case," Birdy said, "what are you going to do there?"

"How do you mean?"

"You're going to reinvestigate, aren't you?"

Kendall smiled. Birdy knew her well now and with Steven gone she felt like there was no one else who really understood who she was, what made her tick. At least anyone who she felt the same way about. Birdy was just like her. She was a puzzle solver. She was the kind of person who liked to pick up a trail and follow it to the very end, no matter how hard, how painful.

How hopeless it might seem.

"I am. I'm going to try to talk to a few of Katy's friends, her father, her teachers, anyone who might give me a little insight. Her mother is pretty wrapped up in trying to do good for the other troubled kids of Kitsap County that I doubt she will really open up. Nothing probably could be harder than being a guidance counselor and having your kid run away. Or worse."

Birdy asked that her second taco be wrapped up to go.

"Elan will devour it in one bite," she said.

"How's he doing?"

"Great. We're both doing great. My sister has backed off and things have calmed considerably. I almost don't want to say it out loud because I'm afraid it will jinx it."

"Say it, Birdy."

Birdy smiled. "All right, Kendall. I hope I get to keep him."

Kendall smiled back and the two women laughed.

"That sounded like he is a puppy or something," Birdy said. "But you know what I mean, don't you?"

"I do. And I hope you get to keep him too."

It was sunny when the detective and the forensic pathologist went through the massive swinging doors after paying for lunch—Kendall's treat this time. The air felt clean and there was a gentle breeze. Wafting through it was the smell of Bonita's amazing corn tortillas. The IMMEDIATE SEATING sign blasted away at a now-empty parking lot.

Brenda Nevins scanned the pages of the Mason County *Journal*. She didn't care what was going on in the Middle East, in politics, in the state of the world.

None of that mattered. Nor did she care about the Kardashians or any other low-wattage celebrity who would come and go. She was above all that. She was beautiful and she knew that her body—however fake her breasts— was a gift to the world. She only cared about one thing, how her little escape from prison was playing in the local paper.

"Janie," she said, her tone impatient, "please stop gasping over there, I'm trying to read and you are annoying the hell out of me."

Janie, tied to the bed, winced and tried to stifle the pain that made her gasp and cry.

"Better, babe. Better little prison bitch," Brenda said, finally finding an article—in an embarrassingly back-of-the-paper section called News Briefs. Her eyes sparked as she read aloud.

"'Nevins is a narcissist,' Kitsap County sheriff's detective Kendall Stark said.

'She craves the spotlight and, like a moth to the flame, she'll be burned by it. She's classic and while we don't know what she will end up doing—predicting human behavior can be as faulty as playing the lottery—you can bet that she'll do something stupid and get caught.'"

She stopped reading and glared over at Janie.

"Damn you! You stupid bitch. Shut up!"

Janie looked away.

"Look at me when I'm talking to you. Don't make me burn you again. Because I swear I will. I'll dip your nose in gasoline and strike a match."

Janie looked at her. Her eyes were pools of terror. With everything that had happened in the days since they'd left the prison, she'd grown more and more aware what Brenda Nevins was capable of. She knew that to make Brenda mad was to have a hanger shoved inside her. To have a cigarette extinguished on her cheek.

"A second one," Brenda had said, "because even in disfigurement you need balance."

Janie tried not to breathe. She tried to will her body in spite of the agony to stop sending her messages that she was going to die.

Brenda looked back down at the paper and seethed.

"Listen to this crap," she said. "Are you goddamn listening to me?"

Janie nodded again.

"'Stark and forensic pathologist Waterman got up close and personal with Nevins when investigating the case of a missing Kitsap County teen earlier this year. Dr. Waterman agreed with Stark's assessment. 'Nevins will turn up. She's not nearly as clever as she thinks. In time, I'm confident that she'll be behind bars where she belongs and this time for good.'"

The switch flipped and Nevins started to laugh.

"Not clever? That's funny. I can think of a million things to do with a screwdriver and some wire that would make both those two-bit county gals wishing they were never born."

Her eyes lingered on Janie. Lasered her, really. Her eyes were knives. The prison superintendent weakly nodded.

"Damn right," Brenda said, dropping the paper and flopping on the bed next to Janie. Janie's body stiffened like a dead cat rolled over by a line of cars on the freeway and she held her breath. She wasn't sure what was coming but she knew that it wasn't going to be good. Not with Brenda. Brenda didn't know the meaning of kindness. Brenda wanted only what she could get and at the top of the list were money, fame, and revenge.

She ran her fingertips through Janie's hair. Brenda's nails used to be her trademark. They were long, lacquered, and usually the kind of brazen red that reminded men of the color of their dream Camaro. But after years in prison without the fawning ladies of the salon, only the negligible talents of a woman who went by the name Cuttlefish to do them, they were less than what she'd wanted. Less than what she deserved. She raked them through Janie's hair, this time hard enough to scratch.

Like a turtle Janie withdrew even more, but carefully so, not so much that Brenda would hurt her again.

"I thought we'd have a little fun, you and me. We'd get dressed up and go out to the casino and maybe find some jerk to roll for his winnings. But now I'm not so sure, babe. I think other things are on the horizon for us. What do you think?"

Janie couldn't speak, even if she tried.

"Are you listening to me?"

Janie's eyes, puddled with tears, indicated that she was.

"We're not going to do any of those things. We're going to make sure that those haters out there are put in their place. I'm not clever? I'm not? Do you think I'm clever? You should because you'd be home with that dope of a husband right now if I hadn't been so damn clever."

Janie winced. It was all she could do.

Brenda nuzzled her like a kitten. A terrified, abused, sad little kitten, but nevertheless, it was better than being tortured again.

Brenda thought about Kendall Stark and Birdy Waterman. She'd met Kendall in prison for an interview about her relationship with a former guard.

"Not impressive, Janie. Not at all. That detective was strictly amateur hour. The pathologist I'd imagine isn't much to write home about either. If she was a decent doctor she'd be working on people who were still alive now, wouldn't she?"

Janie blinked.

"Not clever, huh? I don't want to be narcissistic because I don't like labels, but I've got more than clever in me. I've got a touch of the devil."

Brenda closed her eyes and thought of all the things she could do to Kendall Stark and Birdy Waterman. Some involved flames. Some sharp objects. One an explosive. But as she pondered these things and drifted off to a rage-filled slumber, she knew that the one thing she could do better than anyone was to make someone remember her.

"Night, babe," she said.

And that was that.

CHAPTER NINE

Brit Frazier's words haunted Kendall. She sat in her car in the parking lot of the architecture and design firm that bore Roger Frazier's name. She took a gulp of air and cracked the window. She felt sick, hot. It wasn't from the salsa at Puerto Vallarta, either. It was the nervousness that found a place to rest in her stomach.

Damn, she thought. *I don't like playing clean-up. Not for a partner, not for a departed colleague. It's disloyal and embarrassing.*

It was true that no matter how many cases she'd worked, nor how many grieving mothers she comforted, there was no way she could fully comprehend the disappearance and likely murder of a child. She didn't blame Brit for wanting something to happen with her daughter's dead-end case. The skimpiness of the file was proof enough that no matter how nice a guy Nick Mayberry was, he wasn't the dogged investigator that Katy Frazier's case required. It appeared that he interviewed all the principals, recorded all the details, and then, well, stopped. It was like he'd hit a roadblock and left the Fraziers adrift without any kind of resolution.

Roger Frazier was expecting her. He stood in the doorway to the conference room that looked out over Gig Harbor.

"If your buildings are as beautiful as your view, Mr. Frazier—and I expect they are—then you probably have designed many of the proverbial 'dream homes' for people around here."

He smiled. "They are and I have." His tone didn't suggest smugness or self-satisfaction, but a kind of confidence. Much like his wife's. "Have a seat," he said.

"Thank you for seeing me on such short notice," she said as she slid herself into a steel-framed leather chair and rolled her lap under the glass-topped conference room table. "You have a lot going on right now."

He sat across from her. He was in his fifties, but looked younger. His hair receded and his eyes were sharp and laser-focused on her. He wore a bright white pressed shirt with the sleeves rolled up. There was the slightest smudge of graphite on his right cuff, indicating that he probably still wielded a pencil when drawing the dreams of others on paper.

"We all have a lot going on. But for us, the world stops whenever we think of our daughter. Which is pretty much every hour of every day."

"I'm sorry," Kendall said.

"Sorry is what you tell a kid when you don't have enough money for a popsicle. This is well beyond sorry, Detective."

She understood and nodded.

"Sorry," he went on, unable to stop himself, "is the state of your office when we were so desperate for some help. Sorry is the four years of not knowing what happened, which I put on the Kitsap County sheriff and those who work for him."

Kendall was unsure if this mini-tirade was directed at her or at the fact that his wife had dated the sheriff a few times and he was uncomfortable with everyone in Port Orchard knowing that.

"Look," she said, "I'm here to help. I'm doing the show at the request of the sheriff and against my better judgment."

"My wife and I appreciate that. We know that it's not the conventional route to go, but we've appealed to everyone, every goddamn TV show, magazine, and newspaper of any stature. We think that getting the word out is our only hope of finding Katy."

"I understand," Kendall said. "But really, *Spirit Hunters*? Do you think they will come up with anything?"

He shook his head. "Doubtful. But what I do know is that the publicity won't hurt us."

Kendall wanted to tell him about the woman in Nova Scotia, but part of her figured none of that would matter. The Fraziers were looking for an answer, a shred of hope, and if it came from some psychic TV show it was probably good enough for them.

"What do you think happened to Katy?"

Roger Frazier folded his hands on the table. "I don't know. Do I think she ran away? Absolutely not. Do I think she was abducted by a stranger? Possibly. Look, Detective, I've had four years to run every single scenario through my mind. My wife and I barely have a conversation in which Katy's whereabouts isn't mentioned."

"I'm sure it's all-consuming," Kendall said, hoping he wouldn't challenge her on her feelings—not as his wife had done. She moved the subject quickly toward the reason why she was there. "I'm going to do the show," she said, "but that's not all. I'm going to look at the case and assess each bit of evidence. I'm going to reinterview all the witnesses who Nick Mayberry interviewed and we'll see what fresh eyes can turn up."

The mention of Nick's name brought a look of contempt to Roger's face.

"Your colleague muffed this one, badly," he said.

"He's a good investigator," Kendall said.

"I hope you're a better one."

"That remains to be seen," she said. "Looking at the files, I noticed that Katy had a small circle of friends and each of them was interviewed."

"She was popular, but yes, she valued genuine relationships over numbers. Her best friends were Alyssa Woodley and Tami Overton. She also dated Scott Hilburn, but that had cooled months before she vanished."

"Are they in the area?"

He shook his head. "Alyssa goes to the U and Tami, I'm not sure where she is. Poor kid. She's had some trouble with drugs. I know she's been in and out of rehab a couple of times. Brit did some outreach at a treatment center three years ago and saw her there. She was a mess."

"What about Scott?"

"He's at the U too."

Kendall looked at her phone. The afternoon was winding down. There wasn't time to get over to Seattle and visit Alyssa and Scott at the University of Washington campus, but there was time to see if Tami Overton's parents had any information on her whereabouts.

"I'm having dinner with Juliana Robbins," Kendall said. "I expect you've met her already."

He nodded.

"What's your take?"

Roger pushed back his chair. "Nice girl. Just trying to make a living doing a tough job. Like the rest of us, I guess. She knows the story well and I think she'll do a good job with it."

"You know the Internet is full of complaints about the show."

"Have you ever checked out the Yelp comments on your favorite restaurant?"

"No," she said.

"We'll, if you had, you'll see that not everyone has the same experience as yours. That's just the way it is. I'll bet that *Spirit Hunters* has more supporters than haters, but that's the way I live my life. I always expect the best of people. Maybe in your job, you're trained to look in the opposite direction."

"Maybe," Kendall said, though she hated to think that being a homicide investigator made her suspicious of everyone and everything. She sure didn't feel like that was the case.

CHAPTER TEN

Brenda Nevins sat alone at the end of the bar while CNN replayed a capsule version of her story, the murders that sent her to prison, the escape, the missing prison superintendent Janie Thomas.

"Another Bloody Mary?" the bartender, a middle-aged guy named Chaz, asked.

"Sure," she said. "But put some vodka in it this time."

Her tone was impatient, sharp. She caught his look of annoyance and amended it with a smile. Although she craved the spotlight, she didn't want to stand out in a crowd. Not right then, anyway.

"No problem," he said. "You visiting the area?"

"Yes," she said.

"Traveling alone?"

A surge of adrenaline went through her body. *He wanted her.* All men did. She leaned forward so he could see more of her breasts. She watched as his blue eyes burrowed in her ample cleavage. Her breasts were magnets, she was sure. No man could resist them. When she walked, she imagined they were a pair of bouncing balls coercing men to sing along to her charms.

He wasn't young or rich. So she wasn't interested.

"With a friend," she said.

Chaz shrugged and set down the drink. "Some story," he said, looking up at the TV. "Police were all over this place."

She kept her eyes on him and grabbed the celery stalk and proceeded to dip it in and out of the drink. Up and down. Up and down.

"You don't say," she said. "What happened?"

"Our local prison superintendent went lesbian on her husband, I guess. Fell in love with a serial killer and the two ran off together. Probably to Mexico or Canada."

"Went lesbian?" Brenda asked.

He nodded. "Yeah. I feel sorry for her husband," he said. "Although the prisoner is hot."

She rolled her shoulders and he followed the bouncing balls. She put the celery stalk in her mouth, wrapped her suddenly pouty lips around it, and crunched.

"It sounds like a big to-do," she said.

Chaz was mesmerized. "Yeah, but it's blown over. You know how things go. Front page, top story, then gone when something else happens."

Brenda stuck her now-shortened celery stalk into her drink.

"You staying around here?" he asked.

"I told you, I was with a friend. You shouldn't hit on the customers. Your manager wouldn't like that."

"I'm the owner," he said.

Brenda nodded and looked around. The Grey Gull was nice. He might have some money after all. She reeled in the impulse to pick him up right then. She was sure that he'd follow her to wherever she wanted him to go. He'd beg for more. He'd tell her that she was the best he'd ever had.

They always did.

It had been a long time since she'd had a man inside her. Not since Curt Gomez, a deputy who fell between her Venus flytrap thighs when she was held at the county jail in the Tri-Cities. He was an idiot. He was weak. He didn't follow through with his promises to help her get out. He was lousy at sex too. She wanted to feel a man. She was sick of Sonicare sex. She had tired of luring some new inmate into a corner of the shower so that she could have something to hold over her so that she could get more cosmetics from the canteen. The girls who'd been set up on drug charges by manipulative boyfriends were the easiest prey. Weak. Scared. Malleable. Although she was absolutely sure that Curt would do whatever she wanted, she had let go of the opportunity. Doing everything she wanted when she wanted to do it was what stole her freedom in the first place.

Janie had been a tougher mark. She literally held the keys to the prison. Brenda saw how she looked at her. Like all the others, Janie Thomas had coveted what Brenda possessed. Janie with her silver-helmet hairdo and her sensible oxfords and unflattering attire had never experienced the thrill of the catcall. The hunger of wandering eyes. Whenever a media request was made, it was Janie who was required to tell Brenda in person.

Each time, Brenda would reveal more of herself, pulling Janie in closer and closer.

"My father pimped me out to my uncle when I was six," Brenda had said during one of those conversations. "My uncle experimented on me like a frog pinned to a board in biology class. By the time I was ten I'd been passed around like a happy-hour appetizer at TGI Fridays."

She held Janie's gaze and forced her tear ducts to do what biology and the human psyche meant them to do. It was something she could do on command and with remarkable precision. Just enough to show an observer that she was emotional, but not so much to appear hysterical or manipulative.

Just enough.

"I'm so sorry," Janie said.

"Sorry is for losers, superintendent."

"Maybe so, inmate."

The tear rolled.

"Why do you hate me?" Brenda asked.

"I don't hate anyone. I hate what people do."

"This is my home now," Brenda said. "And you are in charge of everything that I do."

"That's how it works, inmate."

"See! You are doing it. You are treating me like I'm nothing. Like my father. My uncle. My husbands. You don't even give me the courtesy of calling me by name. It's dehumanizing."

Another tear.

"Like I said, this is my job. This is the way it is."

"Can't you call me Brenda? I've heard you call Marian Lockwood by her first name.

Brenda was right. Everyone called Marian by her first name. She was seventy-four and had been incarcerated for forty-two years. She'd come into the institution as a thirty-two-year-old with a long rap sheet, the exclamation point of which was the murder of her two little boys. She'd thrown them off a bridge and was sentenced to life without the possibility of parole. Over time, as she worked in the horticulture building, the chapel, and in the craft area, she became an example of kindness in a place that needed it. She was, in a very real sense, everyone's grandmother.

Everyone who had a grandmother who killed her children, that is.

"All right, Brenda," Janie Thomas said. "I will call you by your first name."

Brenda wiped her eyes. "Thank you. I'm going to be here for the rest of my life and I want to be another Marian, someone you can trust."

Janie smiled.

"I'm sure you'll get there. I see it in you."

Brenda felt a surge of satisfaction go through her body. The hook had been set. Fishing, she knew, took patience. She didn't feel like she had a lot of time. She needed other options. At first, the guard Missy Carlyle seemed a better bet, but that one turned into a disaster. They'd started a sexual relationship, but were caught by records clerk Tess Moreau, who reported everything. Missy was let go, and with her, Brenda's ticket to freedom. She thought of Kitsap County sheriff's detective Kendall Stark and forensic pathologist Birdy Waterman and the mess they'd made of her plans. She seethed with anger as Chaz approached with another Bloody Mary.

Janie was a big fish to hook.

Brenda liked big. She also liked a challenge. If she couldn't win Janie over with her sex appeal—which was almost laughable to her—she'd find another way.

"When do you get off work?" Brenda asked.

"Like I said, I'm the owner. I can get off any time I want."

"I'll get you off," she said, a line that made her skin crawl, but Chaz was dumb enough to enjoy the come-on. "Let me finish my drink."

"I thought you were here with a friend," he said.

"My friend's tied up at the moment."

"Sounds good to me," he said before disappearing into the office behind the bar for a moment. When he returned to her he had a smile on his face. "Told Danielle that I'm heading out for my vacation a little early. Let's get out of here."

"Where are we going?" she asked.

"I have a place at the ocean," he said. "No cell service, just waves and sand."

"Sounds lovely."

"Cold and rainy," he said with a smile. "But that's Washington."

Chaz Masters lived in an A-frame in the middle of the forest. Brenda Nevins parked behind his blue Acura and followed him inside. The deer-head décor suggested a man who lived alone and the clutter of the place indicated that after she was done with him there might be some treasure to be found among the bric-a-brac. Chaz caught her when Brenda slipped on the step down to the sunken living room.

"Sorry," she said. "Feeling a little tipsy."

He smiled.

"Too bad," he said. "I was hoping to have a drink with you now that I'm off work."

"Start the vacation early," she said. "I'll join you."

"For a bar owner, I'm in short supply of offerings. Tequila okay?"

"Love tequila."

"You haven't told me much about yourself."

"Not much to say. I've been away for a few years."

"Oh yeah? Europe?"

"No, nothing so glamorous," she answered. "Out of state."

"For work?"

"Yeah."

"What do you do?"

She hated all the questions, but that was part of his way of seducing her. It was silly because she'd already seduced him.

"Paramedical sales."

He raised a brow. "I thought you'd say modeling."

She pretended to be embarrassed. "Thank you, but no. I mean, I tried. They said I was too busty for that."

He nodded. "They were wrong."

"May I use your bathroom?"

He indicated the first door in the hallway.

Brenda let the toilet seat drop. She opened the medicine cabinet and put her yeoman's knowledge of drugs to the test, fishing through the prescription bottles. *Excellent!* A bottle of Percocet with ten tablets. She dumped

them on the counter and ground them into a powder
with the bottom of the bottle. She flushed the toilet and
turned on the water. Next, she put the powder back in
the bottle and turned off the water.

"Sorry it was such a mess in there," he said when
she emerged.

"I'm not picky," Brenda said.

"Margarita?" he asked, handing one to her.

"Perfect. A bit more ice though?"

He nodded. "Sure." He set down his drink and took
hers to the kitchen. She dumped the pulverized painkillers into his drink, swirled it with one of her red
talons, and stuffed the bottle into the folds of the sofa.

"Cheers," she said. They clinked glasses.

"I'm glad we met," he said. "You're just what I
needed."

Brenda sipped her drink. "Me too. I'm a little drunk,
but I feel the same way."

CHAPTER ELEVEN

Tami Overton's mom, Lynn, opened the door to her house next to one of Port Orchard's always-soggy golf courses. She was a small woman with a mass of curls that looked like a nest of boomerangs. She wore no makeup, but she didn't really need any. She had the look of a woman who didn't fuss much on herself so that she would always have the extra time to help others. Kendall passed a bronze-colored plaque of a pair of praying hands as she was led into the living room.

"Tami's not in trouble again," she said. "Is she?"

Kendall shook her head. "No," she said. "Not at all. I'm just trying to find her so that I can ask her a few questions about a cold case."

"About Katy?" Lynn asked.

"Yes, about Katy."

Lynn motioned for Kendall to sit on the gray velvet camelback sofa. "Want some coffee? Tea? A soft drink?"

Kendall thanked her, but said she was fine on drinks right then.

"Where is Tami?" she asked.

"I used to really hate that question. I hated it more

than anything because I never had a good answer. My ex told me Tami was messed up because I was a bad mother and I just needed to accept that and, I don't know, maybe shoot myself in the head."

Kendall winced. "That's a pretty tough statement."

"Tough is not knowing where your daughter is, if she's dead in some drug house, or turned into some kind of sex slave in Mexico."

"Did that happen?"

"No. Not really. I mean, she lied to me one time when I wouldn't give her any more money for drugs that she'd have to go sell herself to some Mexican drug lord and I'd never see her face again."

"That's pretty dramatic stuff."

"Tami is all about drama. All the time. Twenty-four hours a day. That's why I liked Katy so much. She was sensible. Calm. Alyssa was a little more over the top, but in a fun way."

Lynn got up. "I need that coffee. Sure you don't want any?"

"No. I'm good. You go right ahead."

When Lynn disappeared into the kitchen, Kendall got up and surveyed the contents of the room, looking for signs of Tami. There was a framed photo of a teenage girl on the credenza behind the sofa.

"Is that her senior portrait?" she asked Lynn when she returned with a dalmatian-spotted mug from Disneyland.

"No. I wish. It's her sophomore portrait. Tami never finished high school. She dropped out the fall after Katy went missing. She actually disappeared for five days. I made a report. You probably have a file on that somewhere."

"What happened to her?" Kendall asked.

Lynn tried to drink her coffee but it was too hot. She set it on the table in front of her.

"Don't know. Not really. I know what she told me happened. She said she was picked up in front of the school and held captive by some people in the woods somewhere. She wasn't raped—a detail that I've doubted. Hell, I've doubted her whole story. She'd become a pathological liar by then. I only reported it to the police because I didn't want anyone to think I didn't love her if she was found dead somewhere."

The words were harsh and Kendall's eyes must have betrayed her judgment of the mother.

"I loved her. I did then. I did before. But a kid on drugs, that's a whole different animal, Detective. Do you have kids?"

Kendall nodded. "Yes, a son, but he's young."

Lynn thought a moment. "Give him time. He'll find a way to break your heart like my Tami did mine."

"Where is she now?"

"That's the funny part. She's fine now. She lives over in Purdy. She's got a job. A husband. A baby. Although not in that order. You can't have everything. She's even taking classes at Tacoma Community College."

"So you've repaired your relationship?"

Lynn's coffee had cooled and she took a long drink. Her eyes welled up with tears.

"That just it," she said. "We haven't. Not completely, anyway. All those years when she was strung out on God knows what, well, she blames me for that. Sometimes she won't even look me in the eye. Everything is my fault. I'm the one who stuck that needle in her arm. I'm the one who shoved that meth up her nose. For some reason, it's all on me."

"I'm so sorry."

"It isn't your fault. This one's on me. I didn't do the right thing by her. And now that I can, she doesn't want me around."

A cat jumped up onto the woman's lap. It was gray, the exact same shade as the velvet of the couch. Kendall was pretty sure that her black slacks were going to be covered with cat hair when she got up.

"It's just me and Jeepers now."

"What do you think happened to Katy?"

Lynn petted Jeepers and he purred like a mini-chainsaw.

"I don't know. I thought for a long time that maybe her parents weren't the perfect couple they pretended to be. You know, the type with all the money, all the answers, never a problem that couldn't be fixed. Tami told me a few things about them that gave me pause, but I put that out of my mind."

"What kinds of things?" Kendall asked.

"Nothing that dramatic. I think Roger Frazier was having an affair with someone in his office and Katy found out about it. She might have confronted him. It's all a little fuzzy. My own life turned into such a mess after that I never really had time to worry about other people's problems."

"Did Brit Frazier know?" Kendall asked, leaning in.

The cat jumped down and Lynn got up.

"Like I said, I don't know for sure what happened. All I know is that I've turned into a cat lady without a husband or daughter."

She went over to the desk on the other side of the living room and wrote down an address.

"I drive by the place once in a while. Looks nice. Like I told that producer, Juliana. Tell her I said hello, will you?"

Kendall didn't say a word, but inside she thought Juliana sure got around.

Chaz Masters didn't put up much of a fight. Not that he could anyway. Brenda didn't even need to convince him that it would be fun if she tied him up with two leather belts and the terry cloth tie from a robe that hung on the back hook of the bathroom door. He passed out and she went about scouring the place for anything she might need—setting the spoils on the kitchen table. She took his cell phone. She found $255 in cash in his dresser drawer, another hundred in his wallet. She moved quickly about the house, room by room. She returned to the bathroom where she picked up all the pill bottles that might help her situation later. It appeared that Chaz had hurt his back and she was glad about that. He needed painkillers and lorazepam to sleep.

All good.

She heard him moan and turned to the bedroom.

"You ready for another round?"

He looked at her beautiful naked body. There hadn't been a first round, but he was so high he didn't know that.

"Yeah," he croaked. "Untie me so I can play with those."

She ran her fingertips over her nipples.

"These?"

He smiled.

Brenda pulled a dry-cleaning bag encasing a white shirt from his closest and climbed on top of him, pretending to writhe with ecstasy over his limp penis.

"What?" he asked as she placed the bag over his head.

"Relax," she cooed, stretching the plastic over his face. "This is the best sex you'll ever have."

Chaz's feet twitched and his blue eyes stared up at her from behind the "Fresh in an hour" logo. The bar owner with plans for an exciting start to his vacation struggled only a moment. It was quick, easy. Just the way she liked it.

Brenda climbed off the dead man, a little surprised that he'd managed an erection during the last moments of his life. *Better late than never*, she thought. She watched it return to its unimpressive, flaccid state. The power of the kill turned her on. She didn't understand why that was so. It was as if the taking of a life was the ultimate rush. Seeing the life force ebb from his eyes made her wet. Her fingers traveled downward and she made herself climax.

Only two things felt better than sex. Fame and revenge. She was set on both.

As she found her way out of the bedroom, her eyes caught a small figure of a shark on her dead lover's desk. Its eyes were flat and unblinking. It made her think of someone.

It gave her an idea too.

CHAPTER TWELVE

Cosmo's was both a deli and restaurant with twenty tables and a miniscule but well-stocked bar. It was adjacent to the Staples and across the street from a very busy Starbucks—hardly the best location in town unless you needed coffee and office supplies with your tiramisu.

Juliana Robbins sat at the bar working her iPhone and sipping a glass of red wine.

"Detective Stark! I'm over here," she called from her perch.

Kendall wondered if her cat-hair-covered thighs were some kind of indicator that she was a cop or if her little-bit-longer-than-usual blond hair was another signal. Feminine, but not overly so.

"Juliana?"

"That's me. Sit down. They are getting a table. I'm so excited to be meeting you. I had a feeling that I'd like you the instant I saw you. And you know what, I was totally right."

Kendall wasn't sure how to answer that greeting. "Nice to meet you too."

A waitress offered Kendall a drink and she ordered a glass of wine

"Look," she said. "I want to be up front with you. I don't want to do your show. I don't like anything about TV and how it exploits others, but I understand that the department and Katy's family are all for this. So here I am."

"I get that," Juliana said. "I've run up against the naysayers before. You have to see proof and that's what will happen once Pandora and Ogilvie do their parts. You'll see."

Juliana was dark with black eyes and black hair. She had the exotic looks of someone from the Middle East, though her accent was completely American. Not East Coast either. She wore a short, trendy skirt, and a blouse that was cut a little low for Port Orchard.

"Where are you from?" Kendall asked as the wine came.

"Well, I live in New York, but I'm from the Bay Area."

The mention of the Bay Area made her think of Steven just then. Thinking of Steven made her think of Cody, who was being taken care of by a sitter. She wished both Steven and Cody were with her now instead of this chirpy young woman from *Spirit Hunters*.

"You believe in all this Pandora stuff, don't you?"

"Absolutely, Detective. I totally do. You will too. Pandora is the real deal. She's not some phony that looks for signs about things in a person's life and then rifle shoots to get some answers. There's none of that kind of chicanery."

The word *chicanery* made Kendall think of her mother just then. She'd been gone for more than two years and every now and then a word, a smell, a thought would enter her mind and remind Kendall of what she was missing. *Chicanery* was a mom-word of the highest order.

"I saw some things online," Kendall said.

Juliana was ready. She'd heard that before. "Let's get real. Do you believe everything you read on the Internet?"

"No. I don't."

"Good, because no one with half a brain would. If you're referring to the post made by the woman in Nova Scotia, then let me enlighten you. After we taped the show, she told producers that she wanted twenty-five thousand dollars for her time. Even Pandora doesn't get that kind of shooting fee. No one on cable does. When we told her that she didn't get a dime, that she'd signed away her rights—and by the way we were very clear with her on that as we are with all show participants—she went ballistic, swore revenge."

Kendall sipped some more wine. She knew she'd been drinking more lately and promised to stop at a single glass.

"I saw the video, Juliana."

Juliana shook her head. "Totally fake. Our guys looked at it and could pick apart how it was edited, how voices were dubbed in to make Pandy and Wyo look bad."

Kendall didn't react. She was too busy watching Juliana as she tried to spin some garbage out of what was completely at odds with what appeared to be incontrovertible.

"The mom from Nova Scotia must have had some serious talent in post-production to create such a masterpiece as the one she posted. Looked pretty real to me."

"You can do anything with a smartphone and an app these days, Detective. That's just the way it is. But let's agree to disagree on Pandora and what she can do until after the show."

"Fine. Let's focus on what you need from me. I'm not going to wriggle my way out of this, so I might as well know what's in store."

A waitress came, and since the restaurant was empty, they had their pick of tables. Juliana decided she wanted to stay in the bar, so they moved to one of three tables along the window. Heavy curtains dimmed the light. They ordered.

"I brought the case files," Kendall said.

Juliana perked up. "Perfect. Let's go over what you have."

"We might want to stop at the appetizer section because there's not a whole lot there."

"Don't be so negative, Detective. We're *Spirit Hunters*! We get stuff done. You'll see."

When the waitress appeared, Kendall ordered the lasagna, her husband's favorite dish. He was on her mind. The young producer ordered a wild mushroom risotto and when they were served, she immediately announced it was the best she'd ever had.

"And I live in New York," she said to the waitress. "Repeat that to the cook and tell him that I'm a fan for life."

Kendall showed Juliana what she'd brought and the producer made a big show of how thorough the investigation had been and how Pandora and Wyatt would find the truth—without the documents.

"I brought you copies," Kendall said as she poked at the congealed cheese—Steven's favorite part.

"Oh, and I appreciate that. But I can't take copies. That's not protocol."

"I don't follow. Why did you ask our PIO for me to bring the docs then?"

"I need to see them because I need to make sure that we don't have any loose ends. Wyo does his own investigation. Just like Pandy, he needs to find things out for himself. They are a team. A true team. We want our viewers to enjoy the discoveries they make along the way—not watch them being spoon-fed information from those who already know the substance of the story."

"So, Wyo"—the nickname stuck in her throat a little—"is going to do an investigation of his own, start to finish?"

"That's right. He's interviewed Katy's friends, her parents, and just about anyone else you can think of associated with the case."

"Oh, really?"

"Really. He's found out some amazing stuff already. You're going to love the show."

"I can't wait," Kendall said, without a trace of insincerity. At least she hoped so.

"I'm excited too."

"I understand I'm scheduled to be interviewed tomorrow morning. What's the purpose of that? Wyo has already done all the legwork needed to tell Katy's story, hasn't he?"

Juliana shook her head and pushed the remainder of her risotto aside.

"This tastes like glue," she said.

"I thought you liked it."

"I was just being nice. Force of habit. It's who I am. Now back to you and your interview. It is absolutely essential that you appear on the show. Wyatt will ask you general questions about the town, the investigation. You'll be his safety net. If there are things that aren't computing, he'll go to you for the answers."

"I don't know. Seems like you don't need me."

"Now, Detective. That's silly. You're going to make the show. You are the kind of pretty, no-nonsense cop that our viewers will just eat up for dinner."

The idea of any of this didn't appeal to Kendall Stark, but somewhere at the bottom of the list was the idea the *Spirit Hunters* viewership would gobble her up like a plate of pasta.

"What's the format? Who does what?"

"I basically coordinate everything with the sound and camera team. They're locals who we've never worked with before, so that's a challenge. Wyatt will be doing your interview."

"What about Pandora? When will I see her?"

"You won't. Not unless you want to get up at three in the morning. She'll do her walk through the Frazier home with another cameraman tailing her, capturing everything that happens, everything she's feeling."

"Will she go into Katy's room?"

"Maybe. Honestly, with Pandora you never know what she's going to do. One time she ran off location screaming into the woods and we didn't find her for three hours. I'm not kidding."

"Why would you? So, back to Pandora's part. I've been wondering how much she'll know about the case.

Before she does her walk through the house and then the big reveal."

"Nothing. I'm dead serious. We tell her nothing. Zip."

"Are you sure that Wyo doesn't tell her what's up?"

Juliana made a face. "I wish it was that easy. But if this show lasts another season it won't be because those two get along. Oil and water. I know it looks like they are all buddy-buddy at the reveal but they aren't. Pandy is very possessive of her spirit guides and she doesn't like the way Wyo talks about them. No matter how many times he's seen her in action, he's still a skeptic. Like you."

Kendall nodded. "Just like me."

"The world's full of those who refuse to believe what they can't see for themselves," Juliana said.

Kendall didn't take the bait. "Can I be there at the reveal?" she asked.

"We've never had a cop there before, but I don't see why not. I'll check with my executive producer."

Juliana's phone beeped and she looked down. "Just a sec. I have to take this," she said, leaving the bar for the alcove by the restrooms.

Kendall sat there. She didn't know if she should laugh or cry. A few beats later, Juliana returned.

"Something's up and I have to leave." She put three twenties on the table. "Can you wait for the receipt? Let the waitress keep the change."

And she left.

The change was three dollars. Kendall took the receipt and put down a ten. She waited for a few more minutes for the waitress to return with some buttered noodles.

"For Cody," the waitress said. "That woman you were with was a complete trip and a half."

"No kidding," Kendall said. "But a trip to where?"

"Who knows, but I overheard enough to ensure that I'll tune in when the stupid show airs. I don't know what channel it's on but I bet it's a pretty high number."

"It is," Kendall said. "Way up there in the eight hundreds somewhere."

"No kidding. Didn't know the channels went past five hundred."

Kendall smiled. "Neither did I."

The blue Acura was a nice ride. The best car she'd ever driven. Brenda knew about cell phone triangulation and drove a half hour out of her way to Mason County, where she made the first call to her old friends in Kitsap County. She was pretty sure that the Kitsap County Sheriff's Department didn't have the most advanced methods of tracing a call, but to be more safe than sorry, she decided to call Kendall at home. That was foiled when the operator said she didn't have a listing for anyone named Stark in the Port Orchard area. Brenda asked for Birdy Waterman's number and that one *was* listed. The operator put her through.

"Elan and I aren't home right now," Birdy's voice said. "You know the drill. Leave a message and we'll get back to you. If you have our cell numbers, try those. Bye."

"I hope you and Detective Stark are enjoying your

moment in the sun," Brenda said. "It's me, Brenda. I'd say come and find me, but I don't stay still very long and neither one of you are that good. I've only started. Who is Elan? I like that name."

She turned off the phone and tossed it out of the open car window. It was time to go home to Janie.

Poor thing. She must be so thirsty, she thought.

CHAPTER THIRTEEN

Pandora used her real name when she signed in at the W in downtown Seattle. Carol Kirkowski didn't like to make a fuss about who she was; she preferred the chance encounter with a fan that let her play up the fact that she was the psychic Pandora of TV fame. Her chance came where it almost always did—at the front desk.

"You look a lot like that ghost chick, I mean lady," the young clerk said. "The one who talks to dead people on TV."

"I get that a lot," she said, a self-satisfied smile on her lips. She presented her credit card and the man, a chin-stubbled twentysomething with two gold hoops in one ear, took it.

"Someone close to you isn't feeling well," she said.

He looked up at her. His eyes were wide open. Stuck open. He couldn't even blink. *It was her.*

"You know about my aunt?"

Pandora signed her birth name. "Sometimes it's like just a bunch of noise in my head and sometimes the signals come in very clear. Your aunt is very ill, Kevin."

"How'd you know my name?" He asked.

She looked at his name tag.

"Oh, that's how," he laughed. "But wait a second, how did you know my aunt had cancer?"

"She's a fighter, Kevin, but she won't win this battle. I'm sorry. You'll see her on the other side."

A bellman loaded the cart and Pandora went off to her room on the top floor. She loved that little mind game. Sometimes it felt so good to just take a stab at something as easy as someone close to another being ill. Missing someone was good too. Wanting something that seemed unattainable was also a good one.

"Something you've dreamed about for a long time is about to come your way. Don't miss the chance to grab it."

That could mean anything. It could be a new car, a washing machine, a new job, a cure for an illness. It was whatever the mark had wanted to be true. Pandora, Carol Kirkowski, was good at reading her marks. She always had been.

She used her personal cell, not the company's, to make a call.

"Baby," she said. "I've checked in."

"I had a feeling you were near," a man's voice answered.

"Do you have the feeling that I'm horny?"

"You're always horny, baby."

"When are you coming up to see me? I'm on the top floor."

"I want to get on top of you."

"You can be so corny. But that's okay. I've always liked corny."

"Got some things to do. I'll be over when I can. Get

in bed. Tell the front desk I'm coming and to leave a key for me."

"I'm completely naked now," she said, though she hadn't even unpacked.

"I'm completely aroused," he said.

"Hold that thought. Then I'll hold you."

"Now who's being corny?"

They both laughed a little and hung up.

Pandora was married. Her husband, Bob, was the cameraman who followed her when she did a walk through the haunted feed store, house, crypt, A&P store, or whatever it was that had brought them and the others from *Spirit Hunters* to the Pacific Northwest. She had bigger dreams than a cable show. She'd created a skin-care line called Vanish that was supposed to make all wrinkles disappear, but the FDA wouldn't approve it—at least not when Pandora had presented it as a cure for eighty-year-old wrinkles. She'd had a deal with QVC all lined up and when the skin cream vanished, she schemed for some other product. She had the idea of a home séance game, but that fizzled when a Christian group threatened to boycott the show. For a psychic, Pandora was not very good at seeing what was in her own future.

CHAPTER FOURTEEN

Cody was asleep when Kendall got home. The sitter scurried out the door for a late date and the detective put her focus on a few household chores that the sitter could easily have done—how hard is loading the dishwasher?—and once that was done and the counters were wiped down she assessed herself in the mirror. Was she TV ready? Should she even care? And what should she wear for her not-so-big moment? She looked in her closet and selected a dark blue suit with a light gray blouse and the circle pin that her father had given her mother for their twenty-fifth wedding anniversary. She played with her hair a little, but gave up. It always had a mind of its own. If she made too much of a plan, it would decide to go the other way.

She sat down on the edge of the bed and called Steven. To her surprise, he answered.

"I was wondering when I was going to hear from you, babe," he said.

"It isn't that I haven't been trying. I feel like you're never around."

"I had that deal in San Jose to go to. It was last minute."

"You could have texted me," she said.

"I'm sorry. I should have. You have no idea how hard this is. Everyone is so . . . so young. They expect me to be a leader, but they know more than I do."

"Cody's fine. Thanks for asking."

"Jesus, Kendall. Are you mad at me?"

"No. Not mad. Just irritated. I have a lot going on here and you're not around. You're not even available on the phone."

"Is something happening in the Brenda Nevins case?"

Kendall loosed her grip on the phone. At least he was aware of what she was working on—or part of what held her time in a vise grip.

"No. Nothing on that."

She told him all about the *Spirit Hunters* show and how angry she was that she had to do it.

"Sounds like you didn't have much of a choice there, babe," he said.

"I know. I know. But even so."

"I've never seen the show, but I bet it's a piece of crap."

"You'd be right about that, Steven. It is crap and it's turning this place upside down. I just know they are going to portray the department—and me—as a bunch of bumblers."

"It wasn't your case, Kendall. Nick Mayberry's the one who's going to look stupid if there's anyone they are going to target. Why don't they interview him and leave you guys out of it?"

Kendall had already tried that tactic. "That's what I

suggested, but the show said they can't afford to fly to Idaho."

"Talk about cheap. Now that we've settled that, how is Cody doing?"

"He misses his father. I miss my husband. And honey, I'm kind of scared about us. About where this is all leading . . . Where is this leading?"

"Kendall, don't worry. It's not leading me away from you and our son if that's what you're getting at. I'm yours. I'm never going anywhere. At least not for very long."

"What was that last part?"

"At least not for very long."

"That just kind of struck me. Is there something you need to tell me, Steven?"

There was a slight pause before he answered.

"I'm getting to that. I have to go to Santa Fe for a company retreat next week. I'll be gone a week and there will be no way for us to communicate. It's one of those New Agey things that is supposed to bring the team together."

Kendall didn't like what she was hearing.

"While it rips their families apart?"

"That's not fair and you know it."

"Steven, I don't know anything anymore."

"I love you. You know that. Right?"

This time Kendall thought before answering. She really didn't know. He seemed so far away.

"I guess so. I know I love you."

"I will call you as soon as I get back from the retreat."

"This isn't one of those sweat lodge things, is it?"

Steven laughed. "No, but I understand hot coals are involved."

"Be careful."

"I will. You too. In fact, I bet you'd rather walk on hot coals that do *Spirit Hunters.*"

"I love you. Good night."

"Night."

In her office in the back bedroom of her home on Beach Drive, Birdy Waterman's answering machine blinked its weary red eye. There was only one message on the old, shoebox-sized machine, a relic from the days before voice messaging, cell phones, and texting. Elan had taken to stacking the day's paper on the corner of the desk where the machine stood with its almost-always-empty memory. He noticed the flashing red light, but thought nothing of it. No one called for him anyway. He set that day's *Kitsap Sun* on top of it, leaving Brenda and her message in the dark.

CHAPTER FIFTEEN

Wyatt Ogilvie came with a well-known history. He also came with very expensive shoes, and a suit that had to cost more than two thousand dollars. His glasses were Gucci and his tie was Fendi. Kendall had no idea how she could spot any of those details with a cursory glance, but she chalked it up to a mother who subscribed to all of the best lifestyle and fashion magazines. It didn't matter that she couldn't afford the finer things; she told her daughter one time that what was important was to be able to know the difference between good and great. With Brad James standing beside her in the courtroom they were using for the shoot, Kendall watched as Juliana applied makeup on Ogilvie's forehead—a forehead that didn't look nearly as high as it once had.

"He had micro scalp-hair restoration. No doll-hair look for him," Brad said.

"What a relief that is for the other dolls," Kendall said.

Brad, completely humorless, stood there like a statue, watching the process.

"I always wanted to be on TV," he said. "That's why I went into communications as WSU. I thought I could get a good job at one of the Seattle stations."

"What happened?" Kendall asked, glad for the diversion and glad that Brad James's life hadn't turned out exactly as he'd hoped. He was so full of himself there was barely enough room for him and Wyatt Ogilvie in that big courtroom.

"They said I didn't have the look. To me, that meant that I was too white for what they were looking for. That's why I went for this job. I thought, well, a white guy with the gift of gab—because that's a PR man's gift—was perfect for law enforcement."

Kendall wanted to know how that was perfect, but before she could say anything, Wyatt Ogilvie and Juliana Robbins were swarming her.

"You're right, Juliana," he said, pretending not to look at Kendall and training his eyes on his producer. "She's lovely. The prettiest cop I've seen in a long time."

"I suppose that's a compliment," Kendall said.

"And she has a spark. Just like you told me. I'm going to have to be like our PR lad Brad here and charm her into submission."

"Maybe you can start by addressing me directly, Mr. Ogilvie."

Juliana cut in. "Larger than life, Detective. Doesn't Wyo—that's what his fans call him—live up to my assessment?"

If Juliana had mentioned the sexist and annoying mannerisms at dinner at Cosmo's, Kendall would have answered with a resounding yes. Instead, Wyatt did his own living up to the hype. He tried to charm.

"Forgive me," he said. "I'm exhausted and a little punch-drunk from the interviews we've been doing in your charming burg."

"That's all right. How long is this going to take? I have a pretty good caseload that needs my attention back at the department."

This time Brad butted in.

"No worries, Detective. We've got your back here. You take as much time as you need to do a proper interview. This is very important to the sheriff and to me."

Kendall didn't care that it was important to Brad at all. And, if she'd had a chance to call the sheriff while he was cruising the Inside Passage somewhere around Sitka, Alaska, she would have.

Juliana complimented Kendall on her attire.

"I forgot to tell you no patterns, and yet here you are in a perfect solid."

"I read the press kit and letter you sent," Kendall said.

"Great!" Juliana said as she started toward the jury box, where a sound guy and cameraman stood waiting. The sound tech acted a little bashful when his slid the microphone cords down her back and hooked the transmitter to the waist of her A-line skirt.

"Sorry, ma'am."

This day had barely started, Kendall thought, and it had just taken a dive. No woman wants to be called ma'am in her early thirties. She wondered if she'd crossed over from MILF to ma'am and hadn't even noticed.

"She need a little powder on her crow's-feet," the camera guy said, peering through the lens.

From bad to worse.

Wyatt Ogilvie stood on a steel case just outside of the jury box. He was short, but not that short. Kendall figured that he needed the extra height to look more commanding throughout the interview.

Juliana stood a few feet away and whispered into a microphone, which Kendall was pretty sure went to the earpiece of the expert interviewer.

The camera was on. Silence reigned for a few minutes for the sound tech to capture the ambient noise of the room. Then it started. Juliana did her part. She asked Kendall to state her name, spell it, say what her job was, and state her connection to the case.

"Do you want me to look at the camera or at you?"

"Neither. You'll need to focus your attention on Wyo. He's going to ask the questions, though I might have a few of my own to make sure we get all we need for the story line."

"Detective, you're a lifelong resident of Port Orchard. What sets this town apart from others in the area?"

Kendall gave a rambling answer that she was pretty sure made her sound very, very provincial. It was all about the fabric of the community, the sharing that goes on between neighbors, and the natural beauty that was not equaled anywhere.

"Can you do that again?" Juliana asked. "Try to keep it short. Mention Port Orchard in your bite."

Kendall thought of the mommy blogger and how the producers seemed to put words in everyone's mouth, a story line they had already created, and how they were looking only for sound bites to fill in the gaps between reenactments they'd stage later with cut-rate summer stock actors looking for a little exposure.

"If Norman Rockwell had ever ventured out here, he would have found his paintings come to life. Without the snow, of course," she said.

"Good answer! That's what we like. Short. Snappy. That's just what we're looking for. Are you sure you've never done this before?"

Kendall knew she was being patronized, but she just wanted to get it over with.

"I'm far from perfect," Wyatt Ogilvie said. "People know that. So when I say this, know that I'm not tossing shade on you. I've been there. You guys really screwed up on Katy's investigation, didn't you?"

Kendall wasn't about to fall in a trap. "I don't get what you mean, Mr. Ogilvie."

"Come on. I know you didn't do the investigation yourself, but you have to admit that it was pretty half-assed."

Kendall glanced over at a horror-struck Brad James.

"I can't comment on what was done by someone else, only how I'd handle it myself today."

Wyatt shrugged. "That's easy to say. But what do you say to the mirror at night when you think about the hell the Fraziers have endured because Kitsap County didn't have its act together four years ago? I mean, you know that's why I'm here. I'm here to right a wrong."

He was chewing the scenery. Kendall wondered

how much of that little soliloquy would end up on the air.

"Look, I'm doing this show to be helpful."

"Then just answer the questions."

Kendall felt like she was in the witness box being grilled by a prosecutor just then.

"I didn't hear a question, just a blowhard's statement."

Wyatt put his hands up in the air. "Whoa, now we're into name-calling. That's how we do things in this town. Blame everyone but yourself."

"Can we focus on the case?" she asked.

"I'm trying to. I've been working this case for almost a week. I've talked to everyone who knew Katy. I'm going to solve this on my own, or with Pandora's help."

"Fine. It is a tragedy. It deserves to be solved. We don't know what happened to her."

"I have an idea. I think she was murdered."

"What evidence do you have on that?"

"The blood at the scene."

"It wasn't hers."

"I know. It was her killer's and if you'd have swabbed everyone for DNA samples back then you'd have ended the torture of a family that cannot move forward, a family that is haunted by the memory of a daughter taken from them too soon."

Another big moment for Wyatt Ogilvie, Kendall thought. She wanted to bolt, but she'd made a promise to do the interview.

"Is there another question?"

"Yes, is it true that the original investigator had a gambling problem?"

"I wouldn't know if he did."

"Do you think the case was given all the care that it should have had?"

Kendall thought about that one. She glanced at the camera then over to Juliana, who wasn't even paying attention; instead she was answering an email on her cell phone.

"No. Probably not. I would have done things differently."

Juliana looked at her notes and Wyatt Ogilvie got off the steel case.

"You were awesome," Juliana said.

"I feel used," Kendall said, ripping the mic from behind her jacket.

"I didn't know they were going in that direction, Detective."

It was Brad James, looking horror stricken, and no doubt on his way to the unemployment line.

"We'll talk about this later, Brad."

"Honestly, Detective. You couldn't have been better. You were fire and ice. That's what we like. It makes for good TV."

"I didn't come here to be good TV. I came to help the Fraziers find out what happened to their daughter. I stupidly thought that any publicity on a cold case would be helpful."

Wyatt put his arm on her shoulder. "Hey, don't be mad. You're going to get your wish. I think this case is solvable. And that's not the TV star in me talking. That's the cop."

"The cop who screwed a juror on one of his own murder cases?"

The room went silent. Back to that quiet they'd tested for before the interview started.

"That was a long time ago," he said.

"Well, call me an elephant if you like. I'll never forget. Neither has anyone else in law enforcement. Just so you know."

Wyatt looked like he'd been caught off guard.

"Now you're being mean," he said. "You don't have to be mean, you know."

Kendall wondered if Wyatt was playing her again. He seemed sad, a little lost.

Maybe even full of regret for something that he'd never be able to escape.

Juliana approached.

"Are you still going to come to the reveal? I mentioned it to Pandy and she thought it was good idea."

Inside, Kendall seethed, but she tried not to show it. "I'll be there. Thanks, Juliana. See you later."

"Let's get back to the office, Brad."

Her tone showed complete control, though her adrenaline was pumping as hard as it ever had. She felt like she could lift up a Subaru at that point.

"I thought you were mad at me, Detective."

They kept walking, around a corner to the room where jurors were processed before being assigned a case. Kendall poked her head inside. It was empty. She shoved Brad inside.

The veins on her neck were beyond being covered by any makeup artist's powder, hi-def or otherwise.

"You little shit. You don't even know what you've

done, do you? You think this is going to help the department? Have you ever even heard of the thin blue line? Don't you get that we have to have each other's backs or we'll fail here? You set me up. Plain and simple.

"I swear, I didn't. I thought they would help us. They would spotlight us in a way that would bring goodwill to the department. You know that we care."

Kendall wanted to throttle him.

"We do care," she said. "We have *always* cared. About Katy. About everyone in this community. That's why it's called 'protect and serve,' and if you'd bother to have grasped that you would have seen that this whole thing is going to blow up on us. This will all be on you."

Brad's face reddened. "I didn't go on camera," he said. "I didn't do anything wrong."

Kendall *really* wanted to throttle him just then.

"You made a poor call, Brad, and the sheriff is going to hear from me the minute he gets back from Alaska. I'd call him now but this is the first vacation he's had in three years. I'm so mad at you."

"You should be mad at Detective Mayberry," Brad said, taking a half step away. "He's the one that screwed this up."

"That might very well be true. But when the show airs it won't even mention him. It's going to be me and our sheriff and it looks like they did a . . . what was it that Wyatt called it?"

"Half-assed," Brad said, his voice low. "A half-assed investigation."

Kendall's eyes flashed. At least Brad was paying attention.

"That's right," she said. "Half-assed. I bet that makes

the air. I have you and the fact that no TV station would hire you to thank for that little gem of an assessment."

"I'm sorry."

"I wish you were. And one thing I think you ought to know. You didn't not get those jobs in Seattle because you are white. You didn't get them because you're an idiot."

"Wyatt's right. You are mean."

"You haven't seen mean yet, Brad. And you better hope you don't," she said, opening the door.

"Did you just threaten me?" he asked.

Kendall's face relaxed. "Not at all," she said. "Did you just trash the Kitsap County's Sheriff's Department? I think so. You're a mess. Fix your jacket and tuck in your shirt."

Kendall looked down the hall toward the courtroom. Good. No sign of the film crew that had ambushed her.

Five minutes later, she was in Birdy's office, spilling her guts and asking for a favor.

"It sounds like a nightmare. I'm really sorry, Kendall. I didn't see any of that coming. I thought the show was on the dim bulb side, but I didn't think they'd pull that on you. And for what?"

"Apparently humiliating someone is considered good TV. At least that's how they couched it when it was all over."

"About that favor I need," Kendall went on.

"Yes, anything."

"I need you to watch Cody tonight so I can attend the reveal."

"I guess so. Elan can sleep on the couch."

Kendall shook her head. "It's a bigger imposition

than that, I'm afraid. Cody has to sleep in his own bed.
I hate to ask, but can you two stay over at our house?"

Birdy thought a moment. "I guess we could."

"Are you sure?" Kendall asked. "I know Cody likes
you. *Trusts* you. I wouldn't ask just anyone."

Birdy knew that was an understatement. Kendall
doted on that child. She was a piece of motherly armor
that enveloped the boy since he was first diagnosed
with autism. There were no tears about what could, or
rather should, have been. Just the devotion of a mother
who wanted the best for her baby and was willing to
pull the strings, make the sacrifices, and fight the fight
to ensure that her son could live a normal life.

As normal as possible. Whatever that would be, it
would be forged with everything she and her husband
had.

"Absolutely," Birdy said. "No problem. Let me double-
check with Elan. What time should we be there?"

"As late as you want. You could come over and we
could watch movies for a while. Cody will be asleep. I
have to be over to the Frazier residence for Pandora's
walk-through a little after midnight. Juliana, the producer, said two, but I'm not going to show up and find
out it's all done."

"Okay. We'll be there at ten-ish. Want me to bring
anything?"

"Just your calm, smart self, Birdy. My life's been
unraveling lately and I just need a friend. I need someone I can trust."

"Deal. See you then."

Kendall gave Birdy a hug and thanked her.

"I'm mad as hell at the producers and at Brad James,

but there's no way I'm going to let Roger and Brit face those manipulative, lying bastards without some backup."

Kendall might have been steamed, but Birdy didn't mind. She liked it when someone channeled anger toward a purpose.

"I sense that you're holding back, Kendall," she said.

Kendall let out a laugh, and like her spate of anger, it felt good. "Don't worry. I'm not."

CHAPTER SIXTEEN

Neighbors along the shore facing Seattle in Manchester hated what they called the "Flash Cube" when it first was built by Roger and Brit Frazier in the late 1990s. Most of the homes nestled among old cedars and madrona were Craftsman style. A few were completely redone mid-century modern. The first wave of homes had been built by the well-heeled of Seattle as sprawling summer places just a short steamer ride from the city. As the city grew, so did its skyline, turning the views from across the water into something of unexpected and undeniable beauty. By the time the Seattle World's Fair took place in 1962, the skyline found its exclamation point in the Space Needle. Manchester became a hot location for home development—mostly in keeping with the character of the community.

Until the "Flash Cube," of course. That building changed everything. It seemed that what someone wanted for their personal residence was more important than the character of the place sought by those already there. It was an aberration, a kind of head-scratcher that the locals just didn't understand. It looked so strange. So out of place, so not of the environment they all loved and shared.

It took time, but the Fraziers won the neighbors over. They had two little girls. A Scottie dog. A Volvo, not a Maserati. Their house didn't fit in, but they most certainly did. Brit was a master gardener and made sure that any extra vegetables went to a free box on the main road. Roger, though busy with his burgeoning career, found time to coach the intramural basketball league at Manchester Elementary. Brit spent two hours every Saturday at the library, assisting the overworked librarian in any way that she could. She had a special affinity for older kids who were struggling with reading and research skills. It was a couple of years after they arrived that she went back to school, got her counseling degree, and started the arduous task of trying to help clueless teens at the high school.

When Katy disappeared there was no shortage of support from neighbors on the shore, or of those on the hill above. Nothing like that had ever happened in Manchester before.

And many hoped it would never happen again.

Kendall knew the address. In fact, when the hospital sponsored a home tour for charity, she visited the house with Steven and her mother. She was pregnant with Cody at the time, and a flood of memories came back to her. It was extremely dark now, a little after one a.m. She put on her parking lights and crawled down the fern- and cedar-shrouded driveway to the parking area above the house. There were several vehicles lined up on the gravel lot, two sedans, a rented van, and a Porsche

Boxster. The place was mostly dark, except for some dim lighting in what she remembered to be the main living area.

She turned off the ignition and her door swung open.

"You startled me," she said, looking up and seeing Juliana Robbins, who'd appeared like a ghost outside her car.

Juliana put her finger to her lips. "Pandora is almost done. Your timing is perfect. You need to keep your voice down. I'll take you into the kitchen where the crew is. We're all set up for the reveal."

"Are the Fraziers here?"

"Not yet. You're a bit early. They won't be here for half an hour. It's all good. It's been crazy in there. I think Pandora is really on to something."

"It's all good TV," Kendall said without a trace of sarcasm, a fact of which she was proud just then. That, apparently, was all that mattered.

Juliana didn't say anything, but motioned for Kendall to follow. She led her down the steps to the back door and into the kitchen. At the table were the sound and camera guys, Wyatt Ogilvie, and a bottle of Jack Daniel's.

Before Kendall could say anything, a loud scream came from another room. It was agonal, bloodcurdling.

None of the men at the table batted an eye.

"That's just Pandy doing her thing," Wyatt said.

"Her thing must be painful."

The sound and camera guys, both from Seattle, looked a little upset, but followed their employer's lead.

Kendall eyed the bottle of Jack.

"It helps Pandy relax a little," Juliana said.

"I'm sure talking to the dead is very upsetting," Kendall said, her tone as flat as Kansas.

"You're not mad at me for the interview?" Wyatt said.

Kendall wanted to punch him, but there was no point in that. She'd already thought of a thousand ways to get even, but none would do anything other than make him a star—which she hoped would never happen.

"Not at all. We all have jobs to do," she said, taking a seat at the table.

Another scream and crash came from outside the kitchen.

Again, no one moved.

Instead, they started talking in whispers about why Seattle didn't have a decent baseball team—or at least hadn't in decades.

"At least our football team rocks," the sound guy said.

Wyatt stood up and stretched. He was dressed in the same suit and tie, but it hadn't been marred by a single wrinkle. He must have had a spare, Kendall thought.

"For now their team is doing okay."

"Okay?" This time the camera guy spoke up. "We're number one."

"Yeah," sound guy said.

"Don't get me wrong, Seattle's a nice little town but it's no San Fran and it's a far cry from my new stomping grounds, Manhattan," Ogilvie added.

Kendall just sat there and watched. The disgraced cop was not only a blowhard but also a braggart. She hated when people called San Francisco "San Fran." It was as dorky as a local in New York calling their home

"The Big Apple." Only a tourist would make such a blunder.

Headlights pierced the blinds making everyone in the room appear as though they were printed on sheets of school-ruled paper.

"The Fraziers are here," she said.

Another scream, followed by a strange, soft guttural sound that emanated from the living room.

"Perfect timing," Wyatt said. "Pandy's done her final whimper."

Juliana, looking so very excited, hurried out the door to escort the couple and their daughter Naomi inside their home. Kendall watched as they stood in the parking area.

"What's next?" she asked.

"Showtime, Detective. Be ready. Your world is about to be rocked. Pandora is the real deal. I know you're a doubter now, but that's all going to be different once the sun comes up. You'll see."

The Fraziers looked tired and apprehensive. Naomi looked bewildered, almost swallowed up by the heavy eye makeup she'd put on. She was pretty and resembled her sister a little. Kendall wondered what it was like for her to deal with the specter of a missing sister hanging over every family conversation, every moment since Katy vanished.

"Look," Roger said, "I know you don't believe in any of this hocus-pocus and we're not so sure either. But it can't hurt, Detective. Can it?"

Kendall looked at Roger, then at Brit. "I guess not. I hope not."

Juliana stood next to the table, observing the scene. Wyatt actually got up and gave Brit a hug. He shook Roger's hand.

"I was a skeptic at first too. Believe you me. But I'm a believer."

A Monkees song popped into Kendall's head.

"Are we going to do this here in the kitchen?" Brit asked. "I hadn't planned on that. I would have cleared the counters."

"No. The living room. Let me check on Pandora. I think she's ready." She looked at the sound guy. "Mic up the Fraziers."

With that, the producer disappeared through the restaurant-style swinging doors that led from the kitchen to the living room.

A beat later, she popped her head back in. "She's ready. Come on, guys."

The Frazier residence's living room was the reason the place was nicknamed the "Flash Cube." It was wall-to-wall glass—and capped by skylights. With the lights dimmed as they were, the stars and moon illuminated the space from above. The dining room table had been moved to the front of the window. Outside, a few steps led to the beach and a boathouse. Across the water was the jeweled necklace of the Seattle skyline.

"Pandy's taking a moment to freshen up," Juliana announced.

"I see," Kendall said.

"She wants you mic'ed too. Are you all right with that?"

"I think I've had enough," Kendall said.

"Contract says you have to finish the show if you start it," Juliana said.

Brad! I really hate you!

"Fine. But I don't know what I'll have to offer. I'm not a Spirit Hunter."

"Just relax, Detective. Just go with it. If you go with it, you find the experience a lot more rewarding and less, you know, painful."

It had already been painful.

Despite the late hour, Kendall couldn't deny there was some strange, collective energy in the room. The Fraziers were nervous, but hopeful. The crew from Seattle seemed to be happy that they were making overtime. Wyatt took his place at the table and motioned for Brit and Roger to sit next to him.

"Pandy will sit here," he said, indicating the spot at the head of the table.

"Detective, we want you next to Pandy."

"I don't know about that," Kendall said. "I'm not that important to the show."

Her excuse sounded a little feeble, but she figured that she needed to sound like she was going with the flow.

A man with a black mustache and shaved head entered the room and Juliana introduced him as Rex, Pandora's personal cameraman. Another followed him, who Juliana said was David.

"David's job is to tape Rex and his coverage of Pandora. We don't advertise that he's there, but if you watch the show you will probably wonder who was filming him filming her. Just a little technique that we like to

140   *Gregg Olsen*

keep to ourselves. It's a part of your confidentiality agreement."

"What happened here?" Brit asked.

"They can't say," Juliana said, pouncing before Rex or David could.

"Only Pandora will tell you. She's working with a forensics sketch artist right now translating what—and sometimes who—she saw on her walk tonight. She'll be done in five minutes or so. The artist will complete the sketch while we tape. Everyone ready?"

Katy's parents waited for their cue. Naomi lingered off camera. Kendall wanted to throw up. Make that kill Brad James, then throw up.

Even at that very late hour, Pandora lived up to her hype. She came into the living room wearing nothing but black. Her red hair cascaded down her back and her neck was coiled with silver charms. Moons and stars hung from her earlobes, but at the reminder of the producer she removed them so they wouldn't interfere with the sound. Kendall made a mental note to tell Birdy that she thought Pandora looked more like a witch than a psychic. She didn't say a word at first. It was as if she couldn't be bothered meeting anyone, including the couple whose mystery she'd been called in to solve.

"We need to give her a moment," Juliana said. "Wyatt, can you get her a cup of tea?"

Kendall was pretty sure the tea was coming from the bottle of Jack in the kitchen. She could smell it on Pandora—along with some other kind of heavy scent. Sandalwood? Made her think of junior high when she and her friends thought incense was very, very cool.

Wyatt got up and returned with a mug of tea.

Her hands shaking a little, Pandora took a sip. She closed her eyes. Juliana signaled the guys to roll tape.

Pandora's eyes snapped open and she looked at each person at the table, one at a time. Finally she spoke to Roger and Brit.

"We haven't met until just now," she said. "Is that correct?"

They nodded.

"I need to hear it."

"Yes, we haven't met until now," Roger said.

"Right," Brit added.

"I'm very sorry for your loss," Pandora said.

Brit immediately started to cry. "Loss? Is our baby dead?"

Pandora kept her expression calm and betrayed no emotion. "I will say more in a moment."

Next, she looked at Wyatt and managed a little smile. "Your mom says hello," she said.

He nodded and put his balled-up fist to his mouth.

"Hi back, Mom," he said.

Kendall looked over at Juliana. Juliana mouthed something about how that happens every episode.

Finally, Pandora set her sights on Kendall.

"You're the detective."

"That's right."

"You know she's close by."

"Who?"

"The one you're looking for. She's near."

"Could you be more specific?"

"It doesn't work that way. If it did I'd win the lottery every week."

Wyatt let out a laugh.

Kendall didn't have any idea exactly whom Pandora was referring to—was it her mother's spirit? Was it Brenda Nevins? Was it the obvious choice, Katy's presence?

"There's a lot of bad crap going on in this house. A lot of bad, bad energy here. If I were you," she said, now looking at Brit and avoiding Roger, "I'd tear it down. I'd haul it away piece by piece to the nearest dump. I'd burn it, but glass doesn't burn, does it?"

"What kind of crap?" Brit asked.

"Ask your husband."

Roger looked surprised. "I don't know what you mean. I used the best materials available for this house. It cost almost a million dollars to build."

Pandora kept her eyes fixed on his. "It isn't the house that's the problem. It's what I saw happen here."

"I have no idea what you're talking about."

"You do too."

With that, there was a slight pause. The camera focused on Wyatt next.

"You're right, Pandora," he said. "Something very dark happened here. Hard to believe that such a beautiful place could harbor something so vile, so horrific."

Pandora, her eyes shut, nodded. "Evil seeks the pretty."

She rocked back and forth and the cameraman trained his lens on Wyatt. He opened a folder with copies of the original interviews conducted by Detective Mayberry when Katy first went missing. Even in the dim light of the Frazier living room, Kendall could see that Wyatt had scribbled all over the papers. The word *in-*

competent was written in red, large enough for the camera to pick up.

"While your sketch is being finished by our forensic artist, Pandora, I want to tell you some things that you might not know."

She nodded. "Go ahead. I doubt anything will surprise me. Not after my walk through this place tonight."

When she said the word *place* she made the million-dollar home seem like a crack house.

"I conducted my own investigation here. No offense to the detective here tonight, because she was not involved, but I have never seen an example of more incompetent police work in my entire career. And I've been around the block a time or two."

Pandora nodded. The Fraziers looked over at Kendall. It was not a look meant to comfort, merely to acknowledge they were in complete agreement with what the TV cop had to say.

"Since arriving in Port Orchard I've interviewed several key witnesses to the case and I've turned up some absolutely stunning information—information that anyone could have found if they'd have used a little shoe leather. That's me. That's the way I roll."

Kendall remembered how he'd said something similar on the Nova Scotia show. He was a cop's cop. He was swathed in blue. He was a man of the downtrodden, the abused, and the murdered. She felt like throwing up just then.

"I interviewed three of Katy's closest friends. First I met with a very troubled young woman, an admitted drug addict, Tami Overton. Here's her picture."

He slid a photo over the tabletop to Pandora, who nodded in recognition.

"She's been here, many, many times."

"That's right, Pandora. She was a very, very good friend. She told me something very disturbing."

"She was abused?"

He shook his head and looked at Juliana. "Edit that."

"She told me that in the weeks before Katy disappeared she was acting very, very strangely. She seemed distracted. She didn't have the edge, the focus that she normally had."

Brit jumped in. "That's true. Something was bothering her." She looked at Roger. "I told you that. I told you something was up, but you were too busy with that stupid shopping mall project in Tacoma to give a care."

Kendall looked over and noticed that Naomi had disappeared. She didn't blame her. She wanted to leave too.

"I did too care," Roger said. "I talked to her. She was fine."

"Fine for you is not the same as fine for a teenage girl," Brit said.

Juliana let the argument play out before directing the camera back to Wyatt.

"I told Tami that the truth would come out," Wyatt said. "I told her that there was no way she could hide what she knew forever. It just wasn't going to go on and on anymore. Tami no doubt was shook up by my interview, but I don't care. I'm trying to find out what happened to Katy."

"I'm getting something on Tami," Pandora said, "but I can't quite grab it."

"Give yourself some time. You'll get there. You always do."

Pandora smiled faintly.

"I also interviewed Katy's best friend. She's now a twenty-year-old college student at the University of Washington. She wouldn't go on camera and I can't use her real name, but I think the Fraziers know who she is."

"We do," Roger said.

"I'm a little surprised she wouldn't do the show," Brit said. "Alyssa was like a sister to Katy. She stayed with us two weeks after Katy went missing. We couldn't have made it through that time without her help. She and Tami put posters up all over town. They even made phone calls from a call center set up by the high school."

Juliana spoke up. "That's great stuff, Brit. Can you repeat it without using Alyssa's name? Privacy rules."

Brit nodded and did what she was told to do.

"I also conducted a very interesting interview with Scott Hilburn, Katy's boyfriend at the time."

"He wasn't really much of a boyfriend. He hadn't even earned his driver's license at the time," Roger said.

For the first time, Kendall noticed a small monitor set up on the floor near the end of the table. Juliana put it on the table before turning it on.

"I'm not in the shot here, this will be edited out later," she said. "Also, we're not NBC, we won't be showing the tape made of Scott's interview here in the room. However, Wyo will accurately reflect its substance and we'll pull together some reaction shots."

Kendall was completely confused. Reaction shots of something they weren't seeing? Brad was such an idiot. She was such an idiot. How in the world did she get sucked into this mess? Guilt maybe? Not for what she did, but for what her department hadn't done. What was it that had been going on at the Fraziers' place that set all of this in motion?

She was about to find out.

Pandora jumped to her feet. "Enough! I don't need his taped interview. It makes everything I do look so fake! Stop it. Stop it now! Or I'll leave here and never come back."

Juliana and the crew looked shocked.

So did Katy's parents.

The only one who seemed unfazed was Wyatt himself, and maybe that weird bald guy with the black mustache who'd done nothing but lurk in the back of the room since the cameras started to roll.

"You don't mean that, Pandy!" Wyatt said.

"Don't test me, cop," she said, in what Kendall had already known was a catchphrase that was used on almost every episode. The yin and yang of psychic and cop's relationship was part of the show's appeal. Most thought they had a love/hate relationship. What they didn't know—which Kendall noticed because he wore a matching ring—the cameraman that followed Pandora around was her boyfriend. Maybe her husband.

It was all show.

Juliana stepped away for a second and returned with a piece of paper. She set it facedown on the table.

"Now that I have your attention," Pandora said to the camera first, then to the parents, "I'm going to tell you a story. It is sick and twisted and it makes me so damn angry I wonder why I bother staying here on this earth. So full of sickness. Hate. Death."

Kendall thought that's what kept her in business, but she didn't say so. Pandora's personality filled the room. There was no space for any other words, thoughts, even to breathe. Just her and a tirade against all humanity.

"I talked to Katy," she said, now looking at Brit and then Roger.

Before she could even speak, Brit started to cry. "You mean she . . . she's dead."

Pandora nodded. "Dead would be a gift to her. She's trapped in this house because of what happened to her here."

The refrigerator went on.

"I told you to unplug that damn thing," Pandora told Juliana, who scurried to the kitchen and did what she was told.

"Sorry," she said.

"Katy died a horrible death. Yes. She died in the most despicable manner that anyone could die."

Pandora leaned back and looked up to the stars overhead.

"She's with us, here, right now. And do you hear her cries? Because I do. I want to tell the girl to shut up. That her words are wasted on the living. That she should have used those very words when she was alive."

Roger didn't say anything. He looked like he was sick.

Brit spoke up. "What words? What words?"

Pandora folded her arms across her chest and rocked back and forth. She did that for what seemed like a very long time.

"She's reaching out to the other side," Wyatt told Kendall with a kind of matter-of-factness that seemed at odds with how he might have felt about her after that embarrassing tongue-lashing Pandora had given him. On camera, no less.

Kendall now considered that she was a part of some televised freak show and she made a vow to never, ever mistrust her intuition. She should never have been a part of it. No matter what her boss said.

"Katy is crying out. She's crying out like she did to you, Mrs. Frazier."

"Me? She never cried out to me."

"Oh, really? Can you really sit there and say you were there for your little girl when she needed you?"

"Yes, I was."

"Really? Weren't you off trying to help other troubled teens when your little girl was in trouble?"

"She wasn't in trouble."

"Not that you would know. You weren't listening. You weren't there for her."

"That's not true. Tell her, Roger. Tell all of them. I was a very good mother."

"Look, Pandora, I don't know what your game is here. But I do know that my wife was and is an exemplary mother to both our girls, Naomi and Katy."

Pandora didn't even look at him. "She's gone forever, Mr. Frazier."

"Where? Where is she? What happened to her?"

Pandora ran her fingers over the sheet of paper. She looked at Juliana, who instructed the camera to zoom in.

"One person knows what happened to her and where she is. One person. And that person is here. In this room."

Kendall hoped the sketch wasn't of her. She had nothing to do with any of this, but this show was so full of mind games she wouldn't put it past the producers.

Pandora turned over the white slip of paper and Brit Frazier let out a scream. It was the image of her husband, a near perfect likeness. Brit grabbed Roger by the neck and started to scratch his face. She was so intent on hurting him that Wyatt jumped up and tried to pull her off.

All the while the camera kept rolling.

"You! You!" Brit screamed. "What did you do?"

Roger stood frozen. In shock. A terrified and confused look on his face. He looked over at Kendall, then at his wife.

"I didn't do anything to her," he said. "This is complete garbage."

Brit was a mess. She couldn't even look at her husband. "He molested your daughter," Pandora said. Her tone was ice. "He silenced her by killing her."

"How could you?" Brit wailed. "How could you?"

Kendall didn't know what to do. She'd read the blogs, she should have been more prepared. She felt duped and foolish and didn't know what her role was. Was she a participant? Should she intervene? Should she unplug the camera? It was as if she were frozen in her shock too.

"I didn't," Roger said. "I swear I didn't."

By now Brit Frazier had dissolved into a puddle of tears and the anguish that comes with a revelation that shook the foundation of her being. How could she have been so blind? How could any of this be missed?

"Do you have a boat?" Pandora, still cool, asked.

Tears streaming down her face, and barely able to speak, Brit finally found her voice. "Yes," she said.

Pandora's face started to twist. It was elastic. Almost unreal in its contortions. "Out there," she said. "She's out there in the water. She told me that he tied a boat anchor to her legs. Your baby is out there in the deep."

CHAPTER SEVENTEEN

Finally Kendall found her voice. She'd had enough. Way more than enough. She got up and hurried over to Pandora.

"Look," she said, trying to control her anger, "I don't know what I expected would happen here tonight and I should have figured that something ugly rather than helpful would transpire here. I had some hope, I guess. But you've gone too far."

She spun around and glared at Wyatt, who sat there with an oddly smug look on his face. "You! I expected some crap from you, considering what you've done in the past. How you can sleep at night, I have no idea."

He brushed off her obvious contempt.

"I sleep just fine, Detective. I know that we are doing very important work here," he said.

Before Kendall could say another word, Wyatt turned to the camera.

"You see what I mean. Very defensive, these local cops. They mess up and want to blame everyone but themselves. I'm not buying her outrage. I'd say this detective is more embarrassed than anything."

"I am embarrassed. You're right. I'm ashamed, in fact. And it isn't because you and your psychic here have solved a case that we didn't—it's because I participated in this charade."

With that she hooked her foot on the power cord of the camera and yanked it from the wall.

"Show's over."

"It's not over," Roger said, now standing. "You're not leaving here with those tapes." He started toward the camera guy.

Juliana Robbins, who'd said nothing during the entire out-of-control scene, finally spoke up.

"There are no tapes," she said. "The footage was fed from the camera to our server."

"You bitch," said Roger, his face red and his fists clenched. He pounded the table so hard that the candelabra toppled. "You just did all of this to us for what? To have a show that you could sit around and tell people you produced that got some big ratings or something?"

While there was some perceptible fear in her eyes, Juliana tried to blink it away. There was a very angry man standing ten feet away from her and the star of her show had accused him of molestation and murder. "I do this program," she said, "to help people."

Before Roger could answer, Brit turned to her husband.

"I want you out. I want all of you out. All except for you." She looked at Pandora.

Pandora shook her head. "I'm done here, Mrs. Frazier. What happens next is up to you. And"—she looked over at Kendall—"and I'm sorry to say, her. She's your only hope in finding out where Katy's body is and she's the only one to bring Roger to justice."

"But I need to know more," Brit said.

"You know all that I know. Her energy was fleeting here. Strong, pleading at first, then a very quick fade."

"Please . . . how long was he messing with her . . . how come she never told me? I swear I didn't see any signs. That's my job! I'm her mother!"

"Sometimes we see only what we want to see."

"Please," Brit said

Pandora got up. She put on her pair of colossal moon and star earrings and they tinkled like wind chimes at the beach. "I'm done here."

"Yes. I expect you've done all you could possibly do here," Kendall said.

"How's your husband, Detective?"

The question was a punch in the gut.

"He's fine."

"Oh yes, I'm sure he is."

Kendall looked over at Juliana. She looked away. The producer must have mentioned the geographic separation that she and Steven were dealing with. There was no other reason why Pandora would have known. Unless she was psychic, which Kendall highly doubted.

It was after three in the morning when Kendall pulled her SUV up in front of her house. A light glowed in the window. Although she told Birdy to sleep in the guest room, she knew that she would be waiting up. The grass was covered with dew and the air heavy as her heart as she let herself inside. Birdy was curled up with a blanket and a cup of herbal tea.

"I thought you'd be awake," Kendall said.

Birdy sized up her friend. "You look like crap. I'm guessing things didn't go all that great with The Amazing Parallax."

Kendall slumped on the sofa. "Pandora is her name. And it was awful. Beyond awful. Like a nightmare. How was Cody?"

"No trouble. An angel. We had a nice evening. And by the looks of you, a much happier one. Want some chamomile?"

Kendall, still seething from all that had transpired at the Fraziers' home, nodded. "Sounds good. But I don't have any."

Birdy offered a sympathetic smile. "Of course you do. In case you didn't notice, you have a nice little patch by the back door."

"Thanks. I guess I'm not much of an herbalist."

"I am."

Birdy got up and led Kendall to the kitchen and poured her a cup, added some honey, and passed it to her. Kendall told her all that had transpired that evening. How the producers had obviously planned to ambush the Fraziers with the ridiculous accusation that Roger had molested and murdered his daughter.

"It sounds like more of a freak show than a ghost show," Birdy said.

"More like an episode of that old *Twilight Zone* show."

"My mom used to love that show," Birdy said.

"So did mine."

Kendall went to check on her son. His tugboat nightlight cast a pale yellow glow over his bed. She had the urge to kiss him on the forehead just then, but didn't want to risk waking him. Once awake, Cody wouldn't be able to go back to sleep. She tiptoed out and joined Birdy at the kitchen table.

"I'm sorry for dragging you into this, Birdy," Kendall said.

"That's what friends are for, Kendall."

Kendall drank more of the tea.

"I could use something stronger."

"This will help you rest," Birdy said. "It's Saturday. You can catch up on your sleep later. Now, talk to me. Tell me what you're going to do now."

"You mean with Pandora and that mess?"

Birdy shook her head.

Kendall knew where she was headed.

"I don't know. Steven says we're okay. I want to believe him. I mean, I do believe him."

"Said like you really don't."

Kendall set down her cup. "I really don't know what to think."

"Things will sort themselves out."

"Says the woman with more drama in her family than an episode of *Spirit Hunters*," Kendall said.

As tired as they were, they both laughed.

"You got me there," Birdy said.

CHAPTER EIGHTEEN

Alone in the house with Cody, Kendall Stark tried to fall asleep. She knew her son would be up soon enough and would want to watch TV, so she figured there'd be no point in going to bed. She'd take over Birdy's spot on the couch, crash there, and when her son woke up she could lie there and drift back into sleep.

Sleep. Even the idea of it was beyond any genuine reality. She'd been pulled through a knothole by that awful TV show and the horrible so-called psychic. She felt shame for being part of what felt like was an ambush, an emotional hit-and-run. Pandora had come in with a wrecking ball of accusations, let it swing hard and fast at Katy's parents—her father in particular—and then just like that, pronounced her work done. Like she'd actually provided some kind of service to the couple, to the police, to the community.

She actually accused Roger Frazier of being a child molester and murderer and in the day and age they lived in, it was a coin toss as to which was a nastier label to give a person.

At least a murderer could serve his or her time and start over.

A child molester, good luck on that one.

Kendall searched for the cool side of her pillow. Her face was hot and the chamomile that Birdy had brewed for her did little to calm her nerves. She got up, went to the bathroom, checked on Cody, and tried again to pull the fragments of the longest night into some semblance of order.

She knew that when she returned to the office on Monday there would be a stack of messages for her. She was sure that Roger would get his lawyer involved as the TV show was pretty much endorsed by the Kitsap County Sheriff's Department.

Thanks to that nitwit public information officer, whose name, in her tired grogginess, she couldn't even retrieve just then. She hoped that he'd be long gone. Or at least have the good sense to be in his office tapping out the words for a resignation letter. The sheriff might be on that Alaska cruise just then, but Kendall Stark was pretty sure that he'd already heard about what had happened back home. Kendall was almost glad he wasn't there. She's seen him blow his top before and this one was undoubtedly of Mount St. Helens caliber.

Cody found his way to the couch.

"Hi, Mom," he said.

"Hey, you. Come here."

She pulled him up and tucked him under the blanket on the sofa. He was a hot sleeper, but she didn't care. Cody did something right then that took her mind off of what was rolling around in her brain. She wasn't thinking of the Fraziers, Pandora, Wyatt, or any of the craziness that awaited her.

Her little boy. She had one good thing in her life right then. Cody.

"I love you, Mom," he said.

"Love you too. Let's rest. Mommy's tired."

"But it's morning."

"Let's pretend it isn't. Not yet."

He smiled at her. "All right. I like that game. Let's pretend today hasn't started yet."

Kendall held him and closed her eyes. She wished two things. That her husband was home, and that she could have a do-over for the night before.

CHAPTER NINETEEN

Juliana Robbins didn't especially like being on the other side of the camera, but her executive producer in New York had made it very clear that the cable channel was going to pull the plug on their show if they didn't get a bump in the ratings. *A big bump.* That meant publicity in every town or city that was a show location. Port Orchard was off the beaten track, but Juliana had connections with the producer at KING-TV's *Nightwatch* magazine. She'd gone to school with Theresa Mullins and though they were not close, they shared a kind of sisterhood in broadcasting. One stayed local and the other went out in search of something bigger. Neither really found what they were looking for. Juliana looked up Theresa's number and got her on the phone.

"Oh, it has been forever!" Juliana said, her voice more animated than ever. She wasn't being the caring, understanding Juliana to get her "get." Those were the flavors of her persona she used to get those with a horror story, a family tragedy, to acquiesce to her request.

Theresa seemed surprised. "It has. I've been following your career. I'm thrilled for you. And, honestly, a little envious. I've been doing this for four years now and I don't know how much more I can take. The host is a real bitch."

"That's awful. I love my team. The best ever, but I know how you feel. I've been doing this a while too, and I really would like to get into broadcast journalism. You know, something of true substance."

"I hear you. Hey, you in town doing something?"

"As a matter of fact, I am. That's why I'm calling. I'm over on the Peninsula getting ready to do a show on a Port Orchard missing persons case."

"Wow. That's really cool."

"I'm glad you think so. That's why I'm calling. I was hoping you could do a segment on what we're doing here for your show."

"We're kind of getting away from crime and misery," Theresa said. "I love what you've been doing on *Spirit Hunters*. Wish I could help. But the subject matter is just too dark."

"That's stupid and you know it. People like crime and misery, Teri."

"I *know*. But that's the direction. If I have to produce one more segment on a new winery or a thrift shop makeover I'm going to puke into my Starbucks mug."

Juliana looked at herself in the mirror and smiled. The wheels were turning. If anything, Juliana was quick on her feet. She didn't take no for an answer from anyone. Not some grieving father. Not some cop like Kendall Stark. And certainly not from an old broadcast school chum with a hunger for the big time.

"You can tell your EP that *Spirit Hunters* is about

bringing closure and peace to people," she said. "We're a very upbeat show."

"Jules, you can't bullshit a bullshitter. I've seen the show."

Juliana paused. "But has your EP?"

"Doubtful," Theresa said, her tone giving away her feelings for what she really thought of the woman in charge of the show. "She's the one pushing for all the winery segments. She imagines that she's very high-brow."

Juliana laughed. "TV *is* lowbrow. Lowbrow content gets high ratings. Right now they can't find enough hillbillies to put on a reality show. They're practically trolling the backwoods of West Virginia for the next Honey Boo Boo."

"I know," Theresa said, thinking it over a little. "Okay. I'll pitch it. No promises. How long are you in town?"

"There's kind of a rush on this. I need to do it to-morrow before we do the taping. Stuff happens after the tapings sometimes and we kind of need to leave town."

"Now I'm totally hooked. It sounds like you're really helping people."

"You know the name of the game."

"Yup. Ratings. Ratings. Ratings. Nothing else mat-ters. Nothing at all."

Juliana let a little dead air seep into the phone. She knew that a long pause held power. It made whatever she had to say next seem very, very important. Con-templative.

"I really need this, Teri," she finally said. "You need it too."

"Why do I need it?" Theresa asked.

"Because New York talks and I'll make sure they hear your name."

The next day, a three-member film crew from KING showed up at Swallow Haven for the interview. Juliana had the B and B hosts set up the living room with its view of Gig Harbor's sparkling waterfront.

"I promised that you'd be able to show their sign in the background," Juliana told her friend Theresa. She indicated a large hand-carved sign that featured the name of the establishment and a charming arc of flying swallows.

"No worries," Theresa said. "My executive producer will love that we're spotlighting a B and B in the interview. She'll probably try to score a freebie from the owners. She's done it before."

"I know the type. The industry's full of people with their hands stretched out."

"Glad that's not us, Jules," Theresa said with a laugh.

"So not *us*."

With the camera in place, the mic affixed discreetly on the lapel of her pale pink blazer—Chanel, Teri thought—Juliana Robbins talked about the importance of *Spirit Hunters*, how it brought closure to people, how Pandora's gifts were a marvel.

"She's the real deal," Juliana said. "I'm a skeptic. I'm from New York where we see it all. Pandora is absolutely amazing."

Theresa asked some questions about the show they were doing in Port Orchard.

"It's a real-life mystery. One day Katy Frazier was on the top of the world, top of her class, loads of friends, adored by every single person in town, and then zip . . . she was gone. Not a single clue to her whereabouts."

"Do you think Pandora can unravel what happened to her?"

"The combination of Wyatt and Pandora makes them a true dynamic duo. They make up the force that is what *Spirit Hunters* is all about . . . they are the truth seekers from the world we live in now and world beyond."

Theresa asked some questions about the accommodations at the B and B, and Juliana gushed about the hosts, the food, and the views.

"You haven't lived unless you've stayed here. This place really is to die for."

Theresa grinned broadly. "Queen of the sound bite. That's you. My EP will love that last line."

Juliana rolled her shoulder. "Give them what they want," she said.

Theresa unclipped the mic. "And nothing more."

"Right," Juliana said, adjusting her collar. "When will this be on your air?"

Theresa smiled. "You'll love this. We had to cut a segment on—get this—a boutique pesto maker in Woodinville that the FDA just forced to recall all its outstanding inventory for *E. coli* contamination. Seems like the irrigation water they used for their basil fields was untreated sewage. You'll be on tonight."

"That's good for *Spirit Hunters*," Juliana said. "I love pesto, though. At least until you told me that."

Theresa nodded.

"Yeah, now I think it's just gross. Next time you're in town, give me a heads-up a little earlier. I really would like to find my way out of Seattle. Better yet, put my name out there. You know what I can do. I can get things done. Like this. Like getting this interview set up at the last minute."

Juliana gave her long-lost friend a quick but slightly stiff little hug.

"You're way too nice for New York, Teri," she said, twisting her hair into a messy ponytail and giving her head a little shake. "Try LA or maybe even Portland. But yes, next time for sure. Drinks and dinner on me."

Theresa didn't know what to say. Portland? That wasn't a step up at all. And why in the world would her friend say she was too nice for New York? She'd told off that dim bulb *Nightwatch* host more than a time or two. She even told a hot-air balloonist they were featuring that he was an ass when he said that a woman patron with large breasts could cause "another Hindenburg at the right altitude."

CHAPTER TWENTY

Kendall wasn't sure how to read the look on Brit Frazier's face when she opened the door to the house that would likely become infamous once the TV episode aired. She looked a little tired. And why wouldn't she be? It was a very long night and one fraught with outrageous accusations, hurled at a family who'd been shattered by the loss of their daughter.

"Come in," she said.

"I'm sorry about what happened."

Brit shrugged a little and led Kendall to the kitchen where air was thick with the smell of a freshly brewed pot of coffee.

Katy's mother motioned to a cup. "Want some?"

"Yes, black," she said. "Thanks."

"I was hoping you would come, Detective."

"Call me Kendall. We've been through a war zone together."

Brit smiled faintly as she poured the blackest coffee Kendall had ever seen into two plain white cups.

"It felt a little like that, didn't it?" Brit said.

"Again, I'm very sorry. It never should have happened. Not like that. I had no idea."

Brit stared into her cup. "I really didn't know what to expect. I knew that it was our last chance at the truth of what happened to Katy. You guys—not you personally—didn't do much. I'm not even going into that right now," she said.

"I appreciate that, and again, I can't say too many times how sorry I am."

Brit nodded. "I know. I can see it on your face. I just didn't know where else to turn and, well, I'm a believer in the spirit world and I absolutely believe that Pandora has the gift."

"You really do?"

"I know that being skeptical is part of your job. But I've always been able to tap into things that were not readily apparent."

"How so?"

"With the kids. I've always prided myself on my ability to see what was right in front of their faces, things that were roadblocks to their safety and their health. Issues at home that were bothering them, holding them back from being themselves."

"You're not saying you're psychic?" Kendall said, keeping her tone respectful and as open as she could.

Brit laughed. "Goodness no. I'm not psychic. But I'm sensitive. I have an awareness about things that some people just can't fathom." She paused, keeping her eyes on the coffee cup before looking up. "Makes me sound conceited or stupid. Or maybe both."

Kendall shook her head. "No. Neither."

"Thanks. That's why all of this and what happened last night is so horrible, so damning. It makes me feel like I'm such a fraud. That everything that I thought about myself was so, so wrong."

"I don't follow," Kendall said, though she did. She wanted Brit to dump out everything she was holding inside. The more she talked, the better.

"My husband. Roger. I didn't know. I didn't see."

"See what?"

"What Pandora said happened here."

"You think she's right?"

Brit nodded. "I think so. It crushes me. It makes me want to vomit. In fact, I threw up just moments before you arrived. I didn't see what was happening to my own little girl. She was so perfect. She was so happy. Or at least she seemed to be."

"She never told you her father abused her?"

Brit stood up and offered more coffee, but it was just an excuse to break the tension in the room. The subject matter was so uncomfortable that it just didn't seem like the air in the room could take the words that she was saying and she needed to move away from them.

"No. She never did. She might have told her friends. She might have told her sister, but she never said a word to me. We . . . we . . . we just didn't have that kind of close mother-daughter bond."

"Did you ever see a time when she was uncomfortable around her father?"

Brit thought awhile. She sat back down. "There was one time . . ."

Katy was on the sofa that faced out toward the sunburnished Seattle skyline. Her father sat next to her, reading a magazine every now and then looking up to see if his daughter had stopped crying. Tears were unusual. Katy was always the girl who brought the shine and sparkle to every occasion. She didn't seem to have a care in the world, except being the best she could be. When she hit a brick wall and didn't get the A+ she felt she deserved and worked so hard to get, she sometimes let frustration manifest into tears. Brit was making dinner in the kitchen and she could watch the pair as she went about what she was doing. Lasagna that night. Whole wheat pasta because Naomi, then twelve, was on an attention-seeking quest of her own and was insistent that nothing but whole, healthy foods were consumed by anyone at the Frazier household. Brit didn't mind her youngest daughter's edicts about diet and exercise, but she was less than enthused about the gluey nature of whole wheat pasta.

". . . It will be our little secret," Roger said, putting his hand on Katy's shoulder.

Brit watched as her husband leaned in and whispered something in Katy's ear and then, after doing so, glanced back at the kitchen.

His gaze met Brit's and telegraphed that whatever it was that was going on was going to pass.

Later that night, while Roger undressed for bed, Brit asked him about what had been going on earlier in the evening.

"What is your little secret?" she asked from her side of the bed.

"Nothing."

"Really? Nothing? Katy looked upset all evening. She barely touched her plate."

"She's going through some things," Roger said, sliding his sinewy frame under the covers and moving close to Brit.

"Roger, what are you two keeping from me?"

"It isn't that big of a deal. It's under control. I promise."

"She's my daughter too. I have a right to know."

"She is, but you don't. She's sixteen. It's not mine to tell."

"She's not having sex, is she? Some boy at school we haven't met?"

Roger shook his head and laughed. "No. No, she's not having sex with some boy at school."

"That's what he told me," Brit said to Kendall over the kitchen table.

"You think that's important now," the detective said.

Brit stood and turned away, looking out the window at the grassy lawn as a pair of Mexican landscapers prepared to mow and edge. Kendall wished she could afford some extra help. Her power mower was dead and all she had at her disposal was an old, very sad push-mower. No amount of reminding her that exercise after a long day behind a desk was good for her could convince her that the pain was worth the gain.

The Weed Eaters started and the two men moved in tandem, almost synchronized as they went back and forth over the edge of the lawn.

"You think it is important," Kendall repeated.

Brit turned to face her. Dead eyed, unflinching.

"Yes, I do. I think so now. I mean, look, what kind of

father and daughter have secrets that their mother cannot know about? When he said she wasn't having sex with a boy at school, was he saying the truth, but leaving out the part that *he* was having sex with her?"

By then Brit Frazier was crumpling and reaching back to grip the edge of the sink so she wouldn't fall.

Kendall went to her.

"Mrs. Frazier, please. Sit down. You're making a very big leap here. You're looking back into your life for a truth that might not exist, at the suggestion of a person you don't know."

"Pandora knows. I don't need to know her. I trust her knowledge, her understanding."

Kendall wanted to tell the grieving mother that putting such faith in Pandora was foolish. That there were other people she'd harmed along the way in her quest for stardom, attention, and followers.

"She called me this morning. You don't know her. You don't understand her gifts. I do."

Kendall was surprised. She wondered why Pandora would call after the debacle that left everyone catching their breath and pointing accusatory fingers. The main reason that came to her mind just then was that Pandora was doing a little damage control.

Pandora wanted to make sure that Brit stayed on her side.

"What did she say to you?"

Tears rolled from Brit's eyes to the tabletop. "She told me that Katy was in a better place and that it was good that I knew, that I could protect Naomi and that . . . and that—well, that you, Kendall Stark, you would find where my daughter's body is so I can lay her to rest. That you,

Kendall, that you could bring my husband to justice for the evil that he did to our little girl. That's why you're here. She told me that she'd send you."

Send her?

Kendall couldn't stand the manipulation. She could see it so plainly, but her eyes weren't full of tears and there was no way that Brit had any clarity. She was being fed a hideous scenario and in her grief and in her compulsive need for answers, she was accepting it.

"I'm here because I was worried about you. I'm here because I'm going to investigate the case. I'm here because, like you, I want answers. But I can assure you I'm not here because Carol Kirkowski sent me."

"Who is Carol?"

"That's Pandora's real name. Carol Kirkowski. She adopted Pandora for the TV show, Brit. I thought you knew."

Brit, no longer crying, dabbed a napkin under her eyes, leaving a black smear of mascara.

"I don't care what she used to call herself. She's a miracle worker. And whether you like it or not, she's sent you to me. Now, please. Help. Do your job. Pick up the pieces where that insufferable Detective Mayberry let us down four years ago. I expect and accept that my daughter is dead. I accept that my husband was raping her. That he killed her."

"That's a huge leap," Kendall said, not sure what else she could say. The woman across from her was completely swayed by what the TV psychic had said.

"I'll do my best, of course. I'd like to talk to Naomi."

"Naomi was only a girl when her sister went missing," Brit said. "Leave her out of it."

"Don't you want the truth? Sometimes sisters share things that they would never tell their parents."

"You mean other secrets, 'only between us'?"

Kendall got up and set her cup in the sink. The yard workers were attacking the laurel hedge that separated the Frazier place from the neighbors.

"Something along those lines," she said. "Thanks for the coffee."

CHAPTER TWENTY-ONE

It took some doing, but Alyssa Woodley and Scott Hilburn arrived at the Kitsap County Sheriff's Department for an interview. Kendall called Birdy to see if she wanted to sit in.

"Can't. Up to my elbows in my work."

Kendall didn't like the image that came to mind.

"All right. Will fill you in."

She hung up, went to the reception area where the couple waited, and led them down the hall to the interview room. It was immediately clear from the start that Alyssa was the leader of the pair.

"I want him sitting next to me," she said when Kendall indicated the conference room where she was going to conduct the interview.

"That's fine," she said, making a note of Alyssa's insistent demeanor.

Scott nodded and sat down.

"I'm glad you two made it over here. I was thinking that I'd have to hop the ferry and look for you on campus," Kendall said.

"Well, we saved you the trouble," Alyssa said.

"We're glad to help," Scott jumped in, staving off his girlfriend's abrasive manner. "Katy was a good friend."

Kendall nodded. "Yes, I know. She was your girl-friend at the time she went missing, wasn't she?"

"Yeah, but it wasn't serious," Alyssa said.

"Excuse me, Alyssa, I was asking Scott."

Alyssa made an irritated face.

"Yes, she was, but like Alyssa said, it wasn't serious. Just a high school thing."

"Right. A high school thing," Kendall repeated.

"What do you want to know?" Alyssa asked.

"I'm getting there. You must be on the debate team, Alyssa."

"I'm not. Why would you say that?"

"Because you don't let anyone get a word in edge-wise."

Alyssa looked at Scott. It was a hard, cold stare. "We came here to help and you're treating us like crimi-nals," she said.

Kendall shook her head "No. No. I'm just following up on some things left unfinished by the investigation four years ago."

"Okay. Whatever," she said. "We need to catch a ferry in an hour."

"There's always another boat," Kendall said. This girl was a piece of work. "But this shouldn't take too long." She locked her eyes on Alyssa, then looked down at her notes, the timeline of Katy's disappearance.

"Part of my predecessor's timeline doesn't jibe with all of the interviews," Kendall said.

"Like what?" Alyssa asked.

Kendall glanced at Scott, who was looking over at Alyssa.

"Scott, can you keep your focus on me?" Kendall asked. "I'd like you to answer."

"Okay, answer what?" he said.

"Did you, Alyssa, Katy, and Tami have plans to do something after school the day she went missing?"

He shook his head. "I honestly don't remember."

Kendall didn't like it when someone used the word *honestly*.

"My notes say that you originally said that you did have plans."

"I don't remember."

"Can I say something?" Alyssa asked, in what was the first polite move she'd made since she plopped herself down in the chair across from Kendall.

"Yes. In a moment," Kendall said. "Now, Scott, it was only four years ago. I bet that Katy's disappearance was a very big moment in your life. Surely you remember what happened that day."

Scott looked at the table.

"I wish I could be helpful. It *was* a very big moment. I might have blocked stuff out of my mind."

"Can I talk now?" Alyssa asked, though it was really more of an insistent demand.

"Sure, Alyssa. What do you remember?"

"I have an excellent memory," she said. "I remember being interviewed by that doofus deputy Mayberry. That's what I remember. He wasn't the smartest tool in the shed and I doubt—I seriously doubt—that his notes were accurate."

"Fine," Kendall said. "Then tell me what you remember. What plans did you and Katy have?"

"None," Alyssa said. "That's what plans we had. Katy and I weren't as close as we had been. We didn't hang out that much anymore. I don't know who she hung out with or what she did after school that day or any other day."

"Really, Alyssa?" Kendall said. "You were best friends."

Alyssa thought a moment. "We were. But things had cooled between us. High school relationships are so transitory anyway."

"But you and Scott were high school friends and now you're together, Alyssa."

Alyssa's eyes flashed. "That's different," she said. "We're in love. True love never fades."

Kendall thought about her own relationship with Steven. She wondered when she stopped believing what that twenty-year-old said.

"Why would Naomi say that her sister had plans with you, Tami, and Scott?"

"Naomi was a kid. Who knows why she'd say anything? Maybe to get attention. She was sick of all the family love heaped on her sister. I don't blame her. Not really. Katy and I were close for a time, but I hated how everyone idolized her. God, every time she turned around they handed her an award. Not that she didn't deserve it. Just hard, probably, for a kid sister to take."

Kendall made a couple of notes. "Scott, what did Katy tell you about her family life?"

He shrugged. "I don't know. She hated her mom. I hated mine at the time too. Naomi was clingy, but a good kid."

"What about her dad? What did she say about him?"

"Nothing. She liked him."

Alyssa cut in. "Is this about the stupid TV show that's in town?" she asked.

"No," Kendall said, which was kind of a lie. The truth was they were sitting there discussing a four-year-old missing persons case because of *Spirit Hunters*. "Why?"

"They keep calling us," she said.

"Who does?"

"The whole bunch of them," Alyssa said. "The producer Juliana Something, the cop who's on the show, and the freaky chick who says she can talk to the dead. I don't watch the show. I don't believe in that crap. Not a bit."

"What did they say to you?" Kendall asked Scott.

"Nothing. Alyssa talked to one of them."

"Who was that?"

"The weirdo chick Pandora," she said. "I talked to her."

"What did she say?"

"She wanted us to be on her show. Said that she knew the truth of what happened and that she was going to prove to the world who killed Katy."

"Really?"

"Yes. Really. I didn't buy her BS. Why would I?"

"Did she say anything else?"

Alyssa nodded. "Yeah, something about Katy's dad knowing the truth. But nothing definitive. I mean, think about it. When those psychics make a prediction it's always so stupid and vague, like a earthquake is going to happen next year and some people will die."

"Fine. What do you think happened to Katy?" she asked, this time looking at Scott.

"I wouldn't have an idea about what happened to her," he said.

"Neither would I," Alyssa said, standing up to leave.

"Really, we have to go. I don't want to wait for another boat back to Seattle."

"Don't either of you want to know what happened to Katy? It seems very odd to me that you've just moved on."

Scott stood too. "You can't live in the past, Detective Stark. It'll swallow you whole if you do."

Alyssa reached for his hand. "He's right about that. Scott's always right."

"Have either of you been in touch with Tami?"

"No. Why would we? She's a druggie."

"Yes, but she was your close friend."

"Like I've said, that was ages ago," Alyssa said. "We have moved on from high school. I haven't talked to Tami in years. My mom says she had a kid and got married. I'm glad about that, but I don't care about the past. Tami's the past."

"Yeah, she's the past," Scott. "Like Alyssa says."

Birdy Waterman, thankfully, was no longer elbow deep in an autopsy when Kendall Stark arrived at her upstairs office over the morgue to tell her about the interview with Alyssa Woodley and Scott Hilburn.

"Did I miss anything?" Birdy asked.

"A better show than *Spirit Hunters*," Kendall said. "Although when I think about it just about any show is better than *Spirit Hunters*."

Birdy smiled. "Tell me."

"I think they both know more than they are saying—or more than she lets him say."

"She's the boss then," Birdy said.

"At one point he talked about not letting the past get in the way of living, that if you do, it can swallow you whole. I had a visual of an anaconda named Alyssa disengaging her jaw and eating him. So yeah, she's in charge."

"Say anything about Mr. Frazier?" Birdy asked.

"Nope," Kendall said. "Not really. Talked about how Katy hated her mother, and her kid sister was a pest. They also mentioned they'd been hassled by the folks from *Spirit Hunters.*"

"Who hasn't?" Birdy said. "It seems they certainly are on the case."

"I know. I'm going to talk to the third prong of that friendship, Tami Overton. I'm also thinking that I might need to make a trip east of the mountains."

"Who's there?"

"Mayberry," Kendall said. "I really need to find out what went wrong with his investigation. Between you and me, this really does smack of gross incompetence. Katy was no runaway."

"But what if her father molested her? That would be good reason to run away."

"I know, but I left the door wide open for Alyssa or Scott to say something about it and they never did. I would have thought that if Katy confided in anyone it would have been one of those two."

"Maybe Tami?" Birdy suggested. "Sometimes you make the most private disclosures to those who are close, but not close enough to throw it in your face every time you see them."

CHAPTER TWENTY-TWO

Lynn Overton had a funny feeling in the pit of her stomach. She and her daughter hadn't had the best relationship over the years, but it had improved, and with the birth of Tami's son, Jax, there had been a genuine connection for reconciliation that while tenuous at first, was growing stronger, little by little. When Tami didn't answer her phone, she figured that the battery had died and she decided to drive over to see how things were going. She knew the ghost show had interviewed Tami. She'd had her own interview with Kendall Stark of the Kitsap County Sheriff's Department and there was no doubt that old wounds, old hurts, had been reopened by the TV show that had zipped into Port Orchard to film an episode.

Lynn worried about the show, the attention that it would bring. She'd cautioned Tami on the phone about appearing on *Spirit Hunters* and Tami seemed to be listening. It was a rare phone call, the kind that made her fingers tremble whenever she attempted one.

"I don't know that I want, or that I can do it," Tami said when they talked the night before.

"Then don't. He's telling you not to."

"Mom, don't get all Jesus on me. I have enough baggage from all of that."

Lynn wasn't sure what her daughter was saying and in that moment, she decided that she'd not press her for any details. After Katy's disappearance everything had gone dark for Tami. It was as if her grief over the shocking mystery of what happened to her friend had sucked her into a whirlpool and nearly drowned her. It was only a miracle—and, Lynn thought, God's power to heal— that saved her from becoming another statistic.

She got in her late-model dark blue Volvo and backed out of the driveway, turning on the Christian music radio station that brought her great comfort. The station was playing a song by Mandisa, a gospel/pop singer she'd loved on one of the seasons of *American Idol*. Mandisa's soaring vocals always brought her closer to God. She drove along Long Lake to Mullenix and then on to Highway 16. Lynn always liked the drive over the Purdy Spit's venerable bridge to the neighborhood that her daughter and her family called home.

She'd been there only three times before, but each time felt like a step closer. A baby step. A chance to be a mother to a girl who needed one, an opportunity to be a better grandmother than she was a mother to Tami.

"I failed her. I am to blame," was the brokenhearted mother's mantra. When she told friends that Tami's drug use had been her fault, none could see it.

"You loved her. You were proud of her. You did everything you could to help her get on firm footing," they'd say.

She'd nod in agreement, but those words felt empty when she looked at the damage all around her. Her husband left her. Her child was a drug addict, a drop-out, and a girl of questionable morals. Everything she'd dreamed about when she first held Tami in that hospital room had just turned to nothingness.

Joe, Tami's husband, worked double shifts at an oyster farm not far from their house. Only Tami's old cabriolet was parked in the carport of the tidy red and white rental house tucked into the corner of a neighborhood with an overabundance of speed bumps and cyclone fencing.

She parked and went to knock on the door.

No answer.

The curtains were drawn, and Lynn tried to peer between the slits of the fabric that she recognized as an old sheet set that her daughter had cut and trimmed with gimp for a set of country-style curtains.

She couldn't see anything. She went back to the door and knocked again.

"Tami? It's Mom. Are you home?"

Again no answer.

For a second Lynn wondered if her daughter was avoiding her. She'd felt that their phone call the night before had gone fairly well. At least for them. If Tami didn't want to see her, she should at least have the common courtesy to let her mother know by coming to the door.

She was raised better than that.

The irony of her thoughts tugged at her. She had tried to do her best. She'd gone to group meetings for parents of drug addicts. She'd gone to counseling for herself to see what it was that she could have done to raise a girl who'd stick a needle in her arm.

Lynn went around the back of the house to the slider

and cupped her hands over the glass so she could miti-
gate the reflection and get a better look inside. The TV
was on in the front room. A coffee cup sat on the counter
next to a half-full carafe. On the floor was a fairly neat
pile of toys—mostly stuffed animals and a few little
trucks and things that her one-year-old could hardly
find that enchanting.

Except maybe to suck on. Jax was teething.

Then she saw the baby. Right in the midst of all the
toys, just sitting there, crying.

The door was unlocked—something that she'd hold
her tongue about when she found Tami—and she went
inside, scooping up her grandson.

"Where's Mommy?" she asked, looking around and
finding her way down the hall, looking in each bedroom and the main bathroom. The house was spotless,
which made her feel good, but it also bothered her that
she even cared about that right then.

Something was wrong.

The curtains were drawn in the master bedroom,
making it impossible to see. She flipped on the lights,
but they didn't work. With the baby on her hip, Lynn
pulled back the heavy-lined curtains and let out a
scream.

Tami was on the bed, her eyes open, but unrespon-
sive. A syringe was stuck in her arm.

Lynn, in a panic, started to hyperventilate. She set
the baby down on the corner of the bed.

"Tami! Tami! What have you done! Tami!"

She reached over and pulled out the syringe, throwing it across the room.

"How could you do this to me? To Jax? To Joe?"

She felt for a pulse.

Thank God! Praise Him!

Tami was alive.

Lynn called 911.

"Please hurry! My daughter's alive! But she's over-dosed on drugs!"

The man from the Comm Center told Lynn to hang tight, keep an eye on Tami's vitals, and help would be there. A volunteer paramedic unit was less than a quarter mile away.

"Was she suicidal?"

"No, she wasn't."

"Was she a habitual user?"

"No. No. She was a mother. She's a wife. All of that is in the past. Please, just get here. Save my baby."

Jax was crying pretty loudly by then and Lynn picked him up and tried to comfort him. She hoped against hope that everything would be all right. The baby boy could feel the terror that his grandmother was experiencing right then. He soaked in all her worry, fear, and let out a scream that Lynn was pretty sure God could hear.

She certainly hoped so.

CHAPTER TWENTY-THREE

Tacoma General Hospital was one of those buildings that seemed designed by committee rather than anyone who cared for people. One had to actually work there to find his or her way around passageways and poor signage that directed the distraught and desperate to whatever floor or room they sought. Lynn Overton sat in a small waiting area outside intensive care. A little boy with pudding on his hands painted the sides of a saltwater aquarium while his mother played solitaire on her iPad. Down the carpeted corridor, Lynn's only child was fighting for her life.

Joe, Tami's husband, arrived a half hour after the ambulance blared its way from the neighborhood. Joe was a handsome young man, a few years older than Tami, but not so much that it bothered Lynn. Jax was with his mother at her place in Port Orchard.

"You should have told me she was using again," Lynn said, her lips tight.

Joe shook his head. "She wasn't, Lynn."

Lynn watched the pudding painter. "You really blew

it, Joe. You really messed up. You should not have covered for her."

Joe thought hard for a moment. There was some history between himself and his mother-in-law. She hadn't approved of him at first. Maybe she'd never approved of him at all. He was a peacemaker and he was the one always trying to get Tami to work things out with her mom.

"You don't know anything about your daughter," he said.

She got up. "Don't tell me that. She was my little girl long before you came into the picture."

"Do you really want to have this kind of discussion here? Now?" He looked over at the solitaire mom, who glanced at him and rolled her eyes upward before going back to her game.

"I suppose not," she said. "But it is really hard for me to sit here knowing that she was using again and I had no notice of it. No chance to stop her. To save her."

"Like I said, she wasn't using. And she's going to be all right."

The pair of them sat there in silence. Waiting. Hoping. When a nurse and doctor came out to speak with them, neither needed to hear the words. It was evident by the looks on their faces.

"I'm so sorry," said the doctor, a Pakistani with a sweet face and eyes that seemed to glisten with tears.

"You mean?" Joe asked, now standing and shaking.

"Yes, I'm so sorry. We couldn't save her."

Lynn just stood mute. The room was spinning. It was the feeling of an earthquake and vertigo and a tsunami all at once. She collapsed back into the chair.

"Would you like to see her?" said the nurse, a pretty girl with nutmeg hair and light blue eyes.

Joe nodded. "Yes. Yes. I want to see her." He turned to Lynn and extended his hand. "Are you coming?"

Lynn took his hand. None of what was happening seemed real. She might have expected such a scenario years ago when Katy went missing and Tami fell into despair and sought an end to her pain from the sharp tip of a needle. But not now when she'd come so far, had so much for which to live.

"Why?" she asked, her voice constricted by the anguish in her throat. "Why did my baby do this?"

The window shades were drawn, and a light next to the bed and completely silent monitors illuminated the space. Tami Overton looked as though she was sleeping. Her eyes were shut, her mouth slightly open. One of the nurses had straightened out the light blue blanket that covered most of her body. Her arms were concealed under the fleecy wrapping. It appeared that her curly dark hair had been brushed or combed.

The doctor put his hand on Lynn's shoulder.

"We are so very sorry."

"Thank you."

Joe knelt down beside the bed and buried his face in the blue blanket.

"What happened?" she asked.

"Overdose."

"I know, but how? She was clean."

The doctor nodded. "We noticed some old track marks. Very old. The mark from the needle that killed her today is the only new one. She clearly hadn't been using in a long, long time."

"Did she say anything? Did she say anything at all?"

The doctor shook his head. "Not that I heard. I'm sorry."

The nurse spoke up. "The paramedics that brought your daughter in said she did say a few things on the way to the hospital."

Joe looked up.

"What? What did she say?"

"It wasn't completely coherent. She said something about being sorry. Something about someone named Katy. That she should have told the truth. That she should have been protected."

Lynn asked Joe if she could have a moment with her daughter.

"There are a million things I never got to say to her," she said, her eyes weeping tears, but her voice in full control.

Joe had every right to say something harsh to Lynn—she hadn't been the best mother, but she was far from the worst. His own carried that mantle and he knew that his son would need a grandmother who could tell him the good things about the mom he'd never know. He kissed his wife on her smooth, white forehead and whispered in her ear.

"Oh baby, why didn't you tell me?"

With that, he nodded in Lynn's direction and left the room. The nurse followed behind, shutting the door quietly.

Lynn planted her knees on the floor and stayed very still for a long time, just stroking her daughter's hair, thinking back to the last time they spoke. It was a gift from God that it had not been an argument—that the words were charged with love, warmth, and even a little hope.

"Honey, I thought you were better. I thought everything was going the way you wanted things to go. Your husband, your baby, your education. You told me there were no cracks in the ice . . ." she let her words trail off as she inhaled a deep breath to continue. "The ice under your feet. You didn't need me to hold you up. You didn't need Joe to hold you up."

She pulled herself closer to her daughter, reaching over the metal sides of the hospital bed that held her like she was in danger of rolling to the floor. Tami was still warm. Like she was merely asleep. Maybe this was a terrible dream. Lynn spoke to God to make it so.

"Father, I have been a bad mother. None of this would have happened if I had been what I'd been called to be with this great gift of this child. Please, strike me dead now. Strike me dead and return her to life. Please. Do this for me, for her, for her baby, for her husband. Do not make the world a worse place by taking her and leaving me behind. Dear God, hear me. Hear my prayer."

She looked up and nothing had changed. Lynn still had an unshakable faith, but in that moment she questioned just why it had to be this way. Why her baby, her troubled baby, should do this to herself. It was all so wrong.

She grabbed the edge of the blanket and the sheet that covered Tami's body and peeled it back. She had to see again what it was that had done this evil. What had been the implement of Satan and where it had left its mark.

Her daughter's arms were thin. Almost so thin it seemed impossible that anyone—that she—could find a space to insert a needle.

But there it was. Among a swarm of old faded scars was the red puncture mark of the instrument of Tami's death. It looked like a bug bite, red, slightly raised but with the clear space of an indentation where the needle had struck.

Like the depression a toothpick makes when inserted into angel food cake not yet ready to be pulled from the oven.

CHAPTER TWENTY-FOUR

Janie and Erwin's only child, Joe Thomas, waited for Kendall to come from the coffee stand inside Kitsap County's Administration Building. The woman commanding the front desk told the college student the detective was getting coffee and would be back in a moment. A few minutes later, Kendall appeared.

"Detective Stark?"

She looked at the young man. They'd never met, but she'd seen his photograph hanging in the Thomas home on Long Lake and the family resemblance was remarkable.

"You're Janie and Erwin's son, aren't you?"

He seemed surprised that she knew that.

"Yeah, I am. I'm Joe. I want to talk to you."

"I wish I could help you. We're not working your mother's case," she said. "The FBI is. Do you know something?"

He shook his head. "No. Nothing about that. That's not why I'm here."

"I am very sorry about what's going on with your family, Joe," she said.

"Me too. But I'm not here about that. I'm here about what happened to Tami. I saw it on Facebook this morning."

Kendall didn't have any idea what he was talking about. "Tami Overton? What did she put on Facebook?"

"She didn't. Her mom posted on her wall. Said that Tami killed herself yesterday. Committed suicide or had an overdose. I'm not sure which."

Kendall felt the hair on the back of her neck rise.

"I hadn't heard," she said. "Did you know Tami?"

"Yeah," he said. "We were friends. We both got away from Alyssa and Scott. I was Scott's roommate at the U, but I transferred to Boise State. Couldn't be far enough away from those freaks. Tami got into drugs. I think to escape them too."

Kendall told him to come into her office so they could talk in a more private setting. He followed her inside.

"Were you friends with Katy as well?" she asked as he sat down.

"I knew her," he said. "Everyone did. She was a good person. She deserved better than her supposed best friend and that two-timer Scott."

"What do you mean, two-timer?" Kendall asked.

"Scott couldn't keep his pants zipped. To put it mildly. I think he really liked Katy, but Alyssa was determined to get him into her bed. And in the end, that's just what she did."

"Did Katy know about it?" Kendall asked.

Joe Thomas wasn't sure and he said so. "I didn't hang around them much in high school. If I had I would have run the other way when Scott asked me to be his roommate. That was a joke. He kept throwing me out so he could, you know, have sex with Alyssa."

"I see. So what brings you here, Joe? What is it that you think I should know?"

He shrugged. "I don't know. I mean, I'm not sure. My life's been turned upside down. The press is hanging around the house. My dad is down so low, I'm worried about him. I don't know how much more he can take."

"I really am sorry," Kendall said. "I know it must be difficult."

"You probably don't know," he said, not trying to be unkind, but factual. "My mom's disappeared with her serial killer lover and my dad and I are sitting around hoping that when they find her she's dead because we don't know how we could ever trust her again. I know that sounds terrible, but it's the truth."

Kendall just let his words fill the space of her office. There was nothing she could really say to make him feel better. Words couldn't take away the stinging pain of what Janie had done to her son and husband. She'd turned their world upside down in a decisive and dramatic fashion.

"You said you went to Boise State to get away. Get away from what?"

"The crazy dynamics between Alyssa and Scott. It was like he didn't have a mind of his own. She did whatever she wanted and berated him for any choice that he made on his own. It was big stuff, like what class to take—she wanted him available to her when her schedule was free. And small stuff too. One time she read him the riot act for buying a Husky T-shirt that didn't match hers. It was gross."

The description was an apt one. Alyssa was the anaconda. Scott the passive victim.

"Why did he put up with it?"

Joe waited a beat before answering. "I've asked myself that over and over. It was almost she had something on him. Whenever they had a fight, he'd go crawling back to her."

"And Tami?" Kendall asked.

"I knew Tami in school," he said. "She was a nice girl before she got mixed up with those two. She never drank a beer. Never smoked a cigarette. One time when I came home early from being banished to the library so they could screw, I stood outside the door and heard Alyssa screaming at Scott to do something about Tami."

"What do you mean?"

"I think her exact words were 'shut her up for good.'"

"What do you think she meant by that?"

Joe swallowed. "Kill her. I think she was telling Scott to kill her."

"But he didn't, did he?"

He shook his head. "No. Not then. But with all the Katy stuff being dredged up again I wonder about what happened to Tami. That's why I'm here. Detective Stark, I think they finally shut her up. They didn't like that she was clean and sober."

"You don't have any direct knowledge of this, do you, Joe?"

He shook his head again.

"No," he said. "Not really. Just a feeling."

* * *

Kendall called Birdy and told her what Joe had confided. Birdy said she'd call the Pierce County Medical Examiner's office to let them know they had an interest in the outcome of the young woman's autopsy.

"Let me know how it goes with Tami's mother," Birdy said. "I'll be here."

BOOK TWO
PANDORA

CHAPTER TWENTY-FIVE

B rit Frazier paced the room like an agitated feline in search of a litter box. She was tense, stressed. She hated the house her husband had designed. She looked all around her and her stomach twisted. She wanted to throw up. The design was all about him. Nothing about her. Every suggestion she'd made had been dismissed as being out of character with his vision.

His vision.

His life.

His every need had been more important than hers.

The conversation—battle, really—they had the night after the film crew left was one for the ages.

"I want you out of here," she had said.

"Over what?"

"You're a child molester and killer, that's enough for me, Roger. You make me want to puke. Just the idea that I'm breathing in air that has passed through your lungs makes me want to choke right now. I hate you. I hate everything you've done."

"You're losing it, Brit. This is a goddamn TV show!"

"It's a reality show," she told him. "It's real."

"Oh my God, you're insane."

"Stop saying that. Stop it!"

"It's the truth. That lying producer and that stupid psycho psychic are to blame for your latest break with reality."

"I hate you. I want you gone."

"This is *my* house. I built it."

She stared hard at him, her eyes full of hate. "I will tell everyone what I know if you don't leave."

His face reddened. "What you know?"

"I know what and who you are. Don't test me, Roger. You don't want to be up against me because you might think I'm weak, that I'm fragile, but I have never been backed into the corner like this. Get out!"

"I'm going to call my lawyer."

"Fine. I've already texted mine."

She watched him pack an overnight bag.

"I'll have your other things in the yard."

"You are such a bitch, Brit."

"Whatever. I don't care anymore. I've seen the truth."

In her hand, she held the gardener's business card, with Pandora's personal cell number neatly printed on the back.

"Pandora says I have the gift too."

"That's perfect. That's just perfect," Roger said.

"She told me that you would kill me and Naomi if I didn't get you out of my house."

"You're certifiably crazy. You know that? Why would you listen to some phony psychic? And really, what reason would I have to kill you and Naomi?"

"Child rapists and killers never have a reason for what they do, Roger."

"I'm not a rapist," he said. "I loved Katy. What's gotten into you?"

She looked at him with icicle eyes. "I should never have loved you. Daddy was right about you."

Roger stepped closer, but seemed to think better of it. "Your Daddy is half your problem," he said. "The other half is that you're a messed up, pill-popping bitch."

"You can call me anything you want, but nothing is worse than murderer and child rapist."

Later, after he was gone, Brit went into the bathroom and looked at the mirror. Her rage toward him was multilayered. She wondered how it was that she fit into his vision, his house, or even his life. He was the same age, but he looked younger. He had a career that made him the star of whatever he was doing. She had that too. She tried to, anyway. She didn't tell people that helping troubled teens was more about the accolades that she garnered for doing so than for the support and encouragement she gave young people. She turned on the cold water and splashed her face. She retrieved a towel from the vanity and blotted her face. Brit knew that she was no longer young. No longer the beauty she knew she'd been. There was no denying that the lines on her face had deepened over the last few years. She tried Botox, but it left her vacant looking, and she valued the intensity of her presence.

Her girls. That's all she had. Katy and Naomi. And now, in every sense, both were gone. He'd taken them from her. He'd done the unthinkable with Katy.

Stupid.

Stupid.

Stupid.

And Naomi, she could barely look at her.

Brit opened the medicine cabinet and surveyed a junkie's dream. All of the bottles had her name and doctor on them, but some of the prescriptions had belonged to others. She collected pills from the purses and jacket pockets of the girls and boys who'd come to the coffee shop. It didn't matter what they were—Adderall, methamphetamines, or any number of painkillers.

She could swallow the lot of them right then and there and show Roger just how angry she was. Leave a note that his raping and murder of their daughter had driven her to it. That he'd confessed to her before she took her own life. That would show him. That would make the world see that she had never loved him, never wanted to be a part of the jewel box he'd built for them.

Brit held a bottle of painkillers. It was a confetti-like mix of pills, most of which she could identify. Some not so much. She worried that they were too old, or if the cocktail of pills would make her vomit, kill her, or merely leave her brain-dead.

Brain-dead, she decided, wasn't such a bad option after all. Roger would be stuck with her at least in a small way forever. She knew that he'd foist her off on a nursing home and never visit her, but she'd still be there breathing and reminding him of the ass that he'd always been.

Brit set the bottle on the counter. She realized that, more than hate, she felt the need to punish him. She found a reason she should go on living. Revenge.

She pulled herself together, and, fully composed, punched in the numbers of Pandora's personal cell phone.

"Pandora, this is Brit."

"I've been expecting your call."

"Thank you for everything. I mean, it was an impossible night. Really, really hard."

"Truth is never easy, Brit," Pandora said. "You feel it though, don't you?"

"I do. I mean, I do."

"You know what I'm really getting at, Brit. You feel the truth of the words I said, but also those within your own understanding about what happened to Katy when she disappeared."

"I don't know. I think so."

"You are sensitive, you just are not fully in tune with your spirit guides. Listen to them, like you listened to me last night."

"I'm trying. I need your help."

Long pause.

"I don't know what more I can do to help you."

"I need to see you again."

"I don't do private consultations anymore, Brit. I'm sorry, my time is just too valuable and as much as I'd like to help you find out what happened to your daughter . . ."

"I can pay you."

Pandora let Brit's words linger.

"I don't think so," she said. "I don't want to embarrass you. But I don't think you could afford it. Very few can."

"Please, I'm begging you. I need your help. I'll pay whatever you need. I have to find out where Katy's body is. I have to find her so that my husband can go to prison for the rest of his life, where he deserves to be."

"My plane leaves tonight. I'm packing now."

"Can you stay another day?"

Long pause.

"I don't know. Like I said, my fee is probably beyond your grasp. No offense. No judgment."

"I have money."

"I charge twenty thousand dollars for a private."

Long pause.

"I can get that for you," she said.

"I don't know. It doesn't feel right to charge you, but I can't make exceptions. You can understand the demands on my time, with the show, the other one in development and the skin-care line, Vanish, that I'm so busy with now."

"I know, but I'm desperate. When can you see me?"

Long pause.

"I have to change my tickets and rebook this room."

"Tomorrow then?"

"All right. Fine. I'll help you. Only because I care about you and Katy."

"Thank you, Pandora. Thank you."

Pandora hung up and looked at her lover as he flipped through a magazine.

"That was Brit Frazier," she said.

"Figured."

"Sometimes I think you're the psychic," she said. "You nailed that one. You were so sure she'd want a private consultation."

"You do the heavy lifting," he said. "I just call it like I see it. Nice job on the fee, by the way. I bet she had to think long and hard about that number."

"Sure, it was a gamble, but really some of this bores me so much that I don't mind risking the occasional no."

"What are you going to tell Juliana? You know, the reason for the delay in your return flight. She'll be pissed."

"She's stupid and I don't care one thing about what she says. Without me, there is no show. They can like it or lump it. I'm so over being used by our two-bit network to make money when all they give us is crap."

"I agree, babe. But I think you've got something half wrong here."

"Really?" she asked. "What would that be?"

"I think I have some skin in the game here too. It isn't all about you and your gifts. I have a certain amount of star power all my own."

She rolled her eyes upward and let out an exasperated sigh. It was over the top, like her reactions on the show.

"I have more Twitter followers than you'll have in a lifetime," she said. "Don't ever confuse your past notoriety as an indicator of your value to the network or me. Without me you are a washed-up cop in search of another TV show or a self-published book."

"It was *indie* published," he said, correcting her.

Pandora smirked. "Whatever," she said. "You're nothing without me. Juliana's nothing without me. And as long as we keep her in the dark about our special arrangements with show guests, we're good."

CHAPTER TWENTY-SIX

Lynn Overton had been crying. No wonder. Her child had overdosed and died—a child with whom she'd been working to make amends. She wore a blue sweater, jeans, and a pair of fuzzy slippers. She smelled of alcohol.

"I thought you might come by," Lynn said, her speech slightly slurred.

"Oh, Mrs. Overton, I'm so sorry," Kendall said.

"Thank you, I appreciate that. I don't think anyone understands how I feel right now. I loved her," she said, letting Kendall inside and leading her to the kitchen.

"I know you did," Kendall said.

They sat at the table. A Kit-Cat wall clock above them moved its pendulum tail. Lynn drank from a coffee cup, but didn't offer her visitor any coffee.

"What happened?" Kendall asked.

"I don't know," Lynn said. She swallowed more of what she was drinking. "I really don't. She had everything to live for, Detective. Everything. She had a husband. A baby. I don't know what it could have been that would push her over the edge."

"Was it the TV show?" Kendall asked. "I know they

had planned to call her. Dredging up the past can sometimes be a terrible trigger," Kendall said.

"Her husband told me that she'd talked to the cop on the show, but that was over the phone. She didn't want to do an interview on camera. She said she didn't want any part of it. That Katy's disappearance was too painful to revisit."

"It was a very dark time for her," Kendall said.

More of whatever was in her coffee cup passed Lynn's lips. "Yes," she said. "A very, very dark time. For all of the kids."

"When you say all of the kids, do you mean Scott and Alyssa?"

She nodded. "Yes. After Katy went missing, everything simply fell apart. Tami starting using. The other two stopped coming around. I think everything that happened to her in her life was unhinged by that tragedy. But she was doing better. I wish they'd stayed away."

"Did she see them? Do you know?"

Lynn stared into her now empty cup. "I'm not sure. Her husband said Tami told him that some old friends had called, but she didn't think she wanted to see them."

Kendall's phone vibrated and she looked down and saw that Birdy was calling.

"I need to take this," she said.

"That's all right. You can go in the study if you want some privacy."

As Kendall retreated from the kitchen, her peripheral vision caught a glimpse of Tami's mother pouring some vodka into her cup.

"What did you find out, Birdy?" Kendall asked.

"It was an overdose. The tox screen came back on Tami's blood. She was off the charts with heroin. Something must have really set her off."

"Something or someone," Kendall said.

The drive to the UW that time of day was faster than taking the ferry. Kendall made it there in an hour and parked in front of the house that Alyssa and Scott had given as their address.

"What do you want?" Alyssa asked.

"I want to talk to you," Kendall said

"We've already talked. I have a class. I need to study."

Kendall looked past her and saw Scott sitting on the couch looking at a video game.

"I'm here about Tami," she said.

Alyssa let out an exaggerated sigh. "What about her?"

"She's dead," Kendall said, watching Alyssa's reaction. There wasn't one. "You know anything about that?"

"No," she said. "I saw that she died, if that's what you mean."

"I need to come in," Kendall said. "Scott, I need to talk to you too."

Scott nodded and got up. "If it's okay with Alyssa, sure."

Alyssa made an irritated face. "Come in then," she said. She looked over at Scott. "You dummy. Can't you just keep your mouth shut?"

The three of them stood by the doorway.

"You should just tell her," Scott said.

"I will not," Alyssa said. "It isn't right. Just leave it."

"What?" Kendall asked. "What isn't right?"

"I know you think I'm the biggest bitch ever, Detective. I really don't care. I've never cared about what anyone thought of me."

"I don't think that, Alyssa," Kendall said, in what amounted to the biggest lie she'd told anyone since she told Grace in the records department that the jeans she was wearing didn't make her look fat. "What are you holding back?"

Just then Alyssa collapsed onto a chair and started sobbing. It was loud, showy, and it was unclear to Kendall what it was that she was doing.

"I'm sorry. I should have said something sooner. I really should have. We both should have."

"It's okay, baby," Scott said, now comforting her.

"What should you have told someone?" Kendall asked.

"About what Tami did. I'm not surprised that she killed herself. She was living with a heavy, heavy burden."

"What burden? Go on, Alyssa. This is very, very important."

Alyssa gulped some air. "She killed Katy. She told me she did. She said she was jealous of her and that she just wanted to make her suffer a little but it went too far. I didn't know what to do. Katy was gone. Tami was completely crazy. I kept my mouth shut."

"We both did," Scott said. "We both knew what Tami had done and what she was capable of."

"What happened? What did she do to Katy? Where *is* Katy?"

"I never asked. I didn't want to know. When Katy never came home, I knew it was true. That was enough for me."

"Tami had a guilty conscience," Scott said.

"She really did," Alyssa added, mopping her tears with her shirtsleeve.

"You're going to have to return with me to county," Kendall said.

"Why? We didn't do anything," Alyssa said. "I have a class to go to."

"Me too. I have the same class."

Kendall stayed firm. "You need to come. You need to make a statement. I'll follow you."

"But what about our class? Our professor will fail us," Alyssa said.

Kendall didn't care. The girl had bigger problems than failing a class.

"I'll write him a note," she said.

"What good will that do us?" Alyssa asked.

"It will buy you some time to make up the work."

It would also buy Kendall some time to think about the two lovebirds—the two lovebirds with two dead friends.

It was going to be a very busy afternoon. Brad texted Kendall that Pandora had decided she'd come in for an interview.

I'm sorry about this. Really I am, he wrote.

Not as sorry as Kendall was.

CHAPTER TWENTY-SEVEN

"**I** know you don't agree with my methods," Pandora said as she faced Kendall for the first time since that night at the Frazier place in Manchester.

"That's an understatement, Carol."

Pandora smiled. "You've done some homework. Good."

"Considering what a few clicks of the mouse can come up with, I'd hardly say it was an arduous task," Kendall said.

"Look, haters hate. Lovers love. I'm a lover. Not a hater," Pandora said.

"Is that T-shirt on your website? If so, I missed it."

"No. But it's not a bad idea. Catchy. I just might run with it."

"What are you? Some kind of a human wrecking ball? Do you go around and look for the vulnerable? People you can take advantage of?"

"No. I go around and clean up the messes left behind by the likes of your Detective Mayberry. You know that he botched the case. I know it. The world will know it when the episode airs."

"It won't air, Carol. Our DA is going to file an injunction. I'd be surprised if the Fraziers don't file a civil case against you and the show."

"I love the idea of an injunction, especially one that won't be able to halt the production of the show. The more publicity, the better."

"You like publicity. Don't you?" Kendall asked.

"I like to make money, Detective. Publicity is like revving up a cash machine."

"You really sicken me," Kendall said, doing her best to try to cope with the anger that welled up inside of her. She didn't like that woman one bit. She wouldn't give her a drink of water if she were in the middle of a desert begging for one. Not if she was the last human being on the planet. The world didn't need the likes of someone like Pandora.

"You'll have to do better than that to make me mad," Pandora said. "Remember, I've already got what I wanted. I've produced Katy's killer—something that you and your department failed miserably at. Say whatever you want about me. I hope you choke on your sour grapes."

Kendall laughed. "You are something else."

Pandora smiled. "Yes, that I am. Now tell me what you want from me before this interview or whatever you call it slips any lower."

The words "as long as you are around there's always a new low" passed through Kendall's brain, but she didn't say them.

"Fine," Kendall said, eating her words. "Let's focus on the show and what happened that night. Was it planned? Did you set out to call Roger Frazier a child molester and killer?"

"I don't have the slightest idea what you're trying to imply."

"Get real, Carol."

"Stop calling me that. Carol doesn't exist anymore."

"All right, Pandora. I want to understand."

"People who deal in logic can never understand what they cannot see, Detective. It is absolutely impossible."

"Try me. Humor me."

"Well, since you've calmed down a bit, I'll try. I don't expect you to understand it."

"Like I said, Pandora. I'm all ears."

Pandora's wrist, covered with a sheath of bangles, rolled on the tabletop.

"I have a gift. I don't know where it comes from, but it's real and it is part of who I am. I hear things, see things, that are right in front of the eyes of others. Things they can't see or hear. I know they come from the other side."

"The other side," Kendall repeated.

"I'm trying to help you understand. Please don't mock me."

"I wasn't mocking you."

"I'm extremely sensitive."

"I'm sorry. Go on."

"That night, the information came to me. It just did."

"What about Wyatt? How does he fit in?"

"Wyatt is there to make the producers happy. They don't get it. They can't comprehend the magnitude of my gifts. They have to come up with something for the viewer to grab on to when they are watching the fantastic, the impossible."

The fraudulent.

"I heard that, Detective."

"Heard what? I didn't say anything."

"Right," Pandora said. "You didn't. But I hear and I see your skepticism."

"Did you talk with Tami Overton?"

"No. Has something happened to her?"

"You don't know? I thought you knew everything."

"Is she dead?"

Kendall studied Pandora's carefully made-up face. There was a silky flatness to her complexion. The makeup was heavy. She wondered if Pandora had just done a TV shoot or if she always looked as though she was camera ready.

"I'm not surprised, Detective. From what I understand she was a very troubled young woman."

"Who told you that?" Kendall asked.

"Brit," she said. "Brit told me."

"That's interesting. I was there the whole night. I don't recall her mentioning anything about Tami."

"I didn't say she told me that night. She told me later."

"Later?"

"Yes. Brit and I bonded that night. She wants my help and part of the deal of being born with a gift is to ensure that you use it to help others. I'm all about helping."

That was another load of crap, but Kendall didn't say so. And this time, Pandora didn't call her on what she thought she was thinking.

"You're absolutely certain about what you said you felt or saw that night?" Kendall asked.

"I'm seldom wrong."

Kendall didn't say that her cursory Internet research indicated otherwise.

"I'm very concerned about Katy's case. I'm concerned about the Fraziers. Very concerned, Pandora."

"You think I'm not? I don't dabble in this, Detective. I do this because I must do it. I do it to help others." She paused. "I do this to right wrongs wherever I can."

Kendall's tongue was tired of being held captive. But there was no point in firing back. Pandora had come in for some reason. And it certainly wasn't to tell the truth. Kendall could smell a fraud a mile away.

"Stay in touch, Pandora."

"Oh, I intend to. In fact, I'm always in touch. It's who I am."

Brenda Nevins stood over the bed looking down at Janie Thomas.

"Wake up, lover," she said.

Janie's eyes fluttered open. She was tired, hungry, and completely terrified.

Brenda grinned. "Good," she said. "Would you like me to let you go?"

Janie croaked out a yes from the slit in the duct tape Brenda had cut so she could drink.

"Do you understand that I'll kill your son if you betray me? You know that I'm capable."

Janie didn't react.

"YOU KNOW IT," Brenda screamed in her captive's face. "RIGHT?"

Janie winced and nodded. "Yes. I know."

"Fine then," Brenda said. "I'm going to take a very

big risk that you can do something for me. I know where your family lives. I know your son's apartment in Boise. I know people who know people who can make someone vanish. Do you understand me, Janie?"

"Yes," she said. "I understand."

"Don't even think about double-crossing me. Don't you dare even give it one second of thought, you stupid bitch. I'll take them all out and go off somewhere and have a party."

Janie blinked back some tears.

"Don't be sad, baby. This will all be over soon. Then you'll be free. You'll never be the same, but you'll be free."

Brenda leaned close and whispered. Her hot breath that had been a turn-on was now like the flame of a dragon. Her tongue like a snake's as it darted around Janie's ear. She told Janie exactly what she needed to do.

Janie, who'd been taken in by the devil, promised she'd be good.

"I can do that. But you'll leave my family alone?"

"Yes. I'll leave them alone. And you'll go free."

Janie didn't care about herself. Her life was ruined and there was no point in saving her from anything. She wished she were dead. She knew that death would be the only way to ensure that her family was safe. As long as she was alive, Brenda Nevins would have a bargaining chip.

"I had a husband once," Brenda said as she undid the binding around Janie's wrists. "A daughter too."

Janie already knew that, but she was too terrified to say anything.

"His name was Kirk. Her name was Kara."

"I like those names, Brenda," Janie said.

"Yes. Good names. Sometimes I really miss them. I know how much you miss your son, Joe, and your husband, Erwin. Not such good names, if you ask me."

"Right. Not good names. Joseph is a family name."

"Yes, I know. Your husband's father."

Brenda knew everything about Janie. She knew more about her than Janie knew about *her*. Even though Janie had the benefit of a dossier of Brenda's criminal charges, she had been blinded by her charms. She'd been sucked in like soda though a big, fat straw.

"Kara was such a brat, though. I blame Kirk for that. I never should have had that kid. She nearly ruined my body. God, what a parasite. Always hanging on me, sucking at my breasts, rooting for more. Always more. Like there would never be enough. She was pretty, though. Not like me. But a prettier version of her father's side of the family. Dark hair, dark eyes."

Janie didn't say a word. She wasn't sure what she should say.

"Are you listening to me? Do you understand that I'm just like you?"

"Yes, just like me. Kindred spirits."

"That's how we found each other, Janie."

"Yes," she said.

Brenda stopped and looked away, a gesture of practiced sincerity. "I miss Kara and Kirk," she said. "I really do."

Janie nodded. It ran through her mind that the reason they were out of Brenda's life was that she'd murdered them and burned down the house to cover her tracks. Brenda didn't deny what she did. In fact, she referred to the fire as a "household cleanser" of sorts.

"If you want to ensure that you're not detected, you know, for being what the world considers 'bad,' then burn the goddamn thing to the ground."

Brenda told Janie to take a shower.

"You're a filthy mess."

Janie's legs were rubber bands and she could barely stand as she went into the bathroom.

Brenda primped her hair and regarded her new look in the mirror. She liked it. Chaz had liked it. Others would too. But she knew that it was not a game-changer in her looks. True beauty like hers could never be completely annihilated—no matter what could be done with her hair, her makeup. That's where Janie came in.

She sat on the toilet seat while Janie stepped into the steaming shower.

"Use some conditioner, for God's sake. Your hair's a fright."

Janie stood in the shower and cried into the spray from the faucet.

"Hurry up."

Janie turned the knobs and opened the door.

"*Here.* Put this on your hair."

Janie looked at the tube of hair dye. It was called Chestnut Dream. She opened the tube and rubbed the contents in her hair. Shivering and hoping at the same time. Hoping that her colored hair meant that she would actually be free.

And even so, she wondered where in the world she would go.

CHAPTER TWENTY-EIGHT

Naomi Frazier looked like she'd been sprung from a carnival ride or maybe a carnival poster. She had very black hair with wide blue and pink streaks that looked almost like racing stripes for a baby shower. Her lip, nose, and—Kendall thought—probably other body parts too, were pierced. Although she looked to be the creative type, maybe a little bit of an attention seeker, Naomi almost certainly did not look like the daughter of a buttoned-up architect and his guidance counselor wife.

"I know what you're thinking," Naomi said as Kendall approached her in the Starbucks off Sedgwick Road.

"Everyone's a psychic," Kendall said with a warm, disarming smile.

Naomi gave a little shrug and returned the smile. "Good one. I can just tell the look of surprise, no matter how you want to hide it."

Kendall sat down. "I'm not that surprised," she said. "I knew you went to alternative school, so I figured you'd look, well . . ."

Again, a slight smile. "Alternative?"

Kendall liked this girl.

"Yes, alternative. And by the way, I love your hair. In my day getting a foil was a big deal. Color? We wouldn't have been caught dead with pink or blue. In fact, we'd be killed by our parents, so I guess we would be caught dead."

Naomi grinned. She had braces on her lower teeth. Her eyes were very, very blue. She was pretty and not nearly as hard-shelled as her reputation suggested.

"You want anything?" Kendall asked, glancing in the direction of the barista, a girl with red hair and an annoyed look on her face. "I'm kind of coffee'd out. Your mother makes the strongest coffee on the planet."

"Yeah, Dad says you could eat it with a spoon," Naomi said. "But no thanks, I'm good. I'll stick with my tea."

The color in the cup was a pale yellow. The tea was chamomile. Very herbal, and, Kendall thought, very Naomi.

"I'm here to talk about your sister . . . and your father," she said.

Naomi kept her eyes on Kendall.

"I could have saved you the time and trouble, Ms. Stark."

"How so?" Kendall asked.

Naomi squirted another packet of honey into her hot drink and stirred it with a wooden stick.

"My mom now says that my dad was screwing my sister, which in case you wanted to know, is not the worst thing she's ever said about him," she said. "She hates him. Always has. For as long as I can remember."

Kendall was surprised, but didn't show it.

"They seemed so solid," Kendall said. "Until Pandora, of course."

"That's what everyone thinks. My mom is a total bitch. She acts like she's going out every day to save the world when really she's just messing around on my dad."

"An affair?" Kendall asked.

Naomi shook her head. "*Affairs.* As in more than one."

When the words tumbled out of the girl's mouth, they came with an edge of regret. Naomi might hate her mother, but she didn't despise her completely. In the scale of teenage hate, Brit was probably an eight on her daughter's meter of one to ten.

"I'm sorry," Kendall said. "That must be hard on you."

"Look, I'm fine. I'm going to be eighteen in two years and I'm out of here. I'm leaving Port Orchard and never coming back. That's what I think my sister did, by the way. I don't think she's buried out in the deep, like that twit Pandora told my mom. Katy hated Mom. She loved our dad. I love our dad. No one is perfect, but when you're married to a bitch like Mom—sometimes when I have to call someone for her I say her name is Bitch Frazier until they ask me to repeat it and then I say Brit—anyway, it's the truth. My dad survived her games and stuck with her because he loved us girls."

"You were only twelve when Katy went missing," Kendall said. "You might have been too young to really know what was going on back then."

Naomi stopped. Paused. "Look at me. I'm sixteen now going on thirty. I've never been my age. In that family you couldn't be a kid and survive, not very long anyway."

Kendall knew it was time to focus on the subject at hand, despite the very real possibility that she'd unleashed a volcano of vitriol against Brit Frazier and it would be kind of interesting to hear more. She was there for Katy. She was there to find out what happened to Katy.

"Did you ever see anything back then that might suggest that your father was molesting your sister?" she asked.

"No," Naomi said with great conviction. "Absolutely never."

Kendall prodded. "A secret they shared?"

"They had lots of secrets from Mom," Naomi said. "We all did."

"Why was that?"

Naomi's hands were sticky from the honey pack and she got up and went to get a napkin. "Because my mom knew only one thing to do with any information. She was like a spider with a web. Anytime you confided anything to her, she'd find a way to use it against you. It might not be for a week, or a month. You'd think you could finally trust her."

"Example?"

"They are stupid. Things that shouldn't be betrayed."

Naomi stopped and looked at Kendall. "It's so dumb. But when I got my period, I didn't know what was happening. Stupid right? I had a class about it. And my mom's a guidance counselor! But I was confused and scared. I started screaming in the bathroom and my mom comes running in and then she starts laughing at me, telling me to cool down and it was all normal and stuff."

"She laughed at you?"

"Yeah, like it was a big joke, but I was totally scared."

"It must have felt terrible. Her doing that."

"It was personal and humiliating. Really. Like two days later a girl came up to me and told me that my mom told her about what happened during her counseling session. She told someone else something private so she could win them over. She was always doing that kind of crap."

Brit as seen through the eyes of her daughter was a very different woman than the one people in town admired and praised for her work with the troubled and disenfranchised youth of South Kitsap.

Kendall didn't want to defend Brit Frazier just then. Brit had told her over and over that the Kitsap County Sheriff's Department was to blame for not finding Katy, and that accusation didn't make her like her one bit.

Even if it were true.

"Tell me what you remember about Katy before she disappeared. Anything seem odd at the time? Something that you've been wondering about?"

"No. Not really. I mean, it isn't like I haven't thought of those days a million, gazillion times. I have. I was obsessed with what happened. At one point, I thought I would grow up and be a cop like you just so I could solve the case of my missing sister."

"Other cops have done things like that."

"I'm sure. I get it. It was like a hole punched into my life. Just that quick. She was there, then she was gone. I wanted more than anything to believe she was alive somewhere. Everyone did. When her friends started coming around to support us, help us, I just kind of felt like Katy wasn't ever coming back."

"Alyssa, Tami, Scott?"

"Right. Those three."

"Sounds like you don't like them much."

"At the time I did. I really did. Alyssa practically moved in. Tami too. They were always there trying to help me, my mom and dad. I thought we were friends, but I was a lot younger."

"What about Scott?"

"That's just it. I think Scott and Katy really loved each other. It was weird how quickly he and Alyssa ended up dating. They told me one time that losing Katy was what brought them together."

"Did that bother you?" Kendall asked.

Naomi made a face. "Are you a cop or a counselor, like my mom?"

"Sorry," Kendall said. "A cop. I'm just trying to understand the dynamics here."

"Good. I get enough of that at home. No, it didn't bother me. I liked Scott. I looked up to them. All of them. I wanted to be like them. The day Katy went missing, Alyssa and Tami came by and picked her up to go hang out somewhere. I wanted to go too. Mom was homeschooling me and kept me practically chained to my desk. Not really chained, but I think if she thought of it, she would have."

Kendall took out her notebook and made a few notes.

"What are you writing down?"

"Just a reminder."

"Did I help you at all?"

Kendall nodded. "I think you did. I want you to know that I'll be following up on everything. I'm not going to let this go. I'm not going to let you down."

Naomi wasn't a crier, but she could have cried just then. She felt the emotion well up in her eyes.

"Good, because Katy deserves better. She deserves to be found."

"I know," Kendall said. "Take care. We'll talk again soon. Promise."

Kendall got up and put her hand on Naomi's shoulder. She could feel the slight tremble of emotion that the girl tried to hide from her. Naomi Frazier thought she was older than her years, but deep down, she was a kid sister still. Alone. Still hoping for Katy to come back home.

To be found.

CHAPTER TWENTY-NINE

Birdy Waterman was about to eat a turkey and Swiss sandwich when Kendall let herself into the forensic pathologist's always-strange-smelling autopsy suite.

"How can you eat here?"

"You have to eat somewhere, Kendall."

"Yes, but . . . here?"

"This place is cleaner than any restaurant in town, if you must know."

"I'm sure it is, but it just seems weird to have lunch down here."

Birdy pointed to the ceiling.

"Staff upstairs is having a farewell celebration for Peg's retirement. You know how much I hate to say good-bye to anyone. I'm here to get a little work done, and, yes, to hide out a little."

"Don't let me stop you from your anti-celebration. Go ahead and eat."

Birdy took a small bite. "Want some?"

"No. No thanks."

"How's your day going?"

"Not great. Not awful. Somewhere in the middle, Birdy."

"Most of my days fall somewhere in the middle too."

Kendall sat down on a visitor's chair next to Birdy's desk. She eyed the sandwich while Birdy nibbled on it.

"It grosses me out that you keep your lunch in the chiller with the dead bodies," Kendall said.

Birdy laughed. "I don't do that. We have a refrigerator for personal use. I just told you that because, well, I knew it would be fun for you to mull that over."

"I've been doing all the follow-up on the Frazier case. Talked with the mom, the younger daughter. Talked with one of the friend's mothers. Trying to get a clearer understanding of what happened four years ago."

"Hard to do, isn't it?"

Kendall nodded. "Yes, extremely."

"Even cold tracks on the snow eventually melt."

"Is that a Makah saying or something?"

"No. Just something I thought right now. Are you sure you don't want to share my sandwich?"

Kendall shook her head. "No. I'm sure."

"Tell me what you have so far. Maybe talking it out will help."

"Mayberry didn't do a damn thing with this case," Kendall said.

"Honestly, I was glad to see him go. I would have actually attended his farewell luncheon if I'd been asked."

Kendall took off her jacket. "His reports are about as thin as that cheese."

"Deli thin," Birdy said.

"All right. Enough of the sandwich."

"You brought it up."

"I know. I'm sorry. Back to what Mayberry wrote in his report. He said that Alyssa Woodley had plans to do something with Katy after school, but those plans fell through."

"Right, I remember reading that."

"But when I talked to Katy's sister, she said that Alyssa and a couple of Katy's friends did come over that day and pick her up."

"It's been four years," Birdy said. "Maybe she's mixed up the date, the sequence of what happened when."

Kendall thought a moment. It was possible. "Maybe. I don't think so. She seems to remember a lot of family things. She's got a list of a million reasons why she hates her mother, for example."

"So do I," Birdy said.

Natalie Waterman, Birdy's mother, had found many opportunities to worm her insidious way into many of Kendall and Birdy's conversations.

"I know, Birdy," Kendall said. "But you had reason to."

Birdy set down her sandwich. "Not really. My mom— such as she was—was doing the best that she could. Her best wasn't that great. No argument there. But it's what she could do at the time. I'm doing the best I can with Elan right now. Who knows what he'll say about me when he's grown?"

"He'll say you are the best thing that ever happened to him."

"I hope so."

Kendall got up.

"We barely chatted. Where you going to now?"

"I've got a meeting with Cody's teacher. Then I'm going to track down Alyssa."

"Sounds fun."

"Oh, it will be. It always is."

CHAPTER THIRTY

Kendall parked her white SUV in front of the Cascade School. It had just rained and the parking lot shimmered with iridescent swirls of oil. An old cherry tree had recently fallen victim to some kind of rot and had been cut down by a maintenance worker, and its silvery, smooth bark also shimmered in the wetness of the downpour. Kendall made her way across the parking lot, dodging puddles, to the school's front door. Ms. Donahue, Cody's teacher, was waiting for her.

"You are always right on time," she said.

"I know how important your work is."

Candace Donahue had been teaching children with special needs of all kinds since the early 1980s. She was nearing retirement and anyone who worked with her was dreading the day that she'd be gone. She wore a uniform of sorts, always a twinset and skirt. That day it was a heather gray ensemble, which matched her hair, spun up in a bun, to perfection.

She led Kendall into a conference room.

"I'm glad you come in person. Cody is very important to me and I'm concerned."

Kendall could feel her heart sink a little lower. This was not going to be a happy meeting, not like the last one in which the teacher wanted to let her know that Cody was finding more comfortable ways to interact and socialize with other children. That had always been the biggest concern. His autism was not debilitating. He could function fine on his own. He could read. He could do schoolwork. He just couldn't interact with others, especially those he barely know. At home, Cody was almost just like any other kid. But not at school. Not out in public.

"Something's wrong, isn't it?" Candace said. "I'm not trying to pry."

Kendall knew what she was getting at. She also could easily see that there was a connection between certain aspects of Cody's behavior and his suddenly gone-from-the-scene father.

"My husband has a new job, one that requires him to be away for an extended period."

"In a way, that's kind of a relief, Kendall."

"How do you mean?"

"I was thinking it was something serious, something more permanent. Cody misses his dad terribly and he's been acting out a little because of it."

"What's he been doing?"

"He threw a cardboard box at another child. He didn't hit her, but she screamed like he had and that only made it worse."

"I'm sorry. I had no idea."

"There have been a few other incidents and, well, I've

been doing this long enough to know that when there's a change on the home front it often manifests itself into unusual behavior here at school."

"What can I do?"

"Reassure him, Kendall. Let him know that his father will be home soon and that everything will be back to normal. Cody likes and really *needs* consistency in his life. It's like a building with one brick removed . . . it will stand fine for a time, but at some point it will topple."

"I'm so sorry for all of this, Candace."

"Sorry? You don't have to be sorry. Just love your little boy as you always have, but remind him that his father is only a phone call away."

Kendall nodded. She wished it were that easy. She wanted to tell Candace Donahue the truth, but she was unsure exactly what that was. The two women talked awhile about Cody's remarkable progress with reading and that he continued to show a strong ability in art. His paintings were always a narrative of what was going on in his life. Lately, they were in shades of black and red and showed images of a family disconnected.

Candace slid one over to Kendall.

It almost made Kendall gasp. The rendering of their Harper house was perfect down to the crooked screen door. In the window were three figures: a woman, a man, and a boy. The man's face was smeared and torn as if Cody had sought to erase him from the picture.

"It doesn't take a psychologist to see what he's saying here," Candace said, her finger tapping lightly on the edge of the paper.

Kendall met the veteran teacher's gaze. "No. I guess it doesn't."

"He just needs some reassurance."

"All right. I understand. And, Candace, I thank you so much."

"It's fine. That's why I'm here."

Kendall got up, looked down at the drawing, and did her best to hold it together. By the time she got to her car, she was already dialing Steven.

Again, voice mail.

"Steven, I just left Cody's school. I don't know what's going on with you. Why are you being so distant? Are you seeing someone? There, I said it. Do you have someone else now? Do you not want to be a family with me and Cody anymore? He's falling apart. I'm falling apart. Don't you love us?"

She hung up.

She sat there in the parking lot wishing she could do that call again. Wishing that she could dial him without the frustration and anger in her voice. If he was seeing someone, wouldn't he have the decency to tell her? She knew him. She loved him. Steven Stark was not a philanderer. He was a husband. A father. A family man.

She dialed again.

"Steven, I'm sorry about that last message. I'm scared for us. I don't know what's going on. That's all. Cody and I love you. Call me tonight. I'll be at home waiting for you."

The sheriff's detective turned the key and started for the office. As days go, this one was one of the worst. She'd come up empty on learning anything really new about Katy Frazier, and even worse—her son was drawing pictures that pointed to despair and abandonment issues. None of which Kendall wanted to believe were true.

CHAPTER THIRTY-ONE

Pandora hung up her phone and looked over at the bed.

"How was she?" Wyatt Ogilvie asked as he rolled over on his side to take in the view of his lover.

"Stupid, but that's pretty much what we get stuck with when you do a stupid cable show."

"Come back here. I'm ready for another round."

"Please, Wyatt. Don't kid yourself. You couldn't get it up again without a double dose of Viagra."

"Don't be like that, Pandy."

"Don't call me that."

"Jesus. What's wrong now?"

"I'm thinking."

"You're smart and sexy. That's what I like about you, babe."

Pandora sat on the edge of the bed. She kept her eyes focused on the window. The tops of the Olympic Mountains beckoned like one of those antique saws her mother painted with scenes of the West. She'd come so far from her past, but she wasn't where she wanted to be. Not by a long shot.

"Come on, baby, come back to bed," Wyatt said.

"Can't you see that I'm upset?" She turned around and glared at him.

"What?"

"What? You talk like a five-year-old, Wyatt. I need at least one of the men in my life to be a man. God knows my husband is weak. But at least he isn't obtuse."

Wyatt shifted his weight and sat up.

"Look, I know what you want, but it's out of my hands."

"Really? That's the best you've got?"

"What do you want me to do, Pandy?"

"Maybe you have early-onset dementia, Wyatt! Maybe that's why nothing really tracks with you. I keep repeating myself over and over and each time I do, you act like it's some revelation for the very first time."

"I know this is about the show."

"That's a start. I can't do this much longer, Wyatt. You can. You've maxed out on where you're going in life. I'm different. I'm only beginning. You've had your time in the sun."

Wyatt, who'd heard this tirade more than a hundred times before, held his tongue for a moment, letting the anger fade.

"What are we going to do about it? The show is what it is."

"If you really loved me you'd think a little harder and come up with a way to make something happen for me. I need something really big to happen. I need lift-off if I'm going to attract the big money."

"I've talked with Juliana several times."

"Juliana? That nitwit? She couldn't produce herself out of a paper bag, Wyatt. She can barely get this horrific show produced. It's tired. Lackluster. It's not catching ratings fire like those *Duck Dynasty* guys."

"She says she's working on something really big."

"Really? Her idea of big was to have me guest on a Food Network Halloween cake challenge. That didn't do one damn thing for my visibility. It didn't lead to anything. No *People* magazine cover. Not even a mention on Page Six for the story behind how the Dracula coffin cake blew up on the set."

"That was a good one."

"Is that all I get from you?"

"Sorry. But it was."

"You are so useless."

"Babe, give me a fighting chance. I'm doing everything I can to ensure that the series gets picked up for another season."

Pandora shot Wyatt a disgusted look. "You think it's all about this show, don't you? You are such a smalltimer. I couldn't give a crap about this show. I have a bigger, greater purpose and that means a show in front of millions, not hundreds of thousands. Sometimes you really shock me with your stupidity. How did you catch criminals in the past? Did you just get lucky and stumble on them?"

Wyatt got out of bed and put on a robe.

"I'll do something. I'll get with Juliana."

Pandora sniffed a little. She put her hands over her face. "God, tell me why I put up with this. I have so, so much to give and I'm surrounded by incompetence. Why have you cursed me so?"

Wyatt turned on the shower.

"I hear you. I hear you. I'll do something about it if it kills me. I won't let you down."

She watched him get into the shower. His body was far from an Adonis. His belly protruded and his back was a hairy forest. She never saw him as attractive, just someone she could use to help her get where she needed to go. He was a name. He came with baggage. He was everything that she needed to advance her dreams. The two of them made a marketable pair, hence the TV show. She didn't see any problem in having sex with him as long as he did what she wanted him to do. If he didn't get things going in a positive direction—one that would bring her the world—then she would take matters into her own hands.

Pandora got into bed and picked up her iPad. She went to her secret pin board on Pinterest and looked at the images she collected. Each was there to inspire and move her forward. A Porsche. A house in the Hamptons. A black sable bedspread. A picture of Wyatt. She kept her finger on Wyatt's photograph. So retouched. So not the creature, the *lover*, that was in the shower. She dragged his photo to the trash can. No matter what he was able to accomplish with Juliana, Pandora knew that he was never going to be the man of her dreams. He had a purpose, though. Somehow all the unpleasant sex, the sneaking around her husband's back, the lies, well . . . all of it would be worth it.

If.

Wyatt came out of the bathroom. His hair was damp, but combed. He didn't take the time to blow it dry because Pandora had set the tempo of the day.

"Pinning something on your secret board. I like that," he said.

"Just doing a little housecleaning, baby," she said.

"I love you, Pandy. I would do anything for you. You know that."

She stared hard at him. She looked at him like she was drinking him in, admiring his physique, making him feel as though she desired him.

"No," she finally said, letting him see that her eyes had lingered over his body. "I really don't. I need you to prove it. Don't just tell me you're here for me or that you want to help make my dreams come true. Prove it. Do something. Take a risk."

"Manifest our reality," he said, repeating one of her favorite affirmations.

"That's right." She set down her iPad. "Do it."

"All right. I will," he said.

She had him wrapped around her little finger and she knew it.

"But first, baby," she cooed. "Come and do me."

While Elan did his homework on the sofa in front of the TV, Birdy went about the boring but necessary task of paying the monthly bills in her office. She noticed the blinking light of the answering machine and pressed PLAY.

The voice came at her like a swift kick to the abdomen.

"I hope you and Detective Stark are enjoying your moment in the sun. It's me, Brenda. I'd say come and find me, but I don't stay still very long and neither one

of you are that good. I've only started. Who is Elan? I
like that name."

There was only one Brenda who mattered right then.
And, indeed, there was no other Brenda that Birdy
could think of. Just the one that everyone was talking
about.

She dialed Kendall.

"Just a second, Birdy," Kendall said. "Cody wants
another cup of popcorn. Movie time. Hang on."

"What are you watching? A horror movie?"

Kendall laughed. "Hardly. He's ten."

"Well, listen to this message on my machine," Birdy
said. After it was over, she waited for Kendall's response.

"That sounds like her."

"It sounds like a threat. I don't like it, Kendall. Not
one bit."

Kendall looked over at Cody, who was mesmerized
by the animated movie on the flat screen. "Me neither,"
she said. "Bring the tape in tomorrow. We need to give
it to the FBI."

"I don't like the tone in her voice. I don't like how
she mentioned Elan."

"I agree. It isn't good," Kendall said, hanging up.
She wondered if Brenda had seen the report on CNN.
She'd meant every word, but now she regretted anything that had to do with TV. TV, she thought, was
nothing but bad news. *Spirit Hunters*. CNN. It didn't
matter. There was no time in the sun.

Crap, I've made Brenda Nevins mad, Kendall thought.
Never make a serial killer angry. Doing so is playing
with fire. Playing with fire is something Brenda Nevins
likes to do.

CHAPTER THIRTY-TWO

If there had been any swallows at Swallow Haven, they surely would have perished in the smoke. The homeowners, a young couple from Seattle, stood at the edge of their driveway to the bluff where their house was being pierced by the fire hoses of the South Kitsap Fire Department. Two fire trucks and a tanker arrived within six minutes of the call. They would have been there sooner had a neighbor's goat herd not stymied their entrance by blocking the only roadway that led to the B and B.

A fire captain approached Sonja and Dean Morrison. Sonja had been crying and muttering something about her cat, Seasons. Dean, like his wife, was in his thirties. They'd escaped their high-tech firms and their ever-expanding offices in Seattle's South Lake Union district for a simpler, easier-to-navigate life. Swallow Haven and their adjacent lavender farm had taken every penny of their savings. Now, all of it had gone up in smoke.

"I'm sorry about your cat," the captain said.

Sonja, too upset to speak, nodded appreciatively.

"There wasn't anyone else inside?" the captain asked.

Dean spoke up. "No. No. Our last guest checked out this morning."

"Do you have any idea how it started?"

"It's an old house built in 1920s. We rewired most of it during the reno but maybe we missed something," Dean said, looking nervously over at Sonja. "I don't know. We did a lot of the work ourselves. God, I hate to think we screwed up somewhere. We were very, very careful," Dean said.

"We'll get to that. I promise."

"We were just on TV last night," Sonja said, now able to speak.

"Come again?"

"Our place was featured on TV last night. One of the producers from *Spirit Hunters* gave an interview. The place looked so pretty on camera. I got four calls for reservations this a.m. I guess I'll have to cancel those," she said.

Dean tugged at his wife. She was in shock.

"It's all right. We'll rebuild."

"When can we go inside? No one is letting us get any closer."

"Not today. We'll watch for hot spots. We'll make sure the structure is secure."

"All right," Dean said. "We'll go back to our condo in Seattle."

"I hate that place," Sonja said.

"I know. But we're lucky we have it."

The captain nodded in the direction of a firefighter who'd called over to get his attention.

"Just a minute," he said, heading toward the smol-dering house. "I'll be right back."

Sonja nodded and looked over at the tufts of laven-der, not yet in bloom.

"At least we still have something."

"We also have the condo."

"Don't keep reminding me of that. Our dream just went up in smoke."

"We'll get it fixed."

A lieutenant with the fire department stood next the back door and motioned for the captain.

"Looks like accelerant was used," he said. He indi-cated a large gas can. It was brand new.

The captain nudged it with the tip of his toe.

"Empty," he said.

"Price code is from Walmart, Captain."

The captain smiled. "You used to be a greeter there, didn't you?"

"Everyone starts somewhere. I wonder if those kids got tired of the bed-and-breakfast business. Maybe Swallow Haven was too much for them."

"Maybe. Seemed like they really loved the place. But then again, here's a gas can," he said, stopping and breath-ing in. "And I can smell an accelerant burn better than anyone."

A fireman emerged from inside.

"Better call the sheriff."

"That's what we were thinking," the former Walmart greeter said. "Arson."

"Not just that. There's a dead body in there, too."

"Holy crap," the captain said, looking over at the young couple. "They said no one was inside."

"Looks to be a woman. Pretty bad. She wasn't completely burned up, but singed pretty good. Smoke probably got her."

The captain went inside to assess the scene and then went back over to the Morrisons.

"Did I hear you correctly when you said no one was home?"

"Right," Dean said. "Just Seasons, our cat."

"Did you find her?"

The captain shook his head. "No, but we found the body of a woman."

"Wait a minute. That can't be. Juliana checked out this morning. She was going over to Seattle to meet with friends or something. Isn't that right, Sonja?"

Sonja, now crying, nodded.

"Yes. I told her to turn off the coffeepot and let herself out. I had early errands to run up in Poulsbo. You don't think the coffeepot started the fire?"

"No, we don't. We think it was arson."

"Arson?" Dean said. "That's kind of a relief. That wouldn't be our fault then."

The captain wanted to shake some sense into those ninnies. All they cared about was their cat and whether or not they'd be blamed for the fire.

No one cared about the dead guest.

"What was Juliana's last name?"

"Juliana Robbins. She was a producer for *Spirit Hunters*. She was here to do a show on the disappearance of Katy Frazier. I think she's from Seattle, but now lives . . . I mean *lived* . . . in New York."

* * *

"Sorry I'm late," Kendall said as she joined forensic pathologist Birdy Waterman and crime scene tech Sarah Dorman inside the burned-out kitchen of Swallow Haven.

"Just got here too," Birdy said, kneeling next to the victim.

"Hi, Detective," Sarah said.

"Sarah."

"I had a bad feeling about all of this from the very beginning, but I never thought we'd be at a crime scene with the producer of the freak show I taped."

"Media's camped outside," Sarah said.

"Saw," Kendall answered. "I'll go and make a statement and get them out of here."

"Pandora the magnificent is out there too," Birdy said.

"Ugh. All right. I'll be right back."

Kendall went back outside and the cameras from the Seattle TV stations were pointed at her. A satellite truck was pulling in the gravel driveway, tearing off the limb of an ancient Winesap apple tree in the process. Kendall took a deep breath. She almost wished that PIO twit Brad James was there, but after the debacle at the Frazier place, the Energizer Bunny of PR hacks was suddenly missing in action. If he was sick, then maybe he had a conscience after all.

Kendall identified herself.

"We really don't have much to share tonight beyond the basics," she said.

"Can you say that again, but look over this way? I missed the shot," a cameraman, actually a woman, from KIRO, said.

"Sure. Sorry."

"No problem. We don't want to miss a thing."

There wasn't much to miss, but Kendall didn't say that.

"We have found the body of a female victim in the kitchen of the residence here known as Swallow Haven. We have not identified the victim, nor do we know how she died."

"She died in the fire, right?" a reporter asked.

"Her remains were found in the fire, but we don't yet know how she died. Dr. Waterman will be conducting an autopsy tomorrow and we'll advise the media when the determination of cause is made at that time."

"The victim was the producer of the hit TV show, *Spirit Hunters*, wasn't she?"

It was interesting that the reporter would call the show a "hit" when as far as Kendall knew it was struggling in the ratings. Maybe when you work in Seattle TV everything emanating from New York was a hit.

"I can't comment on that right now."

Just then, Pandora appeared, her hair loose and swirling about her head like red satin ropes. She wore a black tunic with a giant—almost too large to imagine its weight around her neck—medallion of a moon and two stars.

"I'd like to make a statement," she said, the cameras dropping Kendall from the frame like she had typhoid.

"Of course you would," Kendall said, not loud enough for anyone to hear.

The female camera operator did.

"I know the type. My sister works for NBC. How anyone on TV can fit in the same room with another human being is beyond me."

"Cassie," the reporter called out, "get the camera on Pandora."

Pandora gathered herself. Or at least pretended she needed a moment to do so. As Kendall watched her, it passed through her mind that Pandora might be a better actress than she was a psychic.

"As some of you know I was called to the area by the family of Katy Frazier, missing now for more than four years. I was called here because the sheriff's department botched the investigation from the start." She glanced at Kendall as if to say "no offense, just doing my job." And then she started up. "I knew the minute that I got here that something terrible would unfold, that another tragedy would be visited on those connected to Katy's disappearance. I had no idea that it would be my very own producer, Ms. Juliana Robbins. I can't say for sure what happened here today, I'll need to consult my guides for that and that's not something I can do right now. I'm too upset. I'm human too."

"Human too," Kendall repeated.

The cameras parted and Pandora approached Kendall.

"Look," she said, "I didn't mean that you were personally responsible for the botched investigation."

Kendall didn't say anything.

"I will say that I hope you find out what happened to Juliana. I'll be watching and so will my guides."

"Thanks for that, Pandora," Kendall said, choking on her words, but trying to remain civil in front of the news media.

"I'm here to help," Pandora said.

"That's all right. We've got it covered."

With that, she turned, waved away the cameras.

"That's all for now. Coroner's office will issue the report tomorrow."

Kendall was fuming when she returned to the kitchen.

"Pandora Whatshername is a monster! A fame-seeking media whore."

Birdy looked up from a drawing of the scene she'd created. Sarah was clicking away on her camera, documenting everything. "I like it when you hold your feelings in."

"Very funny. Sorry. I just had to vent."

"Venting is good."

"What have you got for me?"

"Not much I'm afraid. The victim—"

"Whom Pandora identified on camera."

Birdy shook her head. "I hate her too. Now let's get on with this. According to the fire responders, the homeowners were both away this morning. Their guest Juliana Robbins was going to check out a bit later. She was told to feed the cat and lock the door. Her bags were packed, so that part checks out. Cat bowl is empty, so she never got that far."

"Unless the cat was very hungry," Sarah said. "My cats gobble everything the minute I set down the dish."

"That's because you have six cats, Sarah," Birdy said.

"I have four."

"They are eating as fast as they can because if they don't they'll starve."

"I was just offering an alternate view," Sarah said, a bit defensively.

Kendall leaned over the body. "Looks like she was

dressed to go somewhere important. That's a Kate Spade suit. So not Port Orchard."

"That's right. See the bruising around her neck?"

Kendall nodded.

"Someone choked her."

"Then lit a fire."

"Right," Birdy said. "To cover his or her tracks."

Kendall stepped back as two assistants from the coroner's office maneuvered Juliana's remains into a body bag. The noise from the zipper sounded a little like a row of firecrackers going off along the shore, as they did every Fourth of July, in front of her house. The sound was unsettling.

CHAPTER THIRTY-THREE

With Stan Getz playing his lonely saxophone over the speaker, Birdy Waterman stepped out of her street clothes and put on pale green scrubs. While there was important work at hand, she still thought of the night before. She hated disappointing Elan. The teenager had been upset about her coming home so late from the scene at Swallow Haven. Maybe even irritated. It was hard to read him sometimes. That probably came with the territory. Teenagers, she knew, were almost another species. She unwittingly had let him down. He'd made her dinner and there was no getting over the fact that her tardiness ruined something that he'd planned to be special. It was supposed to be a surprise celebration. He'd earned the highest score in his English class, an essay about the person he admired above all others—*her*.

"You should have told me," Birdy had said. "I would have hurried home." It wasn't exactly the truth and she knew it. She couldn't just leave a dead body at a crime scene to have dinner with him—or anyone. No matter how special the occasion. No matter how much she loved the teenager who had come into her life when she thought she'd forever be alone.

"It wouldn't have been much of a surprise," he said, looking down at the ruins of his meal. "You know that's the thing about surprises, the other person has no idea about what's in store."

Birdy put her hand on his shoulder. "I get that," she said. "And I'm sorry. I'm not much of one for surprises, but I love you and I love that you thought about me as the most admired person you could write about."

Elan met her eyes. "Well, you are."

"There are lots of people more deserving than me. The Pope, for example."

He rolled his eyes upward. "I'm not Catholic," he said.

She looked at him deadpan. "You're not?"

That made him laugh, which broke the tension in the kitchen. "Besides, I don't know the Pope and the assignment was to write about people who were really, really special in your life."

Birdy was touched and she couldn't hide it. It wasn't like one of those departmental tributes that she always had a good excuse to avoid. This was real, personal, and meaningful.

"Okay," she said, "why me?"

"The obvious answer is that you cut up dead bodies all day and that's pretty cool," he said.

"That got you the highest score?" she asked, teasingly.

"That's not what I wrote. I wrote about how you try to find the answers so that both the living and the dead can be at peace. I called you a bridge from life to death. It's a metaphor."

Birdy smiled.

The dinner was burned, but that morning all she could think about was how it tasted wonderful.

She wheeled Juliana's body from its companion in the chiller—a Jane Doe from Bremerton who'd died of a drug overdose. Birdy's heart went out to all the Janes she'd met in the course of her job as Kitsap County's forensic pathologist. There had been too many. Despite her fractured relationship with her mother and sister, there was no way she'd ever lose track of them. She'd always know right where they were—safe or not.

She muted the music a little and went about the business at hand—the measuring, the cataloging, the recording of every detail that would be used to assess exactly what happened, then, hopefully, forensic evidence that would indicate at whose hands the murder had occurred. There would be the sawing of the ribs, the skull, the buzz saw sound that sent shivers down the spine of most medical students—and some seasoned doctors too. And then the removal, examination, the flash of her camera's strobe on each of the deceased's vital organs. Weighed, measured.

In the even light of her autopsy suite, Birdy could see the distinct bruising around Juliana's slender neck. The marks were made by two hands, throttling the life out of her. Some abrasions indicated that the perpetrator had struggled some, and more than likely left the scene with some of the victim's DNA under his or her nails. Juliana's own fingernails were chipped. Birdy removed some tiny tissue samples from under six of them. They were coded and bagged for the lab.

Juliana's lungs were clear, devoid of smoke, which only reaffirmed what Birdy and Kendall had discussed at the scene. The fire was meant to cover up the murder.

Birdy recorded some notes for the transcriptionist.

"Victim is in her late twenties, Caucasian, normal weight and slight build, she appears to have been in excellent health . . ."

She stopped. She hadn't checked Juliana's teeth. She didn't need to take dental impressions for ID—that wasn't going to be necessary. She was all but certain who the victim was. She did need to check off the box. She opened Juliana's mouth and a flash of iridescence caught her eye.

"What's that?"

She bent closer and swung the light over. It splashed a beam into Juliana's gaping mouth.

"What?"

With a pair of tweezers the forensic pathologist retrieved the intact body of a very tiny bird.

What in the world? Is this some kind of joke?

She set the bird down onto the tray and prepared to bag it as evidence. Birdy, not surprisingly given her name, was a bit of an ornithologist. She knew immediately what the bird was. Everybody's grandmother with a honeysuckle vine could probably identify it. It was an Anna's hummingbird, an all-year resident of the Pacific Northwest. As far as she could tell, the only explanation for the bird being there was some kind of message from Juliana's killer.

Birdy reassembled Juliana and wheeled her back into the walk-in chiller. Five minutes later, she was over at Kendall's office.

"You look sick," Kendall said.

"I feel sick. I just finished the autopsy."

"What we expected?"

"More."

"All right. But before you tell me, I want to show you something."

Birdy let out a sigh. Kendall could sometimes be exasperating like that. She was always so focused on what she was doing that she didn't always see the urgency that others were presenting.

"Okay. Fine. But you really need to know what I found."

"It can't be weirder than this."

Kendall turned her computer screen around so Birdy could see it.

"What are we watching?"

"The surveillance video from Walmart."

"The gas cans?" Birdy asked.

Kendall nodded. She tapped her fingertip to a figure on the screen. It was a woman with a shopping cart with three gas cans and a pair of disposable cellphones. Nothing else.

"Does that look like anyone in particular?"

"Diane Keaton?"

"No," Kendall said. "Look closer."

Birdy was stumped. "I'm sorry," she said. "It doesn't look like Pandora if that's what you're getting at."

"No," Kendall said. "Not Pandora. I can't really say for sure, but I think it looks a little like Janie Thomas."

Birdy stared at the image on the screen, but didn't say another word.

"Well?" Kendall asked.

"Kendall, I'm not sure what's happening here," she said, her face suddenly pinched in worry. She stood. "I got a phone call yesterday. I didn't get it, but the office did. I thought it was a crank. Someone playing a joke. But after what I found in Juliana, I'm not so sure."

"In Juliana?"

"Yes, in her mouth. I pulled out a *Calypte anna.*"

"A what?" Kendall asked.

"A hummingbird."

"A hummingbird," Kendall repeated. "That doesn't make any sense."

"It does now with the tape and the message."

"What was the message?"

"Peg took it. I saved it. Birdy fished a pink slip of paper from her pocket. Underneath the block letters of the slip, WHILE YOU WERE OUT, Peg had written:

Brenda says hi. Will contact you later.

Birdy and Kendall stared at each other in silence. Brenda Nevins hadn't left Kitsap County at all. She hadn't fled to Canada or Venezuela as the tabloids had screamed from the supermarket checkout aisles. Even Drudge had blared one of her so-called sightings with his police siren logo on his mega-clicked-through web page.

"Janie's still alive," Kendall said. "We thought she was dead. I have to tell her husband."

"What are you going to tell him? That his wife is now helping a serial killer?"

Kendall nodded. Birdy was right. She hadn't thought that through. Not at all. What was she going to say to Erwin Thomas?

CHAPTER THIRTY-FOUR

Erwin Thomas answered the door. He looked haggard. Bags hung under his eyes. Stubble covered his chin. He looked thinner than when they first met. Kendall could clearly see that Erwin Thomas was yet another of Brenda Nevins's victims.

"I've already talked to the FBI," he said, letting her inside, "if that's why you're here." He shut the door behind her.

"I'm here because I care about you and Joe."

"I read the papers, Detective. I know you're caught up in this confluence of murder stories. My wife. Brenda. Pandora. Katy Frazier."

"I'm not like that, Mr. Thomas."

"I know you don't mean to be, but I guess it happens."

Kendall wasn't there to defend herself. She was there because she did care.

"What exactly did the FBI tell you?" she said.

"Don't you talk to them?"

"Not really. It isn't our case."

"Coffee?"

"No thanks."

"I've just made a pot."

"All right, then. I guess I could use a cup."

Erwin had stripped the house of any trace of his wife. The house looked like a short-term rental, not a family home with history and personal effects.

"Where's Joe?"

"I told him to go back to school. There's nothing to be done here," he said, handing her a steaming cup. "Black, right?"

Kendall nodded. "Thanks."

They stood in the kitchen and looked out over the placid water of Long Lake.

"The FBI says that Janie and Brenda were involved for months. I honestly didn't see it. I didn't see any of this."

"I'm sorry, Mr. Thomas," Kendall said. "I really am."

"No one is sorrier than me. Not for myself, but for Joe. This has been a nightmare for our son. My son," he said correcting himself.

Janie had been erased. Obliterated. In every way that her husband could devise. Not just her belongings, but even the fact that they shared a son.

"Did they tell you they believe Janie is alive?"

He nodded, but stayed mute for a moment.

"I wish she was dead, but, yes, I understand that she and Brenda are alive. That my wife has been helping Brenda. Did you know she withdrew three thousand dollars from our bank account the day before she ran off with her?"

Kendall didn't know that. Communication with the FBI had been firmly engineered as a one-way street.

"No," she admitted. "I didn't."

"I noticed it when my statement came. I've really been played, haven't I?"

Kendall set her cup down. "There's something you need to know. It's very, very bad."

"It isn't like I haven't heard the worst already."

"No, you haven't."

"Well, out with it."

"All right. I think that Brenda has been using your wife to do her bidding."

"What do you mean, bidding?"

"I think that Janie may have killed someone."

The color went from Erwin's already pale face.

"Who?" he asked. "Who did she kill?"

"A producer from a TV show," Kendall said.

Erwin, whose life had been made miserable by the cameras and the reporters who had stalked his every move, shrugged.

"I guess I'm not sorry about that," he said. "I hate those people."

Kendall did too, but she didn't say so.

"What show?"

"*Spirit Hunters*," she said.

"That's the one that was bugging Joey over that Katy thing."

"They've been bugging everyone," Kendall said.

CHAPTER THIRTY-FIVE

Roger Frazier didn't even try to hide his anger at Kendall. She didn't blame him for that. In fact, she didn't think of any reason to pretend that everything was all right, either. The architect had, indeed, been backstabbed by a TV psychic who was in his presence at least partially because she had been sanctioned by the Kitsap County Sheriff's Department. It wasn't just any backstabbing, either. It was the mother of all accusations that could be made to a father.

Pandora pointed a finger at him and called him a child molester and a killer—and she did it while the cameras caught every ugly nuance of what she was saying.

"Are you here to ruin my reputation some more? Believe it or not, word's already gotten around Port Orchard that I offer candy to little girls when I'm out designing their playhouses."

Kendall approached slowly. The offices were beautifully appointed; the furnishings were the best that money could buy. Leather, chrome, modern. On the walls were renderings of many of Frazier's greatest architectural hits, including a residence that made the cover of

Sunset magazine, one of the West Coast's premier home and garden glossies.

One rendering was of a church. No doubt a client that would not be calling for remodeling contracts any time soon.

"I'm sorry about what happened," Kendall said.

He turned away, toward the rendering of the church. "Sorry doesn't begin to repair what you've done to me," he finally said. His face was completely red and it was clear he didn't want to lose composure. Not like he had during the taping. He'd hoped most of that footage wouldn't make the final edit—though he knew that was the kind of thing reality TV hoped for—the unguarded, the angry, the moment in which the viewer will pause and rewind because they just have to see it happen one more time.

"I didn't do anything," Kendall said.

"Not you personally. But that PIO Bradley James, he's the one I'll name in the lawsuit, along with the sheriff. I'll keep you out of it. Seems to me like you were just as shocked at what she had to say as I was."

"To put it mildly, yes."

"Fine then. Let's sit down and figure out what we're going to do here." He led her into a conference room that overlooked a ravine blanketed with salal and sword ferns.

"I'm not sure what you mean by *we*," Kendall said, sitting in a chair that probably cost more than her car. "I'm here to do a job. The job deals with your daughter's disappearance. I'm not here about what a psychic did or didn't say."

"That's not true, Detective," he said, staring her down.

"What do you mean?"

"My daughter told me you paid her a visit. She told me that you asked all sorts of questions about me and Katy and whether or not I'd been inappropriate with her."

Kendall had been caught. At least it felt something like that.

"I'm just doing my job, Mr. Frazier. That's all."

"Your job is to follow up the made-up rants of a TV psychic?" His face was getting red, but Roger Frazier didn't want to blow his top just then. He didn't want to give Kendall Stark any more reason to think he was anything but a decent man. Not one suspected of being a molester. Of murdering his daughter. Of having anger-management issues.

"Your wife told me a few things," she said, knowing that she was walking on thin ice. "I was following up on those."

He took off his glasses and wiped them with a small cloth before sliding them back on.

"Like what?" he asked.

Kendall went for it. There was no way to step into the subject delicately.

"Like a special secret that only you and Katy could know," she said.

Roger drummed the table and looked out at the ravine. A maple tree dripping with ferns filled most of the frame.

"That?" He sighed, still looking at the tree. "Brit's still hung up on that, is she? It was private. Personal."

Kendall nodded. She could see that Roger Frazier was in a tight spot. His wife had betrayed him; now a homicide investigator was asking him to betray his daughter.

"Tell me the secret," she said, prodding gently.

He was vulnerable just then. She didn't think he was being defensive. It was a different approach to a tough subject and Kendall thought that it might indicate he hadn't been the monster Pandora had made him to be.

And his wife.

"I promised I never would," he said.

"But she's gone now, Mr. Frazier. Maybe it's important."

He waved her away. "No. It has nothing to do with any of whatever it was that happened to her."

"I need to be the one who decides that," Kendall said. "It's my job. You really need to tell me."

The architect with the perfect office and the perfect house began to crumble.

"She was so embarrassed," he said, his words tentative and almost inaudible. "She made me promise never to tell."

A long pause filled the room.

"Was she pregnant?" Kendall asked.

"Oh God, no," Roger said, coming back to the moment. "It wasn't that at all. She was bulimic. My perfect little girl was making herself throw up every night. I caught her one time. I promised never to tell anyone, not even her mom, if she got treatment."

"Lots of girls have that problem," Kendall said, thinking back to a time when she did it a few times to lose weight in college.

"I told her that," Roger said. "But she insisted. She trusted me. I never let her down. That was our little secret."

CHAPTER THIRTY-SIX

In the first days following Brenda and Janie's vanishing from the prison, the media circus moved from the prison perimeter to the Kitsap County Courthouse. A garden of satellite antennae and their accompanying trucks sprung up on Division Street. By the time *Spirit Hunters* came to town, all but one had gone away. Not without the trial by fire of media training that Brad James has pushed both Kendall and Birdy into.

"You are the face of this case," Brad told Kendall as he stood in her office doorway like he knew better than to plop himself on the chair. "You had the last contact with Brenda by anyone in law enforcement."

"It wasn't this case," Kendall said, looking down at her computer screen to give Brad a not-so-subtle hint that she was not at all interested in what he was selling.

"That doesn't matter," he said, before attempting to play her a little. "Look, you are smart and you're easy on the eyes. We need you right now. We're going through a lot of challenges and if we can get your face on *Good Morning America* or something, we're going to really be able to move the needle on our image problem."

"I don't think I'm the right person," Kendall said, though she wanted to call him a complete suck-up. "I don't have anything unique to contribute."

Brad was relentless. Annoyingly so.

"No one is looking for unique, Kendall," he said. "They are looking for somebody to throw some quotes out there so they have an excuse to put up sound bites of Brenda, her case, Janie's husband crying. That kind of thing. It's called news."

"It's called sleazy," Kendall said, now meeting his gaze.

You're sleazy too.

"That may well be," he said. "But get off your high horse. We need to do some things that move the needle."

Kendall tapped on her computer again.

"You've said that," she said.

Kendall didn't want him to sit down. Sitting down meant she'd be stuck with him like a fly on flypaper.

"I'm saying it again," he said, inching toward one of the visitor's chairs adjacent to her desk. "It's called repeating your talking points so that the other party leaves understanding what you're talking about and what you want them to know."

Kendall rolled her eyes. She didn't care if Brad saw her. And, truth be known, *he* didn't care. She stood up to indicate that she had somewhere to go.

"I'll do one or two interviews," she said.

He backed off.

Good.

"You'll do *Good Morning America* and *Inside Edition*," he said without giving her a second to say anything. "You want to know when?"

"When?" Kendall asked, a little startled that he was able to move the needle so quickly.

Brad flashed an excited smile. It was as if he was unveiling some big prize. Maybe a cake for little kid's birthday. A drink of water for a desert traveler. Something wonderful and appreciated.

"*GMA* is tomorrow," he said, looking particularly pleased with himself, a look he'd perfected over his time with the sheriff's office. "*Inside E* is this afternoon. Just be yourself. Talk about the victims. Act like you care."

Kendall could have socked Brad James right then. She *did* care. She cared too much. He was a bonehead. Through and through.

Inside Edition focused on Erwin and Janie and what was happening there. Kendall was swimming upstream on that one. She'd seen him only a couple of times and there really wasn't any news to report.

"He's devastated," she said during the interview, which was conducted in a senior deputy's office with a commodity that was tough to come by in the warren of offices at the Kitsap County Sheriff's Department—a view of some trees. "He wants his wife back. He wants his *life* back."

The field producer, a pretty twentysomething who teetered in her pumps, nodded approvingly.

"It must be awful for him to know that his wife was

cheating on him with an inmate. A female inmate," the producer said.

Kendall didn't take the bait that time, though it was hard to resist. She did her best to flip it all around on where she thought it needed to be—back to Brenda Nevins.

"Look, he's a victim. His wife is a victim. We don't know why Janie Thomas went off with Brenda Nevins, but I can tell you I seriously doubt that it was willingly. Brenda has a way of getting what she wants and using every means at her disposal in order to do so. She's a facile liar, a trickster."

The producer seemed to like what Kendall was saying, and the detective fell into a trap that engulfs many new to the media. She kept talking. She kept the words coming to keep the head nods going, the uh-huhs of approval.

"She's some kind of lucky evil," Kendall said.

That evening the show put out a press release touting the interview with Kendall and the Brenda Nevins story. The *Seattle Times*, which almost never took such headline bait, did.

KITSAP DETECTIVE SAYS NEVINS IS "LUCKY"

Kendall gulped her tuxedo mocha while Birdy read the article the next morning. The detective's eyes were bleary. The *GMA* interview had been brief, by satellite at 5:30 that morning.

"You really didn't call her lucky," the forensic pathologist said.

"I know. But honestly, I don't think I'm cut out for this media crap."

"I think you're pretty good at it."

Kendall set down her cup. "I don't know," she said. "They just look at me and I feel compelled to keep talking. It's stupid. I should just let them stew."

"You were better on *GMA* today. Much better. You really hit that interview out of the park. Honestly."

Kendall nodded even though Birdy was being over the top, effusive. She was trying to be supportive and that was appreciated. Even if it wasn't so.

"Thanks," she said, "if better is being stiff as a board, I guess I was. I didn't say anything truly stupid, did I?"

Birdy didn't answer right away.

Kendall narrowed her gaze. "Birdy, did I?" she asked.

Birdy grinned and patted Kendall's hand. "Not really stupid. In fact, I thought you did a very good job when you called Brenda a master manipulator."

Kendall shrugged her shoulders a little. "Real original, huh?" she said, smiling at the stupidity of all of it.

"Better than lucky."

CHAPTER THIRTY-SEVEN

It was Birdy Waterman's least favorite part of the job, but there was seldom any way of getting around it. Sometimes when such encounters didn't occur she found herself wishing they had. To her way of thinking, as awful as parental notifications were, the idea that someone could die and that there was no one out there with enough of a connection to care was far worse.

"They're in the conference room," the coroner's secretary, Darlene, said. "Super upset."

"Thanks, Darlene," Birdy thought, wanting to tell her that saying "super upset" might be fine if you were a tween, but it certainly didn't fit the decorum of such a sad occasion.

"Mother and father?"

Darlene nodded. "Yeah, Don and Muriel Robbins. Drove over from Olympia."

"All right," Birdy said, taking a deep breath before opening the door to the windowless conference room that had been set up as a family "grief" meeting area by the coroner. In the past, there was no place for the tears and loud cries that came with notifications. The sound of the wailing coming from a child's mother was something that no one wanted to hear.

It just hurt so much.

Don and Muriel were in their fifties. He was a ship-builder and she was a dental hygienist. He was completely bald, and she had a cocoon of brown hair that hugged her small head.

"I'm Dr. Waterman," Birdy said.

Don got up and shook her hand, and introduced himself. Muriel just sat there, unable to say anything.

"I'm so sorry for your loss," Birdy said.

Muriel muttered a thank-you.

"We're really in shock," Don said. "Are you sure? Is there a chance that you got it wrong? I saw on a TV show a few years back . . . can't think of it now . . ."

"*Dateline*," Muriel said. "It was *Dateline*."

"Right, I saw on that show a story when they had the wrong body and that the girl was still alive, but had amnesia. Maybe that happened to our Juli?"

Birdy sat down. She'd seen the familiar machination of hope work its way through the occupants of that room more than a time or two. She'd seen how people grasp at straws, no matter how far-fetched, to give them the impossible.

That their baby is alive.

That this is all a mistake.

That this is just a nightmare.

She's at work and doesn't even know this is going on.

How they will laugh about it later, in that grim way people do when granted a reprieve from the all-too-true.

"I'm so sorry, but it is true. We've positively ID'd your daughter through dental records."

Muriel looked up at Birdy. She took off her frameless glasses and folded them slowly, deliberately. It was as if she needed to eat up some time before she spoke, as if the words that would come from her mouth would kill her right then and there in that awful, sad conference room.

"She was burned up real bad?" Her voice was tremulous.

Birdy shook her head. "No. Very few burns."

"Well, then how did she die?"

This was always the worst question. Only murderers never ask it. Because they already know.

"It wasn't an accident," Birdy said, letting a little out at a time.

"Not an accident?" Don repeated.

"Someone killed her?" Muriel said.

"I'm afraid that's right," Birdy said. "I'm so sorry to tell you that your daughter was a victim of homicide."

"Homicide?" Don said.

Birdy thought of him as a "repeater," the kind of person who echoes all the unpleasantness so that he or she can finally absorb what was so impossible to understand.

"Who would want to kill our baby?" Muriel said.

"How did she die?" Don asked. "The news said a fire."

"Yes, a fire at that bed and breakfast she was staying at," Muriel said.

Birdy was used to the endless questions and the stream of consciousness that came with notifications. She cleared her throat and changed her posture a little to let them know she'd answer their questions the best she could. It was akin to a teacher dragging her nails on a chalkboard to get the attention of the class.

"We're investigating everything and everyone. I know that when you're done here, you'll need to talk to my colleague Kendall Stark. She's the investigator in charge of Juliana's case."

"How did she die?"

"I've determined the cause of death to be strangulation."

Mrs. Robbins put her hands up to her neck, a reflexive move.

"Did she suffer?" Juliana's father asked.

"We don't think the encounter with her killer was a long one," Birdy said. "Your daughter put up a good fight, but she was not able to subdue her attacker."

"She was a strong girl," Don said.

"We never should have let her move to New York," Muriel said.

"This didn't happen in New York, babe. It happened right here at home."

"I know that! I'm saying that those TV people were a terrible lot. She told me about their wild parties and how they made her do things she didn't think was right."

Birdy's jaw dropped.

Seeing the forensic pathologist's reaction, Don jumped into the conversation.

"Not at the parties. Right, Muriel?" He looked at her with pleading eyes.

"Of course not, I didn't mean that. I'm sorry. I meant that the producers and that awful Pandora. They put her up to a lot of stuff that she didn't want to do."

"Do you recall any specifics?" Birdy asked.

"Just things with the show. Pandora was all about . . . you know, ratings. She wanted Juliana basically to trick people into saying and doing stuff on TV so that she could look like an all-knowing psychic. It was rubbish and my daughter knew it."

"A lot of people weren't very happy with the show," Don said.

Birdy already knew that and she could certainly understand why.

"Kendall will be here any moment," she said. "She'll want to get all of this down."

"Are you going to show us our daughter's body?" Don asked.

"Yes," Muriel said. "We want to see her."

Birdy hated when parents insisted, but it was their right.

"Are you sure you want to do that?" she asked.

They both nodded.

"We don't have any other kids. I miscarried twice. She was our miracle baby and . . ." Muriel dissolved into tears.

Kendall knocked on the conference room door, and Birdy let her inside. After introducing Juliana's parents to the Kitsap County detective, she left to prepare the body for viewing in the basement morgue. Kendall offered her condolences and promised that she'd do everything humanly possible to find out who had killed Juliana.

"I'm going to look at those closest to her, like you, to find out what was going on in her life and whether or not she had been targeted by anyone."

"She might have been," Don said. "People hated that show. I mean, the viewers didn't hate it obviously, but anyone who was on it sure did. Some guy in Iowa threatened her after a show."

"Do you know the man's name?"

He shook his head. "No, but he was the man on the Iowa City haunted church episode."

Kendall wrote that down.

Muriel spoke next. "I want to correct something Don just said. I don't know if it's important, but the night before the fire," she said, her throat catching when she realized that it was the last time she spoke with Juliana, "she called me and said she had ended up staying an extra day because of some big exclusive she was going to get."

"I talked to her too," Don said. "She said it was something bigger than the show, something that would catapult her into stardom."

"Right," Muriel said, slightly irritated by her husband. "She was on speaker phone. She specifically said that she'd arranged an interview with a famous—"

"She said 'infamous' person who was in the headlines," Don said, interrupting his wife.

"Did she say anything about who this was? Anything at all."

The Robbinses shook their heads.

Don spoke next. "She said one other thing that I thought was interesting. She said that if Pandora found out that she'd crap in her pants. We laughed about that. Our daughter couldn't stand Pandora. She thought she was so pushy, so fake. She said that the show was within a tenth of a ratings point to be canceled and that if Pandora knew what she was up to, she'd throttle her."

"What'd she think of Wyatt Ogilvie? Did she ever talk about him?" Kendall asked.

"She didn't like him either," Muriel said. "He tried to put the moves on her."

"What, Muriel?" Don asked, his once ashen face turning a little red.

Muriel reached for his hand. "Sorry, she didn't want you to worry. Besides, he moved on. Ended up sleeping with Pandora. Although from what I gather, most of the crew had a go with her a time or two."

None of that surprised Kendall. She'd spent enough time with Pandora to spot a predatory user.

Don and Muriel stood like a pair of garden statues at the foot of the gurney covering their precious daughter's body. Birdy had smoothed out Juliana's hair, but there was no makeup and that meant the remains of the little girl they saw from diapers to a life in the big city would look the color of an unbaked pie shell.

Birdy calmly and haltingly told them what she was going to do.

"I'll peel back the sheet to show you her face, but because of the autopsy and because she suffered some injuries I will not expose any more of her. Do you understand?"

"Yes," they both said.

"You cannot touch her," Birdy said. "She's still in my custody and you will not be able to touch her until I release her to the funeral home employees. Do you understand that?"

They nodded.

Birdy could readily recall the time a mother lurched

at the body, grabbing ahold of it while exposing the Y incision and other cuts made by the pathologist's scalpel that made her son look akin to Frankenstein and not the Little Leaguer that they'd just lost in a joyride auto accident. It was a moment she'd never allow to happen again in her morgue. She doubted the mother ever got over it.

She certainly never did.

CHAPTER THIRTY-EIGHT

Dean and Sonja Morrison arrived at the sheriff's office in Port Orchard looking like a couple who had lost everything, which as far as their livelihood and cat were concerned, they had. They both wore jeans that would cost many locals a week's pay. She carried a Burberry purse—the first one that had likely ever been inside the county building. He wore a dark blue Nautica jacket and shirt and boat shoes that had likely never seen the deck of a watercraft. Kendall led them (by a circuitous route that was a necessity because the building had been added on to so many times) to a conference room to make their investigative statement.

"We're very sorry about what happened to Juliana," Dean said.

Dean looked like he hadn't slept; whether that was because his business was ruined or he felt sorrow for the dead guest was debatable.

"I know," Kendall said, choosing to believe the best of the young couple from Seattle.

Sonja, a smear of pink lipstick on her lips that indicated a shaky hand or haste, slid into a chair next to her husband.

"She was a very nice person," she said. "I thought she was, anyway."

"Yes, I met her too," Kendall said, "in conjunction with the show."

Kendall offered the couple something to drink, but neither was thirsty.

"What can we do to help?" Dean asked. "I mean, we really don't know anything about her, what might have happened, who, you know . . ."

His words lingered in the stuffy air of the conference room.

"Killed her," Kendall said.

"Right," Sonja said, fidgeting in her purse for an elusive breath mint. She found one and popped it into her mouth. "We don't know anything."

Kendall sat down. "In a homicide investigation," she said, "we need to know every little detail about what happened before the victim was killed. What's insignificant to the average person might play a key role in our solving the case."

"I guess," Sonja said, looking at her husband. "I don't think we can tell you much."

Kendall smiled. She wanted to tell Sonja that people often don't know what they know until they are guided to think about it.

"Let's start with the beginning. Did you have any personal conversations with Juliana?"

Dean spoke up. "Not much. She told us that she was from Seattle, but lived in New York."

"She talked a lot about the show and the cast," Sonja added.

"What did she say?"

Sonja answered again. "She didn't really like either one of the people on the show."

"Sonja, that isn't very nice," Dean said.

Sonja crunched on her breath mint. "Well, it's true. She said that she was hoping that she could get a new job after the show was canceled. She thought it was a dead end."

No one remarked on the irony of Sonja's last two words.

Kendall was interested. "What did she say about the cast, specifically?"

Sonja looked at her husband. Dean shook his head slightly. "I'm going to tell her," she said.

"She told us not to tell anyone," he said.

"Juliana?" Kendall asked. "She asked you not to tell anyone something?"

A long silence.

"Yeah," Dean said, finally giving in. "She said she could lose her job for saying so, but she was so angry after that long night of the taping at the dead girl's house in Port Orchard that she didn't even go to bed. I got up early to do some painting, and she and I talked for over an hour. Sonja too."

"What was she so mad about?" Kendall asked.

"She said that she told Pandora and that cop that she was going to quit and that doing this kind of sleazy work was not something she was proud of. She felt like all they cared about were ratings and money and keeping the show going," Dean said.

Sonja thought a second. "Was that what she said?"

Dean studied his wife. He remembered her exact words.

"She said that Pandora and the cop would stop at nothing to make sure that they stayed a viable production and if that meant being completely over the top with their so-called reality episodes then they'd be fine with that."

As Kendall made a note of that, Sonja added more.

"She specifically said that it didn't matter to them one bit if they ruined anyone's life because theirs was more important," she said.

"That remark made me want to puke," Dean added. "That's what she said. I believed her. I think she was probably the only one in the bunch who had anything close to a conscience."

"She really hated those two. That's why she stayed with us. She had friends in Seattle but she told everyone on the show she preferred staying closer to the set and closer to her parents in Olympia."

"Did either Pandora or Wyatt come over to your place?"

"No, but she had a heated conversation with one of them," Sonja said.

"Right," Dean jumped in. "She was on the phone and she was yelling at them that they were charlatans and that if she hadn't signed a confidentiality agreement she'd tell the world."

"Tell the world what?" Kendall asked.

"That they were frauds making money off the heartbreak of others. That Pandora hadn't been in touch with anyone from the other side—not once."

"Most reasonable people already know that," Kendall said.

"You would think so, but I looked at her Facebook

page and it was full of people begging her to come help them find a missing loved one or something like that."

"Did you overhear any other conversations? Did she share anything else?" Kendall asked.

They shook their heads in unison.

"She got a call from someone on our house phone. I think it was a job offer," Dean said.

"Yes, she was very excited. She said that someone very important had seen her on the Seattle TV show that featured our house."

"Did she say what the offer was?" Kendall asked.

"Not that I recall. Dean?"

"She said it was something exclusive and life changing." He paused. "She called it a game changer. I didn't press her for more information, because, well, as nice as she was, she came with a lot of unwanted drama. I like things quiet. Juliana and her rant against Pandora were too much for me."

"I heard that she was strangled to death," Sonja said.

"I can't comment on that," Kendall said. "Anything more about the phone call? How long did it last?"

"A couple of minutes," Dean said. "At the most. She was on, then off."

"I remember something else about the call, Detective."

"What's that, Sonja?"

"That the caller was a woman. She said that she was a bigger bitch than Pandora could ever hope to be."

CHAPTER THIRTY-NINE

"You promised you'd let me go," Janie Thomas said.

"You said you cared about me, but I know that you don't. People only care about themselves," Brenda said.

The words hung in the air. Janie Thomas knew that there was no endgame for her. There was no escape. Brenda had told her over and over that she'd kill her husband and son if she didn't do what she wanted. She'd sent her into the store to get the gas cans, to the service station to fill them up. She made love to her in the kind of way that was neither romantic or even remotely pleasurable. Whatever degrading thing Brenda had done to her, she told herself that she deserved it. Her life was in ruins. Shambles. There was no hope.

And it was all her fault.

It had started innocently. She knew that. She felt sorry for Brenda Nevins. She'd read her file, had seen what had happened to her in life to turn her into the creature that she was. Sympathy was the bridge that led them together. Janie had had it rough growing up too.

Her uncle Jerry had raped her when she was seven. Repeatedly. Her first husband beat her. She loved Erwin, but she didn't trust him completely. She thought that like the other men in her life, Erwin would do something to her. Hurt her.

All the men in Brenda's life had hurt her.

Brenda tried to kill herself after the Missy Carlyle debacle. At least that's what the prison doctor and psychologist had said when they examined her after she was found in her cell bleeding from a not-so-deep slice to her wrist. Brenda noticed the cat pendant that Janie was wearing.

"I had a cat. A white Persian named Devonshire," Brenda said. "That cat loved me no matter what people had done to me. She was everything to me. You know what happened to Dev?"

"No."

"My uncle Kent gave her away to a Mexican family."

"Why'd he do that?"

"Because I loved that cat and he said the cat gave him the creeps."

Janie felt sick. Her own life was so similar to Brenda's. After that first encounter, there were others. Each time, Brenda moving closer and closer. It was like a cold shadow falling on her, so slowly that Janie didn't really know what was happening. It was as if Brenda knew exactly how to draw her in. How to make her feel that she—and only she—really understood her.

"Why do you think you work in a prison, Janie?" she said.

"I didn't start out with that as a dream. It happened."

"Nothing happens. Everything is orchestrated by

people. You and those around you. Think about it. Why a prison?"

Janie thought a moment. "I guess I wanted to do something good for society. I wanted order."

"Not quite. Get real, Janie. You wanted control."

"Control?"

"Control because you had none growing up. I didn't either. But look. I'm on one side of the walls and you're on another."

"Maybe. Maybe that's reaching a little."

"I don't think so. I wanted control too. My path was different. I killed those in my way."

Janie didn't bring up Brenda's child. She couldn't rationalize how an innocent could be in anyone's way. The men, maybe. Though she knew that there were other alternatives. She could have just left them.

"Killing people isn't the answer, Brenda. It's barbaric."

"Holding people in prison for doing what's natural is barbaric, Janie."

"Maybe so. But it's the law."

Brenda changed the subject. "I like your hair."

It started like that shadow. Brenda would dig into Janie's life and Janie would feel that the serial killer inside the walls that she controlled was the only person who really understood her. Brenda was brilliant. No one who knew her or studied her could say otherwise. But she was also funny. And what seemed to matter more as time went on, Janie Thomas felt that Brenda knew her better than herself. She had tapped into her heart, brain, soul. She made excuses to spend more and more time with the inmate, offering her an assignment working in her office. None of the other women trusted or liked Brenda Nevins, but none could say anything about it. Janie Thomas was in charge of their paychecks and their futures. With more potential cutbacks coming from the state's Department of Corrections in Olympia, none dared breathe a word of any concern. When Janie returned home to Erwin every night she found herself in the boring life she'd invented for herself—a control mechanism. What had been comforting was now stifling. What had made her feel calm and safe now agitated her.

How could Brenda Nevins know her better than anyone? Better than her husband? Her son? How was it that at this middle part of her life that she'd finally found a soul mate?

Janie Thomas wasn't a lesbian. She'd never even thought of being with a woman. Or another man for that matter. The connection with Brenda was deeper than sex. In fact, sex was something she was certain would never be part of their special bond.

How could it be? She was Brenda's captor, not her lover.

"Your husband won't want you back. The ladies in the prison will eat you alive when you end up in a cell. That's where you'll be. You know that, don't you, Janie?"

Janie didn't answer right away. Her mind raced over the events that had led her there and what she was certain was about to follow. Brenda was right.

"No one would want me since I've been with the likes of you," she finally said.

"Oooh, I like it when my little prison mouse gets real tough," Brenda said, tightening the cords around

Janie's wrists. "That's a side to you I didn't see coming and it makes me want to laugh."

"I don't want to live anymore. I don't care what you do to me."

"In time," Brenda said. "Did you ever wonder how we came to this moment, Janie?"

"A million times."

"Did you know that it was Missy who brought us together?"

"Missy Carlyle?" Janie looked confused.

Brenda smiled. Her blinding white teeth seemed menacing. Like a tiger's. "Yes, our little Missy. She took pictures of your personnel file and gave them to me. Carried them in her pussy."

"She didn't have access," Janie said, though now feeling the connections being made. Her own psychological evaluation had revealed some of her own trauma growing up. The parallel story lines of their lives were a fabrication, a road map created to suck her into Brenda's world. "You didn't have a Persian cat, did you?"

Brenda shook her head.

"An uncle who raped you?" Janie asked.

"Actually, it was the other way around. I seduced him when I was fifteen. I worked him over good. I got money. A car on my sixteenth birthday. A new car, not a used one. The sex was lousy, but I didn't care. I called his dick my joystick, but I never got a thing out of it. I knew then that I had to use what God gave me if I was going to get out of that godforsaken hellhole alive and make something of myself. I was never like the other girls."

"I don't expect you were," Janie said, her voice suddenly weak with the kind of despair that comes with the realization that everything that she'd thought was true had been built on a lie.

Brenda lifted a straight-edge razor she'd collected from Chaz Masters's bathroom when she did her "shopping" after killing him.

"You've served your purpose," she said.

"Please make it quick," Janie said. There was no fight in her. No purpose in fighting. To fight Brenda while she was tied to a bed was to enrage evil and make the ultimate punishment even greater. Her eyes stayed on Brenda's, away from the blade. The last thing Janie saw was her own reflection. She closed her eyes and waited for her life to ebb into the mattress.

"Goodbye, my meek little prison mouse," Brenda said.

CHAPTER FORTY

Pandora sat in the chair while the technician at the satellite TV station attached a microphone on the inside of her black sweater. She had done her own makeup that morning and asked if she looked all right.

"This is hi-def," she asked, "isn't it?"

"Yeah," a voice in her earpiece said. "Pretty much everything is hi-def these days."

"Tell that to the producers of my show," she said, facing the lens of the camera while the young man named Jerry adjusted everything.

"Cable's pretty cheap, you got that," he said. "Earpiece comfortable?"

She nodded.

"You've done satellite before?" Jerry asked.

"A time or two," she said.

"Great, then you know that you'll need to look directly at the camera," he said.

She looked at the lens. Someone had hung a Post-it note with an eyeball on it, and underneath it had written with a ballpoint pen: *Look Here.*

The voice called into her earpiece.

"This is New York again, can you hear me all right?"

"Yes," she said. "Loud and clear."

"Can you say your name and how to spell it, how we should identify you on the graphic?"

"Pandora. P-A-N-D-O-R-A. Psychic and author."

Jerry excused himself for the control room.

"Got it," she said into the air, toward the lens.

"All right. The talent is Les, one of our top reporters."

Pandora shook her head. "I thought I was going to speak with Diane. I don't know any Les."

"He's great," the producer said. "You'll like him. Diane's on assignment. We're doing this live-taped and she'll intro the piece when it airs tomorrow. All right, Pandora?"

Pandora made an exasperated face, which was certainly seen by New York.

"Five seconds," the producer said.

"Pandora, this is Les. Can you hear me all right?"

"Crystal clear," she said, adjusting to her circumstances.

No Diane Sawyer. Damn!

"Great. I'm going to put together a package with some graphics and photos to introduce the piece, so don't worry about that. Let's get started on the interview. If you want to stop at any time and rephrase that's fine."

"I appreciate that, but I've done this before. I'm good."

"All right then, mighty fine. Pandora, it seems like your show has stirred up a hornet's nest in Port Orchard, Washington. What's going on down there?"

"A hornet's nest is putting it mildly, Les. We came to

do a show on a missing girl, turned up psychic evidence that a murder had taken place, and now it appears that one of our own has ended up dead."

"That's right. Juliana Robbins. She died just after the taping. What happened to her?"

"I'm supposed to have all the answers, I know, but I don't. I have no idea. The sheriff here is laying all of this at my feet, but neither Wyatt nor I brought this on," she said, holding her gaze steadily on the *Look Here*.

"She was strangled and the house where she was staying was set ablaze, right?" Les asked.

"That's what we hear. I mean, we're not getting much information. She was a part of our TV family and the detectives here have shut us out of the investigation. Stonewalled us."

"Isn't it true that they want your participation? Asked for you to make a statement?"

"That's funny. Excuse me for forgetting to laugh, Les. But they are engaging in a modern-day witch-hunt, trying to insinuate that I had something to do with Juliana's death."

"You say witch-hunt," he said. "That's a pretty tough depiction."

"Well, it is, Les. You're right. People with the gift have been stoned, hanged, burned at the stake for centuries. It's funny how every other special group gets the support of the free-thinking nation, but those with the gift are considered charlatans and purveyors of fraud."

"There have been charges that you're a fraud. I'm glad you mentioned that."

"Les, I don't want to talk about that."

"Our viewers really want to know your take on the complaints of others who have been on your show."

"I told your executive producer that I couldn't get into any specifics on past shows. I'm all about the future anyway. My fans know that."

"All right then. Let's get back to the case that brought you to Washington."

"Katy Frazier," she said, doing an imitation of concern—the same one she used on her show. "She was sixteen when she went missing four years ago. My guides told me that she'd been molested and murdered by someone close to her."

"My understanding is that you named her father, a prominent local architect."

"I can't say anything about that," she said. "You'll have to watch the show. I will say that, however, this is the best work that I've done."

"What do you say to the families who think that you've capitalized on their tragedies?"

"I never come looking to hurt someone. Every person who I've tried to find, every crime I've tried to solve, has come by request of those who come to me for help."

"So are you saying that it's sour grapes, you know, when things don't turn out the way they want them to?"

"A bitter pill is more like it. These loud naysayers and complainers need to get in front of a mirror and examine themselves. Evil sought them out for a reason. The price they pay now will be paid over and over until they reconcile that."

"Pretty strong stuff."

"The truth is strong stuff."

"Okay, Pandora. I think that wraps up what we need. You were great. Thank you. Now, is there anything you want to add?"

"A couple of things, Les. Will you mention my upcoming book, *The Heart of the Matter: My Life with the Greatest Gift*? It will be out in a few months. Pre-order now on Amazon."

"All right, will do. What else?"

"People die because they are supposed to die. It's the balance of the earth and it cannot be changed by anyone. Katy and Juliana, while tragic to us, have moved on to a higher level of consciousness and for that we should be grateful. Maybe even jealous."

"But Juliana was murdered, Pandora."

"What difference does it make how someone gets there?"

Birdy pushed her chair back when Kendall appeared in her office.

"I thought you'd be coming by this a.m.," Birdy said.

Kendall made a face. "You saw the show too?"

"Yes," Birdy said. "I can't say I think much of her acting, but I do think Pandora's internal script is a particularly fascinating one."

Kendall sat down. "She really is unbelievable."

"To us. But to others she's, you know . . ."

"The real deal," Kendall said, completing the statement that had become almost a running joke. "Now she's acting like she's being victimized by us, or mostly by me."

"I got that. She wants the world to believe that she's part of some persecuted, protected class of citizenry."

"Exactly. I didn't know liars and manipulators were protected."

"Only those in politics, anyway."

Kendall laughed. It was the first laugh in a long time.

"Maybe she'll run for office," the detective said.

Birdy nodded. "She'd probably win."

"I don't know, Birdy. We'll have to see how things shake out after our interview."

"Did I hear you correctly?"

"Yes, at two this afternoon. She called saying that it was time to clear the air. I think she's just coming so she can go on the news again and complain about harassment or the like. I'll see you there, won't I?"

"Wouldn't miss it."

BOOK THREE
KATY

CHAPTER FORTY-ONE

Madison King thought the half-dead coffee-roasting machine that her cheap-ass boss insisted was still "good enough" had finally given up the ghost when she arrived for work at 4:30 A.M. at the restaurant in downtown Port Orchard that she'd worked at since graduating from college. Madison had wanted to get a job as a teacher, but her student-teaching experience that previous year had taught her a lesson of her own.

She could deal with the fourth graders at East Port Orchard Elementary just fine. Their parents, however, were another matter. They were either absent or so pushy that Madison was all but certain bruises would appear on her body like mini storm clouds the day after any encounter. When she dreamed of being a teacher she never considered the other half of the job—the dads who hit on her, the moms who wedged themselves into every activity, the social workers who could barely remember the names of the kids for whom they were responsible.

Opening up the Bay Street Café for the day was easy enough. She started her day early, which meant she'd end it while there was enough time in the day to chase another dream. There was a problem with that, however. Madison just wasn't sure *which* dream to pursue.

The whiff of what she thought was a burned-out coffee roaster assaulted her when she parked her car behind the restaurant. She'd been fighting a cold and sniffed a little deeper.

It wasn't burned coffee beans and motor oil. It smelled worse than that. It reminded her of the smell of burned hair and maybe something else.

Gasoline?

Madison pinched her nose and went toward the café's back door. Movement filled her peripheral vision.

"Get!" she called as she turned toward a bunch of water rats that were swarming over something by the receptacle where several businesses along that waterfront hid their Dumpsters from customers' view.

Madison hated rats. When she was making her list of career options, she was sure that had never wanted to be a vet.

At least not one that ever had to deal with rodents.

As the large-enough-to-be-completely-gross rats dispersed, Madison let out a scream. It was dark and she was alone but it took only a few seconds for Tim Boyle to reach her. Tim worked at Lunchbox Express, a food truck that catered to the foot-ferry crowd that crossed Sinclair Inlet on their way to their jobs at the shipyard in Bremerton.

"Maddie, you all right?" he called over.

Madison stood still as she kept her eyes on Tim, a big guy with a red beard and two gold earrings.

"What is it?"

"Over there," she said. "Look!"

The light was dim that time of morning, but Tim had no problem seeing what the young woman had discovered.

He didn't know who it was, of course. But Janie Thomas had been found.

Kendall Stark stood next to Birdy Waterman as she conducted the forensic exam and autopsy of the middle-aged female they were all but certain was Janie Thomas. The smell of burning flesh filled the air of the basement autopsy suite. Janie had been naked except for a nylon bra that had melted onto her breasts and a pair of jeans, unbuttoned and pulled down to expose her blackened lower torso.

"It's her, isn't it?"

"All but certain," Birdy said, swiping a light over the teeth. "She had an implant on the front tooth. Cracked it when she was fourteen."

"Must have been a car accident or something," Kendall said.

"Not sure about that," Birdy said. "Records indicate several implants."

Kendall leaned in as Birdy pointed to the right top front tooth. It was white, while the others were darker.

"Porcelain doesn't change with heat," she said.

Kendall thought of the time when Steven had taken them camping and had tried to heat a mug of coffee next to the campfire. The mug exploded, but when they put out the fire before they left, the shards of white sparkled against the sooty remains of the logs they'd used to build the blaze.

"It's her," Kendall said.

"Yes."

"God, I'll have to tell Erwin and Joe. They'll want to know how she died. Can you tell?"

Birdy pointed to a vent-like opening on the right side of the charred neck.

"She was stabbed in the neck. Looks like one clean wound. I'll check the lungs of course, but I'll bet you lunch that she died quickly and the fire was a cover-up."

"Like Juliana?"

"Yes, the cover-up part. Seems like our favorite serial killer likes to mix it up a little when it comes to the killing part. Strangled Juliana, and Janie got a knife in the throat."

"Call me when you're done, Birdy. I'm going to go see Erwin now. I don't want him to find out from the media that Janie's body's been found. Let me know if you turn up anything more."

Birdy nodded and went back to her work. She did everything she needed to do. It was a lot harder to conduct an autopsy with a badly burned victim. The flesh didn't yield. The liquid in the body had dried and tox reports were more of a challenge. She took her time, letting Stan Getz take her on the journey of what the body could tell her. A couple of hours later, she was done. Photos taken. Janie rebuilt the best she could. Her melted bra, pants, and a keychain and some change in her pockets. All of it bundled up for the final report.

Cause of death: Homicide. Manner: A single wound to the neck.

*   *   *

The look in his eyes told Kendall that she was too late. Erwin Thomas had already heard the news.

"A reporter from the *Sun* called and wanted a statement."

"I'm so sorry," Kendall said. "I didn't want that to happen. Not at all."

"Come in," he said, letting her inside. "I thought it would end like this anyway. In fact, it probably sounds awful but I hoped it would. I couldn't ever trust her again. I couldn't be the husband sitting by her side at the trial. It would have dragged on for a couple of years with no real endgame."

He led Kendall to the kitchen.

"Does Joe know?"

"He's not up yet. Late night, I guess. I'll tell him."

"That'll be hard, Erwin."

"I know. But we've talked a lot about his mother. Things about her life that he didn't know. I'm not ever going to defend her, but there are probably reasons why she ended up the way she did." He stopped and offered Kendall water. "Ran out of coffee. Janie used to do all of our shopping."

"I'm really sorry about all of this," Kendall said.

"I know. But it isn't your fault. She didn't run off because of you. I've read the papers. I've seen the TV. I know that you had some kind of connection with Brenda too."

Kendall didn't like the sound of that.

"Let's be clear. I didn't have any connection with Brenda Nevins. I interviewed her for a case. That's it."

"Yes, but she was fixated on you. At least that's what the papers say."

"The papers are wrong. You should know that better than anyone by now."

"I guess so. Anyway, I don't really care anymore. Joe will want to know how his mom died. Do you know? I heard she was burned alive."

"No," Kendall said, still bothered by the notion that Brenda and she were connected in any way. "She died before the fire."

"How? How was she killed?"

"She'd been stabbed. I'm sorry."

"Was it prolonged?"

Kendall couldn't tell if Erwin was interested from a forensic point of view or if he'd been hopeful that Janie had suffered.

"No, it was quick."

He nodded. "I guess that's a blessing."

Kendall was unsure if he was saying the right thing just to say it, or if he'd been a little disappointed.

"You'll catch her, won't you, Detective?"

"The world is after her. She can't hide forever. Despite the lore that's being forged by the media right now, she's not that smart."

Erwin nodded and got up from his chair. "I want to show you something before you go." She followed him back to the living room where he retrieved a single sheet of paper.

"I gave a copy to the FBI," he said. "I found it in Janie's things. None of it matters now. Now that she's dead."

Kendall took the paper and started to read.

All my life I've been running from the past. What was done to me by those who said they loved me.

*I wonder if it is possible that there could be
a genuine attraction between disparate,
disenfranchised people—people who share a
common bond yet have nothing in common.
I'm drawn to her only because she seems to
understand me in a way that my husband and
son never could. I've had all of this locked inside
for the longest time. I feel my resistance is
weakening every day and that I might find
myself doing something that could change the
course of the rest of my life. I find myself
wanting to let go. Abdicate my power. Even be
dominated by a kindred spirit, someone who can
take me places I've never dreamed of going.*

Kendall looked up from the paper. Erwin had moved across the room and was facing out the window.

"Was she writing about Brenda?" she asked, going closer to where he stood.

Janie's husband didn't turn around. He kept his eyes on the small grove of swaying birch trees in the yard.

"I guess so," he said. "Hard to say for sure. It wasn't addressed to anyone. The FBI agent said she thought so."

"I'm sorry," Kendall said.

Erwin rolled his shoulders a little. "You've said that a couple of times today already."

He was right.

"I have. None of what happened is about you, Erwin."

"I've tried to believe that," he said, at last allowing some emotion to seep into his words. "But when I read that note, I realized that I never knew how unhappy my wife of twenty-five years had been. I'd been blind to her suffering. That makes me feel stupid. Like crap. It dawned on me that I didn't really know her at all."

Kendall felt the same way about Steven. She didn't know how he could just move away for a job. Leave her. Leave Cody. She thought that they were solid. Forever. Over the last few weeks she began to wonder if they'd be able to find what they once had.

"No one knows what's inside another person's mind," she said.

CHAPTER FORTY-TWO

At first he didn't know what to think. Wyatt Ogilvie looked at the wad of cash he'd discovered in Pandora's travel bag. He'd had no business going there, but he needed some headache pills—or something stronger—and there it was: $20,000 in crisp, sweet-smelling thousand dollar bills.

He fanned it like a Vegas dealer and looked in the mirror. He wondered where it came from and, more important, if he was going to get a share. He had his eye on a new Armani suit and some Porsche eyeglass frames that made him look both cool and sophisticated.

Why hadn't she said anything?

Pandora was on the phone talking to someone when he returned from his accidental treasure hunt in the bathroom.

"Oh yes. That sounds good. Will Nan be there for makeup? I'm not doing it without decent makeup. My face looked flat as a pancake the last time I was beamed into America's breakfast rooms."

She listened.

Wyatt stood there, hovering over her with a slight glower on his face.

". . . If the car is late, I'll panic. I don't like to be late for anything."

She hung up.

"What's gotten in to you? You look like you're going to hurl. God, I can't catch a bug now."

"I am sick," he said.

"Did you want me to call the hotel doctor?" she asked.

Wyatt knew her well enough to see the practiced concern she had on her face whenever she used it on show, mostly aimed at the parent of a missing child. It was a phony as a three-dollar bill. The thought brought him back to the real bills, the $20,000 that had raised his hackles. He squeezed the wad of cash in his palm, hidden from view.

"No doctor," he said. "He wouldn't know the cure for being double-crossed."

Pandora's face tightened.

"I don't get your meaning, Wyo," she said. "What's bugging you now?"

"Pandy, where'd you get this?" he asked, holding out the money.

Her face relaxed. "Oh, that," she said like it was nothing. "I forgot to mention it to you. I got it from Brit."

Wyatt could feel his blood pressure rise. "You told me she gave you five thousand dollars," he said.

She didn't go as far as yawning, like she was bored, but the look on her face was one of complete dismissal.

"I don't think I ever said that," she said.

"You did."

"I really don't think so, but maybe. A lot has been

going on this week. A lot on my mind. I'm sorry, babe. The usual split, okay?"

He sat on the chair opposite Pandora. The view looked out at the city. She reached over and patted his hand.

"I would never cheat you," she said. "We are partners, babe. Everything we do, we do together."

Wyatt sat there, very still, thinking, *knowing* that he'd been had.

"I don't think so," he said. "I don't know that I trust you anymore." He watched her reaction. She had none. Not that he could really discern. That was unusual. Pandora was always an eager emoter.

"Who was that you were talking to just now?" he asked.

Pandora ran her fingers through her hair and applied a fresh coat of her trademark dark red lipstick—the hue that haters online said looked like she'd been punched in the mouth.

"Which she totally deserves . . ."

"A producer," she said. "They want us to do the *Today* Show."

"When?"

"I didn't commit. I don't think we should do *Today*. They are number two and I am top-tier talent."

He noticed the omission and his face telegraphed it.

"We are," she said. "We are a duo. I won't make a move until we discuss it further."

"I don't believe you," he finally said. He'd seen her work people before. He wasn't blind. No matter what she thought of herself, Wyatt Ogilvie was absolutely certain that she would never be Emmy-worthy.

Her face turned to granite. "Wyo, you are being so

ridiculous and I don't like it one bit. It makes me feel uncomfortable. When I'm uncomfortable I can't do my job. You know that."

He did. She was worse than the most demanding '80s band when it came to her requirements for a shoot. Four bottles of Pellegrino—nothing else—and pity the poor assistant producer who delivered Aquafina. That kid was working as a weather assistant in Sioux Falls. She needed bedsheets of 800 count in her hotel room, a request that was no problem at a place like the W. But in the middle of Alabama farm country, the local Comfort Inn had no idea what 800 thread count meant. She also needed a bottle of Dom, chilled and ready, alongside a welcome basket of black grapes and nectarines.

Wyatt needed her more than she needed him. Nothing was more clear to him. Pandora was making things happen and if he was able to hang on for the ride he'd manage to fill his closet with Armanis.

"I know this has been a hard shoot for you," he said.

"It has. I looked terrible in the footage."

"I meant Juliana. I know you two were close."

She looked out the window. "Yes. I'm sick about what happened to her. I've been trying to grab something that is passing through my mind. About what happened."

The real deal.

"What have you been getting?" he asked.

"I don't know. You know how I've told you that things are sometimes so dark and grainy that I can't quite make out what's going on."

He'd heard that a thousand times before. Whenever Pandora missed his cues, the research that he'd done to lead her where she needed to go, she complained that things were grainy.

"I'm so damn frustrated," she once screamed at him on a show. "I can see it. I can almost see it. Someone is trying to show me something!"

"Were you really going to give me the money?" he asked.

"Of course."

"Is there any more to be had?"

"Oh, babe, there's always more. Remember Wheeling?"

Of course he did. The father of a dead mother of three pleaded poverty and offered her a $2,000 check for a private consultation. He was adamant that his daughter's husband had killed her.

Pandora looked at the check.

"Two things," she said. "I don't do checks. I also don't even turn around for less than five thousand dollars."

"I don't have it," the distraught father said.

Pandora shrugged. "Then you'll never know what happened to her," she said.

His eyes flashed, puddled with tears. "Are you holding some information hostage?" he asked. "That isn't right."

Pandora ignored the man's frustration, his genuine emotion. His complete despair.

"What isn't right is your being so cheap when it comes to your dead daughter," she said. "Honestly, sir, don't waste any more of my time. Move along. Get on with your life."

"But I don't have any more money."

She was in predator mode just then. Wyatt had seen it before when she got the assistant producer fired for bringing her the wrong brand of water.

"I don't drink water from any damn spring in California! What are you trying to do to me? Poison me?"

Pandy the Predator.

"Sell something," she said to the girl's father. "I don't care. I'm not a charity. The truth might set you free, but the truth sometimes comes with a price tag."

The man pulled it together. He would not cry. He would not beg. He gave in.

"All right. I'll get you the money."

"When?" she pushed.

"Now. I have it in my safe."

Pandora shook her head and her eyes met Wyatt's.

"I don't like being deceived," she said, without even the slightest trace of irony in her voice.

Wyatt replayed that moment in his head. He'd seen what she could do. He'd known she was one step above the criminals he'd apprehended when he was a detective in San Francisco. There were times when he hated her. Times when he couldn't wait to be with her. But there was never a time when he trusted her completely.

"Are we good?" she asked.

"Solid," he said. "Solid as a rock."

CHAPTER FORTY-THREE

It's a five-hour drive from Port Orchard to Spokane, long enough to justify a plane ticket, but Kendall decided that she needed the time alone to process everything that had been going on. The drive would do her good. She arranged for a sitter to take Cody to school and pick him up.

"I'll be home late," she said.

"Butter noodles?" the young woman asked.

Cody liked one thing. Make that two. Popcorn and butter noodles.

"Grate some cheese on top. He needs more protein and he's doing a good job of expanding his horizons."

She kissed her sleeping son goodbye and headed out in the dawn of a new day. Seagulls hovered over the inlet in front of her house in Harper and she caught the second boat out of Southworth, grateful that it didn't include a stop at Vashon Island—an inconvenience that irritated many leaving the Kitsap Peninsula. She listened to the news as she looked over the bow of the boat as it chugged across Puget Sound to the dock in

West Seattle. She thought of that first date with Steven so many years ago. They took his car over to a concert in Seattle, but it broke down and they had to hitch a ride back. They'd laughed about it back then. Today, busy as everyone is, there was no time for the unexpected. Every moment had to be programmed to the nth degree.

She longed for Steven to come home.

It was too early to call him, so she texted a short note.

Going to Spokane to work cold case. Cody's with Marsha. Missing you.

She pushed SEND.

As the cars rumbled off over the pier deck, she thought of all that had happened in the past few days. Katy's case had been supplanted by Juliana's. Juliana's had been supplanted by the drama of the disappearace of Brenda Nevins and Janie Thomas from the prison. In the wake of all the tragedy, the murders, the fire, the horrible *Spirit Hunters* TV show, there was the distinct feeling that the world was spinning out of control.

Her world too.

Kendall got on the interstate and absorbed the glorious view of Seattle's skyline, the football and baseball stadiums, and drove east, thinking of everything and nothing at the same time. Everything had been smudged, blurred, altered. She crossed over the mountain pass at Snoqualmie and the landscape shifted from green Douglas firs to the burnished brown grasslands and verdant farmlands of the eastern half of the state. She filled her SUV's tank at Vantage, a truck stop, convenience store, and restaurant perched on the bluff over the mighty Columbia River.

* * *

Nick Mayberry was sitting in the Peacock Lounge at the historic Davenport Hotel. He drank coffee and nervously swirled his spoon in the cup. He was almost fifty with a slight paunch and thinning hair punctuated by white sidewalls. Nick wore a jacket over a uniform, concealing his profession from the casual observers in the bar. Overhead, a magnificent stained glass peacock loomed.

"More coffee, Nicky?" the waitress asked.

He indicated his cup. "Thanks, Carla."

"You okay?" she asked. "You seem, I dunno, sort of distracted. You waiting on someone?"

He nodded. "Yeah."

"You're not Internet dating again? You know that only brings out the losers and the pretenders."

"No," he said. "I'm waiting for someone from the coast."

Those who lived on the eastern side of the state always referred to the western side as "the coast" no matter if the town was a hundred miles inland. Anything on the other side of the Cascades was "the coast."

"All righty," she said. "You take care."

He smiled. "Will do."

Inside there was no smile. There was nothing to be happy about. He'd made a very big mistake four years before and he'd never been able to get it out of his mind. He'd left the Kitsap County Sheriff's Department because of it.

The Davenport Hotel had been resurrected. Opened originally in 1914, it closed in 1985, and had been saved from the wrecking ball in 2000 by a Spokane couple who wanted to bring it back to its former glory. In doing so, they brought back the heart and soul of an inland city that had bragging rights to a gilded past born of mining money that turned a former Indian village into an impressive city. The crown jewel was the Davenport.

After a uniformed valet took her keys and handed her a claim ticket, Kendall found Nick in the bar. She'd known him casually when they were in the department together, but she was working her way up and he was, unfortunately, working his way down. He waved her over to his table and stood to greet her.

"Been a while," he said.

"Yes, it has. How you been, Nick?"

"Can't complain," he said as they both sat down. "You?"

She could complain about a million things, but none that she'd share with him right then.

"I'm fine. I wish I could say that about the Katy Frazier case."

"Yeah. Saw that in the paper."

Carla poured her coffee and asked if they wanted menus. Kendall hadn't eaten for hours and ordered the Crab Louis, a salad that had been originally created at the Davenport. Nick had a four-cheese grilled sandwich. While they waited for their food to arrive they talked about Port Orchard, the department, and its grab-bag mix of personalities.

"I miss that place," he said.

"Why did you leave, Nick? What happened?"

Carla delivered the food and asked if they needed anything else.

"We're good," he said. "Thanks, kiddo."

"Are you a regular here?"

"Kind of," he said. "I mean, I'm not a cop anymore, Kendall. After what happened in Port Orchard, I just couldn't do the job."

He undid his jacket showing the same valet uniform Kendall had seen on the attendant when she arrived.

"Nick, I didn't know. I thought you were in law enforcement in Post Falls."

"Yeah, that's what I told everyone."

Kendall took a bite of the crab. It was delicious, but she didn't savor it as she would have in other circumstances.

"What happened, Nick?"

"Brit happened. That's what."

Kendall's eyes widened. "Katy's mother?"

"Yeah," he said, his eyes cast downward at his plate. "We had a thing. It was before I had Katy's case, but it heated up again when she went missing." He stopped and picked at the fries next to his sandwich. "I know it was wrong, if that's what you're wondering."

"It's more than wrong," Kendall said, setting down her fork and facing him with riveted eyes.

"You can't beat me up any more than I have already."

She knew he was probably right about that. He'd gone from a good job, one with prestige and a future, to parking cars for well-heeled hotel guests in Spokane. That likely wasn't a single person's dream for a career trajectory.

"What happened? How did it affect the investigation?"

"She was going through something. So was I at the

time. I was drinking a lot at the time. Been sober for three years now."

"Go on with it, Nick. Just tell me."

Nick Mayberry stood motionless when he saw Brit. It had been more than a year. Brit had called him over fifty times since he broke it off. It wasn't that he didn't want her. It was that she was married to a nice guy. He didn't want to be party to a divorce. He'd had his own and never recovered. They'd met in a downtown Port Orchard martini bar. He was drinking Scotch. She was mainlining cosmopolitans. He recognized her from the work she'd done with troubled kids.

"This was before her coffee shop. She talked about it back then. I listened. I listened to everything she said. When I'm loaded on Scotch, I'm a very good listener," he said.

"From there, you became involved?" Kendall asked.

He ate some more of his sandwich and shook his head when Carla lifted the coffeepot from the other side of the room.

"Not that night. But not long after. Look," he said, "I liked her. I felt sorry for her. She seemed anxious, angry. A mix of both. She told me that her husband had let his dreams supersede her own. That her kids were sucking the life out of her and she needed a way out. We met a few times after that. At my place because I lived alone and she had Roger and the girls."

"How long did this go on?" Kendall asked.

"Not very," Nick said. "She was clingy and, basically, too much work. We stayed together for six months, but I knew it was wrong from the outset. I kept trying to break it off, but, you know, the sex was good and I was a lonely drunk with few options."

"So you had an affair with her," Kendall said. "And you broke it off. Is that right?"

"Yeah. But there's more to it." He pushed himself away from the table. "Brit was my downfall. Not kidding. I know that I should be accountable for what happened. I know that in my heart of hearts, but damn, she just led me over the edge."

Nick Mayberry knew the address. He'd actually been inside the house twice when Roger was gone and the girls were in Seattle doing whatever a twelve-year-old and sixteen-year-old could do. He was glad he didn't have kids. He'd seen so many come through the justice system with futures written in erasable ink.

"It's you," Brit said, her eyes rimmed in red, as she opened the door. "I'm glad it was you. Roger's here," she said, this time her voice low.

Nick followed her inside the "Flash Cube," looking around as though it was the first time. Roger Frazier got up and introduced himself. Nick took out a small black notebook—one that he now used to calculate tips he'd received from his job as a valet. Back then it was an investigative notebook.

The couple told him that Katy hadn't been seen for hours and they were worried.

"Normally we don't start a missing persons case this soon."

"She's a good kid," Roger said. "Star athlete. Top-ten student. Something is seriously wrong, Detective. Seriously."

"He's right," Brit said, crumpling a tissue in her hands. "Katy is the apple of our eyes."

Nick knew that was a lie. Her daughter was the scourge of her life. She'd said so many, many times.

He made some notes. Captured the names of those who most likely had seen the girl before she vanished. Looking around her bedroom showed just what Roger Frazier had described. A very good girl. A desk set up for homework. A bed with white eyelet sheets, crisp and neatly made. In the bathroom, he detected some small drops of blood.

"What's that?" Roger said, though he likely knew what the oval droplets were.

"Don't know," Nick said. "Could be blood. Lab techs will be down. Don't touch anything."

Carla took their plates and offered dessert, but both declined.

"I interviewed her friends and they told me that they'd planned on seeing her after class, but she was a no-show."

Kendall kept her eyes locked on him. She didn't understand what happened. She pointedly asked him.

"Why did the investigation stall, Nick?"

"Brit and me. That's why. Honestly, that's the truth. In the middle of her daughter missing she needed comfort and I stupidly went there. I know with every fiber of my being that it sounds completely predatory on my part, but the roles were reversed. Honestly. I just let her cry on my shoulder and one thing led to another."

"So are you thinking she got rid of her daughter, is that it?"

"Hell, no. She didn't have a thing to do with it. I'm sure of it. The funny thing was that she wasn't all that broken up about it. She told me over and over that when Katy came back she was going to beat her ass with a yardstick. Does that sound like a mother who killed her kid?"

Kendall thought it sounded like a Port Orchard version of *Mommie Dearest*, but she didn't say so.

"That's all you got, Nick?" she asked. "A feeling that because she was going to discipline her child that she couldn't possibly have made her disappear?"

"I guess so," he said.

"You really screwed up here," she said.

"I told you I know that already. Park some other guy's Lexus for the rest of your life. Drive your Hyundai home every night to your walk-up apartment in a crappy part of Spokane. You'll be reminded every day that you screwed up."

"What happened with Brit?" she asked.

"We broke it off. We kind of had to. One of the kids saw us kiss. Said she'd tell the sheriff and Roger what she'd seen."

"Who was it?"

"Alyssa Woodley. She'd moved into Katy's bedroom. Said she was there to help Naomi and Brit, but I think she might have had other motives."

"Like what? What are you getting at?"

"I'm not sure. Really, I'm not. Part of me thought that Katy had run away from her mother because she couldn't stand her. The other part of me thought that Alyssa had something to do with it. She was just too involved. Always there, listening, checking in on the investigation. A regular junior detective, that one."

"Too helpful?"

He folded his arms. "Like the firebug who befriends

the firemen in his neighborhood and is always there when the sirens sound."

"I know the type," she said.

"I didn't like that girl. Not one bit. But when she caught me and Brit making out I was a little relieved. I knew I'd crossed the line and that I'd compromised the investigation. I gave notice two days later."

"I remember your departure seemed sudden. I thought you'd taken a job in Post Falls that was more to your liking. A better fit."

Nick's face was grim, but his eyes were full of repentance.

"This was my better fit, Kendall," he said. "I'm parking cars and staying away from law enforcement." His voice trailed off to a whisper as Carla came with the check. "There's no forgiving the cop who screws the missing girl's mother."

He reached for the check.

"I'll get this," he said. "I have an employee discount."

"You know that I'll have to report what you told me," Kendall said. "The affair will probably wind its way into the papers. Nothing I can do about it."

He nodded. "I know. I've got nothing to lose anyway. Lost everything that was important to me with I went to bed with Brit Frazier. I just didn't know it at the time."

Kendall waited for the attendant to bring her car into the covered entrance to the hotel. She noticed that she'd received a call from Birdy and dialed her back.

"How did it go with Mayberry?" Birdy asked right away.

"Just got done," she said, stepping away from a young couple in the valet queue. "Said he was having an affair with Brit Frazier. Said his judgment was clouded by alcohol. Said that Alyssa is a puppet master. Did you know she moved in with the Fraziers?"

Birdy didn't. "I guess your trip to Spokane has been fruitful."

"I guess so. It feels a little sad, a little after the fact. Brad is going to have to earn his paycheck when it gets out that one of our own was bagging the mother of a potential murder victim."

"We don't know that she's dead, Kendall."

"I know. But I think she is. And I think that Alyssa knows more than she's saying."

"I know you want to get back here, but I have an address you might want to check out."

"Whose?"

Birdy didn't say. "Texting it to you now," she said.

A beat later, Kendall looked down as the text message appeared on the small screen of her phone.

"No shit? She's here? You're right. This might be fun."

CHAPTER FORTY-FOUR

Spokane's South Hill is rightly known for its stately homes and beautiful parks, the highlight of which is Manito Park, a sprawling oasis of trees, trails, and play spaces for children. Kendall parked in front of an olive green Craftsman-style home sandwiched between a Tudor and a Victorian. The low-slung front porch was painted white and looked clean enough to dress a baby on. Kendall knocked on the door and watched through the window as a woman approached, the cherry-tip glow of a cigarette dangling from her lips.

The woman yanked the door open. "Who the hell are you?" she asked, before giving Kendall a chance to introduce herself.

It was a startling way of greeting a visitor.

"I'm Kendall Stark, investigator for the Kitsap County Sheriff's Department," Kendall answered, half watching for the cigarette to fall from the homeowner's crinkled lips.

"So?" she said. "What do you want?"

Kendall had been greeted with more friendliness from a meth dealer in Seabeck than from this lady.

"Is Pandora your daughter?"

"Pandora. Hmm . . ." The woman smiled and shook her head a little. "I guess you could call her that."

"Good," Kendall said, although she had let it cross her mind that it might not have been altogether bad if she'd been at the wrong address. "I'm investigating a case," she said, keeping her tone even and as warm as she could. Given the circumstances and the older woman's attitude, that wasn't easy. "It's related to your daughter."

The woman sucked on her cigarette again and blew smoke out her nostrils. She looked like a dragon.

"Is the little bitch dead?" she asked.

This was no "Mommy and me" session here.

"No," Kendall said, taking a slight step backward. "She's not. She's fine."

The woman removed her cigarette and let the ash fall to the floor, where it smoldered. "Too bad. She done me so dirty I don't have much feeling for her."

"Mrs. Kirkowski, may I come in and talk to you?"

"Kirkowski was like . . ." the woman said, pretending to count in her head. "Like four marriages ago. I still use it. But there is no Mr. Kirkowski."

Kendall persisted. "Can we talk?"

Rose Kirkowski—or whatever last name she preferred—looked at the interloper on her doorstep with a wary eye.

"You sure you're not with the *Globe* or something?" she asked. "My no-good daughter said that if I talk to you guys she'll, you know, you know."

Kendall didn't know, but she didn't ask. "No, as I said, I'm with the sheriff's department."

Rose Kirkowski swung the door open. The smell of smoke and cat urine nearly knocked Kendall to the gleaming wood of the pristine white porch. It was repugnant and shocking at the same time. Everything outside the shell of Rose Kirkowski's life was perfection. Inside the house, inside her life, was another matter altogether.

"You want a Bud?"

Kendall shook her head. "No, thanks," she said.

"I'm having one. It's hot today."

Kendall stood in the cluttered and smelly foyer while Pandora's mother went into the kitchen and took the top off a beer bottle.

"Come in here," Rose called from the hall to the kitchen. "If you see my Siamese, La Choy, please grab the little bastard. He's a terror and I can't catch him. I think he has worms."

Kendall was not about to catch that cat. She made her way to the sofa while Rose bent over to scoot aside a stack of *Spokesman Review* newspapers.

Rose was wearing a curious outfit. She had an aqua-colored terry bathrobe over a pair of jeans and house slippers. Her hair was the same length and color as her daughter's.

"Yes, we look alike," she said, catching Kendall's gaze.

Kendall started to say something, but Rose cut her off.

"I'm not psychic," she said "I just get that now and then since my daughter became such a famous bitch."

"You don't like your daughter," Kendall said.

"That's an understatement. If you're here to get the goods on her for something she did, I say it's about time and I'd like to help you."

Kendall tried not to gag as her eyes caught a pile of cat feces in the corner next to a deader-than-a-doornail mother-in-law's-tongue plant in a cracked white chamber pot. Kendall knew the plant with its green and yellow blades. In another moment, she'd allow herself to be drawn back to her family home in Port Orchard, reliving a happy memory of a household in which there was boundless love for everyone within its walls.

That clearly wasn't Rose Kirkowski's home.

"I'm just doing some background," Kendall said.

Rose wiped the condensation off the long neck of her beer bottle "She's got a lot of background," she said. "Lots she wouldn't like anyone to know about. Not now. Now that she's all that."

Kendall glanced around the room. A layer of dust covered most of the furniture on its perimeter. A TV in a cherry entertainment center looked as if it was the center of all attention—a worn trail in the carpet suggested plenty of trips back and forth. Kendall wondered if Rose couldn't find her remote control. There were no personal photos out. The only art on the wall was a Navajo-style blanket and a mirror with a cracked frame. In the farthest corner from the sofa, in the window that looked out at the street, was a cat gymnasium. Three cats sat on top, though none were Siamese or the long-lost, worm-infested La Choy.

"I like cats better than people," Rose said, catching Kendall's gaze on her collection of felines. "I like them better than my daughter, but before I tell you anything about her, you'll need to tell me why you're here."

"Just some background on a case, that's all."

Rose tightened her smoker's lips. "That's crap," she said. "And you know it."

Kendall wanted to say, no, that's crap in the corner. But she didn't.

"She was in Port Orchard recently," Kendall answered. "That's where I live in Kitsap County. She was doing her show and she told us some things we didn't know about one of our old cases."

Rose put her bottle down on a nest of water rings on the table in front of her.

"What she say?" she asked, not looking up. "Say someone else was the killer? Someone else did the kidnapping or something?"

Kendall nodded. "Yes, something along those lines."

Rose looked at Kendall, leaned back, and laughed. It was a hard, loud laugh; so much so that Kendall was surprised the chronic smoker had enough lung capacity for such an annoyingly sustained outburst.

"She says that on every one of those stupid shows she's on. Every single time. I don't know who's a bigger idiot, those who watch the show or the producers who put up with that ridiculous crap. Don't you watch?"

Kendall shook her head. "Not really. I have seen part of an episode."

"Look, my daughter's a liar," Rose said, seemingly enjoying the opportunity to toss her under the bus. "She's a bitch. She's my kid. I know her. I know that she's full of crap. She's always thought she was better than . . ." she said, hesitating a beat.

Me.

". . . than everybody."

"I see," Kendall said.

Rose stared hard at the investigator. She stayed quiet a moment, like she had when she was assessing how many marriages ago she'd been hitched to Mr. Kirkowski. "Do you?" she finally asked, "I mean, you're here in godforsaken Spokane and you're asking me about that bitch of a daughter of mine, I'm thinking, oh no, here's another one of those nitwits who think Carol is some kind of high priestess of truth. She's one step above a carny, if you ask me."

Whatever Pandora's mother had to say was going to be good. Good as in an interesting story to tell, but possibly nothing to help advance the investigation into what happened back in Kitsap County.

"So, Mrs. Kirkowski, humor me—"

"Rose, please. Didn't like Kirkowski that much. Not my favorite husband."

"Fine, Rose then. Are you telling me that you know for sure she's a fraud?"

Rose nodded. "I need another beer. And then I'll do better than tell you. I'll show you."

Pandora's mother got up and went toward the kitchen, leaving Kendall in the squalor of the living room amid the feces and the trio of cats, who now had apparently thought that it might be more fun for them to cuddle up on the lap of the visitor. Kendall was all but certain that one of them was going to spray on her. She used the tip of her toe to push away an aggressive tabby as he backed up toward her. She was intrigued by Rose and her venom-soaked discourse on her daughter, but in reality—at that moment—an interview with an inmate in the worst prison she could think of would be more pleasant than sitting in that pretty-on-the-out-side-but-rotten-on-the-inside-residence on Spokane's famed South Hill.

"Sure you don't want a cold one?" Rose called over her shoulder as she fished around the back of the fridge for some beers.

"No, I'm good," Kendall said, pushing another cat away.

"Out of coffee," Rose called out.

Another cat, another gentle toe-kick. "That's all right. I'm fine."

Finally, Rose returned with two beers.

"Brought me a second," she said. "I call it my standby."

Actually, Kendall thought, *that's your third . . . at least that I know of.*

"You said you could show me," Kendall said.

Rose drank. "Show you?"

"Yes. Show me something that proves she's a phony."

Rose nodded and set down her beer. "That's right. I did. Hang on, whatever your name is."

"Kendall Stark," she said.

"Right. Kendall." Rose was on the other side of the room, pulling a box of papers and some photo albums from under a pile of unlaundered, cat-hair-drenched clothes. She took a seat next to Kendall and opened the first album.

Kendall looked down at a photo of what appeared to be a magician and his assistant. The woman in the photograph was blond and slender. Her eyes glimmered in the black-and-white image. She stood next to a big box and a man in a black tuxedo, smiling broadly, who was motioning her to get inside. An enormous handsaw was in his grasp.

"Is that you?"

Again, the overly long and strange laugh.

"Hell, no," she said, when she finally came up for air. "It's my bitch of a mother. She never cared two cents for me and my sister, Alice. She was all about being a goddamn star!"

Kendall leaned closer to get a better look, the smoky air clinging to Rose's terry robe like a smelly, brittle shell. She pulled away.

"She was a magician's assistant," she said.

Rose tapped the page with her nicotine-stained finger and then turned the page.

"Among other things," she said, her tone softening a little. "Yeah, she was." She pointed to the next photograph. It showed her mother on what looked like a Western TV show.

"*Gunsmoke*," she said. "She was a part-time actress and a full-time whore on the set there. At least that's what one of my dads told me about her years ago. She was always trying to make it. I wouldn't live that life for nothing. I just wanted to get away from show business. As far away as possible. That's why I'm here in Spokane. Can you think of a less glamorous place than this hellhole?"

"It's not so bad," Kendall said, almost feeling sorry for the woman. "You live in a lovely neighborhood."

She couldn't say anything about the house, but she bet the Tudor and the Victorian residents had some choice words to say about the house that separated the two of them.

"Whatever," Rose said. "I was stupid to think I

could run away from my past. I literally thought that by living here I could raise my little girl to be, you know, something normal. But my mother wouldn't allow that. No. Not at all."

She turned the page.

On it was a picture of an old woman crouched over a crystal ball. On the wall behind her was the name Pandora.

"Is that your mother?" Kendall asked.

Rose nodded.

"Yeah," Rose said, her voice a little softer than it had been. "She had a little career going for a time. Some TV. That stupid magic act in Reno. Nothing huge. She was always leaving and telling me and Alice that her big break was about to happen and she'd be a big star. Bigger than Marilyn Monroe, if you can believe that. Well, stupid us, we believed her at first. Forgave her for missed birthdays, Christmas, and all that other crap that she insisted wasn't really as important as being a star. To her. That was what she wanted. We hated her. Alice, believe it or not, more than me. Mom was such a liar."

She paused and regarded her beer, took a sip, and then pointed back to the photo of the fortune-teller.

"That's what she ended up doing. She was playing to an audience of one in a hole-in-the-wall in Hollywood as Madame Pandora, the Soothsayer to the Stars. I hated my mother so much for that. I hated her even more when she filled Carol's head with the idea that she too could be a famous star, this time on TV, that she could be psychic."

Kendall didn't know what to say. It was a pathetic story and Rose was living proof that her mother's neglect was generational, born from experiences foisted upon her.

"I'm sorry," she finally said.

Rose closed the book.

"You don't need to be sorry," she said, though not convincingly. "I'm not. I'm glad the little bitch is gone from here. I don't have to watch her implode, like my mother did. I don't have to listen to someone say crappy things about her at the hair salon. If they do, I just try to shrug it off."

Kendall doubted that. Rose Kirkowski was not the kind of woman to do damage control for her daughter. Not one iota.

"Like your mother, your daughter is very ambitious," Kendall said.

"Not even close. Carol would sell me into sex slavery if that meant she'd see her name in lights. She'd screw me over every which way but Sunday. Probably Sunday too. My mom filled her head with ideas. Carol moved out of here and in with Mom when she was sixteen. I've only seen her four times since. That's right, four freaking times. My mom was a bit player at heart. Carol is heartless. There's a difference. I mean, growing up I felt sorry for my mom. I vowed I would never do to my kids what she did to me."

"But she turned on you. Why?"

"Because . . ." her voice trailed off. "That's a good one. I don't like talking about it."

Kendall used the five words she hated to trot out. "But you can tell me."

Those words always felt so disingenuous. Even though she was there to gather evidence and the subject always knew that, it suddenly turned the conversation to something personal. It was as if by using those words it was only "between you and me" and it wouldn't go further.

Which was always a lie.

"I guess so. You have kids?"

"A son."

"I wish I had a boy. Boys are nice to their mothers. Girls, well, they just turn on you when they graduate from T-shirts to bras. There's no putting the genie back in the bottle after that."

"What happened with Carol?"

"My mother. That's what happened to her. She put her through a kind of boot camp to fame. She had a few friends in the business—don't ask me how—I'd have thought everyone she screwed back in Hollywood would have been dead by now—and she made some calls. The son of one of her friends with benefits or whatever you want to call it had a production company and they were looking for someone to play a medium in search of justice."

"*Spirit Hunters.*"

"Right. That piece-of-crap show. Anyway, the producers there wanted her to play a medium who solves crimes."

"Sounds like a great concept, I guess."

"Right. NBC had a show like that. But this one was different. A so-called reality show. The show was far from reality. It is a complete sham. They tell her what to say. She even wears an earpiece so that they can feed crap to her when she's sitting around acting all knowing."

"I guess I'm not surprised," Kendall said. "I can see them feeding her words."

"Yeah, but there's more. The producer in charge was molested by her father so she has it in for every man on the show. She told Carol that whenever the story line can work it in, the target of the show needs to be the dad."

"So they know all of this ahead of time?"

Rose nodded and finished her beer. She was on to number two, or three, depending on where the counting started.

"Yeah. *Spirit Hunters*, what a goddamn joke. That anyone believes it is beyond me."

"Can I take a picture of the photo of your mom? The one as Pandora?"

"You're not going to sell it to the *Globe*, are you?"

Kendall shook her head. "No, for the case."

Rose hesitated, regarding Kendall, and then opened the book. Kendall took out her phone and snapped a couple of photographs. When Rose wasn't looking, she took a picture of the cats and mess all around her. The first one was for the case; the second was to remind herself that law enforcement was sometimes very dirty and not at all glamorous work. She'd show that one to Birdy, who occasionally said that it looked like it was fun to go out interviewing people.

"At least your people can answer your questions," Birdy had said.

"Yours answer too, though not with words."

As Kendall got up to leave, Rose dropped a bit of a bomb.

"Just so you know," she said, "my mother and my daughter are cut from the same cloth."

"I gather that," Kendall said.

"There isn't anything Carol wouldn't do to keep

moving up the charts, or the fame ladder, or whatever. I mean nothing. It's in her DNA."

"What exactly do you mean, Rose?" Kendall asked.

Rose lit another cigarette by striking the match on the rough edge of the beer bottle.

"I mean, she'd kill someone and go have a big breakfast afterward. That's how she's wired. If you're here because of the show, that's one thing. But I read *Radar* and the *Enquirer* online and know about the producer who got off'd in your little burg of Port Orchard."

Rose was surprisingly well-informed, Kendall thought, though her sources weren't the best. She'd never brought up Juliana's death. Not once. The whole time Rose Kirkowski had known about it.

All about it.

After leaving Rose Kirkowski's smelly house, it passed through her mind that there was a great irony to the sweet-smelling name of Pandora's mother. The house stank to high heaven.

So did the family.

In her car, Kendall checked her phone, while two boys played in front of the Tudor. Two missed calls. One from Birdy. One from Steven. Kendall didn't want to talk to him just then and it bothered her that she felt that way. She was hurt, angry, and unwilling to hash out the same thing over and over. If he didn't want to come home, so be it. She'd figure things out. She dialed Birdy.

"How's the Inland Empire?" Birdy said upon answering.

"The what?"

"That's what they call Spokane now. Or at least that's what they are wanting it to be known as."

Kendall grinned. "Really? I thought they called it Spokevegas."

"That too," Birdy said. "How did go with Rose Kirkowski? I'm dying of curiosity here. Before I saw it on the Internet, I didn't think Pandora had a mother," Birdy said. "I thought she crawled out of some primordial ooze somewhere dark and inaccessible to normal beings."

"That's about how I feel about her too," Kendall said.

The boys playing catch almost hit her car, but Kendall just smiled at them.

"So what's the mother's story?" Birdy asked.

"Mother is a chain-smoking alcoholic who despises her daughter and hates her own mother even more. Says that her mom was sometimes an actress and I believe her exact words were 'full-time whore.'"

"Sounds delightful," Birdy said, without a whiff of sarcasm. "I bet Christmas is fun at their house."

The boys went into the house.

"I'll send the photos later and you'll soon grow to feel sorry for me," Kendall said. "Anyway, she said that her mother was the one who gave Carol the Pandora stage name and, along with that, the desire for life in the spotlight. She also said that the show was far from reality."

"We know that, don't we?" Birdy said, struck that Kendall even mentioned the obvious. Maybe she hadn't been sure. It was interesting and they'd talk about that another time.

"Yes," Kendall said. "But there's more. The show is a complete setup. Everyone is in on it. One of the producers—Juliana maybe—had been sexually abused by her father and wanted that to be the story line whenever there was a chance to go for it."

"So Roger Frazier had no chance?"

"Right," Kendall said. "Not against the likes of her."

Next, Kendall returned Steven's call, but after five rings it went to voice mail. Her heart sank, but she tried to leave a hopeful, upbeat message.

"In Spokane doing some interviews. Marsha is watching Cody. Wish you were home, Steven. Or better yet, wish you were here. In any case, I'm wishing."

Kendall looked at the time. It would be dark when she got home. She'd gas up in Moses Lake, stop at the Starbucks in Ellensburg, and get there in time to send the sitter home. She'd be beat, but the trip had been worth it.

CHAPTER FORTY-FIVE

Among the many viewers of the *Today* show was Debbi-Jo Patterson. Her two-year-old was up half the night and she was fueling herself with caffeine and steeping herself in worry. She had been concerned about her boss, the owner of the Grey Gull, when he failed to show up for work the day before. While he'd been known to extend his vacation, Chaz Masters wasn't the type to let his staff twist in the wind to wonder when he'd return.

Debbi-Jo rocked her little one and held him on her hip while she dialed the number for the Kitsap County sheriff and asked for the investigator handling the Brenda Nevins case.

"That case is being run out of the FBI field office in Seattle," Darrin, the dispatcher, said. "You seen Nevins?"

"No. I mean maybe. She was here last week drinking Bloody Marys with my boss Chaz Masters. He's real reliable, and well, I'm worried. He was supposed to be back to work and he's not."

"All right," Darrin said. "Let me take your number.

Hang on a sec. Got another call. I'll give you the FBI's number when I come back too."

"All right," Debbi-Jo said. She waited, but then thought better of it. She was spooked, that's all. She hung up the phone. Maybe Chaz will turn up later that day and they'll have a good laugh over the very idea that he was offed by some sexy serial killer.

Yes, she thought. *We'll have a good laugh over that one.*

After her shift, Debbie-Jo dropped her son off at day care and drove down the long, winding road to Chaz's place in the woods. She knew it was stupid and that he'd probably chew her out for being such a worrywart, but she just couldn't help herself.

His car was missing, but there was another in the driveway that she did not recognize.

"Maybe his car broke down and he had to get a loaner," she told herself as she knocked on the front door. When there was no answer, she did what most people would do. She twisted the knob and swung it open. The air was foul and the stench came at her. She knew immediately what she smelled, but she hoped it was a dead raccoon. Chaz had told her that there was a family of the critters in the attic and he'd done his best to try to get them out of there humanely.

"Chaz? You home?" she called out as her nose pulled her to the source of the smell in the bedroom.

Debbi-Jo let out the scream of her life. Slumped in the bed was the nude figure of the man she'd adored from afar. He was bloated, features distended. His face appeared to be wrapped in a cocoon of plastic. The only thing that told her it was her boss was the tattoo of a seagull across his chest. She'd seen the ink when a drunk patron spilled his drink and he needed to change.

Cody Stark grinned up from the breakfast table. Kendall caught her husband's expression in the little boy's face and it made her miss what had become of their now very fractured family.

Birdy called.

"Turn on the TV. Channel five. Pandora's about to go on *Today*. They are promoting it as an exclusive interview about her close friend and producer Juliana Robbins's murder. Call me back when it's over."

Kendall set her phone down and turned on the small television that sat next to the toaster. She'd purchased it so she could follow along on a cooking show, but that was before she got a tablet.

The toothy but earnest host, Savannah, introduced Pandora, who was on satellite from Seattle.

Kendall wondered when the woman was going to go home. Maybe a trip to see her mother in Spokane would do her some good.

"What I have to say is very disturbing, Savannah. But I've never seen the need to hold back when the dead want me to speak for them. It just isn't right. Keeping them silent would be evil."

"What is it that you're hearing?" asked Savannah, who by then was already looking uncomfortable. "And who are you hearing it from?"

"Juliana Robbins, my producer on my hit show, *Spirit Hunters*."

"All right. Fine then. What is her spirit telling you?"

"She told me that serial killer Brenda Nevins murdered her. She strangled her and tried to cover it all up with a fire."

"Brenda Nevins is the serial killer who escaped with the superintendent of the women's prison in Washington State," Savannah said, cluing her viewers in on a saga that had gripped the nation.

"That's right," Pandora said. "The famed serial killer."

"I don't know if *famed* is the right word," Savannah said. "What else, if anything, did you learn about what happened to Juliana? How was it that she crossed paths with Brenda? It seems a little random."

"I deal with things that most people don't understand. I can assure you nothing in this universe is random."

"Do you know the whereabouts of Janie Thomas?"

"No, but I expect she'll turn up dead. Brenda hasn't stopped killing. She's a mighty and evil force. She's killed at least two people since she escaped."

"Ms. Robbins and Mrs. Thomas?"

"I'm not sure about Mrs. Thomas, but she's killed Juliana and a man named Chaz. I didn't get a last name. A bar owner. Someone who has gone missing not far from the women's prison."

Savannah, who usually was a nimble interviewer, didn't know what else she could say to the medium with the message. Instead, she focused her attention on a statement issued in the wee hours of the morning by the Kitsap County Sheriff's Department's public information officer.

Kendall set down her coffee cup. Brad James's picture appeared on the screen.

The Kitsap County Sheriff's Department can't
confirm anything Pandora has said. Nor do
we intend to. This is an open investigation and
we're supporting the FBI as they search for the
missing superintendent.

And that was it. An awkward segue to the local weather followed.

Birdy was on the phone right away.

"Did you catch that? Tell me you caught that, Kendall!"

"Every last word," Kendall said. "I smell a rat."

"Me too. The rat's name is Brad James."

"Our investigative files were compromised, Birdy. If
Brad's ass wasn't going to be booted out the door for
his botched *Spirit Hunters* 'opportunity' then he's as
good as gone now."

"He didn't mention the hummingbird," Birdy said.

"But he did say a few things only the killer would
have known."

"Except one thing, Kendall."

"What's that?" she asked.

"We never said that Brenda was the killer. Her name
isn't in the file. Not anywhere."

"Then how did he know?"

"I honestly don't know. But I intend to find out."

CHAPTER FORTY-SIX

If one didn't look at what was on the table. Didn't smell it. Just took in the music that Birdy Waterman played on low volume in the background. The slightly gnawing sounds of knives as they cut into flesh. One, quite possibly, could imagine he or she were attending a dinner party of sorts. A dark one of course. But the kind of party that with each moment, each cut, each visual dissected, a little discovery makes itself known.

The forensic pathologist rotated the beam of her light over Chaz Masters's naked body. She'd collected the dry-cleaning bag that had shrouded his face and deposited it into an evidence bag. Bags were often a good source of latent prints—and indeed they'd helped identify the killer in the Moreau girl's case just months before.

It was probably too much to hope for a second time.

Chaz Masters had been dead several days and some of his features were distended in a cruel manner that death does to the former living. In cases in which a body has been disfigured by nature in that way, often a casual friend or distant relative is able to see the remnants of who they are viewing on a coroner's gurney. Someone close to the deceased is frequently so shocked, so disturbed by the visage they cannot readily identify who they've loved and lost. Add murder to the mix and the combination is even more difficult.

Ligature marks on the Grey Gull owner's wrists and ankles indicated what the responding deputies had suggested when they'd collected his remains from his hideaway home. He'd been tied up.

"Sex crime," the deputy suggested.

"Man?" the other asked. "Woman?"

The first deputy shrugged. "Hard to say these days."

"Yeah. Pretty much anything goes now."

Marks left by the bare hands of Chaz's killer indicated a woman or maybe a boy.

"Rough sex," the first one said. "I'd be into it, if I knew this wouldn't happen."

Birdy looked closely at the marks on the neck. She held a ruler to the deceased's neck and took four photographs, each from different angles. While a tox screen would determine if there was any other probable cause—poison, drug overdose—it was a pretty good bet that he had been asphyxiated.

Birdy was about to reach for her older-than-the-hills Stryker saw when she noticed a black triangular piece of plastic protruding from under the dead man's scrotum.

What now? She asked almost out loud.

She lifted Chaz's testes, took a photo, and tugged gently on the black plastic triangle. It came with little resistance.

When she saw it, she was unsure of exactly what it meant. One thing she didn't doubt at all was that a killer with a boob job and a lethal, twisted sense of humor had left it behind.

If that's what she meant.

She draped a sheet over the body.

Kendall looked down at the black plastic shark that Birdy had retrieved and deposited into a plastic evidence bag.

"I don't get it," Kendall said.

"You know it's her work," Birdy said.

"I suspect that it is, but what the hell is this supposed to mean?"

Birdy stared at her. "Really?"

Kendall blinked. "Yeah, what?"

"God, Kendall, don't you know you have a nickname around here?"

"Honestly. no."

"Kendall *Shark*."

"Oh, that. I guess I did know that. How would Brenda know that? And why would she do this?"

"You weren't this upset when we found the hummingbird."

Kendall had been upset, but Birdy was right. Not this upset. "Fine. Fair enough."

"Google yourself sometime. There's a prisoners-and-families website in which they rate and review various members of law enforcement."

"Like Yelp?"

"Sort of," Birdy said. "Anyway, you're the only one from Kitsap who's made the cut. Some drug offender from Poulsbo posted about you. Called you a ball-buster and a shark."

Kendall lifted her eyes from the toy shark. "I guess that's a compliment of sorts."

Birdy smiled grimly. "Guess so," she said.

"After you called," Kendall said, "I thought of someone else who left calling cards like this."

Birdy nodded. "Cecil Reed," she answered.

"Yeah," Kendall said, stepping back from the table. "Reed left a ski lift ticket inside one victim, a watch in another . . . let me see."

Birdy finished the litany of objects hidden from view, only to be discovered by the Provo medical examiner at autopsy. "A lipstick, a tablespoon, the head of a Barbie doll, and . . ."

"The last one was his undoing," Kendall said.

"Right," Birdy said. "The book of matches from his restaurant."

"Uh-huh. Led them right to him."

"Guess we know why Brenda was corresponding with Reed. Maybe she thought of him as a kind of mentor."

"He did get a lot of media," Kendall said. "Don't forget the movie."

"The movie was terrible."

"I don't know. I kind of liked that they shot it in black-and-white. Gave it a kind of noirish vibe, which is right in my wheelhouse."

"Brenda was no Roger Ebert. Any film about her life and crimes would be okay with her."

"Right. Maybe she was hoping for someone like Charlize Theron to play her."

"Charlize has already played the serial killer part in *Monster*. But, yeah, someone like her, but without the ugly makeover."

* * *

After Kendall left the autopsy suite, Birdy went about her business. Music playing. Every detail of the dead man's body recorded and ready for the transcriptionist. She had autopsied hundreds from her medical school days and onward through her career at the county. She knew the exact number, though she never thought of any as merely a number. She knew that Chaz Masters was a proud man. Proud of his military service. Proud of his business. Proud of his body. He'd been in excellent health at the time that he'd been bound to his bed and strangled to death. She wondered if Brenda Nevins had brought the shark toy with her or if she'd merely found it at the scene and seized the moment. Either was plausible. It was patently obvious that she was a facile murderer. One who was clever and always at the ready. One, as they liked to say, at the conclusion of those Investigation Discovery reenactment shows that she watched as a college student, but no longer could tolerate: *She'd stop at nothing to get what she wanted*.

That was Brenda Nevins. Through and through. But just what was it that she was truly after? Fame? Revenge?

More than likely, a murky combination of the two.

CHAPTER FORTY-SEVEN

Roger Frazier sat at the desk of a hotel room in Tacoma and finished the letter that had taken him five shots of whiskey and four attempts with the hotel stationery to complete. There was no fixing his life. The walls had come crashing in. His clients had turned their backs on him. He was a braggart on the surface, the kind of man who boasted about his accomplishments at dinner parties and conventions. He'd won awards for his architectural designs, but there was no way he could fix what hung over him like a blackening thunderhead.

Molester.

Murderer.

Killer of his own daughter.

He folded the note, left it on the desk, and went to the bed where he'd put a glass of water and a party mix of pills. He swallowed each one at a time. He was stoic. Full of resolve. There was nothing he could do to undo what had been done to him. There was no way back after being branded a pedophile, a killer.

He shut his eyes and waited for the relief that would come in the next lifetime.

To Brit and Naomi:

I don't blame you, Brit, for what happened. I know that if the world had conspired to tell me that you were the worst kind of fiend and there was no other option but to believe it, then I would have done so too. I would like to think that I could stand on my own principles and beliefs, but that's a pipe dream. I am so sorry that the turn of events has led me to this point and I know that what I've done will haunt you forever. I'm sorry about that. Sorry is a word that I'd never said to anyone in my life. About anything. But I'm saying it now to you. And Naomi, I am weak. I am not worthy of being called your father. Forgive me for taking the coward's way out of things, but I see no upside to this situation. Both of you are better off without me. I have left all of our financial records in the safe deposit box. Before deciding that this was my best and final option, I made sure that the life insurance that I purchased five years ago was still valid—even in the face of suicide. It is. Both of you will be well taken care of and will not have to worry about money. While the bulk of our assets go automatically to you, Brit, I did name Naomi as beneficiary on the policy so that in the event that you remarry or whatever she will have already had the money she needs to go to college and start a life. And, by the way, that's what I want both of you to do.

Don't think about me, but if you do, remember
me for the good man that I was before the circus
came to town. And forgive me. I love you as I
loved Katy. Now and forever.

Daddy and Roger

Melanie Martin pushed her cart to the door of room
457 at the Hotel Murano in Tacoma. She been working
part-time as a maid and taking classes in the after-
noons at Tacoma Community College. The hotel was
the nicest in Tacoma, but she hated opening the room
doors to find out what disgusting little present the
guest had left for her. She'd been working there six
months and she had serious doubts about the fate of
humanity, having seen what people left behind for others to clean up.

She knocked three times.

"Housekeeping!"

No answer.

She knocked again, and repeated her warning.

And no answer.

Satisfied, she used her pass card and went inside,
leaving her cart in the hallway. The blinds and curtains
were pulled so the room was dark. She flipped on the
lights. The bathroom right by the door looked barely
used, if at all.

Good, she thought. That's the worst place to clean.
Worse than a bus station lavatory at times, she was sure.

The bed was a tangle of blankets and sheets and she
made her way to the curtains to let more light in.

Then she saw him. On the floor on the opposite side

of the bed from the entranceway. It was a man. The
room guest. He was dressed. His eyes were closed.

My first dead guest, she thought, her heart now racing. She picked up the house phone, noticing the note,
but not reading it.

"This is Melanie. I'm in 457. I think we have a suicide. Pill bottles. A note."

Her voice was suddenly shaky and it surprised her.
She prided herself on being unflappable, but she'd
never been confronted by something like this. Not once
in her life. Others who worked on the housekeeping
staff talked about finding couples in the middle of sex,
or a suicide such as this. They talked like it was no big
deal, just part of the job.

But it didn't feel that way. The man looked neat,
clean. Successful. His clothes were Nordstrom, not Pen-
ney's. He was the same age, she thought, as her own father. He had on a wedding ring. He was someone's
husband. Maybe a dad too. And he'd killed himself for
some reason in the Hotel Murano. It was hard for
Melanie to comprehend.

Very hard.

"Security is on its way," the operator said.

As she was taking it all in, Melanie heard a gurgling
sound and looked back down at the man who'd fallen
off the bed and onto the floor.

His hand moved.

"He's alive! I think the man's still alive."

"Calling 911."

Roger Frazier was taken by ambulance to Tacoma
General just a few blocks away. He was there within

four minutes of the 911 call from the hotel. Conscious, but unable to speak, he was going to make it. Doctors and nurses there regarded the suicide note and the empty pill bottles that accompanied him in the ambulance and immediately pumped his stomach for its contents. Roger Frazier was wheeled into a private room where a nurse would be on hand to monitor his every move.

Suicide risk was added to his chart.

From his phone, the primary care physician assigned to Katy's father searched the Internet for his name from his driver's license and learned about *Spirit Hunters* and the allegations that the show had made against him in an article published by the *Kitsap Sun*.

The doctor reread the suicide note and called the Kitsap County Sheriff's Department.

Kendall took the call.

"That architect Roger Frazier who molested his daughter and killed her is here at Tacoma General," he said after identifying himself.

"We don't know he molested anyone, let alone killed."

"Well, if you read his suicide note," the doctor said, with an unmistakable air of inflated ego, "you'll be as certain as I am that he did."

"Suicide?" Kendall asked.

"Right. Attempted. Half-assed, if you want nonmedical verbiage, Detective. We got him in time and I know I should never say something like this, but I wouldn't have shed a tear if he arrived here too late. These guys make me sick. We patch 'em up and they go out to do more of the same."

"We don't know he molested his daughter," Kendall said.

"Once you read his goodbye-I'm-really-sorry note then I'm pretty sure you will change your mind. He bled guilt all over the paper."

Kendall took a breath and reached for a pen.

"Bled? Did he cut himself?"

"No, figure of speech. He was a pill popper."

"All right. Tacoma General? What room?"

"Yeah. He's here just off emergency in a room we use for suicide attempts."

"He's stable?"

"Yes."

"Has he said anything?"

"No, his note pretty much says it all.

"I'll be there as soon as I can. Have you notified his wife?"

"No," the doctor said. "I'll leave that up to you. I figured you'd want a crack at him before the media and family—not necessarily in that order—find out."

CHAPTER FORTY-EIGHT

Wyatt Ogilvie had set his name up for a Google Alert. The automated missives didn't come into his email account as often as he'd hoped when he'd done so, but he felt that as long as he was generating some kind of notice now and then he was still a celebrity. Often the mentions were merely the TV guide indicating that *Spirit Hunters* was on that evening, perhaps a line or two about the episode. A few times there had been some snarky comments online about how Pandora was the undisputed star of the show and that he'd been cast only because they needed "a doofus to move along the story line."

That morning, as he sipped a particularly strong cup of hotel French press coffee, the alert appeared in his email box. From its headline alone, he knew he was in for trouble. He set down his coffee to read. It was from *Radar Online*, a popular gossip and news site—though the editors didn't seem to have a true handle on which was which—that left him reaching for some low-dose aspirin.

Psychic Pandora Leaves
Spirit Hunters For Bravo

The website indicated that Pandora, who was in the midst of a major FBI case, was leaving her old gig for one that would feature her solving "classic true-crime cases that have baffled investigators and left victims' families to cope with the unknown—in some cases for decades." JonBenét Ramsey—with interviews featuring the dead beauty queen and her late mother from "the other side"—was the first installment. Filming was to begin at the start of the following month.

"I'll miss my friends at *Spirit Hunters*," she was quoted as saying. "They'll always be a part of me."

Part of me? Miss them?

"That psychic bitch," Wyatt said as he flipped down the top of his laptop and looked at his face, now very, very red, in the floor-to-ceiling mirror adjacent to the table where he sat, basking a moment ago, now feeling sick to his stomach.

He threw on some clothes, not even trying to look the part of the TV star who in that very moment he knew was ebbing away. Pandora was the star. He knew that. He'd lied to himself over and over. He lied to his own mother when she asked him over for dinner one time if Pandora had the gifts she proclaimed so surely on the show and in interviews. Maybe he was a doofus after all. It was possible that he was doomed to failure from the very beginning, seduced by the woman's charms and promises that he'd ride her coattails into a development deal with HBO. She'd promised that over

and over. If he'd play along with her. Follow her lead.
Do what he was told. She'd see that they'd go far. Network far.

All of that was bull. Just like her. He hated her. He
never liked sex with her. He only slept with her to stay
close.

As in, keep your enemies close.

He got her on the phone.

"Hi, babe," she said.

"Don't *babe* me. I saw the item in today's *Radar*."

Pandora didn't answer right away. She'd had the TV
on and he could hear the volume go lower. It was E!.
She was probably watching to see if her deal made the
entertainment news channel.

"What item?" she asked.

This was how she was going to play it.

"The Bravo deal," he said. His tone was flat.

"God, Wyatt, you sure jump to conclusions. The Internet is full of lies. There's absolutely no truth to that
Bravo story."

"So you know about it?" he asked, letting in a little
emotion and trying hard not to do more than that.

"I know everything."

"Really?" he asked. "Then what am I thinking right
now?"

Pandora let out a breathy sigh. "That you can't wait
to see me."

"Wrong," he said, a little more anger creeping into
his voice.

"Calm down, babe. Please. You're making me feel a
little uncomfortable. I need to stay centered. It's bad

for my health and for my instrument to be challenged by hate. You know that."

Hate was a good word choice just then.

"You bitch," he said. "You've been lying to me for too long. First the money. Now this. We had a deal."

"Oh, Wyo, must you be so dramatic?" she asked in that cool way she'd perfected over time. It was a demeaning affect that she'd managed about once a taping—usually targeted at some poor mother or father torn up about a dead child. Pandora's cold streak was an icicle aimed with precision at the heart. She would always feign that she'd been misunderstood, but she hadn't been. Her fans loved it. It was her duty, she once told Juliana, to give her fans what they wanted.

"If you'd saved this kind of passion for the show," she said, "we'd probably have better ratings."

Wyatt had heard enough. "We're done," he said, before hurling a threat. "I'll take you down so fast you'll wish you'd never met me."

Pandora laughed into the phone. "I already wish that, Wyatt. Every time you're inside me."

Wyatt cut her off and immediately punched in Kendall Stark's office number so hard that he almost cracked the glass of his phone. He took a deep breath. Pandora was crazy. Certifiable. Mean-spirited. Not so great in bed, either. He was calm—or trying to be. As the line rang, he played Pandora's betrayal over in his head. Trying to see how a seasoned investigator who had tangled with the worst criminals anyone could face off with could get things so wrong.

A beat later, Wyatt got Kendall's voice mail. It was

just as well. As calm as he was trying to will himself to be just then, he was furious and needed the drive to chill.

"I'm coming over to talk to you," he said. "Pandora's decidedly *not* the real deal. I guess you probably already know that. At least I hope you do."

CHAPTER FORTY-NINE

Wyatt Ogilvie held out a memory stick. "You need to watch this," he said.

Kendall took it. "What's on it?"

"You need to see for yourself."

She inserted it into her computer. "Where'd you get it?"

"Juliana uploaded it into our show's Dropbox the night she died. She didn't really upload it. It's an automatic upload."

"How did you get it?"

"The three of us have access to it. Me, Pandy, and Juliana. It's where we share the details of the case so that Pandy can look like a real psychic and the executive producers in New York can speak to the media with a straight face."

"I see," Kendall said.

"Click on video 295," he said.

Kendall did just that.

The video started with the familiar face.

"I'm Juliana Robbins and I'm about to score the

biggest interview of my life. Background now. Last night a segment aired on KING TV in which I talked about my experiences with *Spirit Hunters*. It was the local-girl-makes-good kind of story. Anyway, after it aired I got an exciting call. A totally unexpected call."

She waited a beat, like the producer that she was. She knew the value of the pause.

Kendall glanced at Wyatt. The TV detective sat with his arms folded, his eyes on hers.

"Brenda Nevins," Juliana went on. "She called. Yeah, *that* Brenda Nevins. The serial killer who abducted the prison superintendent and who has the local cops and the FBI in a dither because they can't find her. Well, I found her. Or really she found me. She wants to tell me her side of the story and I'm totally down with that. In fact, I know this is make-or-break time for me and my career because outside of Princess Kate, I'd say Brenda Nevins would be the biggest 'get' in the world."

Kendall looked over at Wyatt.

"*Get* means biggest score, interview-wise," he said.

Kendall nodded as the screen blipped to black, then started up again. It was a wider shot this time. Juliana had changed to a different outfit. The camera was positioned behind her back and was facing Brenda Nevins.

Juliana asked her to identify herself, which Brenda did. The effect on her face indicated that she was in her element. Reveling in the opportunity to speak her mind. Share her story. Give the other side.

Or something along those fuzzy media lines.

"Brenda, the whole world is looking for you," Juliana said. "Where is Janie Thomas? And what have you done with her?"

"Oh, Janie's fine. She's my sweet little prison mouse. We're in love. I don't know how long it will last. We don't see eye to eye on everything."

"Where is she?" Juliana asked.

"Safe. She's safe. And remember, Juliana, you know I won't give you details like that. This isn't about having the police find me, is it? Aren't we here for symbiotic reasons?"

"Parasitic," Wyatt said, "is more like it."

Kendall couldn't agree more.

"That's right," Juliana said. "What have you been up to? Can you talk about that at all? Even generally?"

"Some people would say I've been a very naughty girl," Brenda said in a moment that Kendall was sure would make America's skin crawl when the tape went viral, as she was certain it would.

"Naughty? How?"

"Oops, I did it again."

"Did what?"

"Snuffed out a life."

"Did you kill Superintendent Thomas?"

"No," Brenda said. "I killed a man."

"What man?"

"A horny bar owner. I really don't want to say more about that. All right, Juliana?"

"Let's get back to that later," Juliana said.

"Let's not. Let's just say that we did."

"Fine. Let's not. Let's focus on what's going on with you right now. How are you surviving?"

"I'm doing just fine. I'm having fun. No one will catch me. And I've just started. After being in prison, I feel that I can finally breathe, and it feels great being on the outside."

"I'm sure it does," the ambitious producer said. "But you're not really free. You're in hiding."

"Not forever. Just for now. I'm only seizing the moment. I'm trying to make myself the best that I can be. Remember I got caught once before. I don't intend to get caught so quickly this time."

"You were caught for the murder of your husband, your child, your boyfriend," Juliana said, her voice a little shaky.

"She seems scared," Kendall said, pausing the video.

"Yeah," Wyatt said. "She probably knows that she's sitting across from a monster right then and that there is no one else at Swallow Haven to hear her scream."

Kendall pushed the PLAY button.

"Yes, I did those murders. But I'll do more. I've already mapped out my next victims and I intend to get the respect I'm due. Being good at something isn't enough. You have to be proficient. The best. The one that everyone remembers. The one that parents tell their children to fear."

"I guess so," Juliana said, now standing.

"Is the interview over?" Brenda said, now standing.

"Yes. Thank you. You should probably get going so you don't get caught."

Brenda smiled. "I won't get caught."

"How can you be so sure?"

"Two things," she said. "The FBI and those hopeless gals from Kitsap County are not smart enough."

"You said two things. Is that two things?"

Brenda shook her head. "No, that's one."

Juliana leaned in. "What's the other?"

Brenda focused her eyes on the camera just then,

then back to Juliana. "The other is to never leave a witness alive," she said.

Kendall watched with horror as Brenda flung herself at Juliana. Brenda's hands throttled Juliana's throat. Juliana clawed at her attacker and the two of them went down on the floor, out of camera range.

"You stupid bitch!" Brenda screamed out. "You are making me very, very angry."

"Get off of me!" Juliana said.

More screams.

"I'm getting off on you," Brenda said, laughing at her own play on words.

There was more noise, thrashing and screaming, and then silence. When it was over Brenda stood up and dusted herself off. She looked at the lens, winked, and then disappeared out of view.

Kendall, breathless from what she'd seen, turned off the video.

"There's more," Wyatt said.

Kendall nodded and pushed PLAY.

"Fast-forward."

"All right," she said.

Brenda appeared on screen with a gas can. A beat later there was a whoosh of light. The clip was over.

"Pandora screwed me over," he said. "She's a fraud. I guess we're both frauds," he said. "But I'm done. I wanted you to know how it was that she could come up with what happened to Chaz Masters. She also bilked Brit Frazier out of twenty K. Pandora is nothing but a grifter."

"Tell me something I didn't know," Kendall said.

Wyatt shrugged. "Sometimes when you're in the TV

bubble doing a reality show you forget what's real. Like who you are."

"You know that keeping this evidence will likely lead to obstruction charges."

"I brought it to you," he said.

"I know. I'll do my best, Wyatt."

"Thanks. I really am not the buffoon you see on TV, you know."

Kendall knew there was a grain of truth to his personal assessment. He wasn't all bad. She'd leave that designation to Brenda Nevins and Pandora.

CHAPTER FIFTY

Roger Frazier sat up in bed and shifted his body away from Kendall Stark, who stood near the doorway. Tubes ran from a saline bag overhead to his left arm, which was folded over his right. His eyes never once met Kendall directly. They stayed fixed on some crows toggling over the body of a dead rat in the hospital parking lot. The disgraced architect's mouth stayed clamped shut. He didn't want to see, didn't want to talk, and almost certainly didn't want to breathe right then. Roger had been denied the end that he'd sought for himself. His last creation was not a building or fancy home, but had been his death, and even that had been a complete failure.

"Nurse," Kendall said, "can you give us a few minutes?"

The nurse, a middle-aged woman with hair the color of driftwood—and about as stiff—nodded.

Kendall approached the bed. She held the note, now in a plastic sleeve, and spoke once more.

"Mr. Frazier, you had us all fooled. I feel like the biggest idiot in Port Orchard. And that's saying a lot," she said, trying to shake some words from his frozen mouth. "I never once believed you had been sexually abusing Katy. I thought it was some kind of sick suggestion made by the show. Something for ratings."

After what seemed like a long time, after the crows took wing and went to ravage elsewhere, he finally looked up. His eyes were red and his skin very pale. He looked like he'd been through a war zone, and in a way he had. But the damage he'd done to himself at the end of it all was by his own hand. Kendall wasn't sorry for him. It was, she thought, the coward's way out.

"I didn't molest her," he said.

"It says you did," Kendall said, holding the note to make sure he knew she had it. "Not specifically, but a jury wouldn't have a hard time seeing this as an admission of guilt. Why don't you just own up to it?"

His eyes stayed on her. "I didn't do it."

Kendall moved a little closer. "Cowards use suicide," she said. "You did it, but you didn't want the world to know that you molested and murdered Katy."

He looked back at the empty parking lot at the dead rat.

He was a rat.

"Because I didn't," he said softly.

"Let's try this another way, all right?" Kendall sat in the window seat facing the bed. "When did you start molesting her?"

"I told you I never did that. I wouldn't do that. I loved my daughter very much. It was me and her against the world."

Molesters always say that, Kendall thought. *So typical.*

"Why did you try to kill yourself?" she asked.

"Because of you," he said. "Because of everyone."

Kendall blinked. "What have I got to do with it?"

"You're like everyone else," he said, staring her down. "It's how you look at me now. You look at me in a way that I'd never experienced before, with revulsion and hate. I see it in your eyes right now. You think I'm a monster. My secretary of fourteen years, someone who knew me, quit because she didn't . . . how did she say it . . . didn't want the stink of the likes of me on her clothes."

His eyes welled up a little but he wouldn't let that first teardrop go. He was a lot of things, but he wasn't a crier. Not even when it might have been okay to be one.

When Katy first went missing.

"I'm doing my job," Kendall said, almost feeling sorry for the man. "I have to consider that you might have done it."

"Even when the bearer of the news is some phony psychic from a TV show? One that just comes to town to make trouble for the sake of higher ratings? You, like everyone else, gets sucked into the idea of it and in no time at all the idea becomes reality."

Kendall pushed the plastic-ensconced paper at him.

"Your note," she said.

He nodded, still fighting the tears. "My note," he repeated.

"Yes."

"It's just a note about the facts," he said, still looking at her.

Kendall pushed a little harder. "The facts," she said.

"Yes," he said. "The facts are that I've lost everything. All of my clients. All of my very good friends.

Even my high school reunion asked that I not come this year because I would be a distraction. I used to be someone, Detective, now I'm a distraction, a pariah. I'm never going to be who I was before. Never again."

"That sounds like a guilty man speaking, Roger," she said, using his first name.

"A realistic man. I wish I had died. I wish that the embarrassment that has been foisted on my wife and daughter had never happened. I wanted to do the show because I thought it would give me some national exposure. What kind of father would do that? Would trade his missing daughter's memory for a spot on a show because he might sell a condo project?"

"You're being too hard on yourself now."

"Am I? I don't think so. I think I got what I deserved and there's no amount of spinning that can bring back what I was before I let Pandora into my house. She screwed me over. She ruined my life."

Kendall knew that much of what he said was completely, unequivocally true. Pandora's box and its contents had been dumped all around Port Orchard, wreaking havoc wherever she'd been.

Juliana was dead.

Tami Overton was dead.

Roger had tried to kill himself.

It was not a Greek tragedy, but one with a distinct local flavor. At the center of it all was the psychic from Spokane. She might not have had real psychic powers, but a maelstrom of tragedy enveloped everything and everyone that came in her path.

The nurse with the driftwood hair returned and poked her head into the room. She wore an impatient look on her face.

"I'm going to need to take the patient's vitals in a moment," she said.

"Patient wishes you'd put him out of his misery," Roger said.

"One more minute, nurse," Kendall said.

"This note isn't an admission of guilt in your daughter's molestation and murder?" Kendall asked, pointing to the piece of Hotel Murano stationery.

"It was an admission that I am weak and that losing everything precious to me means more to me than living in this world. I'd rather be dead than be a nobody, Detective. Wouldn't you?"

Kendall didn't answer. She didn't want to tell him that she understood, even a little. She opened the door and told the nurse to keep an eye on him.

"He's pretty despondent," she said.

"I'm surprised," the nurse said. "Most of those pedophiles aren't. They don't seem to give a care that they've ruined some poor girl or boy's life. At least this guy has a conscience."

CHAPTER FIFTY-ONE

Kendall was adept at seeing the tiniest fissures in a person's facade. She'd seen it in Scott Hilburn when she interviewed him at the apartment he'd shared with Alyssa. Alyssa had shut him down a couple of times during the visit . . . and she didn't even have to use words. It was out of her way, but Kendall didn't mind. The ferry to Seattle gave her time to process what was happening in her personal life and what she needed to do to ensure justice for Katy, Juliana, and Tami. Steven had left a brief message that morning—more for Cody than for her. It was better than nothing. At that point they were so far apart that she didn't know exactly where things would go. She waited her turn and rolled off the ferry, feeling the bump, bump of the ramp.

She parked in the oil-stained parking lot across from Happy Teriyaki, where Scott had indicated he worked most evenings. It was hot and she rolled down the window, taking in the smells and sights of the University District, affectionately nicknamed the U-District by the grab-bag mix of old, but mostly new, people who prowled the bars, bookstores, and ramen shops there.

Some of the old had started their love affair with the neighborhood when they were young, of course. Kendall had never seen so many gray ponytails in her life. She counted fourteen as she waited in the car.

When she saw Scott head for his car, Kendall got out of her SUV and hurried over.

"I don't want to talk to you," he said before she crossed the parking lot.

"I don't believe you," she said.

He looked around.

Kendall could see the same little fissures she'd seen before. He did want to talk, he just needed a little push.

"I know that you had something to do with Katy's disappearance."

"You're blowing smoke, Detective."

"Scott, you know I'm not. I can tell that you have been carrying the weight of the world for some time. Talk to me. Let me help you do what's right. I know there's a part of you that can grab ahold of some goodness and do the right thing. I know that's not true of Alyssa."

"Don't you talk about her," he said, his tone shifting a little.

It was as if the words were said by rote. Without feeling. Without true conviction. Kendall saw another little chip fall.

"Talk to me, Scott. I can see there's still some good in you. I know that you didn't want things to go as far as they did."

"You don't know anything, Detective Stark."

"I think I do. I've been doing this awhile, Scott. You get a sixth sense about people after a time. When you see true evil like I have a time or two, you know that some people are powerless to stop it."

"You're BS'ing me. I'm not talking to you."

"I can help you, Scott. If you didn't kill Katy, I can go to the prosecutor's office. You just have to tell me what happened. Tell me that I'm right."

"About what? Right about what?"

"That you loved Katy. That you didn't want her to die."

"I can't do this. I can't do this," he said over and over, a monologue that he'd probably practiced in his head the minute he saw Kendall in front of Happy Teriyaki.

"You can. I know that you can."

"You can't tell her I told you."

Another fragment.

"Come sit in my car. I can turn the AC on. It's hot out here."

"She'll kill me. Katy's not the only one."

That wasn't a chip, but a boulder-sized fragment.

"Talk to me. Let's make things right. Don't you know what's happened to that family? Don't you know that Katy's family deserves to rest too? You liked them. You used be a part of the family, didn't you?"

"One of them was part of it," he said.

Mt. Everest.

"Come on. Sit." She swung the door open and Scott Hilburn lingered a little before sliding into the passenger seat.

"You have to protect my family from Alyssa. She said she'd kill Mom and my little brother."

"I'll protect them. I'm going to take you to the sheriff's office where you'll be safe. I'll call ahead to have someone watch your family's house. On Colchester?"

He was crying then and couldn't speak. He nodded.

Kendall decided to take the long drive home, through Tacoma and across the Narrows Bridge—the bridge that had once buckled in a major windstorm and dropped into the deep waters of Puget Sound. It was a lot like Scott Hilburn was just then, bending, breaking, and falling into pieces.

He looked out the window as they passed the Tacoma Dome.

"Katy and I went there to see Britney Spears," he said. "That was one of the really great times we had. I knew she wanted other things. I knew she didn't want me anymore. It crushed me. It hurt so bad."

"Bad enough to make her pay?"

He looked over at Kendall. "Pay, yes, but not die. Alyssa took things too far. She really did. After it was over, I wanted to die. I really did. I even took a bottle of aspirin. Just made me hurl like I drank a fifth of whiskey."

"You said she killed before," Kendall said.

He nodded and returned to the window. "Yeah. But not before. Afterword. She killed Tami. She thought Tami was going to tell that TV show. She said we had to stop her . . . that no one would miss her."

Kendall didn't say anything about Tami's little boy. Her husband. Her mother. There were probably plenty of other people who would miss Tami Overton.

"Killing Katy, that was wrong. I know that. I felt sick about it. But killing Tami, that was just too much. I thought to myself, who was this woman? She could just off anyone. Like a junior Brenda Nevins. She'd kill anyone who got in her way. When she told me that she'd kill my family I saw it as a promise, not a threat. A promise she could make good on and then go to the mall to buy a new outfit."

"You said someone from Katy's family was there."

He didn't answer for a long time.

"Yeah," he finally said, "but she really didn't want any part of what happened."

CHAPTER FIFTY-TWO

Naomi looked up. Alyssa was hovering over her bed. Naomi had never noticed that Alyssa's eyes were so devoid of emotion. Tears fell at all the right moments, but it was more mechanical than emotional. Alyssa sat down on the bed and rested her hand on Naomi's shaking shoulders. Her fingernails dug in a little.

"I have to tell my dad," Naomi said.

"You have to tell him what?" Alyssa said, kneading her nails into Naomi's flesh like a purring cat.

"What we did. What happened to Katy."

"That would be pretty stupid, now, wouldn't it?"

Naomi had cried for two days. She'd gone along with everything. She'd done what Alyssa and Scott had demanded she'd do. She lured her sister to meet up with them. Everything they'd told her made sense. Katy *was* full of herself. Every time she walked into a room people scurried toward her like she was the brightest light and they were moths drawn to her. Naomi had hated being a moth.

"I don't think I can live with this, Alyssa," Naomi said.

Alyssa clenched her grip and leaned in close. Naomi could feel the older girl's warm breath. Her rapid heartbeat. The moisture of her nervousness.

"Really? That's funny, Naomi. We did this for *you*. We did what *you* wanted. And now you're saying that you can't live with it? Forgive me if I laugh out loud right now."

"I didn't want her gone," Naomi said.

Alyssa loosed her grip and pressed her face closer to Naomi. "Sometimes things go farther than you like when you set them in motion," she said.

Naomi knew this wasn't a game anymore. She knew that whatever she said she'd get some kind of verbal punch to the gut. She could lie. She could avoid saying anything to provoke Alyssa. And yet, when she weighed what had happened and what she'd done she knew that only the truth would work.

"I'm going to tell my dad," she said, averting her eyes for the onslaught she knew was about to come at her.

Alyssa didn't disappoint. "You stupid little bitch," she said, seething. "You aren't going to do that. If you do, you'll have hell to pay."

Naomi lifted her head from the pillow and pushed Alyssa away. "I'm not afraid of you and Scott."

Alyssa stayed cool, but those lifeless eyes were now full of rage. "That's fine," she said. "I didn't say anything would happen to *you*. But I can certainly take care of your do-gooder parents."

"You wouldn't."

"Try me, Naomi. Just try me. I'm sick of being second best and I feel a whole lot better now that your sister is out of the way. Scott loves me. I'm empowered. I'm in control and everyone else needs to get out of the way."

Naomi looked away. Alyssa was a monster and she'd never even seen a glimpse of that side of her. She'd played her. She'd made her feel that what she was doing to her sister was something that Naomi needed. Wanted. Couldn't live without.

"Your sister makes me puke," Alyssa said earlier that year. "I can't stand her stomping in and out and getting what she wants."

"She's your best friend," Naomi said.

Alyssa shook her head. "Best friend? She's all about her own self. She doesn't give a crap about anyone but Katy. You know that's true."

Naomi was jealous of Katy, but it wasn't because Katy didn't deserve her accolades. It was simply because Naomi had been relegated to being background sister. She was the one who every teacher felt compelled to tell that the other sibling was going to be a tough act to follow. She was the daughter who tried so hard to get the attention of her parents, but the glow, the noise, the aura that surrounded her competition was too, too fierce.

"I love her and hate her, Alyssa," Naomi had said.

"I know the feeling," Alyssa answered as she pretended to be distracted by a text message.

This was all very casual. Not real. Just a game, right?

"That's why we need to get her out of the way. I mean, she treats Scott like crap and that's not right. Scott's the greatest guy in the world. If he were my boyfriend I'd never treat him the way she does. He told me some of the crap she pulls on him, how she just can't help that all the other guys want to be with her. Poor me. Not my fault. Such a load. Scott is the best."

Naomi nodded. She liked Scott too. He was always nice to her. Other boyfriends didn't even pretend to be kind to her. Scott was different. One time he brought her a package of black licorice because he knew she liked it—and he liked it too. Katy didn't.

"I guess so," Naomi said, thinking back at the list of wrongs her sister either willingly or unwittingly had done to her over the last couple of years. "I guess she needs to be put in her place. We aren't going to hurt her, right?"

Alyssa shook her head. "Oh no. We're just going to teach her a very important lesson."

"What lesson? How?"

"That she's not all that. That the world wasn't created for her exclusive use and that the rest of us have a place in it. You know that I didn't get to try out for the cheerleading team because Katy said she might and that she'd 'feel bad' if I didn't get on it and she did."

"She's such a bitch," Naomi said.

"Yeah, and remember that time she said that it made her feel bad for you because you looked like your mother's side of the family and that you'd probably never really be pretty."

Naomi recalled the incident and what her sister had said, though Alyssa had twisted it. The words had been offered to her as a kind of pep talk when the two of them were in the bathroom getting ready for school.

"You look like Mom. Mom's beautiful, but what I've always liked about her is how she looks smarter than pretty. Pretty fades. Smart is forever. I think you have that look."

When Naomi first told this to Alyssa while they were waiting for Katy to get off the phone one afternoon, she brought it up because she thought it was kind of funny. That even when her sister was saying something that others might perceive as mean, it was offered as a pep talk.

"She said that?" Alyssa said, acting outraged, and reaching out to hug Naomi. "Sometimes your sister is a real bitch!"

"Well," Naomi said, "I just thought it was funny."

"What is this? The Stockholm syndrome around here?"

Naomi shrugged a little. Maybe she was stupid too?

"I don't know what that is," she finally said.

"It's when a bitch like your sister makes everyone else suffer and feel like they should suffer because she's so great and they are a piece of crap. Sometimes I can't stand her."

Naomi started to think. Alyssa was kind of right. Her sister did have a way of making her feel about two inches tall.

Roger Frazier had talked about the house he'd designed on Hood Canal as being the pinnacle of his career. The county planners had moved slowly on its approval and his daughters had taken to using the model he'd built as a place for their Barbie dolls to hang out while they weren't in the pink plastic RV that Katy had been given for her tenth birthday, and which she'd passed on to her sister. The Donaldson place was a postmodern palace conceived for a Microsoft executive who cashed in millions of dollars of stock, flitted about the world funding various causes, and yet still had time to build a monument to his own humble self. It was 5,500 square feet of shiny clean excess with an enormous flagstone terrace adjoining a cozy 2,000-square-foot guest cottage. The neighbors hated what the proposed structure was going to do to their colorful collection of old beach cabins.

"It looks like a godawful alien spacecraft, albeit a clunky one, has set down in the middle of a Norman Rockwell painting," one particularly unhappy local resident said in front of the county review board two summers before the groundbreaking.

"Yeah, and if you ask me, the architect is trying to ruin our community with a design that pushes all boundaries of scale and decency," said another, in a quote that never left Roger's brain.

At the time of Katy's disappearance, the only thing that was under construction was the foundation for the guesthouse and its accompanying six-car garage.

Scott Hilburn, in belly chains and shackles, barely said a word as deputies led him to the edge of the driveway. A backhoe and two teams of searchers waited closer to the garage area. The owner, Calvin Donaldson, approached Kendall.

"She's been here the whole time?" he asked.

Kendall had expected the man, now in his forties, to be worried about the quarried slabs that made up the driveway. She was prepared to tell him that there was a fund for people of lesser means in the event that police work damaged their property, but that he wouldn't qualify. But, she thought, by the look on his face he didn't care.

"We don't know for sure," Kendall said.

"Do whatever you need to do," he said as she handed him the search warrant. "I feel sorry for Brit and Roger. And their girls too. Is Roger still in the hospital?"

Kendall nodded. "Released tomorrow."

"This has been a tragedy all the way around."

"Agreed."

Scott led the searchers to the far corner of the driveway next to the garage doors. He kept his eyes low, ashamed and embarrassed for his role in what happened to a girl he'd once loved—but who'd told him that they were not a forever couple.

"Right around here," he said, touching his toe to the slab of stone that had been installed a few days after Katy had been murdered.

A deputy nodded and another climbed into the backhoe.

A voice called out. "Have you found her?"

Kendall looked up. It was Brit.

"Have you found my baby? Pandora was right, wasn't she?"

Brit looked like a hundred miles of washed-out road. She hadn't eaten. She looked unkempt. The pretty-smart of her looks had ebbed in the days since they met at the reveal for *Spirit Hunters*. There was good reason for that, of course. It had been the second worst time of her life.

Kendall wanted to say "F Pandora" but thinking it was enough given the circumstances. Pandora and the show's ratcheting up of the case had, in fact, led to that moment. Even so, there could be no celebration. No acknowledgment. Tami Overton was dead. Naomi was in juvenile detention. Roger had tried to kill himself. It was as if Katy's case and the resolution they hoped was in store had set off a series of other tragedies that might never have occurred. Pandora had promised Katy's mother that the answer was close by, but she was also very, very lethal.

"I wish you hadn't come," Kendall said.

"I wish my daughter hadn't been murdered, Detective."

That was a statement for which there could never be any kind of response.

"I'll need you to stay back."

Brit pushed closer to the backhoe.

"Really, Mrs. Frazier, you don't want to see her," she said, putting out her hand like a traffic cop with a genuine sense of urgency.

Brit stopped in her tracks. She didn't say anything. She was as close to her daughter as she was going to get. She stood there alone. No husband. No girls. No supporters from the Second Cup, Second Chance coffee shop. Right about then, she needed her own second chance.

The sound of the stone breaking shattered the air. Everyone stood back, holding the air inside. Calvin Donaldson didn't say a word, but gave a sad nod and retreated to the front door of the main house. He didn't need to see any more. Kendall went closer to the equipment and the others.

The backhoe operator lifted the slab and set it aside. A moment later, he gently scraped layer after layer of soil.

"We barely covered her, Detective," Scott said, his eyes finally directly meeting Kendall's. "I'm really sorry about what we did."

Kendall nodded. She would give Scott plenty of credit later for having the basic qualities of human decency. She suspected Tami Overton was that type of person too. Not Alyssa, of course.

"Scott, what happened that night?"

"My dad says I shouldn't say any more. Not without a lawyer."

"You're better than that. I know you are."

"I want to tell you."

"You can. You're an adult. You can waive those rights. You can do the right thing right here and now. We're alone," she said, "but the world is watching."

Scott watched as the backhoe kept moving. It was only a matter of moments before Katy would be found.

"Do the right thing, Scott. Brit and Roger deserve it."

"Naomi does too," he said.

"She was part of this, wasn't she?"

He shook his head. "Not really. She wasn't here when it was all over. She started walking home. I went after her when it was done."

"Tell me."

Katy Frazier was confused and crying. Alyssa had chopped her hair with a pair of scissors while Scott and Tami held her down in the trench dug to hold the cement forms. Naomi stood still. She had wanted to scare her sister. Remind her that she was a person too. She hadn't done a thing but watch and had left before what Alyssa promised would be the "real fun."

"Alyssa! What are you doing to me?"

Katy was crying and shaking. Her hands were held to her head, feeling the patches and unevenness of her best friend's brutal hairstyling.

"You are such a complainer. We're just playing around. Like you do with our emotions every single day, Katy. You're always saying you'll be there. You're always saying come to the Kitsap Mall. I'll see you at A&W. Such a liar!"

"Why are you mad about that? That wasn't anything."

"You don't get to decide what I feel anymore. What any of us feel anymore. Right, Scott? Tami?"

"Right, Alyssa," Tami said, unconvincingly. Alyssa shot her a glare and Tami felt compelled to say more. "We're totally sick of you, Katy."

"Scott! I'm scared. Take me home."

Scott kept his mouth shut. He refused to look at her.

"Scott, what's the matter? Why are you doing this to me? Don't you love me anymore?"

Again, no response.

Alyssa spoke up. "I told him about Trevor and Maxx."

"I don't care about those guys," she said.

"Then why did you go down on them?"

"I didn't, Alyssa. You did."

"You little bitch!"

"You told me you did. Why are you acting like this? I want to go home."

"You aren't going home. Ever. You're gonna die tonight."

Scott looked over at Alyssa. This wasn't the plan,

but he didn't do anything to stop her. He just stood there. Tami did the same. Alyssa held up the scissors.

"Tonight," she said.

Katy was frantic. The construction site was large and with the tide up high, she knew she couldn't get away from any of them. She had to go through them. She started to push past them.

"Stop her, Tami! You idiot! If she gets away she'll tell on us!"

Tami, who hadn't wanted any of this in the first place, but who only wanted to be part of someone's inner circle, threw herself onto her friend, tackling her and bringing her to the ground.

Alyssa pounced, shoving the knife deep into Katy's abdomen. Katy looked up from her future grave. Blood oozed from her mouth. Seeing the blood, Alyssa twisted the scissors and felt the life force drain from her friend.

Her rival.

Alyssa looked up at the others. They stood there frozen, in shock.

"Tami!" she called over to her friend, her follower. "Stab her! Scott, stab her! We are all a part of this! You need to do this now."

"And we did," he said. "I'm really not sure why. Tami and I just did what Alyssa told us to do. Like we didn't have minds of our own. I know we did, but that night it didn't feel that way. I took some psychology courses to see why. The mob effect, I guess. We just did what she said, in the heat of the moment. In the frenzy of what Alyssa had done. We hadn't come there to kill Katy, I swear it. We hadn't. We just got caught up in some-thing."

Kendall knew there was probably some truth to what he was saying, but it was an excuse. And Scott Hilburn wasn't going to prison for Katy's murder anyway. He'd testify against Alyssa.

Scott was going away for what he did to Tami.

"We covered her up and I guess we got lucky," he said.

"Lucky?"

"We thought we'd be caught the next day," Scott said, his eyes wet with the kind of tears that couldn't be faked. "We were sure of it. But we didn't know about the cement pour the next day. I mean, we didn't do a very good job. Not at all. Just barely covered her. I threw the scissors in the water. After we left we found Naomi walking on the road. We didn't tell her all that had happened. At least not right away."

"I see something pink," the backhoe operator said.

Kendall went to the edge of the hole.

"I see it too," she said.

Pink was the color of the shirt Katy was wearing when she vanished.

A deputy with a shovel jumped into the indentation that the backhoe operator had made with his bucket.

"Yeah," he said. "We've found her."

Another deputy approached Kendall.

"They also found Alyssa," he said. "She was picked up an hour ago in King County. We'll transport her tonight."

Kendall looked over at Brit, who was slumped over in the driveway crying uncontrollably. Scott was in no better shape. Both had loved Katy. One was responsible for her death, the other had to come to grips with the blame she'd placed on her husband, an innocent man.

CHAPTER FIFTY-THREE

Back at her desk, going over the paperwork that would close the file on Katy's death and the multiple tragedies that had sprung from it, Kendall Stark longed for the relief that would come on a day without a murder investigation. To say that she loved her work was simplistic. She did see the great value she could bring to the justice system. She could see the sad appreciation on the faces of those who wanted to know the why behind the unthinkable. Sometimes, she knew, the why wouldn't be enough. Not for Tami Overton's mother, her son, her husband. Not for Juliana's parents. Chaz's sister, who kept calling her for an update. Janie's husband and son.

All of them would have some information now, but they would always be damaged by the evil visited upon them.

Kendall's phone vibrated and she looked down. She didn't recognize the number when she picked it up. The voice, however, was chillingly familiar.

"Hi, Detective," the caller said.

It was Brenda Nevins.

"Where are you?" Kendall asked reflexively, knowing that Brenda would never answer that question.

"You can't catch me," she said. "You can't trace this call. But you can listen."

"We know what you did, you bitch. I will find you, Brenda. And when I do I'll think of some reason to be threatened by you so I can shoot you dead."

"That's funny. You are threatened. But what does any of that matter? I'm free. I'm more famous now than I was when you ruined my chance for a TV special."

"Is that all you care about?" Kendall asked, appealing to Brenda's twisted ego. "If it is, turn yourself in right now. You're smart enough to know that you're a hot commodity."

"You think I'm hot? I thought so. I saw the way your eyes dawdled over me when we met. I could have had your tongue between my legs right then and there."

There had been no doubt that Brenda was sick, but she was also a bad judge of character. Kendall was sickened by the fact that they'd shared the same air in that interview room at the prison. She'd seen evil face-to-face before, but never as dark and conniving as Brenda Nevins.

Kendall pushed. "Where are you, Brenda?"

"You are turned on, aren't you?"

"No."

"You're wet right now," Brenda said. "I can sense it over the phone."

"I'm married," Kendall said, not sure why that was her response. "I'm not interested."

"Janie was married too," Brenda said. Her tone was

cool, indifferent. "She wasn't interested either, but I had her."

"Why did you kill her?" Kendall asked. "Why did you kill Chaz Masters? Juliana Robbins?"

Brenda let out a laugh. "Because that's what I do," she said. "Besides riding a man and spinning him like a top, getting a woman to experience her wildest fantasies, I'm good at killing. It's what I do."

"Juliana was a nice girl," Kendall said, knowing that the producer was so much more than that, but stunned by Brenda's sense of entitlement and superiority. Brenda operated in that twisted place occupied by many grandiose serial killers. Bundy and Gacy were two of those who reveled in the attention and their place in history.

"Nice is easy to kill," Brenda said. "No one remembers nice anyway. All they remember is *me*. And my little prison mouse, Janie. Janie was a great help to me too."

"And Chaz? Why *him*?"

"Because I could, Kendall Stark. That's all there is to it. I know that the media wants to ascribe some great plan and messaging on my part but really, killing successfully means killing people randomly."

There was truth to that. Kendall knew that the serial killers who confounded detection the longest were those who killed in different areas, used multiple dump sites, and targeted a seeming hodgepodge of victims. Bundy, however, broke that mold at the end, when he ditched his penchant for sorority girls who resembled his ex-girlfriend for a twelve-year-old Florida girl.

"I got your message. Birdy got hers."

Brenda laughed. "I'm glad. I figured you two ladies

would get a kick out of that. I'm surprised it didn't make the front page."

"We didn't release the information, Brenda. We like to put on a good show too."

Brenda went quiet for a moment. "I'm sure you do. Want to know a little secret?"

"Shoot," Kendall said.

"You'd like to shoot me, wouldn't you?"

"Yes," Kendall said, "but I'd still like to hear your secret."

"About what I left behind."

"Yes, the hummingbird and the toy shark. What about them?"

Brenda paused. "Just came to me at the last minute. I mean, I just thought of it on the spot."

"That's clever of you," Kendall said.

"I thought so," Brenda said, not picking up on Kendall's less than enthusiastic endorsement of her creativity.

"I'm surprised you didn't mention the keychain," Brenda said.

"What keychain?"

"With Janie. In her pocket."

"Oh, that," Kendall said, not knowing what she was talking about.

"You didn't see it, did you? You're a very sloppy detective. Good for me, I guess."

"You need to turn yourself in, Brenda," Kendall said. "Enough people have been hurt."

"I've only just started, Detective. Let's just agree that we disagree. Life's more fun when the world spins wildly. It's like a ride."

The line went dead.

CHAPTER FIFTY-FOUR

It wasn't hard to find Cody Stark's school. Kendall and Steven had been boosters of the school for the past two years—less so at the moment with the change in his job.

Brenda Nevins sat outside watching the kids through the chain-link fencing as they played, mostly quietly, in the school's designated play area. Obviously geared toward younger students, the play area featured what appeared to be a foam rubber tugboat as its focal point. The ground was also rubberized. No kid could get hurt playing there had been the intent. Brenda knew a dozen ways she could harm someone. It spun through her mind that she could tear a chunk of foam off and shove it down some kid's throat.

Not just any kid, of course.

She listened to a rap station on the radio. It was a preset. She imagined the car's owner was a young person, and while she didn't care much for rap she thought that it was good for her to stay current. She thought that the owner was an overprivileged brat who'd been handed the world by doting parents.

Not like her double-crossing mother, who'd always been so cruel to her, who'd seized every moment she could to tell Brenda that she was no good. Not pretty enough. Flat-chested. Stupid. Would never be anything. To kill her mother would be an utter waste of time. So been there and done that.

Mommy issues.

Brenda took the paper bag from the backseat. She checked her makeup in the mirror. It had been applied with a light touch. Her clothes were clean, but not stylish at all. She had lived her whole life to turn heads but in that moment she wanted nothing more than to blend in. The kids scurried back into their respective classrooms. Brenda looked down at the prepaid cell that Janie had purchased. Lunch would be served in an hour. She turned off the radio and started for the door.

Kara Watanabe had been the office administrator for sixteen years and loved every challenging minute of it. She had boundless energy and unbridled enthusiasm. She barely stood still. Why would she? There was always something she could do to help someone. When Brenda came into the office she smiled and waved her over with a disarming smile.

Brenda did her best to fire her own back.

"I'm Cody Stark's aunt," she said. "Staying with the Starks."

"That's lovely," Kara said. "How can I help you?"

"Kendall's working some big case," she said, with a slight inflection that indicated that she'd tired of hearing it. "She asked me to bring Cody some cookies. Call me a bad aunt for spoiling him, but he's pretty precious to me."

"If he were mine I'd spoil him too," Kara said. "I can't very well do that here. Wouldn't be fair, but between you and me and the fence post, Cody *is* one of my favorites. That is if I had been allowed to have one."

Brenda smiled.

"Thank you. I wasn't sure. I'm kind of the black sheep of the family. By default of course. I mean, with Steven and Kendall—who are about as perfect as a couple can be—I'd say there isn't anywhere to go but down."

Kara made a face.

"I mean for me," Brenda said.

"Understood. I hope they work things out."

Kara's comment piqued Brenda's interest, but she didn't indicate so. Instead she did what she was best at—rolling with it. She liked to collect little bits of personal information. Information was a key into places where people wouldn't have wanted her, which is what she wanted in the first place.

Trouble between Kendall Shark and her husband. Good. That might come in handy.

"Me too," she finally said. "All couples have tough times, Ms. Watanabe. It's how they come out stronger for it. That's what I admire. And that's our Kendall and Steven Stark, through and through."

"I hope so," Kara said, searching for the younger woman's name, finally admitting her lapse at an introduction. "I didn't get your name. I'm Kara Watanabe, the office manager, and I do just about everything else that needs to be done around here."

Brenda smiled. "I'm Whitney," she said, picking a name she'd always liked over her prosaic moniker, another crappy gift from her mother. She should have changed it when she got married. Steffi or Whitney had been her names of choice back then.

Not boring-as-the-hills Brenda. She was never going to be a Brenda. *Not ever.*

"Nice to meet you, Whitney. You brought Cody a treat?"

"He and I made some cookies last night. Snickerdoodles. I told him that he could have one today as a little treat after he ate his regular lunch. Is it all right if I leave them with you? I know lunchtime is soon. Kendall told me it's at eleven-thirty."

She knew that not because anyone told her, especially not Kendall, but because she'd stalked the school through the Web.

Kara opened the bag and inhaled the heady scent of cinnamon and sugar.

"They smell divine," she said.

Brenda leaned in and whispered as though it were a trade secret. "My recipe calls for a dash of almond extract," she said.

"I got a whiff of that," Kara said. "You're so thoughtful."

"And you're so busy. I won't take up any more of your time."

"No worries. But before you leave, please log in here." She tapped a finger on a visitors' sign-in sheet.

Brenda took the pencil and signed: *Whitney Nevins.*

Kara Watanabe did have a million things to do. She'd been frazzled since the day started. She was running on bad staff-room coffee and needed a boost before the bell rang and the lunchtime pandemonium ensued. She went over to the cubby where she'd placed the small bag of cookies that Cody's aunt had left behind and set one little cookie on a paper napkin. She was just about to take a bite when student teacher Reeta Anne Marvell scurried inside. Reeta was overly dramatic, overly ingratiating, and overly helpful.

Just flat out overly.

"Ms. Watanabe," she said in her one-speed fast voice, "two boys in C pod are having a fight in the boys' bathroom and I just can't get them to come out."

"Did you go in there?"

"No. It's the boys' room."

"Yes, you said that, Reeta. But did you know that they are just children and you can go in there if there's cause for concern?"

She shook her head. "That wasn't part of our training at the university. Not at all. It would be a major red flag if a woman went into the boys' bathroom. I mean, like a scandal almost."

That was Reeta in a nutshell.

"It wouldn't. But fine, I'll go break it up," Kara said, barely registering the exasperation that she'd felt from nearly the second Reeta came into the office. She picked up the bag of cookies.

"You watch the desk. I'm going to break up the fight, then deliver this to Cody Stark."

"I don't have the training to run the office."

"Reeta, you do. A trained chimp could do it. And sometimes behavior like yours makes me think that this place is no better than a zoo."

"You're mean," Reeta said.

"I don't mean to be. Just sit tight and I'll be back."

Reeta Anne Marvell was a stress eater. Big-time. She looked over at the snickerdoodle on the paper napkin Kara had set next to the sign-in sheet

It was just sitting there. Just waiting for her. Reeta reached over and took a bite. Sugar powdered her chin and she wiped it off. She was going to have only one little bite. She didn't think one bite would matter. But it was so, so good. She took another bite. And then another.

God, this is a really good cookie.

She felt a twinge of something. Guilt, probably. That had to be it. Then she felt a little warm. In the space of a single minute Reeta found herself clutching the counter and fighting to breathe. Her face was bright red. Redder than the school mascot, the American Beauty Rose.

Something's happening to me. Something's not right at all. I don't know what it is . . . I don't have the training for this.

She disappeared behind the counter grabbing the paper towel, the sign-in sheet, and Ms. Watanabe's telephone down with her.

Her fingers somehow managed to dial 911.

Dixie Simpson had come off a break in which she'd managed to negotiate a deal on a used car on Craigslist, call her mother, and proofread a coworker's résumé. The thirty-two-year-old brunette with the ice-blue eyes was the best communications specialist in the Comm Center's office in Bremerton. She took satisfaction in her job and never missed a day of work.

That morning had been slow. Two crank calls, a fire,

and a woman who was stuck in her car at the Port Orchard Fred Meyer parking lot. Routine and boring. She liked things to keep moving. It wasn't that she craved the drama of the calls, but rather she just wanted to be on the line whenever anyone needed help.

It was 11:32 when the call came through.

"Comm Center," Dixie said. "What's your emergency?"

No one answered. Dixie checked the data line and saw that the call was coming from the offices of the Cascade School.

"What's your emergency?" she repeated. She could hear some movement, but no direct response. She repeated her question.

"Help," came a gasping voice. "Help me."

"Are you injured? Talk to me."

Another gasp and the noise of the phone being slammed onto the floor.

Dixie's adrenaline pumped and she swiveled in her chair, catching the eyes of her supervisor, Megan.

She muted her mouthpiece. "I can't get a handle on this call," she said to Megan. "Coming from the Cascade School. Someone's there, but this lady's badly hurt. Maybe a shooting or something?"

Megan did her own swivel and immediately notified the Kitsap County sheriff.

"Not sure what's going on. The caller can't speak. A woman, we think. Something's really wrong there."

Kendall hurried into the evidence room and made a beeline for Janie Thomas's personal effects. Besides her clothes, there was a bindle containing her eyeglasses, four dollars in change, and a keychain. Kendall's heart pumped when she looked down at it. The keychain had already been processed. She signed the evidence receipt, put the keychain in a separate bindle, and hurried over to Birdy's office. Birdy was wrapping up a phone call with the school. Elan had been tardy the last couple of days and they wanted to know if there was trouble at home.

"I'm new at this parenting thing," Birdy said. "Maybe you can give me some pointers, Kendall."

"I'm like every other parent making it up as I go along," she said. "I don't want to be unhelpful, but I came over here as quickly as I could to tell you that I just got off the phone with Brenda Nevins."

"Crap. She called you too."

"Yeah. She's the biggest attention whore in the history of the world."

"Copy that," Birdy said. "What did she say?"

"She wanted to know if we'd found the shark and the bird."

"She wants credit for everything, doesn't she?"

"That's an understatement. She wants the world to know that she's arrived. That she's the best at what she does, which is killing."

"Why didn't she want to be a chef or something?"

"No kidding. She dropped a little hint that we might have missed something with Janie's case. And Birdy, I'm really worried. Tell me I shouldn't be."

"What was it?"

"I brought it." Kendall opened the bindle and held out the keychain.

"Crap," Birdy said, moving to her feet.

"Tell me I'm overreacting."

"I don't know. When it comes to Brenda Nevins there is no overreacting."

Kendall looked down at the brass-colored keychain. It showed the figure of Wild Bill Hickok next to a bucking bronco. Underneath the image were the words "Wyoming's Legendary Cowboy Museum."

"I've been there," Birdy said. "It was one of the few times we left the reservation when I was a kid. Mom had relatives in Wyoming. We stayed in a tent for two weeks. Not the worst time of my life, but in the top twenty."

Kendall smiled. It was a grim smile, but a smile nevertheless. "I'm in the top twenty of mine right now," she said, not saying it was all about Steven and her marriage, but thinking it.

"I'm not a huge fan of Detective Wyo, but I'd better warn him," Kendall said. "He's next on Brenda's list."

"He's probably in his top twenty worst times too," Birdy said. "I feel sorry for him."

Kendall started for the door. "You feel sorry for everyone."

Birdy acknowledged her friend's assessment. Kendall was right. She *did*.

Kendall's phone was dead, so she used her office landline to reach Wyatt Ogilvie.

"What's up, Detective Stark?" he asked. "You looking for more dirt? You're in the wrong place for that. I should have kept my mouth shut."

"Wyatt, you could be in danger," Kendall said. "I think Brenda has a hit list and you're on it."

"What makes you say that?" he asked as he turned on the speaker function of his phone.

Kendall didn't care.

"She left a message with your name."

"Oh, did she now?" he said.

"This is fantastic, Wyo," Pandora said, chiming in with her all-too-familiar opportunistic glee.

"Do you mind, Pandora?" Kendall said. "This doesn't concern you."

"Everything about Wyo concerns me. Bravo might want him too. And just so you know, I really don't like how you tried to manipulate Wyo and turn him against me."

Kendall seethed, but held it together. She was calling him out of a sense of duty, not because she cared about the man.

"Whatever you two have going is twisted and sick and probably, actually unequivocally, unethical," she said. "Maybe illegal. That'll be for someone else to decide. And really, Pandora, stay of out this. You don't know what you're doing. You never have."

"Look, bitch, just because you have a badge doesn't mean you can boss me around."

Kendall ignored the psycho psychic. Disregarding Pandora was the only thing she could think to do. "Look," she went on, "I'm warning *you*, Wyatt. She's very dangerous and your life could be at risk."

She was talking about Brenda, but she felt the same way about Pandora.

CHAPTER FIFTY-FIVE

Birdy Waterman retreated to the green linoleum-tiled kitchen for a cup of coffee. The new offices for the coroner had experienced some construction delays, and while she loved new technology and all the bells and whistles that had been built into her autopsy suite, she'd miss the house on Sidney Avenue. It was old, decrepit, and completely behind the times. Yet it had history and she always loved that. She looked out the window toward the back parking lot between the coroner's office and the other county buildings. All had been built for their ascribed purposes—the courthouse, the jail, and the sheriff's department. The house on Sidney had been drafted into duty.

Her mind went back to that long trip to Wyoming when she was younger. Her sister, Summer, and she were close back then. Booze, jealousy, and envy hadn't supplanted their genuine bond of sisterhood.

Neither had the birth of Elan.

They sat in the backseat of their father's old Ford the whole time from Neah Bay across Washington, the Idaho Panhandle, through never-ending Montana to

Wyoming with nothing but the rustic and rugged western landscape to entertain them. Their mother, Natalie, paid little attention to her daughters—she was always focused on herself. That would never change. When they arrived in Wyoming to camp with a horde of cousins, it was their father who insisted they see the famed Western art museum.

"Not Makah," Mackie Waterman said, "but our people nevertheless."

The museum was massive. Birdy remembered taking in all the paintings, the collections of Plains Indians artwork and the stories told by the docent there. All of it provided a connection with the other Native American people whom she'd seen portrayed on TV, but who seemed so foreign in culture and art. The Makah were people of the Pacific Ocean, shellfish gatherers and whale hunters. The Plains people commanded a vast world of countless acres of rolling grasslands, horses, and bison. They were the Indian people that everyone knew.

Birdy and Summer each bought a seed-beaded bracelet that spelled out the name of the city.

She nearly dropped her coffee cup just then. She was a blur as she ran from the kitchen to her phone. She dialed Kendall, but it went to voice mail.

"Kendall! Call me! The museum isn't just in Wyoming! It's in Cody, Wyoming!"

Brad James kept the sheriff's radio on instead of background music as he went about trying to figure out if he could weather the storm he'd created with the *Spirit Hunter* debacle. He'd set up two K9 officer visits to local schools, an occurrence that usually brought in a measure of good press in the local weeklies. He'd been foolishly ambitious and knew it. He'd burned a major bridge with both Kendall Stark and Birdy Waterman— allies who were needed and specifically requested by media all the time.

Stupid. Stupid. Stupid.

He stopped what he was doing—looking online for a new job—when he heard the code for a potential school shooting. A jolt ran though his body and he jumped from his chair and ran down the hall to find Kendall.

He knew what school Cody attended.

She looked up from her work and glared at him.

"Now what?" she asked.

"Kendall, I just heard it on the radio. Something's going down at Cody's school."

"What are you talking about?" she asked.

"I heard it on the radio. A possible shooting at the Cascade School."

Kendall felt for her gun and grabbed her keys. A second later, she popped the siren onto her SUV and was barreling down the road. Her heartbeat was like a drum inside her. Pounding in her head. Telling her that Cody was all right. That all the kids were okay. That Brad James had screwed up again. And yet, she knew he hadn't. The dispatcher had sent a patrol deputy to the scene. She called in too.

"I'm en route," she said. "I know the school. Is SWAT there?"

"No need for SWAT," the dispatcher said. "Woman in the office had a heart attack or a seizure or something."

Kendall relaxed a little. Not that she didn't care about the woman. She probably knew her. She was just grateful that her son was safe.

"Is she all right?" she asked.

"Looks bad. Paramedics from the fire station are there."

When Kendall pulled up to the school, she could see the logjam of people around its pristine entrance. There were a few kids, some people from the neighborhood, and the whirlwind of activity that comes with a paramedic team. She threw her car into park, wrenched the brake into position, and jumped out. Inside, she felt the kind of urgency that comes when any mother feels that her child is in danger. It's a kind of pleading pain that drives the mother closer to the danger, like a heat-seeking missile that had been launched into enemy territory. No real mother ran from trouble. Kendall was also there as a public servant. She felt for her shoulder holster.

There.

Seeing Kendall, Kara Watanabe ran over to her. For a woman in her sixties, she was fast.

"What happened?" Kendall asked, seeing the unmistakable look of horror on Kara's usually calm face.

"Student teacher collapsed," Kara puffed. "I don't know what's wrong with her. She seemed fine a half hour ago."

"No shooting?" she asked.

"God no. Whatever gave you that idea?"

It wasn't a what, but a *who*. Kendall didn't tell her it was the PIO from the sheriff's office. Brad James had muffed it again. He'd sent her bolting through traffic to get there because the circumstances warranted it. There was no gun violence.

"Are the kids all right?" Kendall asked.

A mother Kendall had seen at a school meeting ran over to Kara.

"Where is Cinnamon?" the mom asked, her voice dripping with desperation.

"She's fine," Kara said. "She's in the classroom. All the kids are fine. It was just Reeta that passed out."

Passed out. It was more than that. It was swift and decisive.

"Is Reeta all right?" Kendall asked.

Still out of breath, Kara kept her eyes on Kendall and shook her head. "Kendall, I think she's dying. She might even be gone. I don't know what happened. I don't. A seizure or something."

The other mother stepped away, taking in the scene.

Kendall and Kara pushed back toward the front door where the paramedics were preparing Reeta for transport. The blank stare in the young teacher's eyes and stillness of her body indicated Reeta was not going to make it.

A paramedic shook his head in Kendall's direction. He didn't need to mouth the words or call over to her.

"She was fine," Kendall said, pulling Kara into the conversation. "Kara Watanabe is the office administrator. She was just with her."

Kara stared to crack a little just then. She'd been unflappable for most of the dramas that come with working at a school, but this felt too close to home. "Yes," she said, her lower lip trembling as she tried to remain composed, "I left her in the office and she was okay. I mean, I don't know if she has any medical issues. If she does, they would have been confidential anyway. I'm thinking she didn't because the teachers that do have, you know, something wrong with them have to take meds in the nurse's office. I never saw her do that." She pivoted and faced Kendall. "She was fine when I left her. I had to run those cookies that your sister-in-law made over to Cody."

Kendall thought she misunderstood. She didn't have a sister-in-law.

"Kara, what are you talking about?" she asked.

"Whitney," the older woman said, her words now mixed with tears. "She came with some snickerdoodles for Cody."

Kendall's eyes flickered. "Steven was an only child," she said, her tone stiff, but her voice louder than it needed to be.

Kara completely lost it. The recognition of what might have happened became so clear just then. She pressed her hand to her stomach. She felt sick.

"I . . ." she said, her words now coming in the smallest bits, the syllables standing alone and away from each complete word. "I did something wrong, didn't I? Whitney was so nice. She knew all about you and Steven. I didn't . . . I'm so sorry."

Kendall grabbed Kara's shoulders. "Where are the cookies?"

Kara flinched. Kendall's grip was strong and while she didn't shake her, there was an implicit promise to do so if she didn't answer quickly.

"I set one aside and gave the bag to Cody's teacher," Kara said, keeping her eyes riveted to the detective's. "She said they were a special family recipe or something like that. I don't remember. Everything is happening so fast."

Drugs could be quick. Some poisons were fast too.

"She had been eating something," the paramedic said. "We found something in her mouth when we intubated her."

"Look around the office," Kendall said, completely unsure about what was going on at the school that she'd scrimped and saved to send her son to for a fighting chance at an independent life. Undone by poison? She could never have imagined that in a zillion years. Who would give poison to a child? Her brain downloaded some cases she'd studied. One in particular had a kind of macabre resonance. It was a case in which a woman named Laurie Dann had delivered poisoned baked goods to kids in her Illinois neighborhood.

Kendall didn't know who Whitney was. Not for sure. But she had a pretty good idea.

Brenda Nevins.

"I'm going after my son," she said.

A few kids were looking out the window at the scene outside, but most others carried on with whatever they were doing. Candace Donahue met Kendall at the door.

"Candace, where's Cody?" Kendall said to the teacher without saying hello.

"He's over there," Candace said, looking alarmed, but not sure why. "Kendall, what's happening?"

"Did you give him the cookies?" Kendall asked as she scanned the room. She couldn't find Cody's shock of blond hair. Not a sign of him anywhere.

The teacher nodded.

"What's going on?" Candace asked.

"I don't see Cody," Kendall said.

Candace looked over. "He was in the quiet area. I don't see him there now."

"What's happening? Is Reeta all right?"

Kendall didn't answer. She couldn't think about Reeta just then. She was probably dead. She'd eaten something before she died. A cookie. She'd been drugged or poisoned. In a second, she was in the quiet area where Cody was lying among the blocks with a cookie in his hand.

She screamed and scooped him up.

"Baby!" she called to him. "Breathe!"

She started toward the doorway, barely turning to call over to Candace.

"Candace, get the cookies! Don't let anyone touch them."

While the rest of the kids and Ms. Donahue looked on in horror, Kendall ran down the hallway carrying the most precious thing in her life. She could feel Cody's heart beating against her own. It was a warning drum. She'd thought of all the times she'd held him and how she'd never imagined a moment like this. She prayed to God that He would spare her son from whatever Brenda Nevins had given him. Cody coughed, struggled for air. He was awake, but having a hard time breathing. Kendall caught the scent of bitter almonds and knew that cyanide had been the poison.

"The cookies are poison," she said as she made her way to the open doors and the commotion outside. "Keep them away from the kids!"

She was fast as she ran toward the paramedics, tears

coming from her own eyes. It was the first time in her life that she'd ever cried without making a sound. It was as though her eyes were raining, dripping, oozing the pain she was feeling inside.

"Guys! My son's been poisoned!" she called out. "Cyanide, I think."

The paramedic team ran to meet her.

At Harrison Hospital in Bremerton, Kendall Stark watched through the ICU window as the team of doctors and nurses kept her son alive. He'd had a small dose of cyanide and he was going to be fine. She managed to get Steven on the phone and he was already on his way home to Port Orchard.

He'd wanted to surprise her.

"I'm north of the Bay area," he said. "I'm going to turn around so I can get to the airport."

"No. Don't do that. They aren't going to admit him. It was a scare. A very big scare at that. But we're going to be all right."

"Are you sure?"

Kendall was speaking about their marriage and their son at the same time.

"We are. We can get through anything."

"I love you," he said.

"I love you too."

"Jesus, Kendall," he said, choked with emotion. "Why Cody?"

Kendall knew the answer. Yet she didn't want to say it to her husband. She knew that she had been the cause of her boy's near demise. Her job. Her relentless pursuit of the bad guy.

"There is no reason when it comes to crazy," she said in the phone

And yet over and over it came to her. This was Brenda's payback. Brenda had made things very, very personal. The Kitsap County investigator didn't know where she was right then. She imagined that Brenda had watched as the scene at the school played out. That she'd loved every minute of Kendall's agony. What Brenda might not have known is that she'd made something abstract very, very personal.

That was too bad for Brenda Nevins.

Kendall would never rest until that monster was put away for the rest of her life. And if Kendall had the chance to kill Brenda, she would be just fine with that. In fact, though she would never admit it to anyone, not even Birdy, that scenario was even better.

"Come home to us, Steven. Drive safely."

"I'm on my way. I'll stop only for gas."

CHAPTER FIFTY-SIX

Kendall was half asleep when her phone vibrated. She reached over and picked it up from the bedside table. She had hoped it was Steven, calling from the road to say that he was almost there. Instead the number on the display was unknown to her.

She answered.

"Hello?" she repeated, when no one spoke.

"Just me," the voice said.

It was Brenda.

"What do you want now?"

"How's that adorable little boy of yours? That was a close one. Wasn't it?"

"I will kill you," Kendall said.

"No, you won't. I've called to say goodbye. I'm traveling. Not sure where I'll end up. And if I don't know, you'll never know."

"I will find you, Brenda." Kendall wasn't making a threat, but an unshakable promise.

Brenda laughed. "That's so funny," she said. "So funny. Goodbye, Kendall. Thanks for making me a household name. It's all I ever wanted."

"You'll be more famous than ever when I find you."

Brenda laughed again.

"Good luck with that," she said. "Bye, Kendall. Oh, one more thing."

Kendall didn't want to hear what Brenda had to say. Yet she couldn't help herself.

Brenda dropped a bomb.

"Your husband is very handsome," she said.

The phone went dead.

Kendall's heart raced. Sweat collected on her brow. It was like she'd been poisoned by those final words. She threw her feet to the floor and dialed Steven. It rang and rang and then, voice mail.

"Steven here. You know what to do."

"Steven! Call me! Steven, be careful. Brenda's out there!"

Kendall ran to Cody's room. He was asleep. His hair, a mass of straw-colored sweetness, glowed from across the room. Tears came to her eyes. Tears and rage. So lost in that moment of fear and anxiety, she didn't feel her phone vibrate at first. She looked down.

Steven's photo appeared on the screen.

"Kendall, missed your call," he said. He sounded alarmed.

"Are you all right?" she asked, her voice low as she left their son's room for the privacy of the living room.

"Yeah, fine," Steven said. "Just worried about you. And Cody. Is everything all right? I just crossed over into Washington. Feels good to be back where there's some fresh air."

"Are you alone?" Kendall asked, standing in front of the window, scanning the yard, the road, for any sign of *her*.

"Yeah," he said. "What's up? You sound weird. Cody's okay, right?"

Kendall sank into the sofa. "He's fine. Steven, be careful. Brenda Nevins won't stop at anything to hurt you. *Hurt us.* Our family."

"I can handle her," he said, trying to calm her.

"I can too," Kendall said. "Be careful. Don't get taken in by her. She's changed her appearance. She's very, very clever. She might come after you."

"You're a little over the top on this, babe," Steven said.

Not the right choice of words.

"You don't understand," Kendall shot back, her voice growing louder with urgency—but not so loud to wake their son. "She's a monster. She's fixated on me. She'll do whatever it takes to inflict the maximum amount of pain. She tried to kill Cody."

"You're breaking up," he said. "See you in less than three hours. I'm going to pull over and get some gas and coffee."

Then the line went dead.

Kendall repeated her husband's name several times into her phone, but he didn't answer. Frantically, she tried his number but it went to voice mail.

"Honey, I love you," she said into the recording, trying to project a sense of calm. "Be careful. We need you. Watch out for her."

Kendall stopped herself from telling him not to talk to strangers. He was a salesman—or at least before the new job he had been one. Steven Stark never knew a stranger. It was part of who he was.

Three hours later, Steven pulled up to the driveway of the old Craftsman in Harper. Kendall and Cody were outside waiting. Just after he turned off the ignition, the little boy bolted for his father. Kendall watched as Steven picked up Cody and hoisted him to the sky. It was a version of "helicopter," a game they had played since he was a toddler.

"You're almost too big for me to do this anymore, buddy," Steven said, setting Cody down on the cushion of lawn next to the driveway.

"I don't think so," Cody said, laughing.

Kendall held that image for a beat, wondering how many more there might be. How the time apart had concerned her. How much she loved Steven, but felt a growing chill between them.

She embraced her husband, but it was quick and somehow strange.

"Cody," she said, "Daddy and I need to talk. How about you take some of his things inside?"

"Okay," Cody said, picking up a small black leather duffel bag.

"Everything we have is right here," Steven said, watching his son carry the bag into the house.

Kendall drew closer. She wanted to jump into his arms, but there was something strange between them. She was unsure. Not able to process all that had happened with Brenda, Cody's school, her husband's distance.

"I've missed you," he said.

She couldn't deny that. "Me too."

His eyes searched hers. "Are we going to be okay?" he asked.

Kendall looked away. "I don't know. I want us to be. But . . ." her words trailed off to silence and the two of them wandered to the stump that had been left behind when the beloved madrona tree died years earlier.

"Talk to me," he said.

She swallowed hard and looked over at the water of Yukon Harbor. It shimmered. A flock of shorebirds landed. A car whizzed by. Everything was normal but the conversation she was having with her husband.

No one spoke for a moment.

"Am I losing you?" she asked.

Steven gave his head a quick shake. He put his hands on her shoulders and looked into her eyes.

"How could you even think that?" he asked.

"You were so far away," she said. "Far away."

"Kendall, you don't understand. Do you?"

She wasn't going to cry. This was a hurt beyond tears. In some ways, after all that had happened, there was nothing left inside to cry out anyway.

"I just thought," she said, trying to get out all the words, yet knowing that saying them aloud would give voice to something she didn't want to be true.

Steven pulled her closer. "Thought what? That I was with someone else?"

She didn't have to say it. *He did.*

"Something like that," she answered, only meeting his gaze for a moment.

He looked right at her. His eyes were bullets at hers.

"Kendall, I don't think you get it," he said.

"Get it? You didn't return my calls."

"I didn't have time," he said.

Kendall pursed her lips. "Everyone has time."

"Look," Steven said, "you don't know what it's like to be kicked to the curb by changes over which you have no control. I was fighting for my job. I was fighting to save my dignity."

She looked at him. In his eyes. Taking him in. Measuring his words.

"You were there to work through some changes in the way you sold advertising," she said.

"You really think that?" he asked, not waiting for an answer. "I was there fighting to keep my job, not be outsourced, show everyone that I could adapt and, as my boss said, 'get with the program.'"

She looked at him. He had laid it all bare. He'd been away not to gain some promotion or work some angle, but he'd been away and very, very absent because he'd been working hard at survival. Not at being with another woman.

"I'm sorry," Kendall said. "I just thought . . ."

Steven reached for her. "Never. Never. You and Cody are my life. In fact the only thing that got me through the training, the sucking up, the trying to hang on to what I'm good at . . . was you two. I was down there fighting for us, not sure I'd be able to make the cut. There are younger, smarter people than me and as the business changes they'll need fewer of us."

Kendall felt foolish and relieved at the same time. Steven hadn't been avoiding her. He was trying to survive. She wrapped her arms around him, pulling him in tight. They kissed. All they'd gone through, the misunderstandings, the terror of over what had happened at Cody's school, faded. She was absolutely sure that they—the three of them—were going to be all right.

* * *

The truck stop was busy twenty-four hours a day. It had a restaurant and bar, a convenience store, and a very basic motel with thirty-eight units. It even had a shower rental for truckers who couldn't stay longer than an hour and needed to clean up for the next leg of their long, lonely drive. Cars were welcome there too.

The man sat at the counter. He wore khaki pants and a dark blue MMA T-shirt. He played with the wedding ring on his finger, loose, like his pants, from a stress-induced weight loss. He looked lonely and preoccupied.

He was perfect.

"Which way you headed?" Brenda Nevins asked as she slithered into the seat next to him.

"Auburn, then east," he said.

She rolled a shoulder forward. She wore a low-cut tank top. And while she considered her breasts her best feature, she thought her shoulders were quite sexy too.

"I have family in Kent," she said.

"Too bad for them," he said, smiling at her. She was a knockout. A little hard, but the kind of woman who made him even lonelier for his wife.

"Tell me about it," she said, taking a French fry off his plate, and inserting it into her mouth, slowly.

"Hey," he said. "I'm not looking for any pay and play."

She made a pissed-off face. It was exaggerated. But subtle wasn't Brenda's strong suit.

It never had been.

"Mister, you've got me all wrong," she said, acting indignant. "I'm not a lot lizard and the fact that you think I am insults me. Big-time."

"Sorry. I just . . ."

"You judged me. I don't like to be judged."

"I'm sorry."

She took another fry.

"My boyfriend dumped me here. We had a big old fight. I'm kind of stranded."

"Sorry about that," he said.

"You're sorry a lot," she said, her eyes softening. "I have some money. I can pay for some gas if you're headed to Spokane. I could use a ride."

The man thought.

She leaned closer, exposing the best breasts that money could buy.

He felt himself get hard and shifted in his seat.

Her eyes lingered on his crotch and he looked away.

"Sure, I'll give you a ride," he said.

She looked at him and smiled. She'd give him one too. One he wouldn't be able to savor for very long at all.

ACKNOWLEDGMENTS

Readers probably know that the author's writing of a book is only part of the process to getting it into their hands. Others, behind the scenes, play important roles. I'd like to share my appreciation for Michaela Hamilton, my editor at Kensington Publishing. Michaela is a wonderful partner in crime fiction—she has terrific insight into story and tone, both essential in crafting a thriller or mystery novel. Our partnership has produced eight novels, including this one. Additionally, I want to acknowledge the contributions of my longtime agent, Susan Raihofer of the David Black Literary Agency. Susan and I have worked together for almost twenty years and I wouldn't have it any other way. Thanks so much, Michaela and Susan. It's been scary fun working with you. And finally, a quick but appreciative shout-out to Jean Olson and Elizabeth Hayes for getting everything right.

Don't miss Gregg Olsen's next exciting Waterman
and Stark thriller

JUST TRY TO STOP ME

Coming from Kensington Publishing Corp. in 2016

Keep reading to enjoy an exciting excerpt . . .

The day Brenda and Janie vanished

Janie Thomas looked at the laptop she'd been ordered to transport to her second-floor office at the Washington State Corrections Center for Women in Purdy, Washington. It was against prison protocol to bring any electronic devices inside the secure facility, but Janie *was* the prison superintendent. When she started to breeze though the checkpoint, she told her favorite officer, Derrick Scott, that she was running late.

"Rough morning," Janie said, an exaggerated look of displeasure on her face. She glanced at her phone. "Have a call with the governor's office in five minutes."

"He's never on time," the officer said. "Not with a meeting or getting a budget approved. But if you ask me, a crying baby in the middle of the night is at the tippy top of the 'rough morning' scale. I didn't sleep a wink last night."

"Tell me about it," Janie said, going through the detector. "I haven't forgotten those days. You'll get through them."

The African American man grinned, showing white teeth, and passed Janie's briefcase over the counter instead of through the scanner. The superintendent was always so nice, asking about the kids, sharing photos of her family from her phone.

Later the officer would say that the briefcase weighed more than usual and he probably should have opened it, but she was, after all, the boss.

"She runs the prison," he said. "What was she going to smuggle in? A set of keys? A file?"

A half hour later that same morning, Brenda Nevins was in Janie's office, purportedly to take on a special work assignment to help other inmates with life skills. Other prisoners saw an irony in that, but didn't say a word. Speaking up against Brenda meant getting cut in the shower with a shank made of a mascara wand and the sharpened edge of a Pringles' can top. Or poisoned at lunch with meds ripped off from the infirmary. Or, worst of all, cut off from visitation with family.

"I run this place," Brenda had said, when a new girl—a meth head from Black Diamond with more body tattoos then brains—challenged her. "You keep that in mind if you piss me off."

In her office the day she disappeared, Janie opened the laptop for the benefit of the woman who had told her to bring it.

"Nice. Does it have video capabilities?" Brenda asked as the pair moved from Janie's office to the records room—the only location in the institution that did not have the prying eyes of security cameras.

They stood face-to-face, a worktable separating them. Brenda had done her hair in the way she knew Janie liked—down, with slight curls that brushed past her shoulders.

The two of them were there to plot the escape. Janie's *and* hers.

"It's an Apple," Janie said. "Top of the line. My husband helped me set everything up."

Brenda watched a flicker of emotion coming over Janie's face at the mention of her husband, Edwin. She moved her own mouth into a slight frown; a mirror of what Janie was doing, sans the slight lowering of the chin. Quivering was too much. Not needed.

"Don't be sad, Janie," Brenda said in a voice dripping with honey sweetness. "I know this is hard. But your life belongs to you and you have to live it as you were meant to do. No more dreaming. No more wondering, baby girl. We are on the verge of our moment. We have to take it together. We have no choice in the matter. You know what we are? You know what brought us together?"

Janie bit down on her lower lip.

"We're soul mates," she said. Brenda relaxed her frown. "Don't ever doubt that. Don't ever. I know that God or some higher power—whatever She is—has brought us together. That's right. The world will be all over us. You know that. They'll be watching and hunting and trying to stop us from doing what we must do."

"I guess so," Janie said, fear evident in her voice.

Brenda reached across the table and grabbed Janie by her shoulders.

"Get a grip," she said. "This moment will not only set us free but will define the future for so many people. The world will be watching and we'll need to tell them the reasons behind everything we're doing."

"To help them, right?"

It was more than a question, almost an affirmation.

Brenda gave her head a slight nod. "Yes," she said. "It isn't about just *us*. Just you and me. I wish both of us could have come from other circumstances. Come from backgrounds free of the torment that sent us here . . . me to be a zoo animal, you to be a zookeeper. But life isn't fair. I get that. Life is what we make it. We're the example of living with authenticity."

Brenda stopped talking to assess. She watched Janie as a cat watches the family goldfish as it twirls in the waters of its bowl.

Like the betta fish.

"And we'll help people, right?" Janie repeated.

Exasperation was in order. Maybe a little bit of the takeaway was called for just then.

"Are you even listening?" Brenda asked as she let out a sigh. It was the kind of nonverbal punctuation at which she was particularly skilled. She was good with words. Good with presenting her concepts, no matter how outlandish. Repulsive even. She could sell peed-on snow to an Eskimo.

"Really?" she asked, drawing away slightly as though she were disgusted by what Janie said. "Really? This isn't about *us*. This is about the world. That's why we need to get our act together and get out of here. I didn't do any of those things they pinned on me. None of them whatsoever."

Janie didn't say another word. Brenda was a lot of

things, but Janie was all but certain a liar was not among them.

"Are you with me, baby? Are you about to let go of the past and be what God wants us to be? She's calling for us. She wants us to be together, and yes, my love, She wants for us to help others."

Brenda was all about empowerment.

"She loves us, doesn't She?" Janie asked. Before Brenda, Janie never used the feminine personal pronoun for God. It felt funny when she did it, but also empowering.

"More like adores," Brenda said.

Janie felt her body relax a little.

It felt so good to be loved for who she was.

"I'll be ready tonight after work," Janie said. "I'll send for you."

After everything happened

Kendall Stark didn't know it, but she wouldn't be in need of a second tuxedo mocha that morning as she arrived in her offices at the Kitsap County Sheriff's Department in Port Orchard. The email link that was about to be forwarded to her would provide enough of a jolt.

The new public and media relations specialist, Daphne Brown, cornered the detective and spoke with a kind of breathless excitement that tempered just about everything that came out of her mouth.

East Port Orchard Elementary wants you to talk about stranger danger safety! Tonight!

We are out of creamer in the break room! Where do we keep it? I need some!

We have a serial killer on the loose!

Do you like my hair this way?

Kendall said good morning and waited for whatever urgent missive only-one-speed Daphne had.

"We've already heard from all the morning shows," Daphne said. "I'm so excited. They want you on."

Kendall shook her head. "I'm not doing it," Kendall said.

Daphne pulled at one of her curls and it bounced back into position. "You don't even know what it's about," she said. "How can you even say that?"

"It's not a *what*, Daphne. It's a *who* and I know that who is Brenda Nevins."

The younger woman's eyes widened a bit, but before she could speak, Kendall preempted her from doing so.

"There's nothing you can do," Kendall said. "I'm not required to go on camera. *You* are. You can do it."

Daphne dialed down her pushy enthusiasm. She'd been to a conference in Seattle the week before and had learned new techniques to influence what she considered a "resistant personality type."

Daphne fiddled with her department-issued smartphone.

"You better watch the link I'm about to send you."

"What link?" Kendall asked.

Daphne glanced up, a satisfied look on her face.

"Watch it," she said. "Then call me so I can work my PR magic."

Kendall didn't acknowledge Daphne's boast. She had no plan whatsoever of encouraging Ms. Brown to do anything, let alone work any kind of self-professed public relations hocus-pocus. She was so sick of Brenda

Nevins that she couldn't imagine enduring one more minute of thinking about her. Brenda was on the front page. Brenda was the top-of-the-hour news. Brenda had even been featured on the cover of *USA Today*. She was a murderous prison escapee and that made her a problem for the special agents of the FBI, not the investigators from the local Kitsap County's Sheriff Department.

Brenda had moved off the front pages. Janie Thomas's husband, Edwin, had buried his wife in a family plot in the memorial park just off the highway in Gig Harbor. TV producer Juliana Robbins's parents had claimed their beloved daughter's remains and placed them in an urn on their mantel—vowing they'd never let her go again. Bar owner Chaz Masters, who had become a footnote to the story in the way the white and middle aged often do, was honored with a wake at the Grey Gull—an event that only brought out a handful of barflies, a blogger, and a local newspaper reporter who normally filled in for the sports editor.

None of those who loved the dead had really moved on, of course. Most never would. The fact that Brenda Nevins had smeared her kind of evil all over Kitsap County had not brought anything but misery to Kendall Stark, Birdy Waterman, or any of the others who'd wanted justice to prevail.

It wasn't that Brenda Nevins, whom federal investigators were all but certain had fled to Canada, wasn't an icepick-in-the-eye kind of torture to Kendall. It was simply that Kendall couldn't do a thing about her.

"She was our Hurricane Katrina," her husband Steven had said a few weeks after the murder spree began.

"She came and destroyed as much as she could and in the morning it was over. Only the wreckage was left behind."

He was right. That's exactly what she was and what she did.

After extricating herself from Daphne, Kendall made her way to her office and, against her better judgment, powered up her laptop and went right to her message inbox.

There it was, an email from Daphne Brown. No message. Just a link to a YouTube clip. Kendall clicked on the link and waited until the advertisement for a trip to Greece on a luxury liner reached the ten-second mark so she could X it out.

The video was entitled: How My Story Began, Part One.

Kendall could feel her heart rate accelerate a little as the clip worked its way from start to finish. Feeling a little sweat collect at the nape of her neck, she pushed her chair away from her desk and dialed Birdy Waterman's number.

"Hi Kendall," Birdy said. "What's up?"

"Are you in your office?"

"Yes," Birdy said. "Gloves about to go on."

"Can you come over here?"

Birdy hesitated a beat. "I'm about to start an autopsy on a crash victim from yesterday."

Kendall pushed. "But you haven't started, have you?"

"No, but . . . what's this about, Kendall?"

Kendall looked at the YouTube video cued up on her screen.

"Put the corpse back in the chiller and get over

here," she said. "Brenda Nevins has posted a video blog. You need to see it."

"Video blog. What is she, fourteen?" Birdy said.

"This is no joke," Kendall said. "Come over as soon as you can."

The image was in high definition—clear and leaving no room for doubt. Brenda Nevins had not ever been a person who could lay low. She took the microphone, looking at the camera.

"The light is on so I guess you can see me. Or you can see me when I post this. I'm not stupid enough to do this live. It pissed me off to lose the chance to be on TV to tell the world my true story. The morons in the legal system really screwed me over. I don't like to be screwed with. I'm the one who does the screwing. Right, Janie?"

She turned and tilted the camera to Janie Thomas, who was bound and gagged on a chair. Silver duct tape cocooned her forearms to the armrest. Her feet were out of view. The gag appeared to be black fabric, some clothing item.

"Looks like underwear," Birdy said. "Wonder whose?"

Kendall didn't reply. Her office was silent. Still. Her eyes were glued to her computer's screen. In particular, Janie's terrified eyes riveted the detective. Though farther back in the shot, there was no mistaking the pleading coming from them, an urgent message that was stronger than words.

Help me.

Brenda let the camera linger first on Janie, then on herself before she started talking again. She wore full makeup and a teardrop necklace that Edwin had reported Janie was wearing to work the day she went missing from the prison. The teardrop, an amethyst, nestled between Brenda's breasts.

Brenda was nothing if not consistent. She was always one to make sure people's eyes landed right there, Kendall thought.

Brenda started talking again. "Janie, you know your baby doesn't like it when you don't answer her. Makes me annoyed. When I get annoyed I need to do something to liven things up. You know, to break the tension."

For the first time, Birdy noticed a curl of smoke in the frame. She tapped her finger on the screen.

"She's going to burn her," Birdy said.

"It's one of her favorite things to do," Kendall said, sliding back into her chair. "She did it to her child."

"Who does that?" Birdy asked, a rhetorical question if ever there had been one.

The answer, of course, both women knew, was a sociopath like Brenda. Maybe no one had seen someone so profoundly evil in the annals of crime. Kendall had. She'd been in the cage with the predator when she interviewed her on the Darcy Moreau case. She'd seen the charm and pretense of being human, the sickening game of those who have no other purpose in life but to win others over and destroy them.

Brenda tugged at the chain around her neck, the amethyst rising and falling, swinging back and forth like a hypnotist's watch.

"I know I shouldn't smoke," she said. "It's a nasty habit that I picked up in county jail and carried over to prison. Not much else to do in that hellhole." She stopped and looked at Janie over her shoulder. "No offense."

Then back at the camera, those gorgeous, but lifeless eyes. "Smoking really scares me. I do not want to be one of those women whose mouth is a sagging sphincter that wicks out lipstick and is an instant sign that she's getting old."

Brenda reached in the direction of the curling smoke. Her fingertips now held a cigarette. She took a deep drag and then examined the filter before exhaling.

"Plus I have to constantly reapply lipstick and in prison—not that that's a problem at the moment—decent cosmetics are hard to come by. I let a hideous creature from Preston fondle my breasts in the shower as payment for a tube of L'Oreal that came in into the institution in someone's butt. Gag me. The things one has to do to look halfway decent."

Brenda let out a laugh.

Kendall shot a look at Birdy.

"She thinks she's a star," she said.

"A Kardashian, maybe," Birdy said, her eyes still on the video.

Kendall was caught off guard. Birdy was more into Kerouac than Kardasian. "You watch that crap?"

"No," Birdy answered. "But Elan's girlfriend Kelsey does. She's over a lot."

The exchange between the forensic pathologist and the detective was that kind of forced break in the tension that people engage in when watching a horror movie.

The popcorn is stale.

Have to go to the bathroom.

I just remembered I left the water running.

"Suddenly," Brenda said, getting up and walking over to a now squirming Janie, "I'm hungry. Do you like Indian food, Janie? I love curry. Don't get me started on tandoori chicken. Love. Love. Love tandoori. Surprisingly, there was a fantastic Indian place in the Tri Cities that I used to go to with my boyfriend. It had the best tandoori in the Northwest. Better than Seattle. Honestly. So, so good. Well, Janie, do you like Indian food?"

Tears rolled down the superintendent's face.

Brenda ignored them.

"When I was a girl," she continued, "we held dandelion blossoms to our chins and if it reflected gold on your skin it meant that you liked butter. Did you ever do that?"

Janie didn't answer. She couldn't if she had wanted to. The black panties used to keep her quiet were tied so tightly that the corners of her mouth dripped blood.

Brenda swiveled around to face the camera. Her eyes met the camera's lens with the precision of a newscaster.

"Did any of you?"

She held her stare for a beat and then turned back to Janie.

"I want to make sure you are seeing this, but it's hard to manage the camera, the shot, the script, *and* the talent. I have newfound respect for TV producers and camera crews. What they do is not as easy as it looks."

Brenda took one more drag on the cigarette, making sure the camera captured its cherry-red tip.

"Let's see if you like Indian food," she said, her tone completely flat and devoid of irony. As the cigarette's red-hot tip moved toward Janie's forehead, the terrified woman turned away, her cries muffled in the lingerie that had so successfully silenced her.

"Don't fight me," Brenda said, in words that were splinter-cold. "You know you can't win. You're weak. I'm stronger. You're smart. I'm smarter."

She grabbed Janie by the hair with her free hand and yanked so hard that it looked as though the captive woman's neck might snap.

"She's a monster," Kendall said.

Birdy didn't say anything. There wasn't anything to say.

"Let's see if you like Indian food!" Brenda said.

And then while tears streamed and Janie struggled, Brenda pressed the lighted tip of her cigarette into the center of Janie's forehead.

"Don't squirm, stupid bitch! Once I moved when the crappy stylist my mother took me to was cutting my hair. I ended up with bangs that made me look like a trailer park kid!"

Through the struggle, Janie's quiet scream was captured.

"A monster," Birdy said.

"Pull yourself together, Janie! You like Indian food! You do!" Brenda said, laughing as if she'd pulled off some practical joke.

Kendall knew it was a pretend laugh. All of Brenda's emotions were as bogus as her breasts. She was incapable of recognizing the pain of others because to her, others were only objects. Things to be used. Things to get her whatever it was that she wanted.

To serve her needs.

Brenda turned to the camera and whispered. The whisper was fake too. Loud enough for Janie to hear every word.

"Everyone who is watching this already knows that Janie didn't get her Indian dinner out. You already know that she's dead."

She paused, looking down at the cigarette she'd ground into Janie's forehead. It was still smoldering, so Brenda took another puff, breathing in the burning tobacco and the incinerated flesh of the woman who'd helped her escape from prison. She made a face and quickly extinguished it.

"Did you find my mark on Janie, Dr. Waterman? Sorry about your little boy, Detective Stark. Kids love cookies. I was a cookie monster when I was a little girl."

Kendall looked at Birdy, gauging her reaction to being named. The reference to Cody and the incident at school was spine chilling. It made her skin crawl. If anything on the video was a shock to her, it was the fact that the two of them had been named.

Birdy stared at Kendall.

"She was too badly burned for me to observe the cigarette burn," she said.

They both watched until the clip found its way to its end.

"I hope this goes viral," Brenda said and the screen went black.

Another advertisement for a cruise popped up.

"She got her wish, Birdy," Kendall said, ignoring the ad and wondering why the advertising tool on YouTube thought she was in her sixties. "More than five hundred thousand views and climbing." She refreshed her laptop screen. "Five thousand more since we started watching."

Birdy looked at her friend. Her expression was grim. "This is going to encourage her, Kendall. She's a narcissist who lives for this kind of attention. She craves it like we crave our morning coffee."

Kendall reached for her lukewarm tuxedo mocha. "Right. She's going to do something big."

"Unless we stop her," Birdy said. "She has to be stopped."

Nail-Biting Suspense from

Gregg Olsen

Closer Than Blood	978-0-7860-2045-4	$7.99US/$9.99CAN
A Cold Dark Place	978-0-7860-1830-7	$6.99US/$8.49CAN
Fear Collector	978-0-7860-2046-1	$9.99US/$10.99CA
Heart of Ice	978-0-7860-1831-4	$6.99US/$8.49CAN
Victim Six	978-0-7860-2044-7	$7.99US/$9.99CAN
A Wicked Snow	978-0-7860-2988-4	$5.99US/$6.99CAN

Available Wherever Books Are Sold!

All available as e-books, too *plus, in e-book only:*

The Bone Box(novella)   978-0-7860-3000-2 $1.99

Visit our website at **www.kensingtonbooks.com**